I0525473

Comeback Girl
The Complete Daily Serial

STEPHANIE BOND

Copyright © 2018 Stephanie Bond, Inc.
All rights reserved.
ISBN: 978-1-945002-38-0
Cover art by Andrew Brown

INTRODUCTION

Hello. I'm Jane Hunnicut, aged twenty-eight. I grew up in Accident, Alabama but I've lived the past few years in London, England with the man I followed there from college. To say I've distanced myself from my upbringing would be a bit of an understatement. I love being a city girl and I've had my share of good fortune, but lately I've found myself in a bit of a slump.

I'm a novelist whose first book sold gangbusters, but the second book—notsomuch. My relationship with my fiancé was flying high… until it wasn't. And to top it all off, my best friend disappeared… like before. When I was at my lowest, the phone rang and in an instant, my life changed—my family needed me.

After escaping the suffocating situation of my childhood, I am reluctant to return, especially since I'm already late on a big deadline. In the small town where I grew up, I never quite fit in, but now after years away, I'm really going to stick out. And I'm not ready to face the ghosts of my past.

Meanwhile, my family and friends in Alabama
think my life is perfect.

I'm in dire need of a comeback.
But my plan didn't include coming back home.

Something tells me my life is going to get worse
before it gets better.

July 1, Sunday

"JANE," MY MOTHER ASKED, "How's the book coming along?"

There are a few drawbacks of Sunday Skyping with my mom who still lives in the same small southern town in the same small southern house I grew up in—the six-hour time difference between Accident, Alabama and London, England, for instance, and the fact that I have to fix my makeup and hair because Sharon Hunnicut expects it. But those disadvantages are bested by the fact that on camera, I can school my face and body language to hide any stress her questions trigger.

And Mom knows how to hit the dead red center of my anxiety target.

"It's coming along great," I lied, nodding and smiling. It's okay when novelists fib—we get paid to make up stuff.

Mom was sitting where she always sat—in front of the laptop I'd given her at the table in the kitchen nook. On the blue wall behind her hung a dated family portrait in a wood frame, where it had always been.

"What's this book about?" she asked.

Ugh—a direct hit. "It's about a young woman... a young mother, actually... who is, you know... struggling to juggle everything... in her life." At least that was the logline I'd given my editor almost a year ago.

"I think it's fascinating how you can write about things you know nothing about."

Shrapnel. "Thriller writers can write about murder without having committed it."

Mom gave a little laugh. "I guess you're right. But you could always call Emma."

Emma is a high school friend who'd taken the married-with-kids route. She still lives in Accident and sends me long

4

newsletters at Christmastime filled with pictures of toothy, chubby kids. I send her pictures of my beloved dog Trudy, and autographed copies of my two published novels.

"If I need insider information, I have friends here who have kids." A reminder that my life was firmly entrenched in London.

"So you're on track to meet your deadline?"

"Absolutely." Not.

"Good," Mom said, nodding... but not smiling. In fact, I noticed the little wrinkle between her thin, arched eyebrows was more pronounced, as if she were squinting into a bright light.

"Are you okay?" I asked lightly. Mom is no fitness queen, but she's a fussbudget, and in constant motion. She's made a living out of helping others—doing housecleaning, running errands, driving people to appointments—a personal concierge before there was such a thing. She doesn't have fancy clothes, but her hair and makeup is always done. And other than persistent insomnia, she's always been in good relative health for her fifty-one years.

Her pretty face morphed into cheerfulness and she gave a dismissive wave. "Yes, of course. How is Hugh?"

My fiancé. I'd met Hugh Green at the University of Alabama and after graduation six years ago, had followed him back to his home country.

"Hugh is fine." Hugh was always fine—he was one of the most easygoing people I'd ever met. "His job is busy, but good. He's out with friends."

"Have you set a date for the wedding?"

Another bullseye. "Not yet," I said casually. "We'll probably wait until I get past my next book deadline."

"That's what you said last year."

"Have you seen Tyler lately?" I asked to change the subject. Tyler is my older brother, who still lives in Accident. I love my brother but we had little in common as kids, and even less so as adults.

"Oh, sure... he was here yesterday to feed the pigs."

Did I mention I grew up on a pig farm? Well, not one of those big operations like you see on television—just a dozen swine or so. Enough for my father—may he rest in peace—to sell and make some money since he never seemed to be able to hold down a job... enough to keep plenty of pork on the Hunnicut table... and enough to ensure a horrible stench permeated everything in sight, including the clothing of the two Hunnicut children, much to the taunting delight of our school friends.

"He's busier than ever now that everyone is ordering everything on the World Wide Web."

My brother drives a package delivery truck. "Mom, you can just say 'online.'"

"Whatever, you know what I mean. No one does things in person these days—like this Skyping thing."

I knew where this was going, so I tried to head it off. "This is better than just talking on the phone, don't you think?"

"Yes, but Jane… do you ever plan to come back home?"

Acid bubbled in my stomach—stress reflux, my doctor said.

"Maybe after my book deadline," I offered. "We'll see."

The little frown returned and her glance bounced around to things, I assumed, off-camera. "I would need a little notice to straighten up. I'm not the best housekeeper these days."

I scoffed. My mother has always been a neatnik, which is why it surprised me that she'd insisted on keeping the pigs after Daddy died. But at the time I was away at college and assumed it was her way of maintaining a sense of sameness. "I'm sure everything looks great, Mom. How's your garden?"

Her face lit up. "The green beans are still going strong, and the okra and squash are coming in nicely."

Every year she added a row or a new crop to the vegetable garden—she loved everything about it and gave the extras to neighbors and people she worked for. And of course, the pigs got the leftovers. I wish I'd inherited her green thumb, but I couldn't even grow herbs here, a place where herbs grew out of the cracks in sidewalks.

"And the muskmelons," she gushed, "well, they're the sweetest I've ever grown."

Suddenly my mouth watered for a taste of the juicy orange melons. The Hunnicuts were not known for touch-feely sentiments—ours had been a sparse, practical household, and when it came to expressing affection, we maintained a don't ask, don't tell policy. But at that moment, I felt a rush of love for my mother, bound up with a sense of sadness that she'd had to be content with a small life when the world was so big.

6

"Mom… why don't you come for a visit?" I asked spontaneously. To my knowledge, she'd never been out of the state of Alabama, much less abroad… but then she'd never had a good reason to travel, either.

Her eyes went wide. "I couldn't come that far. Who would take care of my garden?"

"What about Tyler?"

She looked more anxious. "And my regulars—they depend on me."

Her regular customers, the people she ran errands for. "I'm sure they could do without you for a few days."

But she was shaking her head. "It's just not possible for me to leave, Jane."

"Okay," I soothed, surprised at her vehemence. "I'll talk to Hugh—maybe we can come for a visit during the holidays."

She nodded, seemingly mollified. Then the screen froze.

I sighed. The wireless connectivity wasn't the most reliable in rural Alabama. "Mom? Are you there?"

"… losing… you," her voice said.

Then a chime sounded to let me know the connection had dropped. I stared at the still picture of my mother's face, caught in mid-expression somewhere between a smile and a grimace. She looked as if she were in pain.

But I knew it was just my guilty mind playing tricks on me. Mom was fine, and maybe by the time we talked next Sunday, she'd be more amenable to coming to London.

Because the guaranteed ordeal of getting her here still sounded more appealing than me going back to Accident.

July 2, Monday

THE BATHROOM FLOOR of our flat is freaking gorgeous.

It's covered with one-inch antique porcelain white and blue tile that form a pixelated offset triangular pattern resembling birds flying in formation. I convinced Hugh we needed to rent this drafty flat despite zero closet space and weird electrical outlets placement because this tile spoke to me. For something so rigid, it appeared to be undulating with forward movement, and at the time,

I took it as a sign that living in this place would help me move forward as well. And it had.

After relocating from the States to England with Hugh on a work visa for a pretty crummy marketing job, I had achieved my goal of selling my first novel and quit said crummy marketing job to write full-time. My novel had achieved modest sales and critical success. My publisher had extended a multi-book offer, which I'd happily accepted. And Hugh had proposed.

Well, not technically, in a down-on-his-knee kind of way, but last year when we were attending a friend's wedding we'd been dancing close and he'd asked if I ever saw us getting "hitched" (he likes to tease me with phrases he picked up while going to college in the American South) and I'd said sure. After that he'd started introducing me as his fiancée, even though I didn't have a ring. But Europeans are less uptight about relationships and the formality that trips up us Americans.

My brown cockapoo Trudy gave a happy yap from beneath the sink where she watched me, as if to remind me I was living a generally enviable life.

"I know," I cooed.

Trudy got up and trotted over, taking advantage of my face being close to the ground to lick me silly. She looked like a shaggy teddy bear with black button eyes and could always make me feel better, but her tongue therapy was short-lived. After a few seconds, she retreated to her cool refuge, leaving me nonplused.

Over the last few months things had dulled a bit in my writing and in my relationship, not unlike the bathroom tile, which had over time, lost its shine from accumulated dust, lint, dog hair, human hair, dog drool, hairspray, and perhaps a few spilled glasses of wine when Hugh and I had shared bubble baths. I'd decided if I could restore the tiled floor to its previous luster, I might be able to put the shine back on other parts of my life. To that end, I was using an old toothbrush to systematically scrub clean the postage-stamp size tiles and the grungy grout between each one.

Yes, I had a book due in three months that I'd barely begun writing, and yes, my time might be better spent at the laundromat, but deep cleaning the tiled floor suddenly felt necessary.

"They make special cleaners for that," Hugh offered from the doorway.

I didn't look up. "They might damage the tile. Soap and water is working fine."

"A bigger brush would make it go faster."

"But it would be less precise," I argued. "This way I know it's clean."

I could feel his judgment arrows coming from the doorway.

"Are you going to write today?" he asked.

"I'm letting my story incubate."

"This book has the gestation period of a giraffe."

"Uh-hm."

He grunted. "Jane... maybe you should visit your family now instead of waiting for the holidays."

I lifted my head to take in the concerned expression in his blue eyes. He was dressed for work, the strap of his messenger bag straining across his solid chest. "Why?"

"It's been a while since you've seen your mother and brother in person."

"Four years—lots of people in college or the military don't see their families for longer than that."

"But you're not in university or a war zone," he said dryly. "And it's been six years."

I squinted. "Six? No."

"Yes."

I did the math in my head, incredulous.

"Think about it," he said. "Maybe it would help."

"Help with what?"

He gestured vaguely to the soapy toothbrush I held. "Whatever is making you do this."

I frowned. "Dirt is making me do this."

Hugh lowered his chin. "Okay. I'm leaving."

"Okay, bye."

When I heard the door close, I exhaled in relief, then sat back on my heels. When had I begun to look forward to Hugh leaving in the mornings? Once upon a time, I had hated him being gone, had raced through manuscript pages during the day so he and I could spend the evenings cooking and lying around with some part of our bodies touching.

I sighed. If I were writing my and Hugh's story, this would be the sagging middle. I just had to push through and trust everything in this zany romantic comedy would work itself out.

And it would—after I finished writing my novel… after the bathroom floor was clean.

Renewed, I bent back to my scrubbing.

July 3, Tuesday

IN THE SHORT TIME I've been involved in the publishing world, I've learned Tuesdays are News Days.

Mondays are consumed with internal meetings where decisions are made, then editors are dispatched to deliver rejections for projects (ugh) or to make offers (hooray) or to check on the status of a manuscript (yikes), and follow-up usually occurs the following day. Also, depending what time zone one lives in, some bestseller lists are released on Tuesday. So according to where a writer is in her career, she will either be mentally crossing her fingers the phone will ring on Tuesday, or crossing her fingers it won't.

Since I'm not making progress on my work-in-progress, I'm sitting in the latter bucket. So when my phone rang and my editor's name came up on the screen, my intestines crimped. Jocelyn no doubt wanted an update on The Book.

I paused from scrubbing the tile floor and let my phone ring twice while my stomach churned. Trudy whined at the shrill noise, ratcheting up my anxiety. Each ring seemed more frantic, more demanding. At last the call rolled to voice mail and I exhaled. After a minute or so, the message chime sounded, but I was paranoid about picking it up right away—what if Jocelyn tagged her message with a notification? Then she'd know I was dodging her. I would wait a respectable time before checking her message so she'd think I was out, or better yet—that I was so engrossed in writing I'd turned off my ringer.

"Time for a walk, Trudy."

She understood, yapping happily and running toward the door. I pushed to my feet slowly and stretched my aching back. I took pleasure in the fact that a quarter of the bathroom floor was startlingly clean, but I still marveled over how I hadn't noticed its deplorable state until only a few days ago.

I picked up Trudy's leash on the hall tree next to the door and hooked it to her collar. She licked my face appreciably. She was fairly shaking with excitement, eager to see and be seen. In fact, she's much more sociable than I am. If not for Trudy, I probably still wouldn't know many neighbors.

When Hugh and I had gone to the pound to look for a pet, he'd had his heart set on an English bulldog. But when I saw Trudy, springing up and down to get my attention, I knew she had to come home with us. The fact that she's the product of an American Cocker Spaniel and an English poodle made her even more perfect for my and Hugh's mixed nationality coupledom, and even he couldn't resist her adorableness. Still, she's *my* pet, *my* heart, *my* happiness, and I'm thankful she found me. Growing up we'd had only outdoor animals, so I was unprepared for the overwhelming affection I'd developed for this shaggy little she-pup.

"Ready?"

She barked jauntily with—I imagined—a British accent.

I glanced at my phone, the message light blinking ominously, then set it on the cabinet face-down. When I returned would be soon enough to hear Jocelyn's dreaded inquisition about the state of the nonexistent manuscript... and if I stretched the walk a bit, I could postpone a return call until tomorrow.

I grabbed my sling bag, then walked out the door and down three steps to the small fenced-in back yard that was mine and Hugh's. We sometimes carried our plates out here to eat and listen to music, although I confess I couldn't remember the last time we had, borne out by the layer of furry mold growing on the wood table and chairs. Maybe I'd tackle them after the bathroom floor.

Trudy pounced on a yellow squeaky toy lying in the grass, picked it up and trotted to the side gate. I unfastened the latch and followed her down the stone side path of the house to the sidewalk that had replaced what little front yard the building had once boasted. Only a line of spindly shrubs stood between the sidewalk and the house's front door, which led to another flat where a quiet older man lived.

"Which way do you want to go?" I asked Trudy. She was still holding the toy in her mouth. Without hesitating, she turned left and I followed on our densely populated, tree-lined street, breathing in fish-scented air.

The thing I love most about living in London is the weather. The summers are warm, but not hot; the winters are cold, but not frigid; and every season marinates in rain, rain, rain. I love the mist, the drizzle, the downpours, the storms. I love the clouds, the fog, and the general lushness of everything. Walking around London is like looking through polarized sunglasses—everything seems less harsh and prettily blurred. It's the perfect, cozy, insular environment for writing.

So why wasn't I?

I pushed away the troubling question, telling myself every writer has a process, and every book is different. This one wasn't coming as quickly as the first two, but any day now, I would wake up with the compulsion to run to my laptop and the pages would fly by.

But I had a feeling Jocelyn would want something more to go on than my faith that this book was going to just happen.

Especially after the last book.

A hot flush crawled up my neck when I recalled the reviews.

Hunnicut's sophomore book is a sophomoric look at relationships.

Expected more from this author whose first book delighted.

Alas, some writers have only one book in them and would do well to stop there.

There were kinder reviews, of course, but the ones that mattered had been damaging. The book had floundered. My agent Ron Handler had tried to put a good spin on weak sales—the market was challenging, so small, important books were losing out. Jocelyn assured me we could maneuver around one disappointing title.

But the implication was clear: *We can't maneuver around two disappointing titles in a row.*

So admittedly, I was feeling a little pressure. There's a lot riding on this book—my reputation, my income... my future. Everyone thinks I'm a huge success... including Hugh, all our friends, and my family back in Alabama.

You could say I'm in need of a comeback, something I hadn't counted on so early in my career.

Trudy barked, pulling me out of my thoughts. We had walked past our normal turnaround spot and it had started to rain—hard. I scooped her up with one hand and retrieved an umbrella from my bag with the other, then turned toward home with her huddled against my chest.

But the closer I got to the flat, the heavier my footsteps became, carrying me back to the voice message from Jocelyn I was sure I didn't want to hear. By the time I opened the door and set Trudy down on a towel, my heart was pounding in my wet ears. I picked up my phone with an unsteady hand and retrieved the message.

"Hi, Jane, this is Jocelyn. I just wanted to let you know the sales team loves your title JUGGLING ACT for the new book, so we're going with that. The art department is working on cover ideas and I'll email those in a few days. They know we need to go in another direction this time, so I'm hoping they'll give me some brilliant concepts to go with that brilliant title of yours. That's all—hope you are well. Cheers, then."

I went limp with relief. A reprieve.

Once the bathroom floor was clean—and the backyard furniture—I would focus.

And start writing the brilliant book everyone expects.

July 4, Wednesday

"JANE," HUGH SAID from the doorway of the bathroom. "We're late."

I lifted my head from my scrubbing. "I'm almost done," I said excitedly, gesturing to the expanse of gleaming tile.

He seemed less excited. "Then you still have to take a shower and get dressed."

I gave a little wave. "So we'll be a little late."

He glanced at his watch. "A lot late. And everyone is doing this for you, Miss America."

A Fourth of July cookout at Miranda's for the ex-pat. Hugh's friends had made it an annual party, complete with cheeseburgers, Coke, and sparklers. It always made me feel guilty because all evening everyone would pity me for being homesick, and I wasn't. Still, it was a sweet gesture.

"The sooner I get this done, the sooner we can leave," I

pointed out.

"I can help," he offered unenthusiastically. "What's left to do?"

I gasped. "You can't tell where I've cleaned?"

He scratched his head. "Uh... no?"

"*I'll* finish it," I said, supremely irritated.

He sighed. "How much longer?"

"Ten minutes, max."

"Okay... I'm going to grab a beer and wait in the yard." He whistled for Trudy and she leapt up to follow him. I frowned after them—the least they could do is keep me company.

But I didn't let them put a damper on my mood—I had only a small area left to clean by the loo and it was the worst. Too late, I realized I probably should have let Hugh clean it since it was likely his bad aim that had led to the gunky buildup. *Ick.*

A few minutes later, I sat back, triumphant. The floor was dazzling.

Unfortunately, ten minutes had stretched to forty. I jumped up and took a shower in record time, then slipped into a sundress and pushed my feet into sandals. My knees were red from kneeling and my pedicure had expired, but it would have to do. My shoulder-length hair would dry on the way, I reasoned, and unlike my mother, no one in our group cared if I wore mascara. When I bounced out of the house, two empty beer bottles sat on the table and Hugh was talking on his phone.

He saw me, then ended the conversation and stood. "Ready?"

I nodded and picked up the beer bottles to toss along the way. "Who was that?"

"Miranda, wanting to know if we're still coming. People are leaving."

I winced. "Sorry. But the bathroom floor looks so good!"

"Uh-huh."

"You'll appreciate it when your feet don't stick to the floor."

"They didn't before, but okay."

I pointed at the moldy table and chairs. "Those are next."

He squinted at the furniture, then swung his head back to me. "I think we should hire a housekeeper."

I frowned. "You don't think I keep the flat clean?"

"Lately, the opposite. All you *do* is clean, Jane. I can't eat a sandwich for you tidying up my crumbs along the way."

I wanted to cross my arms in self-righteous indignance, but the beer bottles I'd picked up kept me from it. "It's called being neat, Hugh." I handed him the bottles in defiance. "And it's a lot of work picking up after you."

"So a housekeeper would help you to keep things as neat as you like. And," he added in a quiet voice, "you'd have more time to write."

I bristled. He was implying I wasn't working when I should be. "You obviously don't understand how disruptive it is to have someone underfoot—I'd rather do the cleaning myself."

He pinched the bridge of his nose. "Okay, forget it. Let's get to the party before everyone goes home, how about it?"

"I'm ready. You're the one standing here complaining about me being neat."

"It's more than neat, Jane, it's—" He cut himself off.

"What?" I challenged. I was feeling attacked—and betrayed. I was working like crazy to keep things together and he was fussing at me. I teetered dangerously close to tears.

"Never mind," he said, then gave me a wry smile. "Let's go celebrate your country's independence from mine."

July 5, Thursday

"YESTERDAY WAS nice," Hugh offered from the kitchen table where he was eating buttered toast.

I was wiping the counter and trying not to stare at the crumbs he was getting all over. "Yes, it was really great of Miranda to have us over. The fireworks were a nice touch."

He laughed. "The police didn't agree. If she can't get out of the ticket, I told her I'd pay the fine."

That was generous of Hugh—and fortunate since I'd noticed this morning my bank account was getting seriously low. The royalty payment I'd just received was shockingly small, more proof that sales of the second book had bombed and sales of the first book had tapered off drastically. If I were careful, I'd be able to make it until I was paid for turning in the current manuscript, but it would be close. Anxiety hummed in my belly—I'd promised myself I would never be poor.

Maybe I shouldn't have quit my crummy marketing job after all.

"Now that the bathroom floor is clean," Hugh said mildly, "are you going to work on your book today?"

"Uh-huh." I bent over to scan the contents of the cabinet under the sink. "Do we have bleach?" I was going to need bleach to clean the outside furniture properly.

"I have no idea. Now that I think about it, Jane, I don't even know what this book is about."

That made two of us—three, counting Jocelyn. But I resented him checking up on me. "Since you're not my audience, you really shouldn't concern yourself."

He lowered his chin. "Right."

I'd hurt his feelings, but he'd ruffled mine first.

He pushed to his feet and reached for his work bag. "I'm leaving, then."

"Okay, bye," I said, then walked over to brush his inconsiderate toast crumbs into my hand.

Trudy followed him to the door and whined when it closed. When she came back to me, I let her lick the crumbs from my fingers.

"You at least appreciate me," I murmured.

My phone rang and for a fleeting second, I hoped it was Hugh, calling to apologize and promise we'd cook dinner together when he got home, like we used to.

Instead, Jocelyn's name came up on the screen. My stomach bottomed out, and my chest tightened. Then I exhaled. She was probably calling about the cover concepts—that would be a fun, easy conversation. I connected the call.

"Hi, Jocelyn."

"Jane," she said in a warm voice. "How *are* you?"

"I'm well, thanks. I got your message about covers for the new book."

"Yes, that's why I'm calling," she said, further easing my anxiety. "I just emailed you three concepts the art department is excited about. Take a look and see what you think. I'm on my way to a meeting, so we'll touch base later. Just so you know, number two is my favorite."

"Okay," I said, giddy the conversation would be short.

"Oh, and Jane... how far along are you on the manuscript?"

I broke into an instant sweat. "Uh... not far in pages, but I'm making headway."

"How far is not far? A hundred pages?"

This is where I should explain a full manuscript is about *four* hundred pages. I closed my eyes. "Not quite." Not even close.

Trudy walked over and licked my toes. She could sense something was wrong.

Jocelyn made a concerned noise. "Jane, I don't want to put too much pressure on you, but the book is due at the end of September and expectations are high."

"Yes, I know," I said, forcing confidence into my voice. "But I've put in lots of prep work on this one... I feel good about it." Did I mention that novelists are good liars?

"I'm glad to hear it," Jocelyn said, "but I need to feel good about it, too."

Acid bathed the breakfast I'd eaten.

On the other end of the phone, Jocelyn shifted, and I pictured her leaning forward on her desk. "Jane, in your first book, your great writing compensated for what could have been a thin story, so it worked. In your last book, I sensed you were holding back, being safe with your main character, and I wish I'd pushed you a little more. In this one, don't be afraid to dive deep."

"Okay," I murmured.

"Good, then. Let's touch base on the manuscript in a couple of weeks. Meanwhile, let me know what you think of the covers."

"I will. Bye, Jocelyn."

"Bye, Jane."

I disconnected the call, and heaved a sigh of relief. "Well," I said to Trudy, "that didn't go so badly."

Then I ran over to the waste basket and threw up.

July 6, Friday

"JANE," HUGH SAID, standing in the hallway holding his to-go mug and dressed for work. "I'm leaving."

I was cleaning my bookcase in preparation for cleaning my

desk in preparation for a productive writing day. "Okay, bye."

"Have a good day," he said with a little smile. I could tell he was worried about me, dear man.

I smiled back. "I will. You too."

Trudy followed him to the door for a goodbye scratch, then came back to lie down under my desk. She looked up at me expectantly.

"Not you too," I said. She had practically lived under my desk when I'd written the first two books. "I know it's been a while. As soon as I get these shelves straightened, I'll get back to work."

Several copies of my first two books sat on the shelves in hardcover and paperback, audio, plus German and French editions. Just looking at them had once filled me with pride and inspiration, but now they mocked me. Jocelyn said the story in the first book was thin, and I'd played it safe in the second. On impulse, I retrieved a big cardboard box from our recycling bin and packed all the books inside, then shoved it into a closet. It felt good to see all that empty space on the shelves—space for future books.

Better books.

Reinvigorated, I tackled my desk, filing and tossing papers and rearranging accessories until the only thing left on it was my laptop and a stapler.

I opened the top drawer and dropped the stapler inside.

Now I could write.

I booted up my laptop and drummed my fingers while the various apps loaded, antsy now to finally get some thoughts down. Thoughts to match the cover Jocelyn liked—three blurred plates in midair being juggled by unseen hands. The title, JUGGLING ACT, and my name were depicted in wiry, frenetic fonts, lending "tension" to the jacket which, apparently, was trending in book covers.

When my word processor presented a fresh blank page with a blinking cursor, I smiled and put my hands on the keyboard.

Dive deep.

I frowned, dropped my hands, and sat back. I understood Jocelyn wanted something deep and meaningful, but I didn't know where to begin.

I decided to surf online, hoping inspiration would strike. My character was a young mom juggling responsibilities, and social media was a goldmine for mom communities. I found germane Facebook groups and skimmed entries from all over the world from mothers seeking camaraderie and support for everything from post-partum depression to toddler tantrums to head lice.

And that was only the first page.

And—this is probably terrible of me—I confess after a couple of hours of reading like a voyeur, instead of feeling inspired, I felt *relieved.* Relieved I wasn't a mother with an avalanche of problems so overwhelming it would drive me to seek comfort on forums from total strangers.

And it gave me insight into what my own mother must have dealt with. Two kids with an emotionally distant partner and few resources to keep us entertained and cared for, all while working every odd job she could cobble together. No wonder Sharon Hunnicut had been strict and controlling—she'd probably been deeply unhappy.

Yet as unpleasant as our homelife could be, I'd had it better than some.

I bit into my lip. It had been a while since I'd looked for Deidre... maybe I'd get lucky this time. I brought up a Facebook search bar and slowly typed "Deidre Valentine," then pressed enter.

There were always several hits—typically a couple dozen from all over the world. Some I could rule out quickly from a photograph, but others I had to click on and read further to determine they were either too young or too old or too tall or whatever to be my high school friend. Deidre had spent many nights at my house to escape her own family situation. She'd threatened to run away countless times, and one day our senior year she'd simply disappeared. To my knowledge, no one had heard from her again. I'd always held out hope she would reach out to me. After my first novel was published I'd conjured up fantasies of her showing up at a booksigning to surprise me.

But it hadn't happened.

My toes tingled—Trudy was licking them. She barked, which was rare, signaling she wanted to be walked. I glanced at the clock, shocked to see how late it was and dismayed how much time I'd frittered away. It was past time for Hugh to be home and I strained to recall if he'd mentioned he'd be working late. While I was walking Trudy I texted to ask what time he'd be home.

My phone rang and his picture came on the screen. I groaned and put the phone to my ear. "Since you're calling I assume you're going to be *really* late."

"Actually, Jane, I'm not coming home."

I frowned. "Surely that boss of yours doesn't expect you to pull an all-nighter?"

"No. I mean, I'm not coming home... I'm moving out."

I heard the words, but my mind couldn't process them logically. "Hugh," I said with a little laugh, "is this a joke?"

"No. I told you this morning I was leaving."

Incredulous, I sputtered like a beached fish. "But... but... but you say that *every* morning."

"Maybe so," he said quietly. "But this time I've left."

July 7, Saturday

WHEN I WOKE UP, I couldn't open my eyes because they were crusted shut from crying all night.

It was just a temporary break, Hugh said, to figure out our next step. He said I'd become neurotic and he no longer felt important to me. And this would give me a chance to finish writing my book in peace and quiet.

Once you meet your deadline, we can reassess.

Reassess... like a piece of property falling into decline.

How could he make one more thing contingent on me finishing this book, and at the same time make it harder for me to actually write? I was a mess, and the last thing I felt like doing was schlepping to my laptop to be creative.

Next to me in the bed, Trudy whimpered, then began to slowly lick my face—I'm sure the salty dried tears tasted good to her. I lay there like a statue and let her clean me up. My throat was parched but I didn't want to leave the bed.

Trudy barked, wanting—I'm sure—to know what the heck was going on and where was the big person with the deep voice who normally slept here?

"We're on hiatus," I croaked. Like a television series the writers don't yet have an ending for.

She barked again and I remembered Hugh normally takes her out in the mornings.

"Okay, let me get some clothes on," I muttered, then flailed around until I threw off the covers. When I sat up I realized I was still wearing the same clothes as yesterday. How fortuitous—I was already dressed.

I stumbled to the bathroom and in the absence of a cup, leaned over to get a drink straight from the faucet, then swished a mouthful of water in lieu of brushing my teeth.

When I straightened, I surveyed the shiny white and blue tile and choked back a new flood of tears. Since when was it neurotic to want a clean floor?

Trudy's scratching at the door interrupted my pity party. It was raining, so instead of combing my hair, I grabbed a hat from the hall tree and pulled on my wellies, then trudged after Trudy, carrying her leash. I was descending the steps when my phone chimed. It was a text from Hugh. My heart sped up.

Don't forget to take Trudy out.

I deflated. *On it* I texted back.

Are you okay?

I hesitated, then texted *No, we miss you.*

I waited for him to reply that he missed us, too, that he'd made a mistake and was coming home. I held my breath…

Let me know when you'll be out, I want to come by to get a few clothes.

A misery tumor clogged my throat. So that was how it was going to be.

Now would work

I hit send, then stashed my phone and walked out into the rain. The yard was squishy, and the wood table and chairs, now mold free (thanks to my neuroses), were soaked through, probably sprouting new spores even as I stood there.

I whistled for Trudy, but she didn't come. I sighed, thinking she must have really needed to go. When I rounded the corner to the side path, though, I didn't see her. And when I saw the open gate, my heart jumped to my throat.

"Trudy?"

I trotted along the path and through the gate, slipping and sliding on the wet stones, scanning for her little brown body. She was nowhere in sight. At the sidewalk, I looked both ways, but between the rain and my panicked state, my vision was compromised. Worse, car traffic on the street was heavier than usual—could she have been hit? I ran haphazardly, calling her name, ducking and looking under parked cars and bushes.

Nothing.

I jogged down the sidewalk in one direction for a half block, then turned around and jogged in the other direction. It was raining harder now, and I was gasping for breath. A man approached, scrunched into his coat lapels, and I asked if he'd seen a little brown dog. He shook his head and kept going. I asked the same of a young couple a few yards farther. They seemed more concerned, but said no, and were late for an appointment, else they would help me look.

Someone to help me look...

I ducked under an awning and called Hugh. After three rings, my anger spiked—yesterday morning we were engaged and this morning he was ignoring me?

He answered the call. "Jane, I really don't want—"

"Trudy's lost."

"What? Are you sure?"

"Yes, I'm sure. The gate was open and she got out of the yard before I could attach her leash—" I broke off on a sob. "She's gone."

He made an anguished noise—concern? Irritation? "I'm on my way."

July 8, Sunday

"WE'LL FIND HER," Hugh soothed. He had spent the night on the couch. We were standing in the kitchen staring at Trudy's leash lying on the counter. "Everyone in this neighborhood knows her. She'll turn up as soon as the rain stops."

But after a day and a half of traipsing through our neighborhood and the surrounding areas in vain, I was inconsolable. "It's your fault," I blurted.

He winced. "I know you're upset, but—"

"It is," I insisted. "It's your fault she's gone. You blindsided me—blindsided us—by leaving with no warning. You turned everything upside down and I was so distracted, I must've left the gate open."

Hugh pressed his lips together, then said, "Or the postal carrier left it open, or the wind blew it open, or a half dozen other things could've happened, and it doesn't make any difference anyway. Trudy's probably taking cover somewhere in a flat full of rowdy kids and having a jolly time while we're worried about her."

"*I'm* worried about her," I corrected.

He sighed. "So am I." Then he looked me over. "And I'm worried about you, too."

"Could've fooled me."

"Jane, I didn't want to move out, but I don't know what else to do. I've tried talking to you about your issues, but you don't want to listen."

"My issues? Since when is wanting to live in a clean flat an issue?"

He reached for my hands. I resisted, but he hung on and turned them over. "Since you started cleaning so much, your hands look like raw meat."

I dropped my gaze and surveyed my red, swollen fingers and cracked skin, then pulled them away. "I just need to invest in a good pair of rubber gloves."

"It's more than that, Jane," he said quietly. "You spend all your time taking care of the flat, and you don't take care of yourself anymore." He gave me the once over. "Those are the same clothes you were wearing when I left Friday morning."

I bristled. "I fell asleep Friday night before I had a chance to change, and yesterday I decided I'd take a shower when I got back from walking Trudy, and then last night I was too exhausted."

"I'm not judging—"

"Yes, you are!"

He sighed. "I'm just pointing out that your behavior has become…"

"Neurotic?" I supplied. "I know—you already said that."

"Actually, I was going to say 'compulsive.'"

My eyes flew wide. "Compulsive?"

He took a step back—probably subconsciously—and nodded. "In the clinical sense."

I gaped at him. "Clinical sense? You're saying I'm sick? That I have OCD?"

He put his hands up. "No. Not sick—stressed. Overwhelmed, maybe. Something is making you behave like this." He gave a little shrug. "Maybe it's me."

I blinked. "Is that why you left?"

"Something had to change, Jane. Look at you—you're a mess."

He was right. I was a disheveled, neurotic, unlovable mess.

My phone rang and I fumbled for it, hoping it was word of Trudy. Instead, the area code and exchange was Accident, Alabama. I grimaced. I'd missed my regular Skype time with Mom, so she was probably concerned.

"I should get this," I said to Hugh. I connected the call and tried to force cheer into my voice. "Hi, Mom—this isn't a good time, can I call you back?"

"It's me, Sis," my brother's voice sounded.

I frowned. "Tyler? Is everything okay?"

"No. That's why I'm calling. It's Mom—she's had a stroke."

July 9, Monday

I HAD TO BUY A SUITCASE.

After I moved to London with Hugh, I'd given away my trunks and other big pieces of luggage in favor of cute overnight bags for jaunts to Paris and Rome. There were few stores open in my neighborhood on Sunday, so the pickings for a bag large enough to get me to the States were slim. I stared at the bright pink suitcase as the baggage handler weighed and measured it. I wasn't quite sure what I'd packed, although I have a vague recollection of tossing in a black dress and shoes, just in case.

Tyler said the stroke had happened at home, outside the garage. When Mom didn't show to drive one of her clients to church and didn't answer her phone, the alarm had been sounded. Tyler said doctors attributed the quick action of paramedics and my mother's relative youth to her still being alive... but made no promises what her condition might be by the time I arrived, which would be late tonight.

I was all cried out.

Hugh had offered to come with me, but I wasn't sure how long I'd be away, plus I didn't think this was the best occasion for him to meet my family. I'd kept them apart the entire time we'd dated in college and thwarted an introduction before I moved to London by sending Hugh on ahead and joining him later.

Now that we'd broken up and with my mother critically ill, it didn't seem the optimal time to be breaking bread.

Besides, he needed to stay behind to look for Trudy, and to stay at the flat in case she found her way home.

He'd accompanied me to the airport and given me a long hug with instructions to text him when I'd landed. I wanted to wrap my legs around him, but I'd peeled myself away and said I would.

My mother was in a hospital in Birmingham, which is about forty-five minutes from Accident and has an airport, but no direct flights from London. So I would make the nine-hour flight to Atlanta, then hop a smaller plane to Birmingham where my brother Tyler said he'd meet me.

I was numb through the boarding process and thankfully, my seatmate had fallen asleep before the safety demonstration, so I was left in peace to marinate in misery. Different parts of my life spun like a carousel in my mind, fighting for attention: my career, my relationship with Hugh, my own state of mind, and now, my mother's health.

She was too young for a stroke, I'd argued with Tyler, as if it mattered. I asked if she'd been sick lately, and he said no, then added he didn't see her very often, that he typically squeezed in feeding the pigs between work deliveries.

"I saw her at the diner the day before yesterday," he said. "She looked tired, but she said she was fine."

So the Accidental Diner was still there, serving the four groups—bacon, biscuits, gravy, and grits—to the town's residents. But to be fair, if my mother had high blood pressure, it probably had more to do with her temperament and life experiences than the Blue Plate Special.

As far as my career... I'd decided to wait to contact Jocelyn until I knew what awaited me at home. But even the best outcome of Mom recovering quickly would probably take a chunk out of my schedule, so calls to my agent and editor seemed inevitable.

Weighing most heavily on me was the rock of dread in my stomach at returning to my hometown, and for such a sudden, traumatic reason. Somehow I'd convinced myself I'd never have to come back, that I could have my life in London as a successful novelist and forget what I'd been in Accident, Alabama. And if I did return, it would be when I was at the top of my game, a celebrated bestseller with critical acclaim, and happily married to an exotic foreigner.

Not when every aspect of my life was on a downward slide.

I dozed fitfully and even with the warm washcloths the attendants passed out near the end of the flight, I wasn't feeling very fresh. Then I had to sprint to make my connection and my chatty seatmate on the next flight appeared to be on speed. I should have asked for some because by the time I landed in Birmingham, I felt like a zombie, and was pretty sure I looked it, too.

But I was past caring. When I arrived in baggage claim, it was almost midnight. I scanned for Tyler's ruddy face and big body.

"Jane? Jane Hunnicut?"

The accent was right—thick and deep—but the voice didn't belong to Tyler. I turned to look at the man and recognition banged into me.

Will Story.

A local boy, a few years older than me. Handsome and rowdy, not the kind of guy who noticed mousy girls who smelled vaguely of pigs. Emma and Deidre both had mad crushes on him. Grown-up Will was wearing dusty jeans, dirty boots, and a short sleeve checked shirt. And a cowboy hat, Jesus Christ.

"Yes, I'm Jane," I said, then opted to feign ignorance. "Who are you?"

"I'm Will Story, a friend of your brother's. I came in his place."

My pulse spiked. "Is my mother worse?"

"No. Tyler decided to pull an evening shift and I offered to pick you up." He gave me a little smile. "I hope that's okay."

"Sure. Er, thank you."

"I'm sure you're exhausted," he said, reinforcing my belief that I looked like a hag. "I can take you straight to the hospital or somewhere else first if you want to freshen up."

I gave him a flat smile. "Just straight to the hospital, please."

He nodded congenially. "Which bag is yours?" he asked, jerking his thumb toward the luggage carousel.

"The big pink one," I murmured, feeling foolish, then feeling irritated at myself for feeling foolish around this yokel. I was the one who had left Accident to get an education and had lived abroad and had published two novels. This guy worked with my brother delivering packages. And hey, I'm not knocking home delivery—I order as much stuff from Amazon as the next person. But I'm not going to feel inferior to this truck driver just because he's handsome.

And tall.

He retrieved my obnoxious suitcase, escorted me to the outside curb, then excused himself to fetch his vehicle from short-term parking. My suspicions about his station in life were confirmed when he pulled up at the curb in a behemoth mud-splattered truck. I'd forgotten how big the vehicles in America—and more specifically, the South—are.

Will jumped down from the driver side and ran around to help me up. I was texting Hugh to let him know I'd arrived, and to ask about Trudy. But considering the time difference, I didn't expect him to respond.

"Are you texting Tyler?" Will asked. "He asked me to remind you."

"No. My fiancé in London." I was so used to calling Hugh my fiancé, it just popped out.

"Ah."

"I'll text Tyler next," I said.

"This door sticks a little. Sorry my truck is so dirty—I didn't have time to run it through the wash after work."

"No worries," I murmured, sling-shotting myself up into the seat with the help of a hanging grab handle I was more accustomed to seeing on the Tube than in passenger vehicles. "You must have a very rural route."

He laughed up at me from the ground. "You could say that."

"How long have you worked with Tyler?"

He frowned. "Oh, I don't work with Tyler—we're just friends."

It was worse than I thought—he was unemployed. Suddenly,

I was glad I hadn't brushed my hair—or my teeth. Or put on makeup. Or acted as if I remembered his name.

"I'm a doctor," Will said, then swung the door closed.

July 10, Tuesday

"YOU LOOK LIKE HELL," Tyler said when he walked into the waiting room in the early morning hours.

"It's good to see you, too," I replied.

He grinned and came in for an awkward hug. My brother is a big guy, with dark hair and eyes like our father had. He was wearing a rumpled khaki uniform with his company's logo and was more rotund than the last time I'd seen him.

"I see Stacey is feeding you well."

He patted his stomach. "She does her best."

"How are the kids?" His wife Stacey had two boys from a previous marriage.

"Happy to be out of school for the summer. Stacey took them to her parents in Tuscaloosa for a few weeks, so I'm enjoying some quiet time." Then his mouth twitched downward. "Well, I was before this."

I nodded. "I'm sorry it fell to you."

He shrugged. "I'm used to it."

It was a fair slam to me, but I wanted to point out he could've escaped Mom, too. Instead, I bit my tongue.

"How was your trip?" he asked to cover the moment.

"Long, but uneventful."

"Expensive, too, I bet," he said, then grinned. "Although I'm sure you can afford it, you being a big time author and all."

I smiled back while thinking I was sure he had more money in his bank account than I did.

"People in Accident ask me and Mom about you all the time."

"That's really nice."

"So life is good? You're still engaged? Still writing dirty books?"

My life is terrible. The man I'm no longer engaged to had texted to let me know Trudy is still missing. And... wait, what? "My books aren't dirty."

He laughed. "Well, you know—sexy. At least that's what Stacey told me. You know me—I'm not a big reader."

Apparently Stacey isn't either because as contemporary novels go, mine are pretty chaste.

"Sorry I wasn't at the airport to pick you up," he said. "I hope you didn't mind Will stepping in. He heard about Mom and asked if he could do anything to help out."

"It was nice of him to do you a favor. I don't remember the two of you being friends."

"Will's a veterinarian, so he's been out to look at the pigs a few times and we got to know each other. We go fishing every once in a while."

"So he said." I'd had to bite my tongue not to comment on his 'I'm a doctor' remark—as far as I was concerned, only people doctors get to say 'I'm a doctor.' But I'd hit a wall and didn't feel like debating semantics. Instead I'd passed out and slept until he pulled to a stop in front of the hospital. If I had snored or drooled, he'd been nice enough not to mention it. Still, I'm sure he'd concluded I am not a well put-together package.

Tyler gestured toward the stainless double doors at the end of the hallway labeled "Intensive Care Unit." "Have you seen Mom?"

"Not yet." Visiting sessions were few and far between because—understandably—it depended on the stability of the patients on the other side. I nodded to the nurses' station where I'd made myself known. "They said they'd do their best to get me in next time."

"Any change in her condition?"

"Not as of a half hour ago. She still hasn't regained consciousness."

"I can take you home," Tyler said, nodding to my enormous pink suitcase. "I know you're bushed. I'm sure Mom has kept your room just the same as it was when you left."

No doubt. "I booked a hotel room close to the hospital. I thought it would be easier than driving back and forth from Accident."

"I'll take you there, then."

"Let me try one more time to see Mom."

Tyler followed me down to talk to the nurses.

"Hi," I said, offering a smile to a new face, a perky blonde. "I'm Jane Hunnicut, and I—"

"I know who you are," the young woman cut in with a sugary smile. "We went to school together—do you remember me?"

I did not. I glanced at her nametag—Diane. "Diane, uh..." I trailed off.

"Shipple," she provided. "Well, Diane Yancey now." She grinned. "I married Dale Yancey, the baseball captain."

I vaguely recall she had twirled something—a baton? A flag? And my mouth watered to tell her this far past high school, sports accomplishments mattered only if they were on the professional level... but I digress.

"That's nice. I—"

"Don't you live in England now?"

"Yes."

"Aren't you a screenwriter or something?"

"A novelist."

"You always had your nose stuck in a book," she said, wagging a finger as if I'd been a naughty, naughty nerd.

"Uh-huh. Diane, I was hoping—"

"I'm *so* sorry about your mom. I guess you'd like to see her, wouldn't you?"

I nodded, giving in to her domination.

"Jane's come a long way," Tyler said unnecessarily. He was suddenly animated and flushed. Oh, God, he had a crush on her—would high school never end?

She winked at Tyler. "I'll see what I can do."

Tyler watched her walk down the hall, and I watched him, a finger of unease prodding me. Despite his girth, Tyler was handsome and had always been somewhat of a womanizer. I hoped he was being faithful to Stacey, but I wouldn't be surprised if he wasn't. He hadn't had the best role model in our father.

Diane came back beaming. "You can go in for five minutes."

"You go in, Jane," Tyler said. "I'll wait for you." But he was looking at Diane, not me.

"Through those doors," Diane said. "The nurse inside will help you."

I thought I was prepared, but nothing prepares you to see your parent incapacitated. And when your parent is a force of nature, like Sharon Hunnicut, it's especially shocking.

My mother is a pretty woman who prides herself on her grooming and looking young for her age. But small and pale against the sheets and hooked up to beeping machines, her face drawn and slack, she'd aged twenty years.

Tears flooded my eyes and ran down my cheeks. I reached out to pick up her hand. Her fingers were stiff and curled into her palm.

"Mom," I said, trying to steady my voice. "It's Jane. I'm here."

And from the look of things, I would be for a while.

July 11, Wednesday

I WAS JARRED from sleep by my ringing phone. I was so disoriented, it had rung three times before I remembered I was in a hotel room in Birmingham, and my life was in disarray. When I found my phone, I was happy to see Hugh's face on the screen. My heart leapt in the hope he was calling to tell me Trudy had been found.

"Hello," I croaked.

"You were asleep."

I sat up and swung my legs over the side of the bed. "It's fine. Did you find Trudy?"

"No. Sorry. But I put up flyers all over the neighborhood."

My shoulders fell in abject disappointment. "Okay. Call me as soon as you find her, day or night."

"I will. How are things there?"

"Uh... I don't know—about what I expected, I guess. Not great."

"How is your mum?"

"Still unconscious as of last night. I got to see her yesterday morning for a few minutes." Then I'd checked into the hotel and except for getting up a couple of times to pee and call the hospital, I'd slept all day and all night.

"And how does she look to you?"

I teared up. "Ghastly. And I don't think she knew I was there."

31

"You don't know that," he soothed. "What do the doctors say?"

I sniffed. "Tyler and I are supposed to meet with her doctor this afternoon. Hopefully, I'll find out more then."

"Good. You know, you can call me if you like."

"Okay," I said cautiously.

"I feel really badly about the timing of all of this, Jane."

I pressed my lips together. "You mean you wouldn't have left me if you'd known my mother was going to have a stroke?"

"Damn, this isn't coming out right. I'm just sorry you're going through a rough time and I'm not there."

"So am I," I said pointedly.

After an awkward silence I refused to save him from, he said, "I hope you get good news from the doctors today."

"Thank you. Goodbye, Hugh." I disconnected the call, and the only thing that kept me from crawling back under the covers was the knowledge I might not want to come out again.

That, and the free breakfast buffet closed in forty-five minutes, and I was beyond starving.

I pushed myself up and in the direction of the bathroom for a quick shower, then rummaged through my pink suitcase for something to wear. When I pulled out a wool sweater, I realized I'd done a fantastically bad job of packing for summer in Alabama and if I stayed longer than a few days, I would have to go shopping.

More damage to my bank account.

I found something passable to wear and dashed to the breakfast bonanza, stunned anew at the number of food choices in America and the portion sizes. But today I was grateful for the bounty and I dug in.

When I got back to my room, I cleaned the bathroom— because no way was I going to trust the maids to do a good job— then called the hospital for an update on my mother's condition.

"No change," I was told. "But she's stable."

I thanked the nurse and ended the call, grateful Mom's condition hadn't worsened, but feeling frustrated and helpless. I booted up my laptop to research strokes, and learned just how little I knew about them—my ignorance had been bliss. The more I read about the worst-possible outcomes, the more terrified I became—long-term paralysis, dementia, loss of speech, hearing, and vision. I jotted down a few terms and questions for the doctor, so I felt more prepared when Tyler and I sat down with her later that day.

"Your mother had a intracerebral hemorrhagic stroke," Dr. Amanda Kessler told us in between gulps of coffee from a travel mug. She was, we'd been told, one of the few neurologists on staff who specialized in strokes, and we were lucky she was treating Mom.

"What does that even mean?" Tyler asked.

"It's a common type of stroke—a blood vessel in her brain ruptured and spilled blood throughout the brain, damaging brain cells."

"Do you know what caused it?" I asked.

"Not exactly, although we can narrow it down by excluding risk factors she didn't have, like a family history, or taking birth control pills. And since she's young for a stroke, it leads me to believe it was extreme high blood pressure. Was your mother complaining of headaches or vision problems?"

"Not to me," I said, and looked to Tyler.

He hesitated, then nodded slowly. "When I saw her a couple of days before it happened, I told her she looked tired and she said she had a headache, was having trouble sleeping. But she didn't seem concerned."

The doctor nodded. "Maybe your mother has a high threshold of pain."

I bit down on the inside of my cheek—that applied to all the Hunnicuts.

"She probably ignored the headache," the doctor continued, "even though it would've gotten progressively worse. But according to her records, this time last year her blood pressure was only slightly elevated… do you know if she's been under stress lately?"

Tyler turned his head to look at me. "She's been missing you more and more."

I blinked. "You can't possibly be implying I somehow caused her to have a stroke?"

The doctor held out her hand like a caution flag. "The stress might've come from many sources, such as loneliness, financial difficulties, or even the loss of a pet."

If that were true, I could be ramping up to a stroke of my own. "Can you tell how much of her brain has been damaged?"

"To some extent," the doctor said. "We know it's in the left hemisphere, unfortunately."

"Why is that worse?" Tyler asked.

"The left side controls speech and language," I supplied, recalling my research.

She nodded. "Right. Also, her memory might be affected, so if she does regain consciousness, don't be alarmed if she doesn't recognize either of you right away."

"Right away?" Tyler repeated. "So she could get her memory back?"

"If the brain damage isn't too extensive, then yes, stroke victims can be rehabilitated to recover some or all of their mobility, speech, and memory."

I wet my lips, almost afraid to ask. "What kind of timeline are we talking about?"

The doctor shook her head. "There's no way to know."

"More like four weeks, or four months?" I pressed.

"When it comes to strokes and recovery, I encourage the family to think in terms of months to years."

Months to years? Are you kidding me?

They both stared at me and I realized I'd spoken aloud. I tried to cover by asking, "What happens next?"

The doctor made a rueful noise. "I know this isn't what you want to hear, but for now we have to wait to see how much she can recover with the drugs we're giving her. Hopefully we can move her out of ICU soon to a regular room where you can visit more often. Meanwhile, the best thing you can do for your mother is to be patient." She glanced at her watch. "I'm so sorry, but I have to go. We'll talk again soon."

She stood and strode away, leaving me and Tyler sitting in stunned silence. Finally he grunted. "I guess you'll be on the next flight back to England?"

I turned my head to look at him. "How can you say that?"

"Easily. You and I both know you don't want to be here." He pointed in the air. "That you want to go back to your life over there."

I crossed my arms. "First of all, you're pointing to Canada. And second... you're wrong."

He arched his eyebrows. "You're staying?"

I swallowed. "I'm staying."

"For how long?" he asked suspiciously.

"For as long as she needs me," I said on an exhale, before I could change my mind.

He stood and pushed his uniform hat onto his head. "Good... because I can't lose my job."

Neither can I. And no way could I afford to rent a hotel room indefinitely.

"I need to go to work," he said.

"Tyler... I think I should stay at Mom's house to look after things. I can write there, and drive her car back and forth to the hospital... if that's okay."

"Makes sense. And someone should look after the cat."

"Mom has a cat?"

He nodded. "I've been leaving food out for it. Do you want me to take you there now?"

"The hotel room is already paid for tonight, and I need to pack, so how about tomorrow?"

"Okay." Then impulsively, he gave me a bear hug. "I'm glad you're here," he said, then wheeled away before things got too emotional.

As I watched him walk away, I pulsed with guilt. Because Tyler was right—when the doctor left, my first thought had been to jump on the next flight back to England.

Now I'm stuck.

July 12, Thursday

MONTHS TO YEARS. I was still mulling the doctor's ominous words the next day, standing with my big-ass pink suitcase on the curb in front of the hotel waiting for Tyler. To say I'm not looking forward to staying at my childhood home is an understatement of gigantic proportions. I didn't want to live there when I lived there, so why on earth would I want to go back?

Okay, the cat was one reason. I'm not much of a cat person,

but if I was suddenly incapacitated, I'd want to know someone was looking after Trudy. My heart squeezed. Hugh's text this morning said she still hadn't turned up. I hadn't yet told Hugh how long I might be staying here… I was still getting used to the idea myself.

Months to years.

I checked my watch and contemplated calling Tyler. I'd forgotten how bloody hot it could get in Alabama. I lifted the hem of my shirt to dab at my forehead—something I'd never do in London—then heard the rumble of a monster truck pull up in front of me.

I hurriedly righted myself, frowning at the greasy makeup stain on my shirt—but at least I was wearing makeup today. Some.

The driver side window zoomed down to reveal Will Story.

"Me again," he said, then opened the door and jumped to the ground. "Tyler picked up an extra shift and I was in the neighborhood, so…" He stopped. "Is that okay? I washed my truck."

"Yes, I see. It's very… shiny."

Then he gestured to his dusty work clothes. "Unfortunately, I didn't have time to hose myself down, too."

I gave him a flat smile. "No worries. I appreciate the lift. This will be the last time—I plan to drive Mom's car while I'm in town."

"Tyler told me. Hey, you look nice," he said, surveying my legs beneath the only decent skirt I'd brought with me.

My cheeks warmed. "Thanks."

"And rested," he added as he hefted my ridiculous suitcase and stowed it in the extended cab compartment. "I'm sure the jet lag has been brutal."

I nodded, and stepped up to be catapulted into the passenger seat. Too late, I realized my only decent skirt was too billowy to do it graciously.

Will must've noticed, too, because he cleared his throat and looked away. My face was on fire because my haphazard packing extended to my underwear. I was wearing the Wonder Woman panties a feminist girlfriend had sent me when the reviews for my first novel came out.

Perfect.

He closed my door, then circled around, sprang up into his seat, and set the truck in motion. "How long have you lived in England?"

"Six years."

"You have a blended accent now."

"Do I?"

He nodded, then grinned. "I hear a little Bama and a little Brit."

"And you know something about how Brits sound?" I asked lightly.

"Some," he said. "I spent a year at the University of Hertfordshire studying animal husbandry."

I couldn't hide my surprise. "Really? In Hatfield?"

"Right—north of London."

"And did you enjoy it?"

"Oh, sure, the people were great, and it's a beautiful place. But I was happy to come back." Then he gave a little laugh. "Not that I had a choice."

"Oh?" I was waiting for him to tell me about some family obligation, like a barefoot, pregnant wife. He wasn't wearing a wedding ring, but in his line of work, he probably wouldn't.

"Jefferson County paid for medical school if I came back to practice here. Large animal veterinarians are getting scarce, especially ones willing to make house calls."

"But you like it?"

"I love it. I can't imagine anything else I'd rather do."

The drive from Birmingham to Accident was considered picturesque, but the closer we got to the turnoff, the tighter my chest became. Small talk seemed like a good distraction.

"So you live in Accident?"

"'Fraid so," he said with a grin. "It's central to my territory. I built a house on a piece of property my parents left me."

So he was an orphan. "Do you have other family in the area?"

"A sister and brother-in-law in Birmingham—it's one of the reasons I'm there so often. They have a little girl I adore."

"That's nice. No kids of your own?"

He shook his head. "Never got around to getting married."

As if it were a dreaded project, like digging a ditch.

"You? I know you're engaged, but no kids?"

37

This was an opportunity to correct my earlier misstatement, but I decided it might lead to sticky questions, such as why my fiancé had dumped me. I folded my red, irritated hands in my lap. "No kids. But I have a—" I caught myself.

"A what?"

"A dog," I finished quietly.

"Ah, an animal lover. What breed?"

"Trudy is a cockapoo."

"Let's see—that's a cross between a cocker spaniel and a poodle?"

I nodded.

"Yeah, I've seen them. Cute. I'm sure she misses you."

I wet my lips. "Actually, she disappeared the day before I left to come here."

"Disappeared? You mean, stolen?"

I hadn't even considered someone had intentionally taken her. "I... don't know. The gate to our yard was open and I assumed she ran off." But if someone snatched her, it would explain why mere seconds later, I could find no trace of her.

"Did she have an identifying chip implanted?"

"No."

"Ah, too bad. Well, hopefully she'll turn up before you go back home."

I nodded.

"How's your mom, by the way?"

"The same. Her doctor said to be patient, that her brain is healing, and when she regains consciousness, they'll know more about her long term prognosis."

"I'm sure this is a big disruption in your life," he offered.

"It would be for anyone," I agreed.

"So... can you write anywhere? How does that work?"

I was surprisingly flattered he knew I was a writer—and flabbergasted he was interested. "I write on my laptop, so theoretically, I can write anywhere as long as I have electricity."

"But don't you have to—I don't know what the term is—be in the right frame of mind?"

I smiled. "Yes, that helps."

"So are you in the middle of writing a book now?"

The middle—if only. But I nodded. "My deadline is at the

end of September... but it's not going very well." I could've kicked myself for adding that last part.

"Oh? Why is that?"

I looked out the window. We were approaching the road that led to the house where I grew up. "Turn here."

"I remember. I had to come out and treat your mother's pigs for pink eye last summer."

Nice.

"What a pretty area to grow up in," Will said. "How many acres does your mother own?"

"About fifty, I think, but most of it's wooded."

When the house came into view, my lungs squeezed. The little white clapboard house was exactly as I'd remembered—neatly situated and prettily shuttered with black and green accents. A porch ran across the front of the house, studded with flowering plants and welcoming furniture. The matching detached one-car garage was equally as well-kept and landscaped. The yard was partitioned off from the land around it with a white picket fence that looked as if it had received a fresh coat of paint recently, and the whole scene was framed with majestic oak trees that had soared even taller in my absence.

It was like a postcard, and should've been a welcome sight. Instead I was awash with anxiety because our home had been such a contentious place.

In the distance, past the house, was Mom's flourishing garden—I was sure something or other needed to be harvested. Farther back sat the small barn and the pig pen, thankfully, out of sight.

But not out of mind, I acknowledged wryly when I climbed down from Will's truck where he parked next to the garage. The stench in the summer air was just as I remembered—putrid.

"Ugh," I said, bringing my sleeve to my nose.

"It's an acquired scent," Will agreed with a laugh, retrieving my bright pink suitcase.

"You can leave it on the porch," I said.

"Happy to carry it in for you," he offered.

When I turned to look at him, I was struck by how ruggedly different he was from Hugh. A little curl of awareness unfurled low in my midsection, taking me by surprise. But Will Story was a complication I did not need in my life—assuming he was even interested. And I was sure he was not.

"If you want," he added.

"Hm? I... no, just leave it on the porch, thanks."

He set it down by the front door.

"Thank you," I said abruptly, suddenly eager for him to leave.

"You're welcome," he said, moving back toward his truck. "I hope your mother recovers quickly."

"Thank you."

"And good luck with your book," he called.

"Er... thank you."

"Oh, and Jane..."

"Yes?"

He was standing by the open door of his Jurassic vehicle. "You turned me into a Wonder Woman fan." He grinned, then swung up into his vehicle, and banged the door closed.

I watched him drive away, tongue firmly tucked into my cheek.

Cursing my ludicrous packing job, I located the key hidden in the door frame where it had always been, then pushed open the front door and shoved my suitcase inside the dark interior.

But it stopped, bumping into something solid just inside the door.

I frowned and reached for the light switch. When a light flickered on, illuminating the living room, I gasped.

Jesus God... my mother had turned into a hoarder.

July 13, Friday

"HOLY SHIT," Tyler said, craning his neck to take in the spectacle.

"No kidding," I remarked dryly.

There are people who collect oddball things and display them in their living space. There are people who are content to live with a certain amount of clutter. There are people who are simply bad housekeepers. And then there are hardcore hoarders.

My mom was on the top of the pyramid.

Other than space for the door to swing open and a narrow path through each room, the house was packed wall to wall and stacked floor to ceiling with newspapers, magazines, books, records, clothes, household items and God only knew what else.

"This is like one of those TV shows," Tyler said, awestruck. "Is every room like this?"

I nodded grimly. "This didn't happen overnight. When was the last time you were in the house?"

He shrugged. "I don't know—years, I guess."

"Years?" I was incredulous. "How is that possible?"

He leveled his gaze on me. "How is it possible that you haven't been here in years?"

I frowned. "I live across the Atlantic Ocean—you live a few miles away. And you're here all the time to feed the pigs. How did you not know about this?"

He shrugged his big shoulders. "When I came by, she always walked out to talk to me in the barn while I fed the animals. She'd bring me coffee and give me stuff from the garden. And everything looks normal on the outside."

"She never asked you and Stacey over for dinner?"

"No. She came to our place a couple of times, but the boys got on her nerves so bad we stopped asking." He frowned. "She and Stacey had a falling out."

"Over the boys?"

He nodded. "She said Stacey was a bad mother, and that was that. It's why Stacey won't visit her in the hospital."

I sighed—but I could so picture that angry exchange in my mind. My mother could be a tyrant. I gestured to the towering stacks of junk. "We can't tell anyone about this."

He locked gazes with me. "Yeah... let this be our secret."

Because if she recovered and thought we'd humiliated her in front of her community, well... neither one of us wanted to risk her wrath.

And personally, I didn't want another family scandal. Even after all these years, I was sure there were still plenty of whispers about my father dying of a heart attack while having sex with a much younger woman—who wasn't my mother.

"What are we going to do?" Tyler asked.

"I have to clear out enough space to at least live in."

"Where the heck did you sleep last night?"

"In the garage, in the backseat of her Caddy—it was the only place empty enough to stretch out." Not that I got much rest thinking about the unbelievable situation inside the house.

"Wow."

"Yes, wow. It's roasting out there."

"You can come stay with me," he offered. "We don't have a guest room, but there's a pull-out in the living room. And the boys' bunkbeds will be empty until they get back."

"Thanks, but I think I'll make more headway clearing things out if I stay here. Besides, we don't want Stacey to know something is wrong."

"You're right." He pulled his hand down his face. "This is godawful. I'll help you if I can, but I'm trying to make up for lost time at work." His face reddened. "Things have been tough for us this year financially."

Plus Tyler was such a big guy, it would be a while before I could clear things enough for him to even get inside to help.

"I'll let you know when I get to the heavy stuff," I murmured. "I wonder if she's been sleeping in the car, too. Her bed is piled high, along with everything else."

He pointed. "Except that table over there."

"That's where she sat when we Skyped," I said, noticing the dated family portrait hanging against the blue wall. "She made sure none of the clutter could be seen on-camera." A memory slid into my brain. "The last time we Skyped, she asked if I was planning a trip home. She said she'd need a little notice because she'd have to straighten up."

Hm... I'd thought she was nudging me to come home, but now I realize she was worried I might.

Tyler scoffed. "A little notice to straighten up? It would take months to clean up this place."

Months to years.

"And it's hard telling what you'll find in there," he said, then glanced around. "Have you seen the cat?"

I made a face. "No."

Ugh!

July 14, Saturday

"HERE, KITTY, KITTY."

I walked from room to room—sidled, really, because the pathways were so narrow—in hopes of hearing a scratch or a meow, some indication the cat was alive but possibly trapped somewhere in the unholy mess.

Part of me hoped I found it, and part of me hoped I didn't. Like Tyler, I'd seen too many of the hoarding shows where a family pet was either lost or forgotten amongst the piles of things, only to be found—way too late—by the clean-up crew.

At least I hadn't detected the scent of decomposition. There was plenty of dust to inhale, which is why I was wearing a face mask, but so far, no Dead Kitty smell.

When I was satisfied I'd searched all I could inside, I walked out onto the porch and leaned over to exhale. My chest was tight with anxiety—or maybe mold. The piles of things inside were making me crazy, but every time I decided to clean out a section, I became overwhelmed with the sheer enormity of the task and gave up.

Did my mother feel the same way?

I lapsed into a coughing fit, gagged, then resumed walking, through the yard, then beyond. It was a blistering hot day, and the dozen or so pigs were taking refuge in the shade, their hides ashy from dried mud that helped to keep them cool. They emitted snorts and grunts as I walked by, but didn't bother to get up.

I peeked into the barn, which was stocked with bags of pig pellets to supplement their seasonal diet of leftover veggies from the garden, but no cat.

I circled back to the garden, still calling, alert for any moving plants that might reveal a cat was hiding underneath. I was ready to concede it had run away—like Trudy. I scanned the tree line at the edge of the clearing and spotted something that made me smile.

The treehouse.

I'd all but forgotten about it, although walking toward it now through the deep field grass brought back a torrent of good memories. It was where Emma, Deidre, and I had hung out when they came to my house. In a rare bout of generosity, my father had built the treehouse for us out of scrap lumber and plywood, and we had practically lived in it during our pre-teen and teenage years.

The tall grass around the base of the tree looked snakey so I picked up a stick and beat the ground until I was satisfied no creepy-crawlies were going to get me if I waded in. The boards nailed into the tree for a ladder were surprisingly intact and secure because the tree bark had grown around them. Still, I tested each one before I put my weight on it. I climbed up the trunk and stuck my head gingerly through the square opening in the deck that was the foundation for the treehouse. Since it was open to the air and the elements, the deck was covered with leaves and branches, but again, I was surprised at how solid it felt.

I hoisted myself up through the opening as I'd done a thousand times when I was young, and stood to survey the little house itself. It was eight feet square with a real door and windows, siding and shingles, and it looked to still be mostly intact, proving my father could do something well when he wanted to work and he put his mind to it.

I walked over to the door and opened it carefully. I didn't see or hear a cat, but I was delighted to see the inside was dry and well-preserved. In the middle of the space sat the table and chairs we'd used for so many pow-wows, pizza parties, and late night seances. I stepped in to inspect the dusty table and smiled at the letters we'd carved into the wood—our initials: JH, EG, and ... I frowned.

Deidre's initials had been nearly obliterated with deep gouges. I didn't remember doing it, but Emma and I might have after Deidre had run away if we were angry with her. Or maybe Deidre had done it herself before she'd taken off.

Just looking at it made me sad. I hoped wherever Deidre was, she was happy.

July 15, Sunday

"HOW'S YOUR MUM?" Hugh asked.

We were Skyping. He was sitting in our kitchen, making me terribly homesick. I was sitting on the porch because I didn't want him to see the piled-high interior.

And I didn't want to see it either.

I was basically still living in the garage, sleeping in the backseat of the big car and using the bathroom inside the house. Thank goodness Mom's compulsion for personal hygiene had trumped her compulsion to hoard, so she had left narrow pathways to the sink, shower, and toilet.

"She's the same," I said with a sigh. "But the doctor says the fact that she's not worse is a positive sign."

"Then you have to be optimistic."

I nodded. "Any news about Trudy?"

He shook his head. "Not yet, but someone is bound to see the flyer and put two and two together."

"Unless she's not lost."

"What do you mean?"

"Will suggested maybe she was dognapped."

"Dognapped? Is that even a thing?" He frowned. "And who's Will?"

"Dr. Will Story. He's a friend of my brother's and the local veterinarian. He said it happens. And Trudy is adorable—maybe someone just decided to snatch her and take her home."

"That sounds far-fetched to me. But if someone wanted her enough to steal her, then hopefully they'll be good to her."

I frowned. "Is that supposed to make me feel better?"

His mouth opened, then closed, then opened again. "Yes?"

"I need to go, Hugh." I had the all-overs and was feeling suffocated by... well, everything, really.

"Wait," he said, lunging toward the camera. "I'm worried about you, Jane. Are you okay? This is a lot of stress to deal with at once. Are you... cleaning?"

I wanted to laugh—if only Hugh knew the figurative and literal mess I was dealing with, he wouldn't feel sorry for me—he would feel revulsion.

"Bye, Hugh. Call me the minute you have news on Trudy."

And I ended the call.

July 16, Monday

I HAD RUN OUT OF wearable clean clothes, was down to a wool sweater, a pair of fleece leggings, and a strapless bra.

45

And since the washer and dryer were completely blocked by a wall of cardboard filing boxes marked "The Accidental Post" (the town's defunct newspaper), I decided to pile all my laundry into Mom's car and drive to the laundromat, and run some other errands, too.

I had gone about a half mile on the road before encountering a frantically honking oncoming vehicle and realizing I was driving on the wrong side of the road.

I really had been gone a long time.

The town of Accident was like something you'd see in a William Eggleston photograph—the buildings, cars, and streets are long past their prime and half-heartedly patched until everyone simply gave up and called it "eclectic." There was no rhyme or reason to why some businesses exist (does the town truly need two cobblers?) and why some don't (bookstore, anyone?). There was no metered parking and you're just as likely to see someone cruising town on horseback as a car.

Driving through the shabby streetscape flooded me with good and bad memories—mostly bad. Someone once said writers are usually conflicted about the place where they grew up—presumably the internal struggle gives rise to the storyteller—and I'm no exception. On the one hand, living in an insular place with few entertainment choices fertilized my imagination. On the other hand, I always imagined being somewhere else.

I found a parking spot close to the laundromat and carried in an armful of clothes. The air was sweet with fabric softener and thick with lint. I found an empty washer and dumped the clothes inside, then went to the stooped attendant to get change. The woman looked too old to still be working, but that would probably be me someday.

"Thank you," I said, studying the new designs minted on American coins since I'd left.

She smiled. "You're Sharon Hunnicut's girl, aren't you?"

"Yes, I'm Jane."

"I'm Joann. I heard you were in town visiting your poor sick mother."

"That's right," I murmured.

"Tell her we miss seeing her in here."

Ah—so Mom had been blocked from using her washer and

dryer for a while now. "I will," I said.

While the clothes were on a wash cycle, I walked a block over to the Accidental Diner, the social hotspot, and grabbed a seat at the counter.

"Hi, there," a tired-looking woman said. "What can I get for ya?"

I ordered an egg sandwich and orange juice from a sticky menu, then handed it back to her and fished my hand sanitizer out of my purse. The alcohol stung my hands, but it was worth the pain.

"Hey, you're Jane Hunnicut," the woman said, her face alight with recognition.

"Yes," I said warily. "Do I know you?" She was wiry with dark hair, and tanned within two degrees of melanoma.

"I'm Tamara White," she said in a sing-songy voice. "I used to date Tyler."

"Oh... right," I said, deciding not to mention Tyler had dated countless women. "Nice to see you."

"Nice to see yew," she said. "I'm sorry to hear about your mom. Someone requested prayer for her in church yesterday."

"Er... thank you."

She flashed a sad smile, then wheeled away. I could feel other diners looking over to try to figure out who I was. I heard, "the Hunnicut girl," and murmurs of sympathy. I willed them to stay away and fussed with my phone to look busy until Tamara slid a plate of food in front of me.

"There you go," she said, beaming.

I nodded and took a huge bite of the sandwich so I wouldn't have to talk. Someone plopped onto the stool next to me.

Will Story smiled and touched the brim of his hat. "Hi, Jane."

It was the first time I'd seen him in clean clothes. He looked somewhat... good. I chewed and swallowed. "Hello."

"How's your mother?"

"The same when I called this morning. But thank you for asking."

He signaled Tamara for a coffee order to go.

"Will you let me know if there's anything I can do?" he asked.

I nodded, wondering if he owned a bulldozer.

"Any word on Trudy?"

I was touched he remembered her name. "Not yet."

He smiled. "Don't give up hope—she might find her way home yet. People and dogs always do."

I frowned.

"By the way, there's something I've been meaning to ask you."

Oh, no—he was going to ask me out, and I would have to hurt his feelings. I mean, he was weirdly cute with that absurd cowboy hat, but I didn't need the trouble.

"Weren't you a friend of that Valentine girl who went missing a few years back?"

Okay, a curve ball. "Yes… Deidre."

"Right," he said, nodding. "What happened to her?"

I wiped my mouth with a paper napkin. "She ran away."

"And no one ever heard from her?"

"Not to my knowledge."

"Not even you? Don't you find that strange?"

I gave a little shrug. "Deidre had a bad homelife, so she probably wanted to forget about this place."

He made a thoughtful noise. "Too bad."

Tamara handed him his coffee order, and he pushed to his feet. "Gotta run—Bill Tedder has a mare who's probably going to foal today."

So I knew where his arm would be most of the day. "Give thanks for extra-long gloves."

He laughed. "You're funny, Jane—you should consider writing comedy. Later."

I frowned at his retreating back. It had so been a mistake telling him I was struggling with my book.

And for all he knew, I *did* write comedy.

I finished eating, bounced back to the laundromat to toss my clothes in a dryer, then headed to the hardware store with my supply list.

The white-haired guy manning the counter was the same man who'd worked there when I was a kid. I found it oddly comforting… and a little creepy.

"Hi, there, little lady. What can I help you with?"

I took a deep breath and tried not to think about my dwindling cash reserves. "I need rags, brushes, buckets, bleach, heavy-duty garbage bags…"

July 17, Tuesday

I STARED AT the expiration date on the bottled salad dressing in dismay. "June 2014?"

I chucked it into the nearly full garbage bag, along with all the other expired, spoiled, molded, curdled, and rotted things from Mom's side-by-side refrigerator-freezer. Surely, she hadn't been eating this stuff—if so, no wonder she was sick. The dates on the items gave me some insight into when she might've started hoarding. It had obviously been going on for years.

The last time I'd been here, just before I moved to London, the house had been spotless, just like all through our childhood when Mom had drilled into us to pick up after ourselves and not make a mess. She'd policed our rooms mercilessly—toys left out went straight into the trash, clothes on the floor were first cut into shreds, then tossed… or burned. She loved to burn our belongings in front of us.

So to see what she'd done, what she'd allowed to happen to this house that she'd once been militant about left me angry and confused—but mostly angry. We were little kids, after all.

I wound up tossing everything in the fridge. Even if it hadn't yet expired, it couldn't be good for it to have sat amongst other rotting things. Once the refrigerator was empty, I scrubbed it with soapy water and wiped it down with bleach.

The freezer would take a little longer. The contents were unrecognizable, covered with a thick layer of milky ice. I left the door open to let it defrost while I tackled the first section of counter that was stacked to dangerously high heights with papers, books, and empty food containers. The triumph of seeing the fridge clean gave me the energy to keep going. To keep from getting overwhelmed, I had decided to take things one foot at a time.

I skimmed each paper before I tossed it in the unlikely event it was something important. It was mostly circulars of coupons, long expired. The empty food containers were Styrofoam to-go boxes from the diner, each washed and stacked. I lost count at two hundred of them, but there were easily twice as many. I pictured her standing at the sink, meticulously cleaning throwaway containers to stack and keep. It was so heartbreaking and out of character for the woman I knew, it left me breathless.

As the afternoon went by, I managed to clear a small space. I realized with a start it was like cleaning the bathroom floor tiles one tiny square at a time.

But I moved on before I could get bogged down in comparisons.

Hours later, at the bottom of the last pile stacked on the kitchen counter, my hand closed around a blue binder that struck a memory chord. I wiped the cover to reveal FAMILY FAVORITES written in block letters in permanent marker in Mom's handwriting. Then I remembered—it was the recipe book she used when I was growing up.

I opened the cover to find loose recipes from magazines glued onto pages, and others in her neat handwriting. Next to them she'd made notes: "Tyler's favorite," or "Make for Jane's birthday" or "Dermot asked for seconds."

Dermot was my deceased father, a deeply flawed man, and the love of my mother's life. The fact that she'd maintained observations about what pleased him and us brought me to tears. That was my mother—cruel one moment, indulgent the next. We never knew what we were going to get.

And here she was again, I noted ruefully, lying in the hospital keeping us guessing.

July 18, Wednesday

ON THE SECOND DAY of tackling the kitchen countertops, I found my mother's cell phone.

It was an older model smart phone, and dead as a doornail. I couldn't find the charger—who knew where that was—but luckily my universal charger was compatible, so I plugged it in. Within a few minutes, the message light began to flash. She'd obviously missed calls in the ten days since her stroke. But when I tried to access the phone, I found it locked and requesting a passcode.

I tried all the obvious number combinations—0000, 1234, and

various birth dates—to no avail. Maybe Tyler would know; otherwise, it would go on the list of things we'd have to petition to get access to if she didn't wake up soon, including her bank accounts. She probably had bills piling up.

I looked around, then laughed out loud. *Literally.*

A ring sounded and I realized it was Mom's phone. I didn't have to enter a passcode to accept an incoming call. It was a local number. Curious, I connected the call.

"This is Sharon Hunnicut's phone."

"Hello, this is Nancy Jeffson. I need a ride home from the doctor's office, please."

I squinted. My high school English teacher? "Ms. Jeffson, hello. This is Jane Hunnicut—I was a student of yours ten years ago."

"Jane? Yes, of course I remember you. You were such a good student. And you're a novelist now, how exciting."

Not really, but... "Yes, very."

"I thought you lived in London... are you home for a visit?"

"Yes. My mother suffered a stroke, so I'm back for a while."

"Oh, I hadn't heard. How awful. Is Sharon going to be all right?"

"We hope so. I'm at her house, looking after things."

"Oh, that's nice. I don't suppose you're looking after her taxi service, too? I just left a doctor's appointment at the town clinic, and I need a ride home."

"No, I..." The vision of my dwindling funds stopped me. "Um... maybe. Do you still live in Springer Heights subdivision?"

"Yes."

A quick, easy drive from the clinic to her house—ten minutes, tops. "How much does my mother usually charge?"

"Twenty dollars."

My eyes popped open. Twenty bucks for a few minutes work? That was better than Uber money.

Heck, that was better than *stripper* money.

"I'll be right there, Ms. Jeffson."

"Oh, wonderful! Thank you, Jane."

I disconnected the call, grabbed my purse and ran to the garage. Being careful to drive on the correct side of the road, I sped downtown to the clinic and pulled into the pickup/drop off area. I recognized Ms. Jeffson and waved, pleased to see she hadn't changed, still plump and animated.

I hopped out of the Caddy and opened the back door for her, scanning the seat for wayward bedclothes.

"Hello, Jane. How wonderful to see you."

"Hi, Ms. Jeffson, same here."

"You're just as pretty as ever," she said, tweaking my cheek.

Since I was never considered pretty, it was a true statement. "Thank you."

I closed her door, then climbed behind the wheel and headed toward her address. We chatted a bit to catch up—she was retired now, and busy with grandchildren.

"Jane, I can't tell you how much I enjoyed your two books."

I caught her reflection in the rear view mirror. "Even the second one?"

"Oh, yes, very much."

"Everyone says the second one wasn't as good as the first one," I pressed, eager for her opinion—and approval.

She gave a dismissive wave. "What does that even mean? How can you compare two works of literature? It's like comparing children. They're completely different and they should stand alone."

I absorbed her words like a sponge, and for the first time in ages, I felt calm. I pulled into her neighborhood and she pointed out her house. When I stepped out to assist her onto the curb, she handed me the agreed twenty dollar bill.

But after her benevolent advice, I felt guilty taking her money. "I can't accept it, Ms. Jeffson. Thank you for the pep talk."

But she pushed it into my hand. "Take it, dear. Writing isn't always the kindest profession." She waved and scooted toward her door. "Bye, now."

I felt a rush of affection for her as I climbed back inside. The woman had never set foot in a big city publishing meeting, yet in one sentence she'd given me the counsel I'd been hungry for, words neither my agent nor my editor had been able to supply.

A ring sounded and this time it was my phone. My pulse rocketed when I recognized the hospital's number.

"Hello?"

"Ms. Jane Hunnicut?" a woman asked.

"Yes, I'm Jane."

"Daughter of Sharon Hunnicut of Accident, Alabama?"

My heart clutched at the formality. "Yes," I choked out.

"Ms. Hunnicut, I'm calling to tell you your mother just regained consciousness."

July 19, Thursday

"MOM," I SAID, taking her hand. "It's me, Jane. Tyler and I both are here."

The doctors had been running tests when we arrived yesterday after the call, so they asked us to come back today. It had been enough for me just to know her eyes were open.

She was looking at me now, but her pupils were unfocused. The right side of her face drooped like a fallen curtain. I could barely hold back the tears.

"You had a stroke, so you might feel a little confused," I said thickly.

Behind me, Tyler leaned in. "But you're in the hospital and you're going to get better."

"Yes," I said, squeezing her drawn fingers. "I'm going to stay until you're better."

She blinked and for a second, I thought I saw recognition in her eyes, but whatever it was gave way to fear as she grunted and recoiled. Her hand pulled out of mine, but it could've been a reflex. She couldn't express herself, but it was clear she was agitated.

"You should probably leave now," Diane Shipple murmured to us, stepping in to try to calm Mother. "Dr. Kessler would like to speak to you."

I pushed to my feet, more scared now than ever. I was having a hard time reconciling my strong-willed, obstinate mother to the weak, vulnerable woman in the bed.

We exited the room in silence, but I could feel Tyler's tension mirroring mine. In the hall, Dr. Kessler stood studying an image on her tablet. When I saw it was a brain scan, I assumed it was Mom's. When she saw us, she clicked off the image and walked forward to meet us.

"So," she said with a smile, "this is what we'd hoped for. Your mother is awake, and now we can begin to assess her condition."

"She didn't seem to recognize us," Tyler said.

"She seemed frightened," I added.

The doctor nodded. "All normal. You're welcome to come back tomorrow and try again, but if she gets upset, it's better to leave. It's important that she's calm to keep her blood pressure down, and so we can conduct whatever tests we need to."

"So... more waiting?" Tyler asked.

She nodded. "More waiting. Once we've run all our tests, we'll probably move her to the rehab wing. But we'll keep you posted." She made a sympathetic noise. "This is a glimpse of what's ahead. It's not going to be easy. We have counselors on staff who can help you adjust." She fished out two business cards and handed one to each of us. "Just call if you need to talk to someone."

We thanked her, but we pocketed the cards. The Hunnicuts weren't the kind of people who talk to shrinks—we prefer to implode.

July 20, Friday

I SAT ON THE PORCH, sweaty and dirty from cleaning, and stared at the text from Jocelyn.

Hi, Jane, hope all is well... where are you on the book? Call me.

I realized it had been two weeks since I'd talked to my editor. She was expecting me to have made good progress on the manuscript by now.

So how could I tell her that not only did I not have one hundred pages for her to read, I barely had one hundred *words* for her to read?

Still, if ever I had a good reason not to be writing, it was now.

I punched in Jocelyn's number, half hoping to get her voice mail. But no such luck—she answered on the first ring.

"Hi, Jane, how *are* you?"

"Hi, Jocelyn. And... I've been better."

"Okay… talk to me." I could tell she was preparing herself for the same bullshit I'd fed her during our last phone call.

"Two days after we last talked, my mother had a stroke."

"Oh, no. Jane, I'm so sorry, is she okay?"

"Maybe—we don't have a lot to go on yet. I'm in Alabama, and it looks like I'm going to be here for a while. The bottom line is… I'm not going to be able to deliver the book by the end of September."

She made a painful noise. "That's too bad, and of course I understand. Things happen."

I relaxed a tiny bit. "I haven't talked to Ron yet. I wanted to make sure you're okay with pushing the delivery date, then I'll let you two work out the details."

Jocelyn sighed. "To be honest, I was expecting to have to move the date anyway. It's clear you're struggling with this one."

I closed my eyes. "Yes."

"I can't make any guarantees, Jane. I'll have to discuss this with the editorial committee because it'll mean juggling other books in the schedule. And I won't lie to you—there will be some people on the committee who will see this as a good excuse to cancel the contract because the sales of your last book are down."

I felt nauseous. Canceling the contract meant this book and the next one would disappear, along with the payouts—i.e., my income… plus I could forget getting another deal somewhere else… my agent would drop me…

But this was all my fault. If I'd stayed on pace with the manuscript, if I hadn't let self-doubt erode my confidence, I wouldn't be behind the eight-ball, and we wouldn't be having this conversation.

"I understand," I managed to get out.

"Okay, I need to go unravel some things." Her voice was heavy with disappointment. "We'll talk soon. Take care, Jane."

I ended the call.

And listened to the gurgling sound of my career circling the drain.

I gazed out over farmland. On a distant hill a few black and white spotted cows grazed, their tails swishing flies away. Behind me, the grunting pigs were unseen, but not unsmelled. A mocking bird sat on the white picket fence, calling for others to come and play. Here, no one and no thing was in a hurry to do much of anything. This was a world away from my other life.

And I really, really wanted my other life back. If I stayed here, I would waste away.

A blur of motion caught my attention. Something orange had leapt for the mocking bird, missing, but getting close enough to cause the bird to fly away, squawking.

The elusive cat.

I slowly moved closer, cooing, and stopped halfway. I knew enough about cats to know they preferred to come to you versus being pursued.

Not unlike human men.

The cat was orange and white and scruffy. It watched me warily, crouched and poised to streak away if necessary.

I sat down in the grass, calling to it softly. "Kitty, kitty…. kitty, kitty."

It was a tom, I noticed, and he was limping. He stalked all around me before finally coming close enough for me to reach out, then pet him, then pick him up. He had a wound on his front paw that was obviously hampering him.

There was not a lot in my world right now that seemed fixable—not my career, not my relationship with Hugh, not my mother.

But this… this seemed fixable.

July 21, Saturday

"WILL STORY."

I hadn't expected him to answer so quickly. "Um, hi, Will… this is Jane… Hunnicut."

"Hi, Jane. This is a nice surprise."

I didn't like what that did to my stomach. "I got your number from Tyler. Is this a bad time?"

"To do what?" he asked in a teasing voice.

I closed my eyes briefly. "To see a patient?"

"Problem with one of the pigs?"

"Uh, no. Mom's cat showed up and it has a bad gash on its paw. I tried to wash it, but he won't let me near it."

"Sure, I can come by and take a look at it. I'm finishing a call now, so how about thirty minutes?"

"Sounds good."

I went to the garage where I'd trapped the orange cat so he couldn't run away again, and perused my limited wardrobe stored in the big pink suitcase. I definitely needed more clothes. In the end I opted to stick with the shorts I was wearing, but swapped out my sweat-soaked T-shirt for a lightweight floral blouse. I had time to brush my over-long hair and swipe on some mascara before I heard Will's Godzilla truck coming around the driveway.

I met him by the garage.

"Hi," he said, swinging down.

"Hi yourself."

He removed a black bag from the truck, then gestured to the line of bulging garbage bags sitting next to the garage. "Doing some clearing out?"

"You could say that." The appalling part is the line of bags represented only what I'd cleared out of the kitchen. I hadn't yet ventured into the other, more dense rooms of the house.

"I drive right by the dump on the way to my place," he said. "I can take those bags for you."

I blinked. "That would be... nice. Thank you."

"Sorry, I'm a mess," he said, using his hat to knock the dust off his jeans. "Don't worry, I won't track anything inside."

Good—that kept me from making up an excuse not to invite him in.

"How's your mother?"

How could I say she was worse when at least she was awake? But she still recoiled and flailed around if I came near her. Last night I'd driven to the hospital late when I was sure she'd be asleep, just to sit with her. I'd begun to worry that Tyler was right, that worry over me had fostered the spike in her blood pressure and triggered the stroke. And maybe she realized if I were here, her hoarding secret was out. Regardless, I seemed to be a major pain point in her life.

"The doctors say she's healing," I said.

He nodded, but I had a feeling he knew I was sugar-coating the truth.

"So where's this pussy of yours?" he asked.

57

Our gazes locked.

"Cat, I mean," he said quickly. "The... feline."

"In the garage," I said, heading toward the door on unsteady knees. When I walked in, I saw the orange furball streak under the car.

Will sighed. "Cats make everything hard." He set down the bag, took off his hat, pulled leather gloves out of his rear jeans pocket and lay down on his stomach to inch under the car. I heard him talking to it softly, then I heard a *yeowl*—from cat *and* from man. When he worked his way out from under the car, he had the cat in a secure grip close to his body, and a long red scratch on his cheek for his trouble.

I winced. "Sorry... that looks painful."

"Don't worry about it. After you've been kicked by an emu, everything else is a piece of cake."

"You treat emus?"

"There's a farm not too far from here. Nasty-tempered birds."

He turned his attention to the cat, who was wild-eyed, but seemed to understand it wasn't in a position to fight. "I see why you're so upset, buddy... that's a nasty looking abscess." He looked at me. "Would you mind opening that bag and getting out the brown and white bottle?"

I opened his organized medicine bag and rooted around until I found the bottle.

"Now open it and pour a little on the wound while I hold him."

I did and the cat convulsed, howling.

"It's okay," Will said in a soothing voice. "It only hurts for a few seconds, then it'll feel all better."

Sure enough the cat seemed to relax.

"Now take a bandage out of the yellow packet and wrap it around his leg. It should be pretty tight and it's self-sealing."

I did as he directed while he held the cat down. It flinched when the bandage touched the wound, but didn't fight.

"That's good," Will said. "Now stand back because when I let him go, he might go sideways."

When he let the cat go, though, it zoomed back under the car.

"He should be all right in a few days," Will said, taking off the gloves. "He'll probably chew off the bandage, but by then the wound will be healed over."

"What about your wound?" I asked.

He pulled an antiseptic wipe from the bag and tore it open. "This should do it." Then he dabbed at the scratch.

"You missed some blood," I said, then took the wipe and swiped at the missed spot. He winced when I touched him, but held still.

Suddenly the temperature in the garage seemed to soar. His mouth twitched. My lips were tingling, too.

Will leaned in, closer... closer...

His lips touched mine and I slid out my tongue to beckon him inside. He leaned in to me, deepening the contact. He tasted so good, and his lips were firm, different than...

Jane... you're compulsive.

I abruptly stepped back and wiped away the kiss with my hand. Will straightened, and confusion flashed over his face.

Hugh was right... I had compulsive tendencies, meaning I did things I knew weren't healthy, against my own best interests. And look where it had gotten me.

"Th-Thank you for tending to my cat," I said more primly than I meant to.

A smile curved Will's mouth. "Anytime, day or night."

He picked up his medical bag and walked outside. I watched while he tossed the big bags of garbage into the truck bed as if they weighed nothing. The man was used to getting his hands dirty.

Then he waved and climbed into his truck.

I nodded when he drove past. He must think I'm a ninny—and worse, a slutty ninny since he thinks I'm engaged.

I wondered if I'd see Will again, then decided it was probably best if I didn't.

But when I turned back to the garage, I smirked. I would so see him again.

I leaned over and picked up his cowboy hat and set it on my head. Yee-haw.

July 22, Sunday

"SO YOU HAVE NO IDEA when you're coming home?" Hugh asked.

We were Skyping. He was in our bedroom, and I was in the treehouse.

"None," I confirmed. "And I won't know until Mom's doctor gives us more information."

"I'm sorry to hear that," Hugh said, then backpedaled. "Sorry for you, I mean."

"Thanks. So as it turns out, it's probably best that you broke up with me."

He squinted. "For the record, I'm not telling people I broke up with you... I'm telling them it was a mutual, temporary break."

"Hm, that's nice. Will you do me a favor?"

"Sure."

"I'm going to need some of my clothes—can you ship them to me?"

"Of course. What things do you need?"

I was thinking what I'd need to limit my trips to the laundromat. "Mostly underwear."

"Underwear?"

"Yeah... can you just empty my underwear drawer and send it all to me?"

"Uh... okay."

And if I had more pajamas, I wouldn't have to dirty up all my T-shirts to sleep in. "And all my nighties, too."

"Your nighties?"

"Better yet, just send all my lingerie, period. It shouldn't cost too much because it's all so small."

His eyebrows knitted. "Yeah... I remember."

"No news on Trudy?"

"No, but I've been thinking about the dognapping scenario, and I posted a reward."

I gasped. "A reward?"

"Yeah, like a ransom. No questions asked."

"How much?"

"Fifty pounds."

"Oh. That's..." Not very much, unless schoolchildren had dognapped her. "Nice."

"So keep thinking good thoughts and maybe we'll see her again soon."

"Okay. Call me if that happens." I waved. "Gotta run. Don't

forget to send my underwear."

I ended the call and Hugh's face disappeared from the screen. I missed him, and our flat. But most of all, I missed Trudy. Where could she be?

I climbed down from the treehouse and walked back to the house. Dusk was setting on another productive day of cleaning. Soon I hoped to have the kitchen cabinets cleared and everything in that room back in working order.

Then I'd have to decide which room to tackle next.

It was amazing to me how Mom had compartmentalized her hoarding to just the interior of the house. The outside was meticulously maintained, and the garage. And her car looked as if it had been detailed regularly.

But those were all areas and things other people saw or came into contact with, and it was important to Sharon Hunnicut to keep up appearances... like the one spot in her home she'd left clear for Skyping with me.

What I didn't understand is how she stayed organized with her house in such disarray. If she had important things to keep track of, how would she know where to find them? Obviously she paid her electric and water bills, since those utilities were still working.

Then I thumped myself on the forehead. She'd keep them in her car—the trunk of her car.

I pulled the keys from my purse and hurried to the garage. Sure enough, when I opened the trunk, inside was one large rubber storage container that held neat, hanging files with nicely labeled tabs for insurance and other bills, including her cell phone. And inside that folder, I found the four-digit passcode she'd written down to access her phone.

I hesitated for a few seconds, weighing her privacy against my curiosity. But I reasoned with Mom incapacitated, I needed to know as much about her life as possible. And I could at least keep up with messages people might leave if they needed a taxi.

I punched in the passcode, then clicked on the flashing button to listen to her messages. Most of them were missed taxi requests, no longer relevant. I backtracked and found she had one saved message. Intrigued, I hit the play button.

"Sharon, this is Sheriff Tomlin." The man's thick drawl curled around my eardrums. "This is a courtesy call to let you know someone reported your house is stuffed to the *gill*, to the point they suggested the health department get involved." He sighed. "I've known you for a long time, Sharon, and I don't want to file a report and make this public. So I'm giving you thirty days to take care of it on your own. If you do, no one has to know anything. Okay? Call me back if you want to discuss. Otherwise, I'll be out your way in a month to take a look around."

When the beep sounded, my heart was pounding. The message had been left the week before Mom had been hospitalized. Perhaps *this* was the stressful incident that had triggered her stroke.

And not me.

Then I squinted. Who, I wondered, had turned her in?

July 23, Monday

WHEN JOCELYN'S name came up on my phone, a stone of dread fell to the bottom of my stomach. The next few minutes could dictate the trajectory of my life. After a few deep breaths, I connected the call.

"Hi, Jocelyn," I said, trying to sound bubbly.

"Hi, Jane. How's your mother?"

"Maybe a tad better," I lied. I still could only get close to her if she was sleeping.

"Good, stay hopeful. And how are you?"

"Hanging in there." I exhaled, then crossed my fingers. "Do you have news?"

"Yes. So... the editorial committee was distressed to learn the book wouldn't be delivered at the end of September as we'd planned."

Oh, God, I was getting sacked.

"But I'm pleased to say I was able to convince them this is a unique, unfortunate situation... and they agreed to extend your delivery date to December thirty-first."

I released a huge sigh of relief. "Oh, thank you, Jocelyn!"

"Hold on. You need to know that if you don't deliver the full manuscript before or on that date, the contract will be cancelled, and we will be forced to retract the advance."

Meaning, they'd take it out of my hide if they had to. "I understand."

"Seriously, Jane, there's no wiggle room here."

"Got it."

"Okay then… we'll get an amended delivery date memo over to Ron for you to sign within the next few days."

"Thank you again, Jocelyn."

"Jane," she said in a gentler tone, "you're going through something no daughter should have to endure. But writing is cathartic… try to channel your emotion into your book."

"Dive deep," I murmured.

"That's right. Don't disappoint me on this one."

July 24, Tuesday

I STOPPED AT the nurses' station and set a cardboard box on the counter.

"What's this?" asked Diane Shipple.

"Cabbage," I said. "And okra, green beans, and a couple of muskmelons, all from my mother's garden. For whoever wants them."

It was still a mystery to me why my mother raised such a huge garden. Even the pigs couldn't eat the produce as fast as it needed to be harvested.

"Thanks," Diane said with a smile. "I'll let everyone know. How's your mother doing?"

"I'm going to see her now."

"Oh, I hope she's improving." Diane wet her lips. "And how is Tyler?"

I smiled. "Married… with two stepsons."

Diane's face blanched, but I turned away. I was pretty sure it was too late to warn her to stay away from my philandering brother. And hey, if it kept Tyler coming to the hospital to see Mom, then they could fornicate until the cows came home.

I took the steps to climb to the floor of Mom's room and peeked through the tiny window in the door. Her eyes were open. I hesitated, then decided to go in.

She tensed as soon as I approached her bed, but I forged

ahead.

"Hi, Mom," I said carefully in a calming voice. "I don't know how much you can hear me or understand, but I know about the clean up order the Sheriff left on your phone."

She stiffened, leading me to believe some of what I was saying was getting through.

"I want you to know, it's not going to be a problem. I've already started clearing things. You have nothing to worry about."

A few seconds passed and I thought we'd passed a hurdle, then she began to grunt and flail frantically. Her breath rattled in her throat, a terrifying sound. I ran to the door and shouted for a nurse, then watched from the door and out of her line of sight while they calmed her.

The nurse who'd answered the call gave me a stern look. "Ms. Hunnicut, we've asked you before not to upset your mother."

I shook my head. "I didn't mean to."

"Still… maybe you should rethink coming to visit, at least until she's more communicative and can tell us who she does and doesn't want to see."

Ouch. "Okay," I said, blinking back tears. I exited and walked a few paces down the hall, then sagged against the wall.

How was this going to work? How was I going to take care of a mother who didn't want me to come near her? Anger and fear rose in my chest—my mother had always been so hard to love… was I the same way?

July 25, Wednesday

AFTER A FEW WRONG TURNS, I found Will's house… and was it ever a house. Stone and wood and glass with modern lines I wouldn't have expected out of someone so… Accidental.

I drove up the concrete driveway slowly, expecting any moment for an alarm to go off. I probably should've called ahead, but I just wanted to leave a care package on his doorstep.

It was purely a coincidence I was wearing the Wonder Woman panties and the only dress I'd packed—a black sundress.

I parked my car and self-consciously withdrew the box of vegetables I'd put together from the garden, with his hat sitting on top, then carried it to the massive front door and set it down. There were no signs of life—he was probably still working—but I rang the doorbell anyway. After a minute of silence, I turned to go.

Then the door opened, and a spectacular blonde—wearing a man's robe—stuck her head out.

"Can I help you?"

I was tongue-tied. "I... no... I.... just..." I squinted. "Does Will Story live here?"

"Yes."

I never got around to getting married.

I was an idiot. "Oh... good." I pointed to the box. "Those are for him... and you."

She narrowed her eyes. "Do I know you?"

"No," I said. "No, you do not. You have a nice day, though."

I trotted back to my car and got out of there as fast as I could.

July 26, Thursday

"I SENT THE UNDERTHINGS," Hugh said. "You should get them in a week or so."

"Good... thank you," I said, preoccupied. "Trudy?"

He shook his head. "Nothing yet. But I raised the reward to one hundred pounds."

"That's wonderful. Really... thank you, Will."

He frowned. "Did you just call me Will?"

I blinked. "No... I said 'well'."

"Thank you well?"

"Thank you well... done," I said, improvising. "Good job."

Hugh shifted uncomfortably. "Jane, is there something you want to tell me?"

I sighed. "Yes, in fact. I think you were right about me being compulsive, and I'm going to try to get better."

He leaned forward. "You don't have to get better for me, Jane. I want you to get better for you."

I nodded, swallowing past a sudden lump in my throat. "I have to go. Call me if you have any news on Trudy."

I ended the call before he could say goodbye, then studied my fingers, red and itchy from cleaning and from sanitizing my hands.

I wanted to get my obsessive behavior under control, but how could I when dealing with my mother's compulsion to hoard mainlined into my compulsion to clean?

July 27, Friday

I WAS DRAGGING another bulging trash bag to the side of the garage when I heard a car coming up the driveway. I looked, but I didn't recognize the make or model. I stood and watched while the driver parked. It was, I realized, a very nice car. A woman alighted, balancing something in her hand.

She waved. "Hidy-hoo, Jane!"

When recognition hit me, I grinned. "Emma!"

I met her halfway for a mutual hug. "How are you?"

"I'm terrific," she said, her accent just as dense and sweet as I remembered. She was a gorgeous redhead, and even more voluptuous than before. She was impeccably coiffed, just like her mother, although Emma's car and ensemble were decidedly more pricey than her mother had been able to afford.

"You look well," I said in the tradition of true British understatement.

"So do you," she said, then I looked down at my stained, grungy shorts and T-shirt, and we both burst out laughing.

"Well, I'm sure you do when you're cleaned up," she offered. "Jane, I only just heard about your mother, and that you were in town. How is she?"

"Improving," I said, getting good with the lie. But Mom was definitely getting better at rejecting me.

"Good," she oozed, then handed me the covered plate she held. "I brought peach pie. I was hoping we could catch up over coffee."

"Oh." I glanced back to the house. The kitchen was almost presentable, but we'd have to walk through two overflowing rooms to get there. Emma had married into one of Accident's upstanding families and she was one of the last people I wanted to know about Mom's hoarding. "I, um, can't, Emma. I'm sorry. I... have to work, actually. I, um... am behind on a deadline."

She glanced over my sweat-stained outfit and gave a little

laugh. "I didn't realize writing was so physically demanding."

I flushed. "I'm, um, cleaning out some things to set up a work space." I would've invited her to sit on the porch, but sooner or later she'd ask to use the bathroom, and that was a separate nightmare.

She nodded, but her expression said she knew I was blowing her off. "I started reading your first book, and I got almost all the way through it."

I coughed. "Almost?"

She gave a little wave. "Well, you know I was never much on reading, not like you and Deidre."

I bit into my lip. "It's funny, but her name seems to be coming up a lot lately."

Emma's smile faltered. "Sometimes things are just in the air."

"Did you ever hear from her?"

"Deidre? Gawd no. Don't you remember, she always said if she ever got out of here, she'd never look back."

"I guess you're right." I shifted, still holding the pie. "Listen, Em... I'm probably going to be in town for a while. Let's get together soon and catch up."

She nodded. "My cell number is still the same."

"So is mine."

I marveled over how we'd once been best friends, yet years had gone by since either one of us had reached out to the other voice to voice.

"Okay, then," she said with false cheer. "I'm going to go and let you get back to work, busy girl. We'll catch up soon, okay?"

"Okay," I said, feeling like crap. "Thanks for the pie."

"You're welcome," she sang, then disappeared into her car and drove away.

I'd committed what was akin to a cardinal sin in the south— I'd been rude *and* inhospitable.

I sighed and turned back to the house. If possible, I hated it more now than when I'd lived there.

July 28, Saturday

"HOW IS THE WRITING GOING?" Ms. Jeffson asked from the back seat of the Caddy.

"Good," I said from the front seat, nodding... lying. Even though my deadline had been extended, I had to get down to business soon. Five months was not a long time to write a novel that was still a wisp of an idea in my head. "Did you ever think about writing a book?"

She laughed. "Me? Glory be, no."

"You used to write for the local paper, didn't you?"

She made a scoffing noise. "A feature every once in a while, nothing to crow about."

"What year did the newspaper shut down?"

"I guess it was four years ago? Such a shame. If no one documents what's going on in a town, the fabric of the community will unravel and history will forget about it."

I thought about the mountain of boxes in my mother's house marked "The Accidental Post." I hadn't gotten to them yet, had no idea what they contained.

I pulled up next to Ms. Jeffson's house and helped her out of the car. She handed me a twenty and I took it, blushing. It was going to be a while before I received a payment for my manuscript.

July 29, Sunday

I'M ASHAMED TO reveal I'd forgotten the way to the cemetery where my father is buried.

I could blame it on the winding backroads and the lack of signage, but I'm sure I'd erected a mental block for various reasons. Anyway, I finally found it, an old cemetery that boasted gravestones as far back as the mid 1800s.

I parked and wound my way through the headstones, careful not to step on a grave, both out of respect for the dead and out of fear from the ghost stories I'd read as a kid. I remembered my father's grave was near a massive oak tree, and after I located the tree, I found his head stone.

Dermot Albert Hunnicut, beloved husband and father.

A true sentiment… some of the time. My father could be loving and fun, but he seemed to live a separate life, orbiting outside our family. Even when he was home, I got the feeling he resented being there. Meanwhile, my mother had been manic, at times screaming at him, other times sobbing over his infidelity and seeming lack of ambition. Tyler and I watched them spar through the keyholes of our bedroom doors.

His grave was tidy, and a spray of red silk flowers adorned the headstone. Either Mom or Tyler had been tending to the plot. It was one more family chore I hadn't once thought about since leaving.

I ran my finger over the engraved letters of his name, trying to think about all the sweet things my dad had done instead of the bad. He had died young—only forty-six. Surely that was enough punishment for his sins.

I glanced to the other side of the double headstone, already engraved with my mother's name and birthdate; her date of death had been left blank. Double headstones had always spooked me— to me, they were like the headboard of a deathbed. And how bizarre it must be for my mother to see her own grave waiting for her every time she visited.

It was daunting enough to think about walking side by side a partner in life—lying side by side in death for all of eternity was a mind-boggling commitment… but it spoke volumes for how much my mother loved my father, despite his failings.

Proof there was love in her somewhere.

When I stood to leave, I saw movement in the distance— another visitor, waving. I was shot through with surprise to see Will standing next to two headstones several plots away—his parents, I presumed. I lifted my hand to wave back, then the blonde I'd seen at his house appeared by this side.

I dropped my hand, then turned and picked my way back to the car.

July 30, Monday

"WE'RE MOVING YOUR MOTHER to the physical rehabilitation wing," Dr. Kessler said. "But be aware the maximum stay in rehab is only a few weeks. After that, she'll need at-home care."

"You'll send her home?" Tyler asked, sounding panicked.

"Yes," the doctor said. "Hopefully she'll be much improved by then, but you'll need to be prepared in case she isn't. We'll arrange to have a home healthcare aide visit regularly, but she'll need round the clock monitoring." She gave us a sad smile. "Hang in there."

When she walked away, Tyler and I made worried eye contact.

"Do you think the house will be ready by then?" he asked.

"Not unless you help."

He sighed. "I'm sorry, Jane. I'm claustrophobic anyway and look how big I am. I can't be in that house, not for very long."

I jammed my hands on my hips. "Then maybe you and Stacey should take her in to your house."

He paled. "That's not going to happen."

"Then we need to work together. Especially if we want to keep everything quiet."

"Has the sheriff been by?"

"No. Next week will be about a month since he left the message on Mom's phone. But maybe he heard about her being in the hospital and we'll get a reprieve. Regardless, we have to get a move on and get the house cleared. I'll tackle her bedroom next." I sighed, feeling remorseful for snapping at Tyler. "I'm sorry if I'm irritable. I do appreciate you coming by regularly to take the garbage bags to the dump."

Tyler frowned. "What do you mean?"

"You know, the garbage bags I fill and line up next to the garage that you haul off every few days?"

He shook his head. "That's not me."

I stuck my tongue into my cheek. That left only one other possibility.

July 31, Tuesday

MY MOTHER'S PHONE RANG and a number with an Atlanta area code appeared on the screen. Probably a telemarketing call, but since it could be legit, I answered.

"This is Sharon Hunnicut's phone."

"Hello," a deep male voice said. "Is Sharon available?"

I didn't recognize the voice, but it had a commanding tone. "No, I'm sorry. Sharon is in the hospital and unable to communicate."

He made a thoughtful noise. "I'm sorry to hear that. Who is this?"

I bristled. "Her daughter Jane. Who is *this*?"

"Sorry. This is Detective Jack Terry of the Atlanta Police Department."

My pulse blipped. "What's this about, Detective?"

"Um... maybe I should call back when Ms. Hunnicut is feeling better."

I set my jaw. "Unfortunately, that could be a long while. She suffered a stroke."

"Oh. I'm very sorry."

"How do you know my mother and why are you calling?"

More fidgeting, stalling. "Well... actually, I'm returning her call from earlier this month. I took some time off and I'm only now getting around to responding."

I frowned. "My mother called you? Why?"

"She didn't leave a lot of information in her message, just that he needed to talk to me."

Now I was really mystified, but he had my attention. "Did she say what it was about?"

"She said she had information about the disappearance ten years ago of a young woman from the town of Accident, Alabama—a woman named Valentine... Deidre Valentine."

August 1, Wednesday

I WAS WORKING in Mom's wildly overgrown garden, using a hoe to chop down the tallest of the weeds and keeping an eye out for copperhead snakes that were known to lie in wait under groundcover. (I didn't have to worry about copperheads in England—one more reason to be homesick for my adopted country.)

In between picking wax beans, yellow squash, and spiny cucumbers, I replayed the previous day's conversation with Detective Terry over and over in my mind.

I'd forgotten his name, but I remembered what a big man he was from when he'd investigated Deidre's disappearance eleven years ago. "Investigated" might be too strong of a word—the newly-minted detective had been working for the Birmingham Police Department at the time, and had come to Accident to follow up on a missing person's report filed by a truancy officer when Deidre hadn't shown up for school for several days and her family couldn't account for her whereabouts.

He'd come to the high school to question me and Emma and a handful of Deidre's other friends, plus her teachers. Everyone, including me and Emma, told the same story: Deidre had threatened to run away at least once a week and habitually stayed with friends rather than going home to her dysfunctional family. In fact, she'd spent the night at my house—or more specifically, the treehouse—the day she'd disappeared. When she hadn't come to the house to shower or walk with me to the school bus stop, I'd assumed she'd left early—or in the middle of the night. There was a shortcut through the woods to get to the main road and Deidre often hitchhiked. When she hadn't shown up at school, I still wasn't alarmed. Deidre had been prickly and fended for herself and in fact, became angry if anyone pried into her personal business.

My mother had never shown more than a passing interest in Deidre—or any of my friends, for that matter—except to warn them not to make a mess in her house. So the news that she'd reached out to the detective with alleged information about Deidre's disappearance, and had gone so far as to track him down at his new post in Atlanta, was unsettling, to put it mildly.

And told me just how muddled my mother's mind had become in the past few weeks.

I'd told the detective about her stroke and apologized for the intrusion, adding she'd become compulsive of late, to the point of hoarding. I assured him she'd barely known Deidre, and more likely—as much as I hated to admit it—my own absence had triggered her confusion.

He'd been gracious about the false alarm and said he hoped my mother recovered quickly. I'd thanked him and ended the call.

Then had lain awake most of the night in the back seat of the Caddy, marveling over just how distorted my mother's life had become, and now mine as a result.

The August sun was high and blisteringly hot. I'd found Mom's gardening hat, boots, and gloves in the barn next to the pig pen, but their protection felt suffocating. My scalp was roasting, and my shirt was stuck to my back. Sweat dripped off the tip of my nose and gnats swarmed around my eyes. Exasperated, I cursed and yanked off the hat, swinging wildly at the buzzing offenders that seem to represent everything assaulting me at the moment. I missed them all, but managed to knock myself off balance.

I fell solidly on my back in the dirt, and the impact took my breath away. I lay blinking up at the white blur of the sun gasping for air, feeling the weight of the world pressing me down into the soft pungent earth.

Tears escaped the outer edges of my eyes and ran down into my ears. Everything here was so bloody isolating… and stifling… and harder than it needed to be. And I was accomplishing nothing.

I wish I'd never come back.

August 2, Thursday

I WAS CLEANING the kitchen again, scrubbing every surface with bleach water. I'd lost count of the live and dead roaches I'd found, which made me dread starting on the other rooms because I knew for every roach I found, a hundred more were hiding. After another thorough cleaning, maybe I could start putting dishes back into the cabinets and stock the refrigerator with more food. I'd been existing on individual cartons of Greek yogurt and produce from the garden.

I stopped and stared at the eleven sets of dishes and fourteen sets of glassware I'd uncovered in the piles—and that was just the stuff that matched and was in boxes, all unopened and with price stickers still on them. The unmatched pieces—most of them chipped or broken or just downright odd—had gone into the bags headed for the dump. And I'd lost count of the dish towels—a hundred?—most of them still wrapped and tagged with their original packaging, while it appeared Mom had used and reused the same two stained and holey towels over and over.

There were three blenders, four crockpots, six toasters, eight coffeemakers, and countless waffle irons, panini presses, and other novelty appliances advertised on late night television.

The moldy or broken items were easy to throw away. But what would I do with the stuff that wasn't garbage, yet wasn't needed?

And when I looked past the kitchen to the jam-packed rest of the house still waiting for me, a tide of panic rose in my chest. I picked up my phone and brought up Tyler's number, then connected the call.

"Pick up," I muttered, listening to it ring. When the call rolled to voice mail, I sighed, then waited impatiently for the beep.

"Tyler, it's Jane." I fought to keep my voice steady. "I... I..." I exhaled. What could he do to help, right at this moment? Nothing. "I just wanted to remind you of the appointment we have with Mom's doctor tomorrow. It's important we're both there. And we need to talk about some other things, too. Bye."

I wondered if Mom had mentioned to Tyler she was going to contact Detective Terry... or if she'd mentioned it to anyone else. Probably not since Mom was so private and it was such a crazy thing to do.

But then again, crazy people didn't know they were crazy.

I decided to go through my mother's phone to see who she'd been talking to leading up to her call to Detective Terry. I scrolled backward in her phone log until I found the phone call with the Atlanta area code around the time he said she'd left the message. The call had lasted two minutes—assuming she'd been on hold and listened to his voice mail intro, her message had indeed been short.

I scrolled backward and a week earlier, found a call to a Birmingham number that had lasted around ten minutes; I pressed the call button.

A few seconds later, a woman's voice said, "Birmingham Police Department."

"Sorry, I misdialed," I said, then ended the call.

So Mom had called the Birmingham Police Department, presumably to find Detective Terry, and probably was told he now worked in Atlanta.

A week had lapsed before she'd called him... had she been working up her nerve? Second-guessing herself? Conferring with someone else?

I scrolled through the list of her other calls. The numbers were local, and all had contact names attached to them—her regular taxi clients, I realized: Nancy Jeffson, Keller Miles, Pat Crombie, Bessie Calhoun. Since Mom couldn't possibly know anything about where Deidre had run away to, had one of her regulars told her something?

A thumping noise sounded on the front door, sending a stab of fear through me. I looked out the kitchen window, but didn't see a car. All this time I'd been depending on the nearly zero crime rate in Accident to make me feel safe... but what if someone had heard Mom was in the hospital and had decided to rob the house?

Even as I crept toward the entrance, I acknowledged that throwing open the doors and windows to thieves might solve all my problems. Although I suspected the towering clutter would scare away even would-be looters.

When I reached the front door, I stopped to listen, but there was no discernable sound on the other side. I opened the door and frowned at the emptiness. Either I'd imagined the sound, or someone was skulking around the exterior of the house.

Then I looked down to see a dead mouse, centered perfectly on the Welcome mat.

I smirked. The orange and white cat must be feeling better if it was hunting again—and leaving me gifts.

And what did it say that the stiff little rodent was the nicest thing anyone had given me in a while?

August 3, Friday

"THE GOOD NEWS," Dr. Kessler said, "is your mother's condition remains stable, and her vital signs are strong."

We were sitting in uncomfortable chairs near the nurses' station on the floor of my mother's hospital room in the rehabilitation wing.

"She's breathing on her own," the doctor added, "and all of her organs appear to be functioning properly."

"Except her brain," I pointed out.

She nodded. "Except her brain. That's going to take a while." She wet her lips. "I understand your mother still reacts, um, negatively when you're in the room, Jane."

A flush warmed my face. "Yes."

"She's probably still confused and doesn't remember you," the doctor said smoothly. "Since she's still worked up from the move, why don't you wait a few days, and the next time you go in, try sharing a good memory?"

Tyler and I exchanged glances. That was a tall order. "Okay."

"Or maybe bring a family picture?" she suggested. "Something to help her make a memory connection."

Tyler and I exchanged another glance. Who knew where the family photo albums were in the hoarding heaps?

"Meanwhile," the doctor said, "Ms. Hunnicut will receive rehab every day."

"What does that mean, exactly?" I asked.

"Rehab specialists will move her limbs for her, and try to engage her, encourage her to speak. We'll do everything we can to get her in the best possible health for the next phase of her care."

I swallowed. "You mean sending her home?"

She gave a curt nod. "Unfortunately, your mother doesn't have health insurance."

"She had an insurance card in her wallet," Tyler shot back.

"Her coverage had lapsed," Dr. Kessler said quietly. "Quite a while ago."

"Will Medicaid cover her?" I asked. At least I thought that was still the backup plan for the uninsured in the States.

"Maybe," she said, with an unconvincing nod. "The business office will have more information. But it might mean your mother will have to leave the hospital sooner than we'd originally planned."

I swallowed hard. "When?"

"We might be able to stretch her stay until the end of the month, but I can't make any promises."

Considering how long it had taken me to clear out the kitchen, that was practically no time. "Unfortunately, Mom's house is, um, not really fit for her to come home to."

The doctor's brow furrowed. "Can you be more specific?"

"It's just really messy," Tyler said quickly. "We're trying to get it cleaned up."

Now it was my turn to frown. "But it's going to take a while. Is there another option?"

"A nursing home, but Medicaid beds are hard to come by. My guess is she'd have to go on a waiting list."

"If necessary, she can go to Tyler's house," I said.

Next to me, Tyler made a sound of protest.

"For a while," I said firmly, cutting him off.

The doctor looked back and forth between us.

"We'll figure out something," Tyler groused.

"Good," Dr. Kessler said, then stood, obviously eager to make her escape. "We'll talk again soon."

She had barely gotten out of hearing distance when Tyler sputtered, "She can't come to my house—no way. Stacey would never stand for it."

"Really?" I asked mildly. "Because it appears she stands for a lot of other things."

His face darkened. "Mind your own business, Jane."

"At the moment, Mom is my business. If you don't want her to come home with you, I'm going to need some help."

He threw up his hands. "I'm feeding the damn pigs—"

"I'm feeding them more than you are," I cut in.

"—and I'm trying to hold down a job, plus sit with Mom since she can't bear the sight of you."

I blinked to absorb the sting.

He sighed. "If it were me, Sis, I'd douse the place with kerosene and toss in a match."

"Really? Well, if the house burned down, she'd definitely have to move in with you."

He leaned in and lowered his voice. "All I'm saying is that situation in the house... that creeps me out. I mean, that's not the behavior of a normal person."

"No," I agreed. "And for the record, it creeps me out, too."

He looked pained. "Is there anything I can do to help without going in the house?"

"Do you know anyone who resells things?"

"You mean, like a junk dealer?"

"Yeah... someone who will take some of the stuff off our hands after I sort through it."

He nodded. "Jim Powers runs a flea market out near the interstate. He'll probably take it."

I exhaled. "Okay. Talk to him, please. But first we need to visit the business office and find out how we're going to cover Mom's medical bills."

He gave a laugh. "We? You got a frog in your pocket? I told you Stacey and I are barely making ends meet. You might have to fork over some of that big book money you're pulling down."

I opened my mouth to tell him the only thing I was pulling down was the reputation of my publishing house, but his phone chimed.

He glanced down. "I have to get back to work. See you later, Sis."

He stalked away and I turned toward the elevator, dreading to learn the particulars of the financial fallout of Mom's stroke. This could bankrupt her—and then what?

I suddenly remembered I'd forgotten to tell Tyler about Mom's phone call to Detective Terry, but when I turned back, he was down the hallway chatting with a blushing Diane Shipple Yancey. So the chiming phone hadn't been about work.

I stopped, turned, walked onto the elevator and stabbed the button.

What did it even matter that Mom had called the detective? I had enough on my plate without digging into something that wasn't even a mystery—Deidre had simply run away.

And right now, that sounded pretty darn good to me.

August 4, Saturday

I STOOD IN the doorway of my mother's bedroom and felt a little dizzy.

If I fell, the towering stacks of boxes and files and magazines and books would've kept me upright, but I held on to the wooden doorframe anyway.

As kids, we hadn't been allowed in our parents' bedroom— and we hadn't wanted to go in. This fifteen by twenty feet room was where our parents had retreated for the worst of their fighting. Tyler and I would turn up the music on our headphones to block out the shouting and the thumps.

There was no longer space in the bedroom for that kind of activity. From what I could tell, the bed was the same one my parents had slept in—I could see the curve of the wooden headboard between the piles stacked on the mattress, and snatches of the pea green bedspread I remembered.

I glanced around, looking for a logical place to begin clearing things, but couldn't find one. Every stack looked just as formidable as the next.

Plus, truth be told, I didn't want to go through this stuff. Clearing the kitchen of spoiled food and collected dishes was one thing, but it stood to reason the items she'd hoarded in this room were more personal... and it felt like an invasion of her privacy on the most intimate level.

If she hated me now, she would loathe me after this.

The longer I stood there, the more I felt as if I was suffocating, so without thinking, I simply reached forward and opened the first cardboard box I touched.

It was full of empty perfume bottles. Some of them were quite pretty, but all of them were dusty and scratched. There had to be two or three dozen of them, along with a hand-lettered sign that read "Box of bottles 5 bucks."

It was becoming clear my mother had haunted flea markets and estate sales and had bought whatever struck her fancy. From the timeline I'd pieced together of when she'd stopped paying for her health insurance and when she'd started hoarding, it led me to believe she'd begun buying things with the idea of re-selling them... and at some point, the items had simply taken over.

But even if Tyler found someone to take some of this stuff off our hands, it wouldn't make a dent in the staggering bill she had accumulated at the hospital—and the meter was still running.

Tears threatened when I thought of her being strapped financially—it was scary for me to contemplate and I had skills and a college degree to fall back on. But Sharon Hunnicut had only her wits and looks to sustain her. It broke my heart to think she'd had to choose between paying her health insurance and paying other living expenses. I'd never once asked her if she needed money, and she—like Tyler—probably assumed I was making bank. But of course, her pride would never allow her to ask for money.

It was my oversight, my failing.

Then as soon as guilt descended, anger was fast on its heels.

If she'd needed money, why hadn't she sold off those vile pigs? According to Tyler, between the feed bills and the vet bills, they were barely earning their keep. Selling all of them would've paid for maybe a year of health insurance... but then my mother, ever stubborn, would probably think, "Then what?"

And if she was broke, why keep plowing money into all this useless stuff? I put the lid back on the box of empty bottles and shuffled around awkwardly to open the next box—a jumble of lace doilies, moth-eaten and stained. The next box held two years' worth of *McCall's* magazines. With each box of junk worse than the last, the lump of misery in my throat expanded.

How lonely and sad was my mother that these items had seemed valuable to her?

The sound of an approaching vehicle caught my attention. I hurriedly wiped my tears and worked my way back to the front of the house. When I stepped out onto the porch, Will Story's humongous truck was pulling to a stop. I was irritated that he'd interrupted me at such a personal moment, but then I reminded myself I didn't care what this man thought of me.

The driver side door creaked open, and he alighted with a wave. He wore dusty jeans and a checked shirt, and mud-covered boots. Oh, and the ever-present cowboy hat. "Hi, there."

I moved to the edge of the porch and squinted into the afternoon sun. "Hi."

"How's it going?"

"How's what going?"

He gave a little shrug. "Life."

"Oh." I crossed my arms. "Life is just dandy."

He bit into his lip. "How's your mother?"

Broke and broken. "Maybe some better." Not true, but it was what everyone wanted to hear.

"Good." He looked around. "I came to check on your cat."

Was it me, or did the good doctor pass a glance over my lady parts? "I haven't seen him, but this week he left me a dead mouse and a dead bird on the Welcome mat."

Will laughed. "That's a good sign—it means he's back in hunting form. And isn't it amazing that cats understand the hierarchy of power and the importance of gift-giving?"

I nodded. "I never asked you... do you have a cat at home?"

He smiled. "There's always a few roaming around my place."

I smirked. "You don't say?"

He reached up to scratch his chin. "Are we talking about the same thing?"

"I don't know—what are you talking about?"

"Cats," he said. "The four-legged kind. What are you talking about?"

"The, um, two-legged kind."

His eyebrows climbed. "Come again?"

"Your girlfriend answered the door when I returned your hat... and I saw her at the cemetery with you."

"Ah." He bit back an infuriating smile. "Tiffany isn't my girlfriend."

"Oh? Your maid?"

"No. Well, she does pick up after me sometimes... and she's loaded the dishwasher a time or two."

"She sounds... helpful."

He grinned. "She's my sister."

My lips parted. "Oh. Well... she's very pretty."

He was still grinning. "Yes, she is."

"Is she the one who lives in Birmingham with her husband?"

"And their little girl, yes." Then a little frown passed over his face. "Tiff and Carl are having some problems, so she's been staying at my place some."

"Sorry to hear that," I murmured, wondering if his brother-in-law had the same loose interpretation of his marriage vows as Tyler—and my father. But that was a bit sexist, I admitted, because women cheated, too. Diane Shipple Yancey, for example.

And hadn't I kissed Will when I was supposed to be in love with Hugh?

"Thanks for picking up the garbage bags," I said to change the subject. "I thought Tyler was doing it all this time."

"No problem," he said, then nodded to the empty space next to the garage. "Are you finished cleaning?"

I wanted to laugh... and cry. "No. Just taking a little break."

"Your mom must be a bit of a clutterbug."

"That's one word for it."

"Oh, I brought you something," he said. He opened the door to his truck and reached inside, then came out with a little jar. He walked to the porch and up the steps to stand next to me, then nodded to the swing. "Can we sit?"

I didn't see a graceful way out of it. "Okay."

I walked over and lowered myself to sit on the wood swing, and he followed suit.

"This isn't as special as a dead mouse or bird," he said, holding up the jar, "but I thought it might help."

"What is it?"

"It's hand salve," he said, unscrewing the lid. "I wash my hands at least fifty times a day, and it's the only thing I've found that works." He glanced at my red, cracked hands. "I couldn't help but notice."

I curled my fingers into my palms.

But he dipped his fingers into the jar and came up with a white, creamy dollop, then set the jar aside, and reached for my hands.

"Tell me if it hurts," he said, then gently massaged the cream into my skin.

It didn't hurt.

Will's fingers were long and strong, tanned from the sun and softer than I expected, although I could feel the nubby calluses on the heels of his palms. The warmth of his touch made my heart beat fast and I was finding it hard to breathe.

"A writer needs to protect her hands," he murmured.

I didn't like the implied intimacy. A kiss was one thing, but intruding on my writing process cut too close to the core. I pulled my hands from his. "That's enough. Thank you," I added primly, then stood. "I don't want to keep you from your patients."

"Okay, Jane." He returned the lid to the jar and slowly pushed to his feet. "You know what I think?"

"What?" I responded, suspicious.

"I think you wanted me to have a girlfriend."

I frowned. "What do you mean?"

"Then you wouldn't have to worry about something happening between us."

I frowned harder. "Nothing is going to happen between us."

"Something already did," he said, staring at my mouth.

I pulled my traitorous lips into my mouth to hide them from him. "I have a boyfriend in England," I mumbled.

He squinted. "I thought he was your fiancé."

I ignored his astute observation. "And I'm going back as soon as my mother is well enough." Maybe even before.

He walked back down the steps and to his truck nursing an infuriating little smile. "I hope you change your mind."

"I won't," I said, feeling compelled to add, "and that cowboy hat is ridiculous, by the way."

He tipped it to me, then climbed back into his redneck truck, fired it up, and drove away with a wave and a smile.

August 5, Sunday

"YOU'VE NEVER mentioned your friend Deidre," Hugh said.

We were Skyping. "Surely I did."

"No. Just Emma."

"Well, it was the three of us."

"So... Deidre just ran away and you never heard from her again?"

I shrugged. "Yeah."

"What about her family?"

"I don't know."

"Don't you think you should start by asking them?"

"Start what? It's not as if I'm looking for Deidre. If she wanted to contact me, she would have."

"I guess you're right," he said.

"Speaking of looking for things, I don't suppose you have any news about Trudy?"

He shook his head. "No. Sorry, Love."

The endearment rolled off his tongue casually, and sent tears to my eyes because I had to question the meaning of it. "You're not trying hard enough," I accused.

"I increased the reward by fifty pounds."

"Have you been to the dog parks to look for her?"

"Not all of them," he admitted.

"Well, go to all of them," I said, my voice shrill. "And put up more flyers."

"I will, I promise. How's your mother?"

"It's hard to tell... she might be getting some better."

"Good. Is she talking?"

"No. She's awake some of the time, but she doesn't respond to questions. We're not sure she even knows where she is."

"But her doctor is optimistic?"

"Guardedly."

"Hey, I just noticed you're sitting inside."

I nodded. "It's raining here." I could hear the patter on the roof, could feel the moisture in the air. Great—more mold.

"What's the picture on the wall behind you?"

I was sitting at the table where Mom Skyped with me, keeping my phone camera strategically pointed so it didn't reveal the piles hemming me in. I craned my neck to look at the photo. "It's all of us, a family portrait."

Dad stood behind, his hand on Mom's shoulder. Tyler sat next to Mom, and I sat on a stool in front of them. We all looked wooden and uncomfortable, as if we didn't want to be there. I seem to remember it happening after one of their rows, so perhaps it was Mom's way of reminding my father he was a family man. I squinted... was his hand digging into her shoulder?

Hugh laughed. "How old were you?"

"Fourteen, I think."

"What's wrong with your hair?"

"That's called a perm."

"What's that?"

"A permanent wave, or as I like to call it—a permanent excuse to be made fun of." As if I needed one more thing at that age to feel self-conscious about.

"I think you should use it as your author photo."

"Very funny."

He wet his lips. "Are you getting to work on your book?"

I shifted on the chair. "No. But with the deadline extension, I have more time. Of course," I added lightly, "by extending my deadline, I'm extending the decision on us getting back together."

Once you meet your deadline, we can reassess.

He seemed agitated. "For now, you should focus on your mum getting well and you coming back home as soon as you can. I really miss you," he said earnestly.

My heart buoyed. "I miss you, too. Oh, thanks for sending my underwear."

He frowned. "You're welcome. So have you reconnected with your friend Emma?"

"Briefly. I'm going to call her soon for a proper visit."

"Good. So... have you reconnected with any other, um, old friends?"

I shrugged. "A former teacher of mine, Ms. Jeffson."

"Ah. Good." Then he gave a little laugh. "I'm sure you have some old boyfriends in the closet."

I would check once I cleared a path to my closet. "Oh... you know," I said vaguely.

"You're still staying at the house alone?"

"Yes."

He looked relieved, then backpedaled to pensive. "Is that safe?"

I wanted to tell him this was the safest I'd ever felt in the house—no one was yelling or throwing things. "Yes. And Tyler comes by regularly to feed the pigs. And Will checks on me."

"Will? The guy who thinks someone kidnapped Trudy?"

"He's a doctor."

"An animal doctor is not a real doctor," Hugh said with a laugh. "He sounds dodgy to me."

"He's not. And get this—he spent a year training at the University of Hertfordshire in Hatfield."

"Oh... well, then. Hey, why don't you show me your bedroom? I'd love to see where you spent all your time growing up."

Since I could barely get inside the door of my bedroom, that wasn't going to happen. "Um... now's not a good time. The house is a mess."

He gave a little laugh. "Don't tell me you're cleaning?"

"Some," I said flatly. "Listen, Hugh, I'd better go."

"Okay," he said. "I miss you."

Tears pressed on my eyelids. "I miss you, too. Please find Trudy."

He nodded and waved, then I ended the call.

August 6, Monday

I WAS WALKING a wheelbarrow full of muskmelons toward the house when I heard a car coming around the driveway. My stomach pinched to see the markings of the sheriff's car approaching. By the time the car came to a stop, I had stripped off my gloves and stood there, awash with dread.

The door opened and a portly man stepped out. I recognized Sherriff Tomlin from seeing him around town when I was younger, although his hair was much grayer, and his belly a little lower.

"Howdy," he offered, then wrinkled his nose, darting a look toward the pig pen.

"Hello, Sheriff."

"You must be Sharon's girl, the one who lives in England?"

"Yes, I'm Jane."

"You're a book writer, aren't you?"

"That's right." Although at the moment, my editor would probably disagree.

"Really sorry to hear about your mom. How is she?"

"Recovering, but she'll be in the hospital for a while."

He grunted, then put his hands on his hips. "This is a might touchy, Jane, but my office received a report that your mother was, um, *accumulating* a lot of stuff in her house, to the point that it might be a health concern."

I nodded. "Neither my brother nor I knew anything about it, but we're working to get it cleared out. We want it to be clean and safe to bring her home, of course."

"Good. I need to take a look, though."

I relented, then turned to walk toward the front door. He followed me onto the porch, studying the windows. Mom had closed the curtains and secured them with clips so no one could see in. A full-body flush descended as I turned the doorknob. When the door swung open, I stood back, knowing both of us couldn't go in at the same time.

"Jesus," he muttered, then stepped one foot inside. "Is the whole house like this?"

"I cleaned out the kitchen. Now I'm working on her bedroom."

"Do the utilities still work?"

"Yes, thank goodness."

He stepped back out and pulled the door closed, his expression slack with shock. I squirmed as he surveyed the exterior of the house, and the fenced yard. "Did you clean up out here already?"

"No. Mom kept the exterior tidy… and the garage."

He nodded, pulling on his chin. "Yeah, the last time I saw Sharon, she was at the car wash cleaning the Cadillac. I remember commenting on how good it looked. And she always looked so put together." He smiled. "Your mother is a pretty woman."

I managed to smile back. "Yes."

He jerked his thumb back toward the house. "So what's that all about?"

I lifted my hands. "I don't know. Maybe she was having cognitive problems leading up to her stroke."

"Makes sense, I guess." He sighed. "Okay, Jane, I'm glad to see you're taking care of things for your mom. I'll be going, but I'll have to check back in a few weeks to make sure this is gone." He frowned. "We don't need another reality TV show in town. That dang Bigfoot hunter show made us all look like a bunch of rubes." He turned to head back down the steps.

I followed. "Do you mind telling me who reported my mother? I'm not angry," I added. "My mother is so private, I just wondered if she had a friend I'm not aware of."

"I wouldn't mind telling you if I knew. My office got an anonymous letter in the mail. Guess the person didn't want Sharon to find out they'd reported her."

That was... strange. "Thanks anyway." I trailed him to his car. When he opened the door, I blurted. "Sherriff, do you remember when a girl in high school ran away from Accident about ten years ago?"

He stopped. "You talking about Deidre Valentine?"

"Yes. She was a friend of mine. Do you know if anyone ever heard from her?"

"No, I don't. Funny you ask, though—I got a call from a detective in Atlanta asking about the Valentine girl."

My heart sped up. "Did he say why he was calling?"

"Said it was just a routine follow-up on some old cases from when he worked in Birmingham."

"Ah. What did you tell him?"

He shrugged. "I told him there was no case. Girl ran away is all."

I nodded. "Right."

He looked at my overflowing wheelbarrow of melons. "If you have an extra, I'll take one of those off your hands."

I smiled. "Sure... take two."

August 7, Tuesday

SHE SAT DOWN with the novel she'd been saving for a quiet afternoon. She had read one full paragraph before the baby monitor screeched with the sound of her nine-month-old daughter crying. The noise pulled on her heart. She set aside the book and rushed toward the nursery.

I stopped and reread the block of text I'd written. Jocelyn's voice rang in my head.

Don't disappoint me on this one.

I backspaced and started again.

She sat down with the novel she'd been saving for a quiet afternoon. She had read one full paragraph before the baby monitor screeched with the sound of her nine-month-old daughter crying. The noise felt like an indictment on her mothering skills. She set aside the book and started crying, too.

The last time I'd talked to my mother, she'd commented on my credentials for writing about a woman juggling family and worklife. *I think it's fascinating how you can write about things you know nothing about.*

I backspaced and started again, this time inserting how my own mother might have reacted in the situation.

She sat down with the novel she'd been saving for a quiet afternoon. She had read one full paragraph before the baby monitor screeched with the sound of her nine-month-old daughter crying. The noise worked her last nerve. She reached over and turned off the monitor, then turned back to her novel.

I sat back, feeling the familiar push-pull of emotions any time I thought about my mother, or any mother-daughter relationship, for that matter. Good or bad, mothers impressed their own experiences onto their daughters, either to follow the same path, to do the exact opposite, or to straddle the line between. How many times had my mother advised me to never have children? *They will ruin your marriage, and your life.*

Her experience, obviously.

I looked up from the table where I'd set my laptop, the one area Mom had left clear so she could keep her hoarding secret, and glanced around the living room. Every other inch of space was packed, including the area underneath the table. Was the hoarding a manifestation of a lifetime of unhappiness? An accumulation of misery?

I picked up my phone to search on "hoarding" and was sickened by the sheer number of results, most of them pictures and videos of hoarding situations. I clicked through them, wincing at how eerily similar some of the scenes looked to the one I was dealing with. It was like watching a car accident, or a graphic surgical procedure—it made you sick to your stomach, but you couldn't look away.

The title of one video caught my eye: "I've Kept My Hoarding a Secret From my Family." I clicked on the link and settled in to watch. Maybe I'd learn something.

I would work on my book later.

August 8, Wednesday

I WAS TACKLING my mother's bedroom again, comparing her mess to the ones I'd seen on the programs I'd watched yesterday. Her accumulation was similar in scale, although fashioned in orderly stacks rather than shapeless piles. And Mom bore little resemblance to the hoarders themselves, who seem confused and disconnected from society, sometimes frail and nervous.

Although did I really know her anymore?

I had begun creating stacks from the stacks. Tyler said the junk man who ran the flea market was well acquainted with Mom and was willing to take the sellable items off our hands. So those items I carried to the garage and arranged around the perimeter. Tyler's suggestion to set the house on fire had actually given me an idea—I could burn most of the paper in the brick firepit at the edge of the property. So those items—magazines, newspapers, and old books—all glued shut with moisture and mold, went into a wagon to dispose of later.

There were at least fifty sheet sets for beds of all sizes, plus lap blankets, wool blankets, electric blankets, and the pillows—ack. There were foam pillows, feather pillows, throw pillows, most of them in plastic bags and still tagged.

And the clothes—oh, my *gawd*. Boxes and boxes and boxes of jeans, T-shirts, sweaters, and coats, most of them terribly dated and smelling old. I picked out a few wearable items to fill in around the meager wardrobe I'd packed, and set them aside in the hopes a good washing would dispel the funky scent that seemed to permeate all used clothing.

To me, the word "vintage" was a trumped up term to make you forget the people who once wore the clothes are probably dead.

There were lots of craft items, too—yards of fabric and sewing notions, tin after tin of loose buttons, countless skeins of yarn, and enough scrapbooking supplies to supply a hobby store.

I was starting to think I should've just called the flea market man to come and get all this stuff without me having to go through it.

But then the next box I opened held cards and letters I'd never seen. At first I thought they were yet something else Mom had picked up from a yard sale, until I saw the envelopes were addressed to her, from Dad when he was in the Navy and stationed overseas. The stamps were exotic, mostly from the Middle East. And there were collections of letters from her to him, held together with rubber bands.

The letters had obviously meant enough to her to keep... him, too. I was stunned—and wildly curious. I picked up an envelope, pulled out a letter Mom had written to Dad, and began to read.

My Dear Lover...

I stopped and absorbed the shock of learning my mother was once a romantic, sexual being, then resumed reading.

August 9, Thursday

I PULLED THE CADILLAC onto the wide driveway and parked in front of a three-car garage. I climbed out, surveying the sprawling columned house that looked like something out of *Southern Living* magazine. Emma Gaines had done very well for herself by marrying her high school sweetheart, Eddie Hopper—*Dr.* Eddie Hopper.

A people doctor.

The door opened and Emma appeared, all waves and curves and smiles. "Hi, Jane!"

I walked to the entrance, brandishing a basket of beets and corn. "It's not a peach pie," I said in apology, "but I hope you can use them."

"Of course," she gushed, giving me a quick hug. "I'm so glad you called."

"Me too."

She swept her arm behind her like a game show model. "Welcome to my home."

"It's gorgeous, Emma. Thank you for inviting me, although I'm afraid I can't stay long."

She made a mournful noise. "How is your poor mother?"

"Better," I said, out of habit.

"Good."

She gave me a tour of her mansion, which seemed even more palatial because it was uncluttered—I was starting to realize how claustrophobic Mom's house was making me. And I met Emma's three children—two girls and a boy, aged five through nine. They were beautiful and boisterous, giggling and dressed in soaking wet swimsuits.

"I thought we'd have a drink by the pool where I can keep an eye on the kids,'" Emma said.

"Sounds good," I agreed. I stopped at a picture in the hallway of her and her husband Eddie. "You both look like you're still in high school," I said. They had been connected at the hip back then, and had continued the "first love, only love" fantasy, going to college together, then marrying as soon as Eddie had finished medical school.

She gave a little wave. "We feel like we are—well except for the kids, they run us a little ragged."

"But you're happy?" I asked.

Emma gave me a little frown. "Of course. What's not to be happy about?"

She had me there.

"Oh, before I forget, I'm having a birthday party for Eddie Sunday—will you come?"

"Here?"

"Yes, a pool party—no kids, thank goodness. Just some adult friends."

"I'll try to make it."

"Good."

We settled into chaises by the pool, a pitcher of lemonade between us. I gazed out over the turquoise water and lavishly tiled outdoor space, which included a full kitchen. "Wow, Emma... did you think you'd have it this good when we were teenagers?"

She laughed. "Actually, I always pictured my life would be great. But then, I'm content with living in Accident, as long as I'm surrounded by the people I love." She smiled. "This is enough for me, being a wife and a mother. I never aspired to do great things like you did."

I shook my head. "I haven't done anything great."

"You're too modest, Jane. I'm sure your life is so exciting. And how is your fiancé? I'm sure he misses you terribly."

"He says so," I murmured.

"And your sweet little doggie—Trudy, isn't it?"

I just nodded, didn't want to go into the fact that she'd disappeared.

"We have it pretty good," Emma said, lifting her glass of lemonade to clink with mine. She heaved a happy sigh and drank deeply.

I sipped the sweet, tart liquid—the taste of summer itself—and had to agree that up until recently, my life had been going well. Hopefully I'd get back to that place.

"I wonder what Deidre is doing right now," Emma mused.

My pulse jumped, but I gave a little laugh. "Probably this same thing, except overlooking the Mediterranean Sea."

Emma laughed. "With a half-dozen hard-bodied men waiting on her." She made a noise like she was remembering the old times. "I've missed you, Jane. It's good to have you back."

"Thanks. I've missed you, too." And I meant it. Emma and I didn't have a lot in common now, but we were bonded over our shared history. And she was a good person—better than me.

"I wish your mother a speedy recovery," Emma said earnestly. "But I hope you'll be staying for a while."

I nodded. "Probably." Unfortunately.

August 10, Friday

I PEEKED THROUGH the tiny window in the door to mother's hospital room and saw her eyes were closed. Gingerly I opened the door and stepped inside. She didn't stir as I approached. For a moment, I feared the worst, then I saw her chest was moving rhythmically.

One side of her face still drooped. She looked pained, even in sleep, and my heart crimped for her.

I didn't dare touch her or do anything that might disturb her sleep. Instead, I set the family portrait I'd removed from the wall on the table next to her bed. I dearly hoped the doctor was right, that her adverse reaction to me was because she didn't remember me, not because she didn't want me there.

On the way out of the hospital, I took a detour. When I found the door I was looking for, I took a deep breath and knocked.

"Come in."

I opened the door to see a bespectacled women I estimated to be in her forties going through a file cabinet behind a desk strewn with papers. She smiled. "Can I help you?"

"Anne Warford?"

"Yes."

"Hi. I'm Jane Hunnicut. My mother is a stroke patient here."

"I'm sorry to hear that, Ms. Hunnicut."

"Thank you. Her doctor, Amanda Kessler, gave me your card—she thought I might need some... help."

She closed the file drawer. "You're having trouble dealing with your mother being ill?"

"It's not the stroke, actually." I wet my lips. "What can you tell me about hoarding?"

"Your mother is a hoarder?"

I nodded. "I've lived away for a while, and didn't know about it until I came back for this."

"She lives alone?"

"Yes."

She walked over to a bookcase and rifled through pamphlets, then extended them to me.

Obsessive Compulsive Behavior and Compulsive Hoarding.

"These should give you some basic information on the disorder," she said.

I scanned the conditions listed on the front of the first brochure. *Overeating, self-harm, excessive hygiene, addictive cleaning...*

"If you'd like to set up a time for me to visit your mother, let me know. Or I can talk to Dr. Kessler."

"My mother isn't communicative yet," I offered.

"Ah. Well, then if you'd like to talk to me—"

"This is good," I cut in, holding up the pamphlets. "Thank you." Then I vamoosed.

August 11, Saturday

I NAVIGATED THE Caddy over a deep rut in the gravel road, regretting that I'd brought the car to this remote corner of Accident. I'd only been to Deidre's house once, and it had not been a good experience. But it had been memorable, so I knew at the end of this road I would find the Valentine clan.

When I pulled up to the sagging house, a handful of curious kids were playing in the sparse yard, just out of reach of mangy dogs chained to trees. A teenage girl sat in a lawn chair reading a book. My appearance riled up the dogs, who strained at their collars and barked ferociously, letting me know they'd happily eat me if only they could get to me.

The uproar brought a woman out of the house onto a wooden stoop. Even at a distance, I could tell Deidre's mother had not aged well. She was emaciated and the baggy dress she wore made her look more haggard. She removed the cigarette she was smoking from her mouth long enough to bellow for the dogs to stop barking.

When they did, I got out of the car and closed the door as quietly as I could. "Hello, Ms. Valentine."

The woman squinted at me. "Who the hell are you?"

I swallowed and took a few steps closer. "I'm Jane Hunnicut. I was a friend of Deidre's."

Her expression blanched. "Deidre ain't here. She run off a long time ago."

"I know. I remember when she ran away. I was wondering if you've ever heard from her?"

She shook her head violently. "Nah. I figure she's in a big city somewhere—that's where she always said she wanted to be, away from this place. Guess it weren't good enough."

Or not happy enough. "Ms. Valentine, did Deidre tell you she was leaving?"

The woman crowed out a laugh. "About a hundred times."

"Did you ever receive a phone call from her after she left? Or a letter or postcard?"

"Nah. And truth be told, I'm glad she's gone. Mouthy girl. Weren't nothing but trouble anyway."

She would've been more believable if she hadn't burst into tears.

"I'm sorry," I called. "I didn't mean to upset you."

"You get on out of here," Ms. Valentine yelled, shooing me with her bony arm. "Let sleeping dogs lie." She hustled back into the house and slammed the door.

The dogs started growling again and the kids began to yell at me to get the eff away.

I climbed back into the Caddy and drove away as fast as I dared with the car dragging bottom and the kids throwing rocks at the bumper.

Small wonder Deidre had left.

August 12, Sunday

I RANG THE DOORBELL of Emma's big house. When no one answered, I followed the noise around back to the pool.

I was late to the party, it seemed. A couple of dozen adults stood around the edge of the pool grazing on finger food and holding drinks.

"Jane!" Emma called, waving. "Come over and meet some friends."

Some of the people and names were vaguely familiar and they reminded me of classes we'd had together in high school. Many of them, like Emma and her husband Eddie, had gone away for college, but had returned to Accident to open businesses or commute from jobs in Birmingham.

"Jane is a successful novelist," Emma said. "And she lives in *England*."

You would've thought she'd said Antarctica. People oohed and ahhed and asked if I'd met the Queen. It was a happy, party crowd, but I couldn't help but compare them to my friends in London and the time we'd gotten together on the Fourth of July. My friends there were laid back and hipster cool, content with their individuality. Here, it seemed the opposite—everyone was tanned and shiny and trying too hard.

Except for Emma's husband Eddie—he seemed just as agreeable and charming as he'd been in high school. "Welcome home, Jane," he said, and gave me a hug. "Someday I want you to write about me and Emma and our happy ending." He gave Emma a noisy kiss on the neck and I experienced a little pang of jealously.

I wish I was more like Emma—agreeable and happily content with whatever came my way. And in Emma's case, it was a self-fulfilling prophecy… good things had come her way because she was agreeable and happily content.

Emma laughed at Eddie, then pushed a pink vodka slushie into my hand. "You brought a suit, didn't you?" she asked. "Everyone always winds up in the pool."

"I didn't have time to pack much before I left London."

She winked and crooked her finger. "Come with me, I have just the thing."

Feeling wary, I followed her inside the house to her lavish bedroom and the adjoining dressing room that housed as many clothes and shoes as some retail stores.

She rifled through a few hangers, then plucked one off the rack and handed it to me. "Here. I bought it, it's too small, and I haven't bothered to take it back."

I stared at the triangles of fabric. "Where's the rest of it?"

She giggled. "Jane, you always could make us laugh. Put it on, it'll look great on you. And here's a coverup if you're feeling shy. I need to get back to my guests."

Emma sashayed out and closed the door behind her. I surveyed her luxurious personal space, once again squashing a pang of envy while being happy for my sweet friend. Three dress-me mannequins wore complete outfits, each prettier than the last. The carpet under my feet was plush, the racks and cabinets were custom. A large gold "E" adorned an accent wall surrounded by a collage of photographs floating between large plates of glass, photos of Emma growing up, from her wedding, of her children.

I undressed self-consciously and pulled on the two-piece bathing suit. It was peacock-green and a nice color for me, I admitted—if only there was more of it. But a diet of yogurt and garden vegetables had winnowed my waist, and working in the garden had warmed up my pasty English pallor.

I had looked worse.

When I turned away from the mirror, my gaze landed on one photograph in Emma's collage, and a memory chord vibrated. It was a selfie of me, Emma, and Deidre in the treehouse. Obviously we were having a sleepover because we were wearing PJ's, and quilts were draped over our shoulders.

I zeroed in on the quilt wrapped around Deidre—it was the quilt she carried in her backpack, I recalled, handy for her transient lifestyle. Her grandmother had made it for her, and she took it everywhere.

But it was the pattern on the quilt that held me rapt—a flying geese pattern that mimicked the pattern in the bathroom floor tile of the London flat.

Was that why I'd been so attracted to the tiled floor, because unconsciously it reminded me of Deidre?

Shaken, I shrugged into the coverup, pushed my feet back into my sandals, and returned to the party. As Emma had forewarned, while I was away, everyone had gone from poolside to the water. And the bathing suits were so skimpy, mine seemed practically chaste by comparison.

"There you are," Emma said, dazzling in a white cutout one-piece. "Let me see."

I opened the coverup and she squealed as she eased it off my shoulders. "You look great, come on, let's get in."

Admittedly, it was a scorching hot, muggy afternoon and I could think of less fun things to do than float around in a pool. Like sort through a hoardy house.

Or write.

"Oh, but first, there's someone I'd like for you to meet," Emma gushed, gesturing to a man who'd just climbed out of the pool and was drying off his muscled chest and arms. "Jane, this is Will Story."

He looked up and grinned. "We've met."

August 13, Monday

"IT'S SO GOOD to see you again, Jane."

"You too, Ms. Jeffson." I held open the door to the rear seat of the Caddy.

"Knowing I'll be seeing you makes going to the doctor a little more pleasurable. How is your mother, dear?"

"Better," I said, then closed the door and climbed behind the wheel. "But still in the hospital."

"Bless her heart," she offered. The Southern panacea. "I'm sure you've been passing the time working on your next novel."

"Absolutely."

"What's this one about?"

"It's about a woman who's juggling a lot of things in her life, trying to find balance."

"Is there a man in there somewhere?" she asked.

"Um... not yet. Does there have to be?" I was feeling cross after dodging Will at every turn yesterday afternoon.

She laughed. "Of course not—look at me, I'm a fat and sassy old spinster with no regrets. But even 1 like to think there's true love and romance in the world."

Romance? The man wore a cowboy hat with swim trunks. Even for Accident, that was over-the-top redneck.

"Surely you have some young man pining for you back in London? I believe Sharon mentioned you were engaged."

I squirmed. "We hit the pause button on getting married until I get things here under control, and until after I finish writing my book."

She laughed. "The book about the woman who doesn't have a man in her life. How ironic."

I tucked my tongue into my cheek. "The main character is more focused on her baby and her job."

"So there's a baby, but no man?"

"She chose a sperm donor."

"I see," she said in a non-committal tone. "Go on."

"But she has other things going on, too—her best friend is sick and her parents are going through a divorce, and her flat is being turned into a condo so she has to find another place to live."

"Sounds like a bestseller," she said, nodding.

I exhaled in relief. "My editor certainly hopes so. The book business has changed so much. Every title is expected to be a hit."

She laughed. "The book business has changed, but storytelling is the same as it's ever been."

I soaked in that little tidbit, then awkwardly segued into my main purpose for the taxi ride.

"Ms. Jeffson, coming back to Accident has resurrected a lot of memories for me."

"Mostly good ones, I hope."

"Um, yes," I lied. "Do you remember a girl in my class named Deidre Valentine?"

"Yes, I remember Deidre. Dark hair and tall. Rather exotic-looking, I believe."

"Yes." Since the age of twelve, Deidre had looked and dressed older than she was.

"A bright girl, and a decent student, if I recall."

"She could've been a straight-A student," I agreed, "but she didn't have the best home life."

"That was true for many of my students," she murmured, avoiding making eye contact in the rear view mirror.

So Ms. Jeffson had been aware of the strain in the Hunnicut household.

"I remember she ran away," Ms. Jeffson said. "What year was that?"

"We were seniors, so 2007. "It was near the end of the school year."

She made a mournful noise. "That's right, because I wondered why she hadn't simply waited until she graduated."

I'd wondered the same. "Do you know anything about the circumstances of her running away?"

She shook her head. "No. Why would I?"

I shrugged nonchalantly. "No reason. I just wondered if the teachers were privy to information that wasn't shared with the students."

The woman appeared to be thinking. "I remember a couple of the male teachers were reprimanded for being too friendly with some of the female students, and Deidre's name always came up, but I don't know if that happened around the same time."

No surprise there—Deidre drew male attention wherever she went. "Did any teacher resign or disappear at the same time Deidre did?"

"Not that I recall."

I wet my lips. "And, um… did my mother ever mention Deidre to you?"

Ms. Jeffson frowned. "No. Why would she?"

I scrambled. "Because… Deidre and I were best friends, and Mom would've known you taught both of us. I thought it might've come up some time."

"No, it didn't. You never heard from Deidre after she ran away?"

I shook my head. "As far as I know, she never contacted any of her friends or family."

"That's sad," she said. "But I understand a young woman's need to get away from a place like this and never come back." Ms. Jeffson finally made eye contact with me. "And I'm sure you understand that desire as well."

I didn't say anything. I didn't have to.

August 14, Tuesday

"HI, THERE," Will said, plopping onto the stool next to me at the diner. "I almost didn't recognize you with your clothes on."

Tamara the waitress arched her eyebrows at us.

"Ignore him," I told her, then looked back to my eggs. "I plan to."

"Don't be like that," he said, then gave Tamara his coffee order. When she walked away, still eyeing us suspiciously, he said, "Sunday was fun. I didn't realize you were such good friends with Emma."

I nodded. "She and Deidre Valentine and I were best friends."

"Yeah, I remember that now," he said, nodding slowly. "So you and Emma have stayed in touch."

"Not as much as we should have," I admitted. "But that's mostly my fault."

"So when you left Accident, you wiped the slate clean."

I shrugged. "Not consciously, but I guess so. I don't have a lot of good memories of this town."

"I'm sorry to hear that," he said, and sounded as if he meant it. "When I saw you at the cemetery, whose gravesite were you visiting?"

I took a bite of eggs and chewed it slowly. "My father's."

"Were you close?"

"Not really. He was closer to Tyler."

"And you were closer to your mother?"

I took another bite and chewed. "Not really. Mom was... is... a hard person to get close to."

"You don't say." His tone was mildly amused, as if he'd just figured out a puzzle. "How is your mother, by the way? I haven't seen Tyler in a while."

"He's been working a lot of overtime." Allegedly. "And Mom is... better."

"How goes the clearing out?"

I nodded. "Slow, but sure."

"Just call me if you want me to come back up to take a load to the dump."

"Okay… thanks."

"Or just call me."

His eyes twinkled, which, I was pretty sure, he could do on demand. I gave him a flat smile, but no commitment.

Tamara brought back his coffee, and he stood to go. "I'm glad your mom is better," he said. "But I also hope you and that green bikini will be sticking around for a while." He lifted his coffee in a salute, then walked out.

"Mm," Tamara said, staring after him. "That doctor man is a tall drink of water."

"He looks taller because of the hat," I said dryly. "And he's an animal doctor—that doesn't really count."

"That's perfect," Tamara said with a grin. Then she made a growling noise in the back of her throat. "Because I'm an animal."

I stared at her.

She pointed her index finger at me and winked. "Feel free to use that line in one of your books."

"Thanks," I murmured.

August 15, Wednesday

"ANY NEWS OF TRUDY?" I asked Hugh.

He sighed. "No. I'm sorry, Jane."

"Did you visit all the dog parks?"

"Yes, I spent all last weekend at the dog parks looking for her and posting flyers. By the way where were you Sunday?"

"At a pool party," I murmured.

"A pool party?" he asked, leaning forward. "I thought you'd be too busy visiting your sick mother and finishing your book to be going to a pool party."

"It was at Emma's house," I said. "She was having a birthday party for her husband."

"Really? Well, speaking of birthdays…"

My mind raced, then I glanced at the date and gasped. "Oh, Hugh! It's your birthday! I'm sorry, I completely forgot."

"It's okay," he said, but I could tell his feelings were hurt.

"How can I make it up to you?" I asked.

He pulled on his chin. "Well, since you brought it up… we could… you know."

I squinted. "What?"

"Have Skype sex."

My eyes flew wide. "Are you serious?"

"Yeah, Jane. I miss you."

I sighed. "I miss you, too."

He leaned into the camera. "So how about showing me some of that sexy underwear I sent you?"

I hadn't seen this side of Hugh in a while. I grinned and began to unbutton my blouse.

August 16, Thursday

SHE SAT DOWN with the novel she'd been saving for a quiet afternoon. She had read one full paragraph before the baby monitor screeched with the sound of her nine-month-old daughter crying… and another sound—a strange man's voice. Someone was in the house.

I stopped, then pressed the heels of my hands into my eyes. Ugh! This book did not want to be written.

I glanced around the dark, claustrophobic living room. No wonder I couldn't get inspired—this place was like a mausoleum.

I carried my laptop outside to the porch and sat on the swing. The fresh air and open space were stimulating, but it was awkward to hold my laptop steady, and the sun rendered my screen almost unreadable.

I sighed and scanned for a more shady place to write, and my gaze landed on the treehouse. I walked through the deep grass of the field to the treehouse, then contemplated how to climb and manage my computer. Then I remembered the rope and box we'd used to bring things up. It was still intact, and it still worked. I climbed up, then carefully hauled my laptop up through the opening in the deck. I looked around, nodding. With a little cleaning, it could be a great place to work.

And heaven knew I could clean.

I pivoted to look at the view that was opposite the house's porch, due west. Rolling hills, heavily wooded, with a few houses here and there. Then I squinted. Was that Will's house? Mentally I mapped his location to where I stood. And while I watched, his monster truck came into view, then disappeared around the back of the house to a garage, I assumed, since I could only see the roof. Then Will came walking around the front of his house, carrying his medical bag. He set the bag on the porch, then walked out into his yard, sat down, and stretched out on his back, pulling his hat down over his face.

The man napped in the grass. It spoke volumes for how much he loved his life.

Here.

In Accident, Alabama.

We were complete opposites, but I couldn't deny the man's appeal... and his forthright outlook on life.

You're funny, Jane—you should consider writing comedy.

I frowned, then booted up my laptop and sat cross-legged on the leaf-strewn deck to pick up where I'd left off.

She sat down with the novel she'd been saving for a quiet afternoon. She had read one full paragraph before the baby monitor screeched with the sound of her nine-month-old daughter crying. She closed the book, then used it to bang herself on the forehead. She would never have sex again.

I pursed my mouth. Hm. Better.

August 17, Friday

I'D FINISHED READING the letters my parents had written to each other, and I was stunned—not just by the way they'd felt about each other, but how they'd been able to express it... especially my mother. I'd never thought about where my love of words had come from—I had selfishly assumed I'd developed it on my own from escaping into books to avoid the tension in my house.

But reading my mother's words made me wonder if she and I had more in common than I realized.

I re-stowed the letters and set them aside for safekeeping. These were the kinds of items I was glad she'd kept, and it made me hopeful not everything in the boxes represented, as the brochures the therapist had given me indicated, the desire to keep worthless things in an attempt to elevate those things and ultimately reduce everything in one's life to the same level of importance. Because if everything was important, nothing could be *more* important, so it didn't have to be addressed.

As indicated by the box of preserved letters, Mom did understand some things were worth keeping.

The next box held legal papers—the deed for the house and property, my father's military papers, and his death certificate, among other things. There were less critical items, like manuals for every household appliance, but useful nonetheless. Near the bottom of the box was an unmarked folder. I opened it and scanned the papers, confused as to what I was reading. The papers concerned Tyler and...

An arrest report dated five years ago? My pulse pounded as I read the charges. *Physical assault, filed by Karen Womack... guilty plea, probation.*

Womack was a common name in Accident, but I didn't know the woman. Another of Tyler's conquests, it seemed. Had this one gone too far? I sat in shock, trying to absorb the fact that while I had inherited my mother's way with words, Tyler had apparently inherited my father's violent tendencies.

Then I looked around Mom's bedroom, still far from being cleared of clutter, and wondered what else I'd inherited from her? I realized I was chewing on my thumb nail and it was down to the quick and bleeding.

The adult version of sucking one's thumb.

Disgusted, I retrieved my purse and pulled out Anne Warford's business card, then reached for my phone.

August 18, Saturday

"BUT MY MOTHER was a complete neat freak when we were growing up."

"Surprisingly, that's not uncommon," Anne Warford said. "Many hoarders were once orderly people, some very much so. Then something happened to trigger the hoarding."

We were sitting in her cramped office, she behind her desk and me in a chair opposite her within hugging distance, if I were a hugger.

"What kinds of triggers?"

"Usually, it's a traumatic event in the person's life. Like losing a loved one. You said your father is deceased."

"Yes, but he died when I was in college, and mother was in mourning, of course, but she wasn't hoarding after that."

"Do you know when your mother began to collect things?"

"It had to be sometime after I moved away when I graduated college."

"Where did you move to?"

"To England, with my boyfriend."

"Ah. So you weren't able to visit often?"

I shifted in my chair. "This is the first time I've been back."

She nodded, obviously trying not to pass judgment. "Were you and your mother close?"

"As close as one could be to my mother."

"And do you have siblings?"

"Yes, an older brother. He still lives in Accident, but he has his own family and only sees Mom sporadically."

"Was there violence in your home?"

I hesitated, then nodded. "Sometimes my parents would... strike each other."

She wet her lips. "And did they strike you and your brother?"

"No, they never hit us. It took... other forms."

"Verbal abuse?"

"Sometimes."

"Emotional abuse?"

"Usually."

She nodded. "It could be that you leaving affected your mother more than you thought it would... and sometimes it's simply a buildup of traumatic events. So losing her husband, then her children leaving home—maybe the totality of it was too much."

"You mean she filled up the empty house with stuff?"

"Possibly. Until your mother is communicative, we can only conjecture."

"So people who hoard are all struggling with emotional trauma?"

"Usually, but sometimes suffering a physical injury can lead to a neurological trauma. You said your parents used to hit each other... do you know if your mother ever went to the emergency room or suffered concussions?"

"Not to my knowledge," I said slowly. But I covered my mouth with a shaking hand, realizing this could be so much more than my mother surrounding herself with junk. And no trigger on the spectrum the therapist mentioned sounded like a cakewalk.

She checked her watch. "I'm sorry, but we're about out of time. Can I answer any other questions for you today?"

I swallowed. "Is... what Mom has... hereditary?"

She sat forward slowly. "It depends on the underlying issues that caused the compulsive behavior. Certainly, anxiety and depression can be hereditary... and in some cases, the compulsion is simply a learned behavior."

"Learned?"

She nodded. "Compare it to a family where the parents are obese, and so are the children. The children didn't inherit the weight issues, but they probably learned from their parents to deal with emotional issues by using food."

I sighed. So I'd picked up my mother's off-putting peccadilloes. "Thank you." I stood and shook her hand. I saw her frown at the adhesive bandages covering my entire thumb, but she didn't comment.

On the way out of the hospital, I decided to check on Mom. She'd been awake earlier and I hadn't dared to risk upsetting her. But this time her eyes were closed and remained closed for the two minutes I stood there. When I was convinced she was sleeping, I opened the door and stepped inside.

She looked frail and deathly pale. And I realized with a start the half-inch long roots of her hair were almost completely gray, as if they were pushing her health and her youthful color right out of her.

A tiny stream of drool leaked out of the drooping side of her mouth. I pulled a tissue from a box on the bedside table and pondered if I could wipe her chin without waking her.

My foot nudged something under the bed and I looked down.

Our framed family portrait lay face up, the glass shattered across the photo in a spider web pattern. And I didn't have to guess at who had knocked it to the ground.

I used the tissue to dab at my own eyes on the way out.

August 19, Sunday

"I RECEIVED A CALL from someone claiming they found Trudy," Hugh said.

My heart leapt in my chest.

"But it turned out to be a hoax—they just wanted the reward money."

My heart fell to my knees, and I teared up. "We're never going to get her back, are we?"

"It's only been a few weeks," he said in a soothing tone. "There are stories in the news all the time about lost dogs finding their way back home."

I nodded, then wiped at my tears.

"How is your mother?" he asked.

"Better," I said automatically.

"Good. And how is the book coming along?"

I nodded. "Actually, it's starting to flow." That, thank goodness, wasn't a lie. The offhand comment Will had made about me writing comedy seemed to have unleashed something in me I didn't know I was holding back.

"That's great news. By the way, a mail packet arrived from your agent, shall I forward it to you?"

"Yes. It's probably the contract extension."

"Hey." Hugh leaned forward. "Hold your hands up to the camera."

I did, spreading out my fingers.

"Your hands look great—they've healed."

I studied them, then nodded. "I guess so." The salve Will had brought me was working miracles.

Hugh sighed. "I'm glad to hear you're not cleaning anymore."

My gaze bounced around to take in the hoarding stacks he couldn't see. "Uh-huh."

August 20, Monday

I WAS PICKING BEANS in the garden, filling a bucket with the fat pods, when I heard a vehicle approaching the house. Will?

Ridiculously, my pulse picked up, then normalized when I saw it was an SUV I didn't recognize. When it drew closer I noticed it had rental plates, which only puzzled me further.

I picked up the bucket of beans and headed toward the house. By the time I reached the driveway, a man had alighted and was standing with his back to me, looking out over the landscape. He was tall and wide-shouldered, dressed in jeans and a black T-shirt.

"Hello," I called.

He turned, and flashed a friendly expression, walking toward me. "Jane Hunnicut?"

I knew him from somewhere, but couldn't place him. "Yes."

His stride was so long he reached me in no time. "I'm Detective Jack Terry. We talked on the phone a couple of weeks ago."

I froze, then set down the bucket.

"Your mother left me a message about the Valentine girl's disappearance?" he prompted.

"Yes. But I told you—my mother was confused. Deidre didn't disappear, she ran away."

He nodded. "I remember that was the conclusion I and everyone else drew at the time."

"So why are you here?"

He smiled. "Came over to do a little fishing around Bayview Lake. Figured while I was in town, I'd follow up, that's all. How is your mother, by the way?"

"She's still in the hospital, but she's not communicative, so don't even think about trying to question her."

He held up his hands. "I won't."

"We're not sure how much brain damage she might have," I added.

He dipped his chin. "Really sorry to hear that."

"Thank you."

"I drove out to talk to the Valentine girl's mother, and she said you were there a few days ago, asking about Deidre."

I felt my guard go up. I chose my words carefully. "That's right. Since I'm in town for a while, I just wondered if she knew where Deidre was living now."

"And what did she tell you?"

I crossed my arms. "That she hasn't heard from her since she left."

He nodded, as if to indicate that's what she'd told him, too. "Has anyone heard from her?"

"I wouldn't know… I've been away from Accident for the past six years."

"Where do you live now?"

"London."

"London, Kentucky?"

My mouth tightened. "London, England."

"Ah. Have you met the Queen?"

"No, I have not."

"Too bad." He pulled a notebook from his back jeans pocket and flipped through it. "I looked over my notes from eleven years ago when I first came to Accident to follow up on the missing person's report." He stopped on a page and skimmed it. "Deidre spent the night with you the day before she ran away?"

"Sort of." I turned and pointed. "She stayed in the treehouse. It was our teenage hangout. She came and went."

"So you saw her the next morning?"

"No. Usually she came to the house to shower, but she didn't that morning."

"You didn't think that was strange?"

"Not really. Deidre did her own thing."

"You never noticed anything strange in the treehouse after she disappeared, no signs of a struggle?"

"No."

"Care if I take a look now, just to scratch an itch?"

I relented and walked with him to the treehouse, then climbed up ahead of him. When he pulled himself onto the deck, he stood and looked all around. "Nice view."

I opened the door to the treehouse and he stooped over to walk inside.

"I can see why you would've spent a lot of time here," he said, glancing around. "It's a neat little place."

I nodded. "We liked it."

"You and Deidre?"

"And Emma, our other best friend."

He checked his notes. "Emma Gaines?"

"Emma Hopper now."

He walked over to the table and chairs and his gaze latched onto our initials carved into the wood. He squinted at the gouge marks that nearly obliterated Deidre's initials. "Did you do this?"

"No."

"Do you know who did?"

"No."

"Do you know when it was done? Before Deidre left? After?"

"I truly don't remember."

He nodded. "Is there anything else you'd like to tell me, anything at all that you've remembered since that time that might be important?"

I shook my head. "No. Sorry."

"Me, too," he said agreeably. "Thanks for your time, Ms. Hunnicut. I'll be going. I hope your mother recovers soon."

"Thank you, Detective. Goodbye." I didn't want to accompany him back to his vehicle because I didn't want to answer more questions. "If you don't mind, I think I'll stay up here for a while."

"Don't blame you."

He flashed a smile, then climbed down and strode back through the tall grass to get to his SUV. He stood for a moment, then turned, giving the property a three-hundred-sixty-degree scan. Then he threw up his hand in a wave, got into his vehicle, and drove away.

But something told me I hadn't seen the last of Detective Terry.

August 21, Tuesday

THE NEXT MORNING I had to take a load of clothes to the laundromat. I asked Joann for quarters and she seemed happy to be useful.

"How is your mother?" she asked as she counted out my change.

"Better." Maybe if I kept putting it out in the universe, it would happen.

"That's good to hear," she said. "Sharon has spunk, she'll come out of it."

I wet my lips "How well do you know my mother?"

She shrugged her thin shoulders "Well enough. Your mother wasn't much of a talker, though. She was in and out, lickety-split."

"How long has she been bringing in her laundry?"

Joann looked off to the side. "Let's see... it's been about four years, I guess." She looked back. "Said her washer and dryer both broke down. I gave her the number of the man who services our machines, but I guess she never called him."

Because they probably weren't broken down... and even if they were, he couldn't have gotten to them to fix them.

While my clothes were washing, I walked to the diner to get breakfast. But when I stepped inside, my feet stalled.

Sitting at the counter was Will Story... and Detective Jack Terry, deep in conversation.

I started to leave, but Tamara spotted me and waved. "Mornin' Jane, got a seat waiting for you right here." She grinned and pointed to the stool next to Will.

The men looked up and saw me. Will waved, but the detective didn't act as if he knew me.

I slid onto the seat, feeling antsy. Was the detective telling people my mother had phoned him with crazy talk about knowing something about Deidre's "case"?

"Hi, Jane," Will said easily. "This is Jack Terry. He's a police detective from Atlanta. He's in town doing some fishing."

"Nice to see you," Jack Terry said with a little smile.

"Likewise," I muttered.

Will smiled. "How's your mother?"

"The same," I said, not wanting the detective to think she was in any condition to be questioned. "But thanks for asking."

"I was telling Jack about all my favorite fishing holes at Bayview Lake."

"That's… generous," I said. "How long do you think you'll be in town, Detective?"

He lifted his big shoulders in a shrug. "As long as the fish are biting."

August 22, Wednesday

I WAS SITTING in my mother's hospital room watching her sleep when my phone rang. Tyler's name came up on the screen. I hurried to answer it before it woke her, stepping near the door.

"Hello," I whispered.

"Jane," he said, sounding agitated. "What do you know about an Atlanta detective coming round asking a bunch of questions about Deidre Valentine?"

I grimaced, but tried to keep my tone light. "He came by the house and asked me some questions about the day Deidre ran away, no big deal. He said he was just in town fishing and thought he'd follow up on an old case."

"Why would he be asking questions now?"

"I don't know," I lied. Did I mention novelists are good at lying?

"Well, thanks a lot for telling him about my arrest."

I blinked. "I didn't tell him about your arrest. I didn't even know about it until I found some papers in Mom's bedroom the other day. What the hell, Tyler? You assaulted a woman?"

"No," he said. "We had an argument and things got out of hand. You should've seen the bruises she left on *me*."

"We'll talk about it later," I said. "Don't worry about Detective Terry—he'll lose interest when he realizes Deidre simply ran away."

"I don't like this," Tyler said, his voice shaking with anger. "I don't like any of this."

"Join the club," I hissed, then ended the call. I peeked around the corner to see Mom was starting to stir in her bed.

And since I didn't need another upsetting incident, I left.

August 23, Thursday

THE NEXT MORNING I was waiting in the kitchen before dawn, watching for Tyler's vehicle to arrive to feed the pigs. When he drove up in his delivery truck, I poured two cups of coffee, then headed outside.

"Good morning," I called.

He was coming out of the shed with a bag of feed pellets on his shoulder. "Hey."

"I brought coffee," I said, extending a cup.

"Okay." He dropped the bag, pulled a folding knife out of his pocket and stabbed the bag with unnecessary force, splitting it open. Then he picked it up and poured the pellets into the troughs. The pigs squealed loudly in their dash to get a good spot to feed.

Tyler tossed the empty bag back into the barn, then walked over to take the coffee cup. "This doesn't make up for the fact that you sicced that detective on me."

I scoffed. "Tyler, I did no such thing. First of all, your arrest is a matter of public record. He could see that if he looked."

"Why would he look?" Tyler bellowed. "I didn't have anything to do with that Valentine girl going missing."

I blinked at his eruptive anger—and his choice of words, "going missing." "Then you don't have anything to worry about," I said lightly.

He grunted, then tossed the rest of the coffee on the ground, climbed back into his delivery truck, and peeled away.

I drank my coffee and watched the pigs, shaking my head. If Deidre could see what a fuss everyone was making over her, she'd be laughing her ass off. It seemed as if she was suddenly on the minds of everyone in town... what was it Emma had said? That her name seemed to be in the air.

And my mother's nonsensical rambling had set it all in motion.

August 24, Friday

THE NEXT DAY I was opening more boxes in my mother's bedroom and still mulling Tyler's over-reaction to Detective Terry's presence in town when my phone rang. I smiled to see Emma's name come up on the screen—I needed a distraction.

"Hi, Emma."

"Hi, Jane."

I could tell from her voice she was upset. "Are you okay?"

"Not really. There's a detective in town asking questions about Deidre."

I sighed. "Yes. He came to the house to talk to me."

"What did you tell him?"

I frowned. "Nothing... the truth. That she stayed in the tree house the night before she ran away. Why?"

She made an anguished noise. "I made the mistake of telling him about Deidre's boyfriend."

"What boyfriend?"

"Don't you remember? Deidre talked about a guy she was seeing... she said if everyone knew, they would freak out. She was always teasing about how her diary would make a bestseller."

Her words were stirring dormant memories. "I remember the diary."

"It was red, wasn't it?"

"I think so. And it locked."

"And she wore the little key around her neck," Emma said.

"Maybe... yeah... I do remember something like that." Then I gave a little laugh. "But Deidre was always making up stories to be dramatic."

"I know. Funny, I always thought she'd be the writer."

"Maybe she is."

"Yeah. And you're right—it probably was one of her made up stories. Which is why I should've kept my mouth shut. Oh, Eddie just got home with the kids... I gotta go."

"We'll talk later," I said. But she'd already hung up.

I cursed. Everything was starting to snowball.

Now I would have to tell Detective Terry the truth.

August 25, Saturday

I WAS IN THE treehouse writing on my laptop when I heard a car approaching the house. I walked out onto the deck and my stomach clenched to see a familiar SUV rental rolling to a stop. I climbed down and walked back to the house. Detective Terry was standing in the driveway waiting for me.

"Hello, Ms. Hunnicut."

"You can call me Jane," I said.

He smiled. "I looked you up—so you're a novelist, huh?"

I nodded. "I hear you've been making the rounds, asking questions about Deidre."

"In between catching my limit of small mouth bass." He put his hands on his hips. "What did you want to talk about?"

"It's nothing titillating," I said. "I just wanted to tell you I know for a fact there's nothing suspicious or criminal about Deidre's disappearance."

His eyebrows shot up. "Oh? How's that?"

I sighed. "Because... I was supposed to go with her."

He crossed his arms. "You both planned to run away?"

I nodded. "The night Deidre stayed in the treehouse, I came back to my room to pack the things I was going to take, and I fell asleep. When I woke up the next morning, she was gone. I assumed she thought I'd changed my mind, and just left without me."

"I see. And why didn't you tell me this back when it happened?"

I pressed my lips together. "My mother is... was... very controlling. If she'd thought I was going to do something like that... well, I don't know what she would've done."

The detective nodded. "Okay... fair enough."

"So... this is over?" I asked.

He nodded. "I've asked questions all around and everything points to the same conclusion as before." He reached into his pocket and withdrew a business card, then wrote something on the back. "I'm staying at a fishing cabin on the lake for a few more days. If you remember anything else that's pertinent, give me a call."

I took the card. "I don't think that will be happening."

He gave me a flat smile. "I hope your mom gets better." Then he climbed into his vehicle and drove away.

I released a long exhale.

August 26, Sunday

"WHERE ARE YOU?" Hugh asked.

"In the treehouse," I said, moving my phone camera all around to show him.

He smiled. "If I hadn't lived in Alabama, I might find that odd."

"I've been coming here to write."

"And how's that going?"

"It's going," I said vaguely. "Any news from Trudy?"

"No, sorry," he said. "Maybe... maybe we should let it go, Jane."

I gaped at the camera. "You mean, stop looking for her?"

"It's been a long time. I don't know what else we can do."

"If I disappeared, is that what you'd do?"

He blinked. "What? No."

"You'd stop looking for me when it got too hard?"

"Of course not."

"Then don't stop looking for Trudy," I said, practically shouting.

"O...kay," he said. "Jane... are you alright?"

"No," I said, feeling teary. "I miss you, and I miss Trudy... and I miss my life."

"Don't cry," he said, then he leaned forward. "I'll bet it would make you feel better if we had Skype sex again."

I counted to ten silently.

"Jane?"

"Goodbye, Hugh. Find Trudy." I ended the call, then pulled up my manuscript document in the hopes that something good came to me. Or even something mediocre. I wanted to be able to send Jocelyn some pages soon.

In the distance, I heard a pounding noise. I walked out onto the deck of the treehouse to see a bicycle turned over in the yard. A young woman stood on the porch, knocking on the door. Probably selling something for school or church, I surmised.

"Hello," I shouted.

Her head turned toward me, then she loped off the porch and strode through the tall grass toward the treehouse. She was willowy and long-legged—and vaguely familiar.

"Hi," she called up, shielding her eyes from the sun. "You're Jane, right?"

"Yes. Do I know you?"

"I'm Kelly, Deidre's sister."

I flashed back to the girl at the Valentine house who'd been sitting in a lawn chair, reading a book.

"Yes, Kelly. I remember you when you were a little girl." I put her age at around sixteen. I lowered myself through the opening in the deck, then climbed down the ladder. "Do you know something about Deidre?"

She shook her head. "Only that I don't believe she ran away."

My heartrate sped up. "Why?"

"Because she promised me if she did go away, she'd come back to see me, no matter what."

My heart squeezed. "And I'm sure she meant it... but maybe she thought your mother would object, or maybe she moved somewhere far away."

The girl shook her head again. I could see her resemblance to Deidre, and she appeared to have the same independent streak. "Deidre promised, and I know she would've kept her word."

"You were young," I said. "I'm sure she didn't want you to worry about her... and I'm sure she still feels that way. Hopefully, she'll reach out to one of us someday soon. If she does, will you let me know?"

She looked as if she wanted to argue, but she nodded.

"Okay, and I'll do the same," I pledged.

Kelly turned and trudged back toward her bicycle. I wanted to reach out to her, but to what end? She was obviously defying her mother simply by being here.

Besides, I didn't want to give her false hope. Because once Deidre had run away, she might have decided to cut ties with everything and everyone in Accident, including her sister... or maybe she'd gotten into trouble, had landed in jail.

Or worse.

August 27, Monday

I HAD MANAGED to clear Mom's bedroom, and thank goodness, I hadn't found any more incriminating or shocking documents.

I turned around in the empty room, reveling in the daylight. I surveyed the pea green bedspread, wondering how long it had been since it had been washed. Clearing a path to the washer and dryer was definitely high on my list. In the meantime, I'd have to haul the linens to the laundromat.

I leaned over and stripped away the bedspread, folding it as neatly as I could, then dropped it in the floor. Surprisingly, the white pillowcases and sheet beneath looked clean—but I knew better. I removed the top sheet and the fitted sheet, then decided the mattress cover would have to go, too.

When I lifted the corner of the mattress to remove the cover, I spotted the edge of a manila folder. I frowned, wondering if this was the stash of porn I'd been dreading I'd find.

But when I opened it, the contents sent a stone to my stomach: a dozen articles about Deidre's disappearance, all dated at the time she had first run away.

Why would my mother be so interested in Deidre, unless—as her voice message to Detective Terry indicated—she knew something about her disappearance?

August 28, Tuesday

"TWO EGGS SCRAMBLED, coming right up," Tamara said, writing in her order pad. Then she grinned. "Jane, is something going on between you and the animal doctor?"

I gave her a flat smile. "No."

"Are you sure, because I have a sense about these things." She leaned in to whisper. "I'm an empath."

"You don't say?"

"Yeah, I can feel things that other people can't feel."

"Okay. But still no—there's nothing going on between me and Will."

She wagged her eyebrows. "Yet."

I smiled. "Ever. Um, Tamara, there is something I'd like to talk to you about."

"Sure." She leaned in. "Is this for a book of yours?"

"Um, no. I was wondering if you know a woman named Karen Womack."

Her thin eyebrows climbed, then she nodded. "Yeah... she dated Tyler after I did."

I wet my lips. "I understand there was some incident between her and my brother that led to him being arrested."

Tamara glanced all around to make sure no one was within earshot. "You mean when he beat the hell out of her?"

I grimaced. "He said they were both, um, physical with each other."

She sighed, and looked away again, as if she were contemplating what to tell me. "Listen, Jane, I like yew, I really do. But your brother is a bully. He never hit me, but he came close. But then maybe I wasn't his type, if you know what I mean."

I shook my head. "What's Tyler's type?"

"Tall, dark hair... you know—exotic looking."

I swallowed hard. Like Deidre.

August 29, Wednesday

I PUSHED A wheelbarrow of damaged and spoiled produce to the pig pen, holding my breath against the stench I would never get used to.

When they saw me coming, they began to squeal in earnest, jumping up from their mud baths and lumbering to the troughs.

"Ugh," I muttered, leaning over the fence to toss in the vegetables.

A motion on the ground caught my eye. Too late, I realized it was a copperhead. It struck at my hand, barely missing. I yanked back, terrified.

But when the snake fell back to the ground, the pigs attacked it, stomping it into the dirt. One pig was struck on the snout, but there was no stopping the stampede. Not only did they kill it, but they ate it, too, slurped it up as if it was a big worm.

I staggered backward, my heart still racing. I had a new appreciation for the pigs. And now I felt beholden to the one who'd taken it for me on the snout.

August 30, Thursday

"IT MIGHT'VE BEEN a dry strike," Will said, examining the pig's nose.

"What's that?" I asked.

"An adult snake doesn't always expel venom on the first strike."

"You mean it's a courtesy strike?" I asked, dryly.

He laughed. "Kind of. It's a nasty bite, but she'll probably be okay." He patted the pig on her big neck, then let her go to scramble back to the herd.

Will climbed over the fence and used his hat to dust off his pants.

"Thanks," I said, then walked back to his truck with him. "What do I owe you?"

He waved me off. "No charge."

"You can't make a living like that," I protested. "Tell me... and for the cat, too."

He did that thing to make his eyes twinkle. "Okay... I'll take a kiss."

My eyebrows went up. "A kiss?"

"Make that two—one for the pig, and one for the cat."

I scoffed. "That's not what I had in mind."

"Really," he said, leaning his head close to mine. "Because kissing you is all I can think about, Jane."

My throat convulsed, and my heart was doing acrobatics. He leaned in closer, then closer. My lips opened in anticipation of meeting his. This certainly beat further draining my meager cash reserves. I closed my eyes.

Then I felt a pull on my hand. My eyes popped open to see Will lifting my hand toward his mouth. He kissed it once, twice, then returned it to my side.

"Consider your bill paid, ma'am."

Then he twinkled his eyes, dammit, and left.

August 31, Friday

I WAS WORKING in Mom's garden, chopping down the relentless crop of weeds in the unrelenting undulating heat. The events of the past few weeks were starting to take their toll—my breakup with Hugh, the loss of Trudy, my shaky career, Mom's illness, my return to Accident, the hoarding, the interest in Deidre, Will's kisses.

I was on edge. And the more I sweated, was bitten and stung, and gritted through my lower back pain, the more I felt as if I was teetering.

The hoe slipped and instead of whacking a weed, I caught the base of a tall stalk of corn. Heavy with unharvested ears, it fell with a thud.

I stared at it lying on the ground and instead of feeling remorseful, I was struck with relief that it was one less plant to water, weed, and harvest.

And I lost it.

I raised the hoe and chopped down another corn plant, then another, felling them like trees. When I had decimated the corn, I moved to the cucumbers, hacking the plants and the vegetables to pieces.

When the hoe hit something solid, I thought I'd hit a rock, or maybe a bit of clay. But when I crouched down to look, I saw the torn edge of a green garbage bag. I whacked it again, and realized something was inside, probably a sack of garbage left in the garden that had somehow gotten covered over with dirt.

I dug around it, growing more curious when I saw whatever was in the bag was uniform in size—about the size of a briefcase—and it was soft.

I used the blade of the hoe to cut through the layers of the plastic bag, squinting at the spot of color revealed—white and blue cloth. I squatted down and used my hands to tear the opening wider...

And gasped.

It was a quilt... Deidre's beloved flying geese quilt.

September 1, Saturday

I COULDN'T REMEMBER the last time I'd driven out to Bayview Lake, and truth be told, I didn't want to be driving there now.

No one had told Accident, Alabama it was September because the three-digit temperature and wet-blanket humidity hadn't budged a bit. Although admittedly, the sweat sliding down my back probably had little to do with the stifling weather. In the backseat of the Caddy sat a black garbage bag holding my high school friend Deidre Valentine's flying geese quilt in the torn but original plastic bag in which I'd found it.

Buried in my mother's vegetable garden.

I swallowed past the bile backed up in my throat and fought the steering wheel that seemed to want to turn the car around and drive straight to the Sheriff's office. Or to the dump to dispose of the quilt for good. I'd lain awake all night thinking through the ramifications of each option. I'd even considered re-burying the quilt and covering it over with black dirt... but frankly, I was terrified of what else I might uncover if I put a shovel into the ground.

If I showed my discovery to Sheriff Tomlin, I suspected he would explain it away by saying Deidre could've buried it herself to lighten her load before she ran away... or maybe she'd simply dropped it as she'd left our property and my mother had buried it where she'd found it versus bothering to carry it to the trash.

Or to burn it, as she'd often done with offending items.

Before the hoarding had set in, that is.

Yes, Sheriff Tomlin would probably relieve me of the quilt and re-bury it himself—in the back of some evidence room because he wouldn't see the use in reopening an old case he and the Birmingham Police Department had rubber-stamped as a runaway.

What was it Deidre's mother has said?

Let sleeping dogs lie.

127

It could be the official town motto.

Which was why I'd turned the Caddy in the direction of Detective Jack Terry, who had come to Accident on a fishing trip and to poke around into Deidre's disappearance after receiving a cryptic phone message from my mother that she had information. Allegedly. Because by the time he'd returned her phone call, my mother had suffered a stroke. Which was why *I* was in Accident in the first place, far away from my real life as an engaged published novelist in London, England.

Okay, so I'm no longer engaged... and my status as a published author is on shaky ground... which puts my United Kingdom work visa at risk... but I digress. The point is, I don't want to be here, and I really don't want to get mired deeper in the emotional quicksand of this place.

But neither did I want to leave loose ends when I left.

When I'd seen the quilt around Deidre's shoulders in the picture of the three of us girls on Emma's wall, it occurred to me the reason I'd been so drawn to the bathroom floor tile of the London flat was because its pattern mimicked the flying geese pattern.

So call me weird, but it seemed like a subconscious connection to Deidre that left me feeling... obligated.

Mine was one of many cars heading toward the entrance to the lake, although most of them were trucks or sport utility vehicles. Many pulled boats, presumably for fishing, since it was what the lake was known for. Each time I glanced in the rear view mirror, more vehicles had chained onto the back of the line. The sheer volume of traffic confounded me until I remembered it was Labor Day weekend. The proverbial end-of-summer marker in the States, so everyone was rushing to get one last sunburn.

I sighed and tried to tamp down my impatience as I slowly wound my way through the entrance of the lake property. After all, everyone else looked as if they were having fun—as usual, I was the one who didn't belong.

Detective Terry had written the number of the cabin he was renting on the back of his business card. I followed the signs around the perimeter of Bayview Lake through lots of hardwood trees, passing picnic shelters, boat docks, and loading ramps, keeping an eye out for the number I was looking for.

The fishing cabins ran the gamut from cinder block buildings to simple clapboard houses to elaborate two-story weekend homes. I'd been here a few times when I was younger. Tyler and my father were both avid fishermen, and sometimes when my father was working, he would rent a cabin for a weekend or even the entire season. On other occasions, though, they had crashed with buddies who owned or rented, or even pitched a tent at the nearby campground.

The cabin Detective Terry had rented was a small A-frame that was more well-maintained then most of the buildings. It was hard to tell from the road, but it looked as if he might have a dock in the back. I knew I was in the right place because I spotted his SUV sitting in the gravel driveway. I hadn't called him mostly because I wanted to give myself time to change my mind on the drive.

I pulled the caddy behind his SUV, still wavering. I had silently accused my mother of opening a can of worms with her irresponsible phone call to the detective, yet here I was making matters worse for no good reason. I put the car in reverse—this was madness.

I had almost cleared the driveway when I heard a shout. I turned my head to see the cabin door open and Detective Terry standing in the doorway, shrugging into a shirt. I was caught.

As the big man strode toward my car, my mind raced for another excuse to be there, but I still hadn't thought of one by the time I rolled down my window.

He gave me a curious smile. "Good morning, Ms. Hunnicut."

"Good morning," I mumbled.

"To what do I owe the pleasure?"

I hesitated… for a long time.

"Ms. Hunnicut?"

"I, um, found something I thought you should see."

"What is it?"

"Something that belonged to Deidre Valentine."

He crossed his arms. "You have my attention."

I swallowed, then put the car into park, opened the door and climbed out. Then I opened the door to the back seat and gestured to the garbage bag. "It's a quilt—a flying geese pattern. Deidre's grandmother made it and Deidre always had it with her."

"Where did you find it?"

I wasn't ready to answer that question, so I didn't.

He leaned in and opened the bag, but didn't touch the still-folded item. "What's with the dirt?"

"I, um… found it… in the garden."

He straightened then leveled his gaze on me. "It was buried in your garden?"

His serious tone sent my pulse higher. I nodded.

"Do you know how it got there?"

"No."

"And you're sure it belonged to your friend?"

"Positive."

"Can I ask why you're bringing it to me instead of taking it to Sheriff Tomlin?"

"I have my reasons," I said evenly.

He pursed his mouth, then leaned back in for a look. "Did you handle it?"

The question was jarring—he was treating it as evidence. "Just to put it in this other bag."

"Good girl."

I frowned at the "pet" reference, but he'd turned and was walking toward his SUV. He opened the hatch and rummaged around, then emerged pulling blue latex gloves onto his hands. When he walked back to me he was carrying a folded plastic tarp, which he spread on the ground.

"Let's take a look," he said. From the garbage bag, he lifted the quilt and carefully separated it from the dirty bag through the opening I'd already created. He used his phone to snap a photo, then he slowly unfolded the quilt on the tarp. What looked like a compact square shape was actually made up of smaller diagonal folds.

"Is that how Deidre folded it?" he asked.

"I really don't remember, but it looks about the right size for a backpack, which is where she kept it."

"It's folded sort of like a flag," the detective said, then took more pictures.

"Does that mean something to you?"

He lifted one shoulder. "It has a military feel to it—was Deidre in ROTC?"

"No. But it was offered at our high school."

"Was anyone in your family in the military?" he asked lightly.

I bristled. "My father was in the Navy for a short stint when he was young, before he married my mother."

"Where is your father now?"

"In the cemetery," I said bluntly.

"Sorry," he murmured. "When did he pass away?"

"When I was in college, eight years ago."

He nodded, then bent over to continue unfolding the quilt until it was spread out fully. "A flying geese pattern, did you say? Oh, yeah... I see the formation. Pretty."

But I didn't respond because my gaze was riveted on the rusty brown stain in the corner. About the size and shape of an eggplant—definitely too big for chocolate.

Blood?

"Do you remember the stain being there?" he asked, his voice an octave lower.

"No," I squeaked.

He made a rueful noise. "I need to pow-wow with the sheriff."

September 2, Sunday

"I DON'T UNDERSTAND," Hugh said. "Why would your friend or anyone else bury her quilt in your garden?"

We were Skyping. "I have no idea."

His face was scrunched in incredulity. "What kind of place did you grow up in?"

"Now that you mention it, Accident just might be an alternate universe. That would explain a lot."

He gave a little laugh. "I'll say. What happens next?"

I shrugged. "Maybe nothing. The detective took the quilt to the Sheriff and they're both supposed to come to the house today to talk to me and walk around the garden."

"Okay.... wow. Keep me posted. How's your mom?"

"Better," I said automatically. The truth was my mother was still in the rehab wing of the hospital, but was still uncommunicative, and the only inkling I had that she even recognized me was because she reacted so violently to my presence that the nurses had practically banned me from her room.

"Good... maybe she can clear up the mystery of the quilt soon... and you can come home."

I gave him a weak smile. "Any news on Trudy?" I assumed no, but I had to ask... I just liked saying her name to someone who had memories of my little brown cockapoo that had vanished just before I'd left to come back to my home town.

"No, love. Sorry. Oh, and I forwarded another parcel of your mail—you have some past due bills, I'm afraid."

Great—more bad news.

He glanced at his watch. "Sorry—I have to run. Miranda is having a cookout."

My heart sagged with homesickness. "Tell everyone I said hello."

"I will. Bye for now."

I ended the call. A dam of tears pressed painfully behind my eyeballs, and for no single reason. My entire life was in the toilet, and my prospects for improvement in the short term looked dim. Why had I taken the quilt to the detective when I could've simply put it back where I found it, covered the dirt with collards seeds, and no one would've been the wiser.

Right on cue, I heard the crunch of gravel announcing an approaching vehicle. I looked out the kitchen window to see the Sheriff's car crawling up the driveway, and Jack Terry's SUV following a few yards behind. My stomach dipped—I didn't want to do this. I glanced around at the hoarding mess in the living room and considered hiding—they'd never find me.

Then I sighed, thinking since I'd set this in motion, I might as well get it over with. I walked out and met them on the driveway, my heart thrashing in my chest. They were both alighting from their cars. Jack looked friendly... Sheriff Tomlin much less so.

"Ms. Hunnicut," Jack said with a nod.

"Hiya, Jane," the Sheriff said.

"Hello." I crossed my arms, not sure what to expect.

"How's your mom?" the sheriff asked.

"Better," I said.

"That's really good news, truly." The Sheriff put his hands on his hips. "So Detective Terry here brought by a quilt he said you dug up in the garden?"

"That's right."

"And you think it belonged to the Valentine girl?"

"I know it did."

Sheriff Tomlin smiled. "Sure are a lot of quilters in town, and I'd say every one of them have made at least one flying geese quilt."

"Maybe so," I agreed. "But the one I found is Deidre's. In fact, Emma Hopper has a picture of the three of us, and in the picture, Deidre has the quilt around her shoulders."

The Sheriff still looked doubtful, but pursed his lips. "Can you show us where you found it?"

I nodded and walked them to the garden. It was another hot, humid day and the stench from the pig pen was especially strong. I had read somewhere that the stink alone could raise a person's blood pressure—perhaps the pigs were to blame for the Hunnicut family being on edge all the time. How ironic if the pigs my father had bought and raised to help provide for his family had instead contributed to its splintering.

"Here," I said, pointing to the hole in the black dirt.

Sheriff Tomlin glanced at the withering corn stalks and cucumber vines I'd decimated in my tantrum that had led to the unearthing of the quilt. "What happened here?"

I squirmed. "I thought I might plant... something else."

He bent over to pick up a cucumber I'd hacked to death.

"I, um, was going to feed it to the pigs," I mumbled.

The Sheriff picked up the hoe I'd left lying on the ground. "How do you think the quilt got here?"

"I don't know."

"Assuming the quilt does belong to the Valentine girl, is it possible she buried it?"

I shrugged. "I suppose so, although I don't know why Deidre would."

"Maybe she thought it'd be found sooner and it would create a big stir, that someone might think something bad happened to her instead of her being just another runaway."

Detective Terry shifted, but didn't say anything.

I wanted to be angry, but Deidre had been an impulsive girl, with a penchant for drama. "Anything is possible," I agreed.

The Sheriff used the hoe to scrape aside loose dirt, then used it to dislodge big chunks of earth. Suddenly the metal blade connected to something with a *chink*.

I froze and waited for him to lift the hoe to see what he'd hit.

"Rock," he said, tossing it aside with a scoff. "There's nothing here."

"Shouldn't the area be dug up just in case?" Detective Terry asked.

The Sheriff tossed down the dirt-covered tool. "Why? We don't even know the quilt belonged to the Valentine girl."

"It did," I insisted.

The Sheriff blasted me with a frown. "Even if it did, we don't know a crime has been committed here other than the destruction of some perfectly good corn and cucumber plants."

"What about the blood stain on the quilt?" I asked.

Another frown. "Who said it was blood? Could be tomato juice for all we know. And even if it is blood, it could be natural."

"Natural?"

A third frown. "You know—menstrual." He seemed irritated I'd made him say the word.

"Can forensics tell the difference?" I asked.

"Yes," Detective Terry spoke up. "New techniques can differentiate between menstrual and peripheral blood."

"How long will that take?" I asked.

"No time at all," the sheriff said dryly. "Because I'm not sending the quilt to the state crime lab for an expensive test when *no crime has been committed*."

I glanced at Detective Terry.

"Sheriff Tomlin has jurisdiction," he conceded.

"Damn right I do," the sheriff said sourly. "Sorry for the trouble, Detective. We'll let you get back to your fishing vacation. How are the bass biting?"

"Fair," the detective said, then locked gazes with the other man for a few seconds, before swinging his head to look at me. "Guess I'll be shoving off. Take care, Ms. Hunnicut."

"Thanks, Detective," I said, then watched him stride back to his SUV.

Sheriff Tomlin heaved a sigh. "Now why did you go and involve an outsider, Jane?"

I blinked. "He's the law, same as you. Besides, he seemed interested in Deidre's case."

He gave a little laugh. "There is *no* case. You're under a lot of stress right now. I think your writer's imagination is getting the better of you—you're seeing a story where there simply isn't one."

I couldn't argue—the man could be exactly right.

"But if you do find something else," he said gently, "call me. I know how to handle things around here without them getting blown all out of proportion. Okay?"

I nodded, contrite. "Okay."

He smiled, then gestured toward the house. "How are things looking in there? I sent the detective off so you and I could talk in private about the, um... hoarding."

I appreciated the consideration—I didn't want to see the judgment in Jack Terry's eyes, although perhaps it would help him to see my mother's state of mind when she'd left him the voice message.

"In addition to the kitchen, I've cleared Mom's bedroom, so when she's ready to come home, she'll have a place to sleep." I walked toward the house and the sheriff fell in step beside me. "It's easier to see if you look through the window," I offered, gesturing.

He gave me a flat smile, then stepped into the bushes, cupped his hands over his eyes and peered inside. "Looks good, Jane. Sharon will be happy."

I wasn't so sure about that.

"Did you, um... find anything interesting in all that stuff?"

A finger of unease ran up the back of my neck. Something about his tone...

He stepped back from the window and looked at me. "Well?"

Then I realized what he was referring to. "Oh, you mean the papers on Tyler's arrest... yes, I found those."

He hesitated, then gave a curt nod. "A messy situation, but it was all smoothed over."

By him? "Good," I said mildly. "I'd hate for anyone to think Tyler is... was... a bad guy."

The Sheriff nodded. "And now that you're clearing out the house, that little business with the hoarding report can be smoothed over, too."

I managed a smile. "Thank you."

He began walking toward his car. "I'll be back in a couple of weeks to check on you," he called.

But why did his promise seem more tinged with warning than with comfort?

September 3, Monday

I WAS SLEEPING in my mother's bed now that her room was cleared of the hoarding mess, but with my mind running on a constant loop, rest was still hard to come by. So when the headlights of Tyler's delivery truck bounced over the uneven driveway pre-dawn, I was already on my second cup of coffee. Our last few exchanges had been tense, but at least he wasn't forsaking the pigs. I expected this encounter to be equally uncomfortable, but I wanted to give him a heads' up about the quilt in case Detective Terry or Sheriff Tomlin questioned him about it.

And maybe I was being paranoid, but I hadn't called to tell him because I wanted to gauge his reaction in person.

I poured him a cup of coffee, and reached the fence of the pig pen just as he was coming out of the shed carrying feed. Tyler was a big, strong man, and unbidden, the words of Tamara the waitress came back to me. *Your brother is a bully. He never hit me, but he came close.*

The temperature was already in the eighties, but I shivered.

"Hi," I offered.

"Hey," he said. "What's up with Petty?"

"Hm?"

He nodded to one of the pigs standing by itself. "Petty. She's moving slow."

"Oh. She took a copperhead bite on the snout. Will thinks she'll be alright."

"Will, huh?"

I squirmed. "Isn't that what he does—makes house calls for animals?"

"Sure. But seems like he's been making lots of calls to this particular house."

Will's extraction of two kisses—on my hand, Jesus Christ—for veterinary services rendered came back to me. The man simply had been showing off how his salve had healed my ravaged hands.

I studied my smooth fingers and nails, then scoffed. "I think he feels sorry for me—for us," I corrected. "How's Mom?"

"Same," he bit out. "I had a delivery to the hospital yesterday and stopped by. She's still not talking or responding to yes or no questions. Diane said they'd tried putting a pen in her hand for her to write, but she can't."

Or won't?

At least there was an upside to Tyler having an affair with one of the married nurses—she was keeping him informed between the sheets.

"I got Mom's bedroom cleaned out," I offered. "But I still need to get a pathway cleared through the living room before she can come home."

"Glad you're making headway," he said, folding the empty feed sack. "I talked to Jim Powers at the flea market and he said he'd come by soon to take some stuff off your hands."

"Off *our* hands," I corrected, feeling sour, then I handed him the coffee and took a deep breath. "I was digging in the garden and I found something."

Tyler's eyebrows went up over the rim of the mug. "I hope it was a big box of cash."

I gave a laugh. "Not quite. It was a quilt."

He frowned. "A quilt? That's bizarre."

"I thought so, too... then I realized it was a quilt Deidre Valentine used to carry around with her."

His mouth tightened. "So?"

"So... don't you think that's strange?"

He shrugged. "She buried it, thinking she'd come back for it?"

I hadn't considered that possibility. "Maybe." And maybe the Sheriff was right—maybe I was letting my imagination get the better of me.

"Where is it?" he asked lightly.

There was the tickle at my neck again. "The quilt? Sheriff Tomlin has it."

His face darkened. "Why did you give it to him?"

"I thought it might be important."

"But why?"

At his sudden and unexpected anger, I decided to change tack. "I thought her family might want it back. It was an heirloom."

He relaxed a bit. "Oh. Right."

I lifted my cup for a sip, but my hand was shaking a bit. I didn't like seeing this side of my brother... it reminded me too much of my father. "Are you off for the holiday?"

"Yeah, thought I'd do some fishing."

"I could use your help here."

He shook his head. "No way, it's my first day off in months. Will is taking me out on his bass boat."

Ugh—of course Will Story had a bass boat. Else why have the behemoth truck?

Then Tyler grinned, back to his charming self. "I'll tell him you said hello."

"Don't bother," I said. Tyler's laughter mocked me as I turned back toward the house.

September 4, Tuesday

I SIDLED PAST the nurses' station, headed toward my mother's hospital room.

"Ms. Hunnicut?" a women's voice said sharply. "Ms. Hunnicut!"

I swallowed a curse and turned back. "Yes?"

The dark-haired nurse narrowed her eyes. "You're not supposed to be in your mother's room. You know how upset she gets."

I held up a stack of garments. "I brought some of her night gowns. I thought they might make her feel more at home."

The woman's body language softened a bit. "That's nice of you."

"I'm her daughter," I said, taking advantage of the opening. "I want her to get well. And I want her to know I care." I wet my lips. "Please?"

She hesitated, then sighed. "How about if I go in with you? Then if she gets upset, you can leave and I'll stay with her until she calms down."

I gave her a grateful smile. "Thank you."

I stood in the hall and let the nurse go into the room first. I heard her speaking to Mom in a low, comforting voice. "Hello, Ms. Hunnicut. I see you're awake. How are you feeling? Can you nod or shake your head if you understand me? Okay, well we'll keep trying. Meanwhile, you have a visitor."

I stepped inside the door and made my way to my mother's bed. My heart lurched. She looked thinner even than the last time I saw her, and her right arm was drawn up to her chest.

"Your daughter is here," the nurse said. "Isn't that nice?"

I walked up to the bed in her line of sight and smiled. "Hi, Mom."

She didn't react violently, but neither did she seem to register what she was seeing. Her eyes were unfocused. She wasn't looking at me, but through me.

The nurse gave me an encouraging nod.

I stepped closer and held up the stack of soft garments I'd brought. "I thought you might like some of your own gowns to wear. I cleaned up your bedroom and washed all your linens, so it's all ready for you when you're feeling well enough to come home."

Her gaze fell, although I couldn't be sure she saw the garments. Then in the blink of an eye, she stiffened and began to flail, making guttural noises in her throat.

"Okay, okay," the nurse soothed, reaching across the bed to hold my mother's swinging arms. She looked at me and nodded to the door. Disappointed, I retreated back to the hallway. One step forward, two steps back.

As I walked back to the parking garage, I thought back over my mother's reactions over the past few visits. Was she responding violently to me... or to the fact that I was cleaning out her house?

And was she responding to items I had already found... or something I had yet to uncover?

September 5, Wednesday

I SLOWED THE CADDY to pull up to the curb at the Accident town clinic where Ms. Jeffson waited patiently on the sidewalk.

The happily rounded woman smiled wide. She had been my favorite teacher and had fostered my love for reading and writing. It wasn't lost on me that if she'd chosen a different profession, I might have, too. And although I was struggling in my career at the moment and in desperate need of a comeback, I loved being a writer. Most of the time.

"Hello, Jane."

"Hello, Ms. Jeffson." I got out to open the rear door and see her safely settled inside. "How are you?"

"Right as rain," she sang, ever the optimist. "How's the book coming along?"

Normally I hated that question, but Ms. Jeffson seemed to understand more than most that writing had its ups and downs. "It's not going as well as I need for it too."

She smiled. "You're in control, not the story. Take it where you want it to go."

I nodded. "You're right. I need to be more disciplined."

"You have a lot on your plate at the moment. How is your mother?"

"Better," I said. Then I sighed. "But not well. I'm starting to worry she's not going to recover fully."

"Be patient," she urged. "My mother had a stroke and she was much older than Sharon, but with physical therapy, she was back to herself within a year."

A year. I swallowed a groan, feeling guilty. "My brother and I are trying to be hopeful."

"Tyler is your brother, right?"

"That's right." I caught her reflection in the rear view mirror to see if her face revealed anything about him I should know, but she was looking out the window. "Did you have him as a student?"

"Yes, for one year, I believe." The corners of her mouth turned up. "He wasn't as good a student as you were, too distracted by the girls."

I wet my lips. "Yes... Tyler is quite the ladies' man." Then I caught myself. "*Was* quite the ladies' man. He's married now, with two boys."

She nodded. "Family is important. What does he do for a living?"

"He delivers packages and his territory includes Birmingham, so he's all over."

"Sounds like he gets around," she said, nodding.

I tried to decipher if she was speaking in double entendre, but since her sweet tone held no sarcasm, I decided the reference to Tyler's philandering was unintentional.

"Jane, I have a favor to ask."

"Sure," I said.

"I've been substituting at the high school for an English teacher who's on maternity leave, and I wondered if you'd be willing to come in and speak to the class."

My eyes widened. "Me?"

"Yes, you. You're a homegrown published author, after all. You can let the students know they can do it, too."

If they wanted to be broke, frustrated, and full of self-loathing. "If you think it would be helpful."

"I do. How about next Monday?"

I swallowed a sigh. "Okay."

September 6, Thursday

I STOOD TO TAKE IN the towers of hoarded stuff packed into the living room so high—mere inches from the ceiling—it was dangerous. I couldn't understand how my average-height mother had been able to stack items so high until I spotted a narrow step ladder wedged between two cabinets. It was staggering to think her hoarding was limited only by the height of the ceilings.

If there was one good thing about this room it was that the items were mostly furniture, so they were larger. But the endless number of end tables, lamps, shelves, foot stools, and side chairs were jammed together in a barrel of monkeys scenario—before I moved one piece, I had to figure out how it would affect the item next to it. Once I managed to dislodge a piece, I determined whether it was salvageable or destined for the dump, and added to the piles I'd accumulated in the garage. There was no longer room for the Caddy inside.

I hoped Mr. Powers the flea market man came soon.

As I sorted Mom's piles into piles of my own, and as the morning progressed, I could feel my energy waning and my focus wandering. Each item seemed to require more brain power than I could devote to it, and the claustrophobic nature of the work had me on edge, so by lunch time, I was shaky from mental exhaustion, and despite my dust mask, my airways felt fuzzy and compromised.

I took refuge in the cleared out kitchen, grabbing a bottle of tea and sitting down at the table to recharge. It was the same table I'd grown up with and around. We'd had family meals here, although much of the time the meals had been punctuated with my mother's angry body language as she slammed plates down in front of us, and glared at my father who sat at the other end of the table, seemingly oblivious to her moods. On the rare occasions my mother would invite my friends to eat with us, things were better. Mom and Dad both wanted to portray a happy family to outsiders, and my friends bought it. Deidre had often expressed how lucky I was to have a father who lived with us and parents who believed meals at the table were important. Emma, too, because her father, like Deidre's, was MIA from his family.

I hadn't talked to Emma since her distressed phone call about her regret over telling Detective Terry that Deidre had spoken of a secret boyfriend. I'd forgotten about Deidre's bragging, and at the time had chalked it up to her taste for drama. And Emma had jogged my memory about a locked diary Deidre wrote in, and the key she'd worn around her neck. In my mind I could see my exotic-looking friend talking and mindlessly sliding the gold key back and forth on a brown leather cord.

On impulse I picked up the phone and brought up Emma's number, then connected the call. She answered on the second ring.

"Jane! Hi."

"Hi, there. Are you busy?"

"Not really," she said. "What's up? How's your mom?"

"She's better," I said. "And nothing much is up, I was just thinking about you and checking in."

"All is well here. Have you seen Will Story lately?" she teased.

I flushed, thinking about running into him at Emma's pool party in my teeny borrowed bikini. "Not lately," I said smoothly. "Actually, I've been thinking about our last phone conversation. You seemed upset."

She scoffed. "Oh, that. I don't know why I was so flustered about the detective questioning me. I guess all this talk about Deidre in general just got me remembering how upset you and I were when she ran away. But that's all water under the bridge."

"Right," I murmured. "But how strange is this? I found Deidre's quilt."

"Her quilt?"

"Yes, remember her flying geese quilt?"

"I... maybe."

"I'd forgotten about it myself until I saw the picture of the three of us in your dressing room."

"Hm... I'll have to look for it. Those pictures have been up for so long, I don't even know what's there. Did you find the quilt in your bedroom?"

I almost laughed—I could barely get the door of my bedroom open, much less find anything nostalgic inside. "No. Actually, I found it buried in the vegetable garden."

"What?" She gave a little laugh. "That's... bizarre."

"I know, right?"

"And you're sure it's Deidre's?"

"Yeah. The one she always carried in her backpack."

"Do you think she buried it there before she took off?"

"Could be. Maybe she thought she'd come back for it. I honestly don't have a better explanation for how it could've gotten there."

Emma made a thoughtful noise. "Regardless, I'm sure Deidre's mother will be happy to have a family heirloom back."

"Yes. Sheriff Tomlin is going to return it."

"What does the Sheriff have to do with it?"

I gave a little laugh to dispel Emma's worried tone, lest she get upset again. "I went to see Deidre's mother to ask if she'd ever heard from Deidre, and she wasn't exactly welcoming. I thought it would be better if the Sheriff took the quilt to her."

"Oh. Good thinking."

"Do you want to get together sometime soon, get a bite to eat?"

"That would be great," Emma said, then made a rueful noise. "But the kids are back in school, so this week is crazy. Can I ping you when I come up for air?"

"Absolutely."

"Okay, gotta run."

"Bye," I said, then disconnected the call with a sigh.

I was lonely. I considered calling Hugh, but at the moment, it felt as if he was even farther than half a planet away.

A thump sounded on the front door. I went to investigate, but when I opened the door, no one was there. Then I looked down to see a little dead vole lying on the welcome mat. The cat had sensed I needed a lift.

September 7, Friday

SINCE I WAS supposed to talk to Ms. Jeffson's class Monday, I decided I probably should spend some time working on my book— the book I was supposed to have finished by the end of December else my career as a novelist would be over.

I wasn't sure what I'd talk about, but at the moment inspiration seemed like a good topic since I couldn't seem to find any myself. I was in the treehouse with my hands on the keyboard of my laptop and out of desperation, had resorted to typing out questions to jumpstart my brain.

What's the worst thing that could happen now?

What's the best thing that could happen now?

What's the weirdest thing that could happen now?

It occurred to me that nearly everything I thought of paled in comparison to the drama going on in my own life at the moment.

While I waited for a good idea to float into my head, the sound of a vehicle approaching reached me. Ridiculously glad for the distraction, I stood and walked to the window to see Will Story's giant truck bouncing up the driveway.

Unbidden, my mood buoyed higher, which was indicative of just how bored I was.

He got out of the truck and headed for the pig pen. From my perch I watched him climb inside the fence without hesitation, then lean down to examine one of the animals—Petty, no doubt. He withdrew something from his black bag, then gave her an injection. When he walked back to his truck, I shouted and waved.

He looked up, then grinned. "Hi."

"Hi yourself," I called.

"Want some company?"

I shrugged. "Sure... come on up."

He stopped by the truck to drop off his medical bag, then walked across the field, carrying two cans of soda. He juggled them while he climbed the ladder, then I took them so he could hoist himself through the opening in the deck. He stood and turned all around.

"Wow, what a great view."

"I like it," I said.

"Who built this place?"

"My dad, when I was little."

"For you and Tyler?"

"Tyler was a little too old for it then, he didn't spend much time here. It was more for me and Deidre and Emma."

"The Three Musketeers?"

I laughed. "Something like that."

"So this is where all the magic happens?"

Naughty images popped into my head. "Uh..."

"Your writing," he said, nodding to my laptop.

"Oh... right, my writing. Not much magic happening today, unfortunately."

He cracked open a soda and handed it to me. "Maybe you need some caffeine."

"Can't hurt," I agreed, then lifted the can for a sip. "Mm, thanks."

He turned around to take in the landscape, then squinted. "Hey, that's my house."

I followed his gaze. "Is it?" I asked, feigning ignorance.

"Ah, so you can spy on me."

I scoffed. "You wish."

"We need a sign so we can signal each other."

"For what?"

He grinned. "To rendezvous, of course."

I laughed. "That's a mighty big word for a country boy."

"I'm a Renaissance man."

"Ooh, two big words."

He held up his hand. "I'm going to stop while I'm ahead."

I nodded toward the pig pen. "Did Tyler tell you the pig was still ailing?"

"Yeah, he mentioned it when we were fishing, so I thought I'd check on her. Gave her a shot of antibiotics, so maybe she'll pep up. Keep an eye on her, though."

"Will do."

"Your brother seems to think I have a crush on you."

I took another drink from my can. "And do you?"

He nodded. "Yeah."

My jaw loosened a bit... and other parts due south.

"You don't have to say anything," he said. "I just wanted you to know."

"I... okay." I would have to let that declaration digest.

He pointed to the treehouse. "Are you going to show me around?"

"Not much to see, but sure." I led him inside and he admired the sturdy craftsmanship. "Your dad knew his way around a toolbox."

"He was handy when he wanted to be."

"Nice table," he said. "Did he make this, too?"

I nodded.

He ran his fingers over the three sets of initials. "Hm, too bad about the gouges—was someone mad at someone else?"

I shook my head. "I don't remember. Those were Deidre's initials."

"Looks like someone used a chisel to erase them."

I frowned. "How can you tell?"

"Tool markings here... and here." He said, pointing to flat gashes.

I raised my eyebrows. "Sounds like you know your way around a toolbox, too."

He wagged his eyebrows. "Yeah, I'm good with my hands."

A warm sensation settled in my stomach. I lifted my can for another drink. "I'll take that under advisement."

September 8, Saturday

SINCE I STILL hadn't cleared a path to the washer and dryer, I had to make another trip to the laundromat.

While a load of my clothes and another load of dust mite-y linens were churning, I walked to the diner to get some nourishment. The first person I saw when I walked in was Detective Jack Terry, who was hard to miss since his big body practically took up two stools.

He nodded. "Ms. Hunnicut."

I nodded back. "Detective."

I sat at the other end of the counter to avoid him, although I felt his gaze on me while I ordered a bagel sandwich from Tamara, the chatty waitress.

"That police detective is checking you out," she said when she brought back my juice.

"Not in the way you think," I assured her. "Any good town gossip?"

She angled her head. "Yeah... but it's all about your brother."

I frowned. "What?"

"That he's boinking Diane Shipple Yancey."

"Oh, that. Anything else?"

"I heard his wife isn't coming back."

I frowned harder. "Oh. That's news to me."

She shrugged. "A friend of mine knows her sister, so it's straight from the horse's mouth."

I squinted. "Well, not really..."

She winked. "Don't look now, but here comes Detective Hunky."

I rolled my eyes at her, then turned to smile at Jack Terry. "Hello, Detective. I assumed you'd gone back to Atlanta by now."

"Nope," he said congenially. "The fish are biting so well, I decided to rent the cabin a little longer. I'll be going back and forth some, but I'll be around if anything interesting gets dug up." One side of his mouth lifted. "Again."

I squinted. "I thought you told the Sheriff the fishing was only fair."

He pursed his mouth. "Did I?" Then he turned and sauntered out the door.

September 9, Sunday

"SO THEY'RE NOT going to do anything with the quilt?" Hugh asked.

I shrugged. "Return it to Deidre's mother, I assume."

"But you think something bad might have happened to her on the quilt?"

I pressed my lips together. "I don't know. Maybe the Sheriff is right—maybe I'm making more of this than it is."

I waited for Hugh to agree, to say I was being compulsive, or neurotic, or I was sabotaging myself by trying to invent a reason not to work on my book. I pretty much checked all three of those boxes.

"But what if you're not?" he asked. "What if something really happened to your friend? If it did, and everyone thinks she ran away, someone got away with murder."

I blinked. "I didn't say Deidre was murdered."

"I know," Hugh said. "You've said everything but that. I think you're afraid to ask questions."

I frowned. "Don't you think I have enough on my plate?"

"Absolutely," he said. "So how can I help?"

His offer flummoxed me a bit because it meant he didn't think I was crazy. Still… he'd broken up with me, which was an assy thing to do. "You're supposed to be looking for Trudy," I reminded him.

"And I still am… but I can multitask. Give me something to do to help your family."

"Well… it would help me to get my hands around my mother's financial affairs if I could access her laptop." I also

148

wanted to check out her search history. "She has a password on it, but I can't find it anywhere. Can you help?"

"Sure. Send me the IP address, ISP info, and access to your home network. I'll get right on it."

I felt a rush of appreciation and love for Hugh. "Okay. After."

"After what?"

I started unbuttoning my blouse.

"Oh... *after*," he said with a grin.

September 10, Monday

"SO THAT," I said brightly, "is the life of a novelist in a nutshell."

The classroom of English Lit students stared back at me with slack, bored expressions. If any of the teenagers had been considering becoming a writer, I had probably just convinced them it was a one-way street to a dead-end life.

Ms. Jeffson stood and clapped until a few brown-nosers joined in. Then she beamed at the class. "I'm sure *many* of you have questions for our hometown best-selling novelist, Jane Hunnicut."

After an awkward silence, a hand went up in the back, and I exhaled in relief. "Yes?" I strained to see the student.

She leaned forward, into my line of sight. I gasped. It was Deidre's little sister Kelly.

"I have an idea for a book," she said. "Would you like to hear it?"

"Of course," I said, unsure what to expect.

"So it takes place in a small town, and a high school student goes missing, a girl."

I swallowed hard. "Sounds... interesting."

"Maybe we should take another question," Ms. Jeffson said in a rush.

"And everyone thinks this girl ran away," Kelly continued, her voice stronger, "but actually she was the victim of foul play, and there's a cover up."

"Cover up?" I squeaked.

"Yeah... a coverup by the local police because the girl comes from a poor family, and the men she went out with were upstanding members of the community—you know, like teachers, ministers, and married men."

A flush was traveling up my neck. "That sounds like an interesting piece of fiction alright."

Kelly gave me a flat smile. "And the person who could help, doesn't because they don't want to get involved."

"M-maybe that person has a lot going on," I offered weakly. "I mean, that could be the character motivation," I added.

"In literature, that person is known as a reluctant hero," Ms. Jeffson said helpfully.

Or heroine. I swallowed hard. "May I ask how your made-up, fictional, unreal story ends?"

"Happily ever after," the teen said dryly, "for everyone except the girl who disappeared."

September 11, Tuesday

I WAS STILL slogging through the living room hoard stash, but I couldn't get Kelly Valentine's accusing dark eyes out of my mind. She seemed sure Deidre had run into trouble and was the victim of a crime... and she seemed to think I was in a position to help.

More likely, though, Kelly was spinning a story to justify why she hadn't heard from her beloved sister. She'd rather think something terrible happened to Deidre than believe she could've reached out to her and hadn't.

A few minutes later, I tugged a packing blanket away from a tall object and uncovered a row of three metal school lockers that had been painted many times and had a pleasant retro patina. The lockers, I realized, would look great in the treehouse and the metal would withstand the elements.

But no way could I move it to the treehouse on my own.

I picked up my phone and texted Tyler. *I could use your help with some heavy lifting.*

A few seconds later, my phone pinged. *Can't, working... maybe Will can help*

I frowned. *Thought we were keeping the hoarding a secret? Will's a good friend, he won't judge*

I worked my mouth back and forth. I hadn't even told Hugh about the hoarding, so sharing with Will seemed a little *intimate*. On the other hand, it would be a relief to share the secret with someone... but I didn't want to intrude on Will's workday.

He was probably somewhere with his arm up a cow's butt.

I rummaged through my things for a scarf and found a bright yellow one that would do. Then I walked to the treehouse and climbed up, and fastened the scarf to a pole so it was visible from Will's house.

If he was looking.

I had no idea when he would get home or if he'd notice the signal, so I went back to my unpacking, with the story Kelly had told me once again running through my head. Suddenly I was spinning variations and what-ifs and embellishing the story with a colorful cast of characters.

And I realized the story forming in my head was much more interesting than the one I was writing. I scrambled to make notes, my hands flying over the keyboard of my laptop.

A few minutes later, the sound of Will's truck pulled me from my musings. I walked out onto the porch and waved as he swung down, grinning. "You signaled?"

I smiled. "I did."

"I hope this isn't a pig problem?"

"Nope." Then I winced. "I need a hand moving a piece of furniture."

"I'm your man," he said, touching the brim of his dusty hat.

I sighed. "And I have something to show you."

His eyebrows went up. "I'm all in."

I gestured him to follow me inside, and I braced myself for his reaction. He climbed the steps to the porch, then gingerly stepped into the living room, now only three-quarters full of stuff stacked to the rafters. My face burned for him to see my mother's shame... my family's shame.

He stood and took in the towering stacks of stuff. I waited for him to bolt, or to shrink back in revulsion. Instead he put his hands on his hips and nodded absently. "So your mother is a bit of a collector?"

In my abject relief, I gave a little laugh. "That's an understatement."

"I assume the entire house is like this?"

I nodded. "I've cleared the kitchen and her bedroom, but there's still a lot to do."

He looked at me with... admiration? "That's what you've been doing all this time?"

"It has to be cleared out so she can come home from the hospital when it's time."

Will nodded. "How can I help?"

"For now, help me move these lockers to the treehouse?"

"I'm on it," he said, springing into motion.

It struck me I had two distinctly different men offering to lighten my load... this was getting sticky.

September 12, Wednesday

I'D FINALLY UNCOVERED a decent piece of furniture in the bowels of the living room hoard, a large oak cabinet whose doors had been bungeed shut. It was too heavy not to contain something, and I prayed it was something valuable, like stacks of gold bars. After a bit of tugging, the aged bungee cords fell away. I opened the doors to find...

Hundreds and hundreds of empty baby food jars.

I burst into tears.

In the midst of my crying jag, a vehicle came rolling up the driveway. I wiped my eyes and opened the door to see a pickup truck with a wire cage around the bed. The side of the truck read "Junk Man Jim."

It seemed Mr. Powers had finally made good on his promise to stop by and take some things for his flea market.

He waved and parked his truck, climbed out, and offered me a toothless grin. I balked, wondering how much of a businessman he could be if he couldn't afford dentures.

"Hiya, young lady. You must be Sharon's daughter."

"Yes," I said. "I'm Jane."

"Your brother Tyler asked me to come by, said you had some things you wanted to sell."

I nodded, then led him to the garage that was now practically full of kitchen gadgets, linens, dishes, books, clothes, furniture, whatnots, gewgaws, and tchotchkes, all sparkling clean and sorted, like a retail store. If he didn't take at least some of the things, I wasn't sure what I'd do.

"Hm," he said, pulling on his grizzled chin. "I recognize a lot of this stuff. Sharon sure has been a good customer over the years. Between you and me, I wondered if she was planning to open her own flea market." Then he shook his head, turned, and walked back to his vehicle.

"Mr. Powers," I said, trotting after him, "please... don't leave." I choked back a sob. I didn't realize how much I'd been counting on him to make some of this clutter disappear.

"Got to," he said, then opened the door and climbed in, flashing another gummy grin. "Gotta go get a bigger truck."

I watched him pull away, so happy I burst into tears again.

I was still stuck in Accident, Alabama, but finally, it felt as if I was getting somewhere.

September 13, Thursday

THE NEXT DAY I had to drive Ms. Jeffson to the hospital for a checkup, and while I waited for her, I decided to test my theory about why Mom reacted so violently to me each time I went into her room.

But when I got there, I heard the murmuring of a man's voice. I stopped—it sounded familiar.

Detective Terry?

I poked my head into the room and saw he was sitting next to my mother's bed... reading the newspaper aloud?

While I listened, he went through the *Atlanta Journal-Constitution* section by section, reading everything from sports scores to wedding announcements. I marveled at his soothing tone. It was as if they were having a conversation, yet my mother remained silent.

But apparently, she could tolerate his company.

I was standing in the hall when the detective walked out with the thick newspaper folded under his arm. When he saw me, he did a double-take.

"Ms. Hunnicut... hello."

"Don't hello me," I said, my voice shaking. "When you first came here, I told you my mother isn't well enough to be questioned, and you said you wouldn't."

He nodded. "That's right."

"So what are you doing in her room?"

"I was reading the paper."

I frowned. "I heard. But why?"

He shrugged. "I wanted to read the paper, and I figured she wouldn't mind hearing what's going on."

I waited for more of an explanation.

"And believe it or not, I have some experience with unresponsive patients, and I thought it might help. Plus I'd like to question your mother—"

"No way—"

"—when she's well," he emphasized, cutting off my attempt to protest. "And I thought it might be helpful if she gets used to my voice."

I glared at him.

The big man sighed. "Ms. Hunnicut, if I'm going to get to the bottom of what happened to your friend, it looks as if I will eventually have to talk to your mother."

I crossed my arms. "So do you think there's more to Deidre's case than her running away?"

He crossed his arms. "Do you?"

"I asked you first."

"Then yes, I do."

"Okay," I said. "So do I."

September 14, Friday

"HI, NADINE," I said. "It's Jane Hunnicut. Is Jocelyn in?"

"You're in luck, Jane, she just walked in. Hold, please."

The line clicked. "Jane?"

"Hi, Jocelyn. How are you?"

"Fine. How's your mother?"

"Better," I said. "But it looks as if I'm going to be in Alabama for a while longer."

"I'm sorry to hear that," she said.

"I did manage to do a local personal appearance recently."

"Oh? At a bookstore?"

"Um, no… at my former high school."

"Oh," she said, sounding somewhat deflated. "Although, sales for both of your books were really strong in the area around your hometown, so every publicity event helps." She paused. "I hope you're calling with an update on the manuscript?"

I took a deep breath. "That's what I wanted to talk to you about."

"I'm listening."

"Another story idea has… presented itself, and it's something I'd like to write."

"Something other than JUGGLING ACT?"

"Yes."

"Jane, it's too late in the game to change direction editorially."

"But you told me to dive deep," I added quickly, "and this is that kind of story."

She made a rueful noise. "Okay, you have five minutes to convince me. What's the story?"

"It's a bit of a mystery."

"Jane, the market is chockablock full of mystery series."

"This isn't a series, not the typical amateur sleuth… this is a story about a woman whose friend goes missing, and when the police won't follow up, she decides to find out what happened."

She was silent—not a good sign.

"It's loosely based on a true story," I added.

"Whose?" she asked.

"Mine."

"Keep going," she said, sounding intrigued.

I made a fist and pumped the air. "The story is centered around a threesome of friends…"

September 15, Saturday

"I DID IT!" Hugh crowed.

"You found Trudy?" I asked excitedly.

He deflated. "No. I cracked your mother's laptop password."

"Seriously? What is it?"

Hugh bit into his lip. "Before I tell you, Jane... don't you think it's a bit of an invasion of her privacy? I mean, won't she be angry?"

"I only hope she gets well enough to be angry."

"Good point," he said. "Okay, it's 'Treehouse, zero five zero seven, question mark.'"

I squinted. "Treehouse?"

"Yeah, one word, capital T, then zero five zero seven, question mark."

"Okay, thanks," I said, writing it down. "I have to go. Keep looking for Trudy."

"I will." Then he leaned into the camera. "Before you go, can we... you know?"

"Not today," I said, eager to see what information, if any, I could learn from Mom's laptop. "Find. Trudy."

September 16, Sunday

YOU'D THINK I'D be used to going through my mother's things by now, but pilfering through her laptop seemed even more personal than looking under her mattress. When people are online, they tend to feel anonymous, and I wasn't sure what I'd find. Once I got into her laptop, she'd used the password saver program I'd recommended, so I was able to access almost everything. No surprise, she had accounts on several online auction houses, although I was surprised to see how many game sites she visited, and her most used application was a version of solitaire.

It made me sad to think of her sitting at the table, surrounded by her hoard, playing solitaire for hours and hours... another compulsive activity at an almost unwinnable task.

Her search history revealed little—she'd looked online for garden seeds and how to get rid of dandelion weeds. And I was surprised to find she'd performed searches on my book reviews. Interesting.

As I continued to scan her search strings, I froze. DEIDRE VALENTINE.

So Mom had been looking for Deidre, too, days before she'd phoned Detective Terry. She'd probably covered the same online ground I had, and come up empty. Hm.

Her most recent searches seemed incongruent, almost scrambled. But a couple did stand out. SEVERE HEADACHE, NUMBNESS.

I covered my mouth with my hand. Symptoms of a stroke—had she realized it was happening? It occurred to me the nonsensical searches might have been a result of blurred vision.

I hesitated a bit before accessing her email because there, you find out not just who a person communicates with and the newsletters they subscribe to, but also how well they write and their personal peccadillos.

My mother, I was pleased to see, was just as expressive in her emails to a couple of far flung friends as in the letters she'd written to my father. One older saved email caught my eye. It was dated nearly five years ago. There was no subject line, and the address appeared to be machine-generated.

My mother had written:

Thank you for what you did for my boy. No matter what happened between us, I will always be grateful to you for your kindness to T. All my love, always, S

I squinted. Was "T" Tyler?

The person had responded:

S, I was happy to help your boy, but tell T to lie low. The girl's daddy is on the warpath, and if he goes after T, my badge can't save him. I still think of you at night, S. Take care.

Badge?
Sheriff Tomlin?
He still thought of her at night?
Ew.
But there it was, in black and white. The Sheriff had admitted to me he'd smoothed over the assault charge against Tyler, and

157

now it was clear he'd done so because he'd once had an intimate relationship with my mother. What wasn't clear was just where their relationship stood at the time she'd fallen ill.

September 17, Monday

"JANE," SHERIFF TOMLIN said with a smile. "What brings you in?"

I turned and closed his office door.

"No need to be so formal," he said. "You can't keep a secret in a small town anyway."

"You're having an affair with my mother?" I asked.

His face blanched. "Oh. That's different."

"You're a married man."

He stood, then gestured to a chair. "Have a seat, and let's talk."

I sat.

He sighed and crossed his hands over his big belly. "How did you find out?"

"I read her emails."

"Oh." He winced, no doubt mentally scanning the intimate things they'd exchanged. "First of all, your mother and I did have a brief affair six years ago when my wife and I were separated, and we really cared about each other." His mouth went flat. "But my wife and I got back together—you know, for our kids—and I ended it with Sharon."

"But that left my mother out in the cold."

He sighed and lifted his hands. "Maybe... I don't know. I thought she was okay with it. We were able to remain friends and honestly, I can say things to Sharon I could never say to my wife." Then he looked grim. "But I do wonder if my breaking things off with her is what triggered the hoarding."

I sighed, my heart breaking for her. After spending her life with my cheating father, she'd found love with another man... only to become the other woman herself, and then be left alone yet again.

It seemed as if my mother had had reasons galore to become a hoarder.

September 18, Tuesday

"SO WHILE YOUR mother isn't demonstrating as much improvement as we'd like," Dr. Kessler said to me and Tyler. "We're almost to the end of the line as far as the services and the bed we can offer her here."

She stood. "I've set a release date for two weeks from today, unless her condition changes. I hope that will give you time to make arrangements for her home care. A social worker will be in touch to help you coordinate a home health aide, plus a bed and any other equipment you'll need."

"Thank you, Doctor," I managed to get out. But inside I was screaming.

When she walked away, Tyler wiped his hand across his mouth. "Will the house be ready?"

"Maybe," I said. "But Tyler, how am I going to be able to lift her and take care of her? It would be better if she came to your house."

He shook his head. "Absolutely not. Stacey would have a fit."

I frowned. "I've heard Stacey isn't coming back."

His face reddened. "That's a lie. She's coming back... soon."

"Then maybe you can move in with me and Mom until Stacey returns."

"No." His expression was stony. "I looked after Mom the four years you were in college, and the six years you were on the other side of the world. It's payback time, Jane. She's all yours."

September 19, Wednesday

THIS TIME I remembered the way to the cemetery, but it still took me a few minutes to find my father's grave.

I hadn't felt particularly compelled to visit today, but I'd driven a taxi run for one of Mom's regulars to get groceries, and when I realized their home was close to the cemetery, I decided to drop by.

I guess I was feeling slammed about revelations I was having about my family, and I needed to see that one thing, as sad as it was, remained the same.

My father was still six feet under in the cold, cold ground. My mother once joked darkly it was the longest she'd ever been able to keep tabs on him.

The red silk flowers were faded and scattered. I made a mental note to replace them soon.

"Dad... what am I going to do with Mom?" I asked aloud, as if he might answer. "I don't know how to take care of her... and honestly, I don't want to." My cheeks felt frosty with tears. "I don't think she even likes me that much."

I came hoping a sense of peace would come over me, a sense that life would turn out okay even if it didn't turn out the way we'd planned.... but I was disappointed. Instead the sky opened up and dropped buckets of rain. Before I could make it back to the car, I was drenched to my Wonder Woman underwear.

I sat in the Caddy and watched the rain pound against the windshield. I'd never felt so thoroughly alone and at loose ends. My mother had never been the soft, happy mom who tickled me breathless or read me bedtime stories. She hadn't enjoyed being a mother, and I hadn't enjoyed being her daughter. But as I'd gotten older, I'd taken solace in the fact that she was so iron-willed, she'd never need anyone.

Least of all me.

And now that she did, I was positively terrified.

September 20, Thursday

THE RAIN continued to fall all night and into the next day. I didn't want to leave the house, but I had to take a break from cleaning or I was going to lose my mind.

At least the writing was going well... or starting to. I woke up thinking about my book and went to sleep thinking about it, so that was a good sign.

But there was one item outstanding I needed to take care of.

I drove to the high school and checked in at the front office.

"Hello," the receptionist said, smiling. "You were here a couple of weeks ago weren't you? You're the writer."

"That's right," I said with a smile, then I held up a book. "I brought this for one of Ms. Jeffson's students, Kelly Valentine. Would it be possible for me to give it to her? It would only take five minutes."

He checked the wall clock, then shrugged. "Sure... classes are changing in a few minutes anyway. Let me page her to the office. You can wait over there."

A few minutes later, Kelly arrived, looking pensive. I stood and waved, and she seemed surprised to see me.

"Hi," I said. "I brought you this book on writing... it helped me when I was getting started."

She took the book. "Thanks... but I don't want to be a writer. No offense, but you made it sound pretty boring."

Ouch. "Still, don't count it out. Meanwhile, I wanted you to know I'm going to try to find Deidre."

Her dark eyes lit up. "Really?"

I nodded. "Really."

She threw her arms around me and squeezed, catching me off guard. "Thank you."

"I can't make any promises. But I'll do my best to get some answers—for both of us."

She grinned, then pulled back when a bell sounded. "I have to go. Thanks again."

I smiled and waved.

But as she glided away on youthful optimism, I worried that the "answers" to Deidre's disappearance might not be as happy as she and I hoped.

September 21, Friday

SINCE EVERYTHING was nice and wet, I took advantage of a break in the rain to haul a mountain of paper out to the farthest corner of the property to the burn pit. I approached the black, sooty patch of ground with a bit of trepidation—I did not have good memories of the brick firepit.

A vivid recollection surfaced of Mom bringing home a dress for me that had made my heart sink. It was brown and frumpy and altogether wrong for a fourteen-year-old to wear to a Valentine's Day dance—at least in my mind. I'd shortened the dress and removed the sleeves to reveal a little more skin, and my mother had lost her mind, said I'd ruined it and wasted her hard-earned money. First she'd shredded the dress with shears, then had made me watch while she burned it in the pit.

And needless to say, I'd skipped the dance.

I transferred the paper from the wagon to the burn pit, wondering how many Hunnicut mementos had been incinerated here, and when my mother had lost her taste for it.

When Tyler and I were no longer around to torment?

I used a lighter to start a flame and added a few boxes at a time to make sure the fire didn't get too high or out of bounds. While stirring the ashes with a stick, I hit something metal, and looked closer.

It was a chisel, the handle scorched but otherwise in usable condition. And it didn't look as if it had been exposed long—it wasn't rusted. I wondered what it was doing here—maybe mixed in with something else and accidentally tossed in the fire?

Then I remembered what Will had said about the gouge marks in the wood table in the treehouse—that it looked as if they'd been made with a chisel, and maybe recently.

I frowned. Why would my mother gouge Deidre's initials out of the wood table?

September 22, Saturday

DETECTIVE TERRY turned the chisel over in his hands, then held it up to the gouges in the table.

"It's possible this tool could've made the marks," he said with a nod. "But I'm not sure that buys us anything."

"I'm not sure either," I admitted. "But I thought someone should know."

He looked at me. "You didn't call the Sheriff?"

"No."

"You're going to get me in trouble again."

I sighed. "Sheriff Tomlin and my mother… have history."

"What kind of history?"

"The screwing kind," I said flatly.

He nodded. "So you hate him?"

"No," I said, choosing my words carefully. "But I think he has a bias for my family that's getting in the way of finding out what happened to Deidre."

The detective pursed his mouth. "So you think your mother does know something?"

I shrugged. "I can't say for sure… who knows if or how much her mind was scrambled when she made that call. But I believe she *thought* she knew something."

"She's still not communicating?" he asked.

I shook my head. "We're bringing her home in a few days to continue her rehab."

"Maybe she'll recover more quickly in her own surroundings."

I winced. "I don't know about that." Then I sighed and nodded to the house through the rain. "Come with me—I need to show you my mother's state of mind when she called you."

September 23, Sunday

WHILE RAIN hammered on the roof of the treehouse, my fingers flew across the keyboard. The story of a trio of friends splintered by the disappearance of one of them.

Deidre had been our keystone. Without her, Emma and I had fallen away from each other.

But I was careful to make the names and places different, and I changed lots of small details and backstory to ensure the story I wrote would be unrecognizable to anyone who lived in Accident and knew Deidre.

My phone lit up and Hugh's face came on the screen. It was time for our Skyping call. I reached over and hit the decline button, which was rude, but I was ecstatic because I couldn't remember the last time I'd wanted to write more than do anything else.

I was still plotting the story and although my enthusiasm was off the charts, one thought kept nagging at me.

I'd never written a story before when I didn't have the ending worked out ahead of time.

But I couldn't seem to think of a good ending for this one.

September 24, Monday

I'D SCHEDULED ANOTHER session with Anne Warford, the therapist at the hospital who specialized in Obsessive Compulsive Disorders.

"Can you tell me how a hoarder would react to knowing someone is going through their things?"

"You mean if they aren't there to watch and participate?"

"Yes."

She winced. "That would trigger every anxiety a hoarder has. They would see it as an invasion of their personal space, and a violation of trust. Remember, a person's hoarding collection might seem random to us, but to them it's very personal and specific. They remember each item they collected and when they pick it up or look at it, they relive the thrill of finding it."

"So if I don't clean out her house, she can't come home from the hospital. But if I do clean out her house, she will hate me."

The therapist looked sympathetic. "You're in a tough spot, Jane. There's no easy answer here. You have to do what's in the best interests of your mother's immediate health. Her home has to be safe and secure. Once that's in place, your mother can receive the mental health support she needs."

I nodded, reviewing the last few times I'd tried to talk to my mother. I'd told her not to worry, that I was going through her things and "fixing" the situation. I was starting to realize, though, that my mother wouldn't see it that way. No wonder she was reacting so violently to me... in her mind, I was making absolutely everything worse.

"But maybe it won't be as bad as you think," she said. "It's possible your mother will be so relieved the clutter is gone, she'll be grateful to you for helping to set things right again." She smiled. "Especially if the reason she began to hoard is because she was lonely. The fact that you cared enough to visit and help put her house in order might be enough to get her back to a healthy place."

"So it all depends on why she started hoarding in the first place?"

She nodded.

I chewed on my lip. Then I might be screwed... because I was starting to think my mother had started to hoard in an attempt to cover up something.

Literally.

And here I was, unwittingly revealing skeletons.

Literally?

September 25, Tuesday

"UGH, THIS RAIN!" Emma said, waving me into the foyer of her home. "Will it ever stop?"

"I don't know," I said, wiping my feet on the mat inside the door and shrugging out of my raincoat. "Sorry, I'm getting water everywhere."

"Don't worry about it," Emma said with a wave. "The kids are running in and out like animals, there's mud all over. Between them and the workers, I'm going a little batty."

"Workers?" I asked.

Emma dimpled. "We're having our bedroom remodeled."

"Wow, it was already pretty gorgeous."

"Thanks," Emma said. "But it was time for a refresh. We thought about selling the house, but then we decided to just overhaul the areas where we spend the most time." She leaned in. "And we spend a lot of time in the bedroom, if you get my drift."

"I do," I murmured. Emma and Eddie had always been nuts for each other, and their amorous hijinks had been legendary, even in high school.

"Want to see?" she asked.

"Sure." I followed her up the sweeping staircase, once again marveling at the display of good taste. Emma had a knack for making things beautiful. She'd loved to perform makeovers on me and Deidre, flat-ironing our hair and making us learn how to apply false eyelashes.

"Ta-da," she said opening the door to the massive bedroom. "The painters haven't finished and of course all the light fixtures will be changed out."

"Nice," I said, nodding, and trying to take it all in.

"We remodeled the bathrooms, too," she said, waving her arm. "New vanities and shower tile and fixtures."

"Beautiful," I breathed.

"Oh, and new closets, too," she said, opening the door to the expansive dressing room where I'd been tricked into a skimpy bikini. Bare of furnishings and clothes, the room looked completely different, except for the large gold "E" on the wall.

"Where is the photo collage?" I asked, remembering the photo of the three of us.

Her face crumpled. "It's gone. The workers who dismantled it threw everything in the trash by mistake."

I gasped. "Your wedding photos?"

She nodded, looking pained. "I can get more copies of those, but there were lots of photos of the kids I don't know if I can replace."

And the photo that proved the flying geese quilt was Deidre's... that was gone, too.

September 26, Wednesday

IF ANYONE HAD DRIVEN onto the property at this very moment, they might think I'd gone completely mad. Using a big tarp, I'd erected a makeshift tent over the area in the garden where I'd dug up the quilt. It was muddy from all the previous rain, but at least the tarp kept most of the moisture off me.

I was using the hoe and a shovel to systematically cut down plants and dig up the ground. If Sheriff Tomlin wasn't going to do it, I would. No one could stop me from digging up Mom's garden, except Mom. And she wasn't there to stop me.

Plus I wanted to do this before she came home.

But I was dirty and achy and hot and wet and miserable. I wanted to find something, and yet, I didn't.

The sound of Will's big truck coming up the driveway was such a relief, I was almost teary.

He climbed out of his truck and headed to the pig pen, clad in a gray slicker and rubber boots, with a plastic cover over his dumb hat. He hadn't yet noticed me. Through the rain I watched him check Petty, then smile and give her a pat on the neck. It was such a small thing, but something about the gesture moved me.

Then he looked up and saw me. He waved and I waved back. He strode toward me and laughed as he stepped under the tarp and shook the water off his arms. "Are you digging a grave?"

I felt my face crumple.

"Hey, hey," he murmured, moving in to comfort me. "It was a joke. What's this all about?"

I told him about the quilt and he listened, stone-faced.

"I just want to make sure there's... nothing else here," I whispered.

"I'm sure there's nothing else here," he said.

He thought I was losing my mind. And maybe I was.

Then he gently took the shovel from my hand. "But let me help."

September 27, Thursday

WE HADN'T FOUND ANYTHING, of course. Will had offered to spend the night, but I wasn't ready to sleep with him.

But I'd thought about his goodbye kiss all night and now all day. I'd spent another rainy day in the treehouse, writing, plotting, thinking. It felt good, but I was feeling bored and antsy.

And yes, a little horny.

I emerged from the treehouse facing a long evening alone, then turned to look toward Will's house.

Billowing from the knob of his front door was a yellow cloth... a signal.

I grinned and grabbed my laptop, then climbed down in record time, heading for the Caddy.

And marveled over when the idea of staying longer in Accident had become... tolerable.

September 28, Friday

"GOOD MORNING," Will said in my ear.

I gave in to the smile that teased my well-kissed lips. "Good morning."

"I have to leave for an early appointment," he said. "Will you be all right to make yourself some breakfast and lock up?"

"Yes."

He gave me another really good kiss, then left.

I lay in his bed for a few minutes, enjoying the luxury of a wonderful mattress and a ceiling fan overhead. The man had good taste, and he tasted good. I could get used to these sleepovers.

At length, I crawled out of bed and made my way to the gourmet kitchen. More opulence, ugh.

While I waited for the espresso machine to do its thing, I padded around the kitchen in my underwear, looking at all his really nice stuff. On the counter was an electronic picture frame, with a gallery of photos changing every few seconds. Some of them were of Will and his sister Tiffany growing up, and I was riveted. Since he was a few years older, I had only vague memories of Will, and the crushes the girls had on him from a distance.

When my espresso was ready, I blew on the top and sipped as the photos slid by, giving me a peek into the man's background.

But the next picture stopped me cold—it was of a younger Will and his blond sister... and both their arms were slung around a young exotic beauty in the middle.

Deidre.

September 29, Saturday

IT WAS STILL RAINING with no end in sight. I was awake when I heard Tyler's delivery truck come down the driveway. If he could get out in this soup to feed the pigs, the least I could do was take him a cup of hot coffee. Although considering our last conversation, I wasn't sure we were still talking.

I got the coffee going, then bundled up and carried a thermos of coffee out to him. He had just finished emptying a bag of feed into the troughs, and had ducked back into the barn. I followed and held up the thermos.

"Thought you could use this," I said over the sound of unrelenting rain on the metal roof.

He hesitated a long while, then inclined his head. "Thanks," he said, folding the cloth feed bag. But he didn't look good. His face was long and his eyes were bloodshot.

"Are you okay?" I asked.

"Not really," he said. "I'm going to Tuscaloosa to get my family and bring them home."

I wondered if it had more to do with wanting Stacey back, or ensuring I didn't insist Mom be taken to his house. Probably some of both. "How does Stacey feel about coming home?"

He shrugged. "I don't know... I don't care. I can't stand this."

"I understand, Tyler, but you can't make her come back to you."

He scoffed. "Yes, I can."

"But do you want to do that? Do you want the boys to see that?"

He set the feed sack on a shelf with a stack of other empties. "I want them to see how much they all mean to me."

"Then by all means, go visit them," I said. "But don't go angry and say things that can't be taken back." I handed him the thermos. "You and I saw plenty of that around Mom and Dad... it never ends well."

He nodded, then sighed. "Okay... I'll be on my best behavior."

I smiled. "Good."

He suddenly reached forward and clasped me in a hug. "Thanks, Sis."

"You're welcome," I murmured.

He released me abruptly, then walked out before things got too emotional. I watched him climb into his delivery truck and waved goodbye. He gave me a grin and a thumbs up as he drove away... the man could swing from alarm to charm in a matter of seconds.

I raised my jacket hood and prepared to run back through the rain when I noticed the bag Tyler had just left on the shelf. It was folded in triangles… like the way Deidre's found quilt had been folded.

September 30, Sunday

I NOW KNEW how Noah had felt. The rain didn't seem to want to stop. And it wasn't the nice gentle rains we got in England, with shrouds of comfy fog. It was ruthless sideways-blowing sheets of water, one after another.

I waited for a break to feed the pigs, but when none seemed forthcoming, I put on my mother's yellow slicker and rubber boots and braved the weather.

When Tyler got back, I was going to talk to him about selling the pigs.

The precisely folded feed bag was where I'd left it in the barn. I bit into my lip. When Tyler got back, we needed to talk about a lot of things.

If the ground around the pigpen was a river, the pen itself was a slopfest of gooey thick brown-black mud… and the pigs were in their glory, rolling and wallowing, their thick hides impervious to the driving rain.

Except for Petty, I noticed. She was struggling, and I realized her hind quarters were stuck in the mud. She squealed for help, and I had to do something.

I poured the feed into the troughs to distract the other pigs while I tended to Petty. Then I climbed over the pen fence and dropped into six inches of sucking muck. Walking was an exhausting feat, but I finally made my way over to her. She was frantic, squealing and flailing. I put my arms around her thick butt and lifted with all my might, finally freeing her hind legs. She kicked and leapt way, knocking me off balance. I fell face down in the mud and it held me like cement. This would not be a good way to go.

I managed to push myself up and roll over, wiping mud from my eyes and mouth. I gasped and rallied my strength to get to my feet. I made a lunge for it, but something unusual caught my eye.

It was white, sticking up and in sharp contrast to the black mud.

I squinted, and when I realized what it was, I stumbled backward.

It was a leg bone.

October 1, Monday

WHEN I HEARD the sound of a car door slamming, I shot up from Mom's bed where I'd huddled on top of the covers since reporting my discovery of a leg bone in the pigpen the previous day. Sounding somewhere between dubious and angry, Sheriff Tomlin had bellowed he had a hundred more important things to tend to in this godawful weather and would stop by this morning, *maybe*, then forbade me to tell a single soul what I *thought* I'd found, especially "that interfering detective, dammit."

I had obliged. I couldn't think of anyone I wanted to tell about this particular development, even my boyfriend—er, *ex*-boyfriend—Hugh in London. Especially Hugh—he would think my family were complete barbarians.

Because that's what I was thinking.

In fact, I'd come close to not even calling the sheriff. I'd been around pigs long enough to know if I'd simply left the bone exposed, they would've devoured it and no one would've been the wiser. The fact that it existed at all meant before the rains, it had been buried too deep for them to unearth.

But my conscience had gotten the better of me. So I'd shooed the pigs out of the muddy pen and fastened the gate, leaving them to find shelter under trees.

And I'd left the bone sticking up out of the mud where I'd found it.

Sleep had not come easy. I would've absconded to my brother Tyler's house except he was out of town fetching his long-suffering wife from her parents' house. My friend Emma would've taken me in for the night, but not without an explanation. Ditto for Will Story, but on top of everything else, I was still reeling from the discovery of a photo proving he'd spent time with my missing high school friend Deidre.

Missing.

When in my mind had she gone from "runaway" to "missing"?

I peered out the window to see Sheriff Tomlin's wide form emerge from his car and move toward the pigpen, his shoulders hunched in the driving rain. I was dressed, but it took me a few minutes to get into a slicker and rain boots I'd left near the front door. The hood did a laughable job of protecting my face from the slanting rain. As I splashed through puddles to reach where the sheriff stood, I almost hoped the bone had washed away, but when I stopped next to him, I could see it was still there, sticking up like a middle finger.

He turned his head and acknowledged me with a loud grunt. "Jane."

"Sheriff. Do you think it's human?"

"Hard to say."

"It looks like a leg bone to me."

"Don't go speculatin'," he said gruffly. Then he unlocked the gate and waded over to it. I didn't have to be told to stay put. He glanced around and found a long stick, then drove it in the mud next to the bone. I realized he was marking the location with the stick, then he used his gloved hand to give the bone a tug.

I held my breath, praying it didn't have a foot attached.

It came away clean, but the other end was broken off, so it was impossible to tell how long it had once been.

He carried it back to where I stood, his expression pinched. "Did you tell anyone about this?"

I couldn't take my eyes off the bone. "N-no."

"Not even Tyler?"

I frowned. "No. You told me not to say anything, so I didn't."

He nodded, satisfied.

"What are you going to do?" I asked, suddenly nervous that he could make this bone, like Deidre's quilt, disappear if he wanted to. I'd learned he and my mother had had an affair and he'd gotten Tyler out of trouble at least once. He could smooth this over, too, out of loyalty to my mother.

"I'm going to turn it over to an expert," he said.

A rumbling noise sounded on the driveway, and my womb contracted like Pavlov's dog. Will Story's enormous truck materialized through the rain and lurched to a stop a few feet from the Sheriff's marked car.

"There's my expert now," the Sheriff said with a smirk.

I swallowed a groan—of course the area veterinarian would be the person who could tell them if the bone was animal or human. I should've called Will myself... except for the little tidbit where he might be connected to Deidre.

And just like that I admitted to myself what I hadn't wanted to before—that this could be Deidre's remains.

The realization hit me so hard, I took a step back just as Will strode up to meet us. He was dressed for the weather and his ridiculous cowboy hat had its own raincoat. It was a startling contrast to the last time I'd seen him—stark naked.

He nodded hello to both of us, but his gaze lingered on me as if he were thinking thoughts similar to mine and wondering why I'd been dodging his calls.

"What do you have there?" he asked the sheriff, staring at the bone.

Sheriff Tomlin handed the mud-stained bone to Will. "I was hoping you could tell me."

Will turned it over in his gloved hands, bringing it closer to his face to examine. "Looks like a tibia."

"Leg bone?" the sheriff asked.

Will nodded.

"Of a pig?" the sheriff pressed.

"Probably... but human tibias look the same in some places when they're fractured like this."

My heart thudded against my breastbone.

"But it's probably pig," the sheriff urged.

Will nodded slowly. "Since you found it in the pigpen, that's a good bet."

The sheriff nodded, as if the matter was settled, then took the bone back. "Thanks, Will. That's what I thought." He looked at me. "See? Nothing to get excited about."

"Wait," I said. "That's all? You're not going to have it examined?"

Sheriff Tomlin glared. "I just did. You don't trust the good doctor's word?"

Will shifted. "Sheriff, it's just my opinion."

"Good enough for me," Sheriff Tomlin said, then touched the brim of his wet hat. "Now if you don't mind, I haven't been to bed yet." He was already walking toward his car. "Y'all try to stay dry."

I watched him disappear into his car, feeling an odd mingling of relief and frustration.

"You okay?" Will asked, breaking into my thoughts.

I glanced up, shielding my eyes from the rain. "Sure."

He squinted. "I'm almost certain it's a pig bone, Jane."

"Okay... good."

"I've called several times. Are you avoiding me?"

"No. I've been busy. My mother comes home from the hospital tomorrow."

His stance eased. "Oh. You must be relieved."

I was so far from relieved, I wanted to laugh, then cry.

A vibrating ring sounded, and Will touched his side. "I should go, my phone's been ringing nonstop. This rain is causing havoc with livestock."

I nodded. "Go. Thanks for... helping."

He hesitated, then gave me a little smile. "Call me anytime, day or night."

I stood there until he pulled away, churning. *I'm almost certain it's a pig bone.*

Almost.

I bit into my lower lip. And if it was a pig bone, why had the sheriff taken it with him?

October 2, Tuesday

As THE PHONE RANG on the other end, I tapped my foot with impatience. I steeled myself to have to leave yet another voice message for Tyler, but the call unexpectedly connected.

"Hi, Sis."

"Tyler," I hissed into the phone. "Where are you?"

"I'm still in Tuscaloosa," he said calmly. "Is everything okay?"

Incredulous, I gasped. "No, everything is not okay. Mom will be released in twenty minutes. You said you'd be back to help me with this."

"I'm sorry, Jane, but my own family comes first."

Except when he was sleeping around behind his wife's back. I blinked back frustrated tears. "How am I supposed to take her home by myself? She can barely walk, and she's still not talking." *And she hates me.*

"You're the smart one, Jane. You'll figure it out. Besides, I thought you said a nurse would be coming every day."

I closed my eyes. "An aide will come by every day for a while, and to help with physical therapy, but what about getting her settled into the house?"

"You said her room is cleaned out, and the living room and kitchen."

I studied my hands, red and raw again from cleaning nonstop the past few days. "Yes."

"Then you have nothing to worry about."

"What if she reacts badly to having the house cleared out?"

He scoffed. "Are you kidding? She'll be ecstatic you did it for her."

I didn't think so, but I didn't have time to educate Tyler on the emotional triggers of hoarding and the attachment our mother might have to her "collection." "When are you coming home?" I asked, hearing the pleading note in my own voice.

"Soon," he said. "And I'll stop by often to help—I promise."

"Okay," I murmured, hoping he meant what he said. "I need to go."

I ended the call, trying to squash my anger. Before he'd left town, Tyler had reminded me he'd watched over mother for years in my absence, and now it was my turn.

He wasn't wrong.

A discharge nurse told me where to drive around to pick up my mother. When I pulled the Caddy around, the sight of her sitting in the wheelchair on the curb made me suck in a breath.

She looked small and frail in the gray sweat pants and sweat shirt I'd brought, her right arm drawn up under her breasts, her hand fisted. A plastic bag of medications sat in her lap. At least the rain had ceased, but in the bright sunlight, the droop of the right side of her face was more pronounced. Her eyes were open and trained straight ahead. When I walked into her line of sight, she tensed and her gaze darted away... looking for Tyler? But at least she didn't flail or spasm. If anything, her body sagged as the attendant pushed her toward the car, as if she were resigned to being handed over to my care. The attendant helped her from the chair into the passenger seat. She could at least stand and walk, although not unaided, and not far.

"Tyler couldn't get away," I said cheerfully as I fastened her seatbelt. "So it's just me and you."

She didn't respond.

The drive from Birmingham to Accident seemed interminable. I chatted like a magpie about the weather and to catch her up on things that had happened since she'd been hospitalized. I wondered if she had a sense of time passing since she'd had the stroke.

"I took care of the garden all summer. Your corn and muskmelons were especially plentiful. I gave away what the pigs and I couldn't eat, and put lots of okra and beans in the freezer."

She didn't respond.

I took the opening to start easing into the revelation that I'd cleaned up her hoard, keeping in mind the advice the OCD therapist Anne Warford had given me. "I hope you don't mind, Mom, but I had to tidy the kitchen a bit to have room to handle all the produce."

She stiffened.

I held my breath and waited a few minutes before venturing, "And I had to tidy your bedroom so you'd have a comfortable place to come home to."

She made a small noise, but I couldn't tell if it was from anger or pleasure or pain.

"You have a lot of clothes," I offered with a little laugh. "I didn't know what to bring you, I hope that sweat suit feels good."

No response.

I let another few minutes slide by, then said, "And I had to tidy the living room a bit to make sure you can move around the house while you're recovering. The Sheriff said not to worry about the report that was filed about your, um... collecting."

She made another noise, this one louder, but again, I couldn't make out the emotion behind it.

"I moved some of the extra stuff out to the garage," I added quickly. For now, she didn't need to know Junk Man Jim had removed it from there. Or that Will had hauled countless bags of junk to the dump. Or that I'd burned enough paper and boxes to incinerate the state of Alabama.

"I haven't touched my and Tyler's old rooms," I said, then gave a little laugh. "I guess storing things in our rooms was insurance we'd never move back home to live."

Did she tense again, or had I imagined it? She seemed to understand some things, so maybe I was getting through. If so, how frustrating it must be for her not to be able to tell me how wrong I was for interfering and how I was going to pay.

"Your cat misses you," I said to change the subject. "He keeps leaving dead animals by the front door."

No response.

"And the pigs are fine. Well, except for the one Tyler calls Petty. A copperhead got her on the snout, but she's bouncing back. All this rain flooded the pen, so we had to let them out."

She made another noise, this one of clear displeasure... so either she understood me, or she was in pain. I realized, though, she was probably worried about her precious garden.

"Yes, I'm afraid the pigs are rooting through the garden for leftover food, but with all the rain, it was a lost cause anyway."

Was she worried the pigs would unearth the quilt that was buried in the garden... or did she even know it was there? That question would have to wait until she could communicate. Today had been challenging enough, with still one big hurdle.

We were at the turn off for the road leading to the house, and my heart was beating fast. Would my mother freak out at the sight of her hoard being gone? Would I be able to control her if she reacted violently? Would she, as Tyler had suggested, be relieved? Or would the shock of the loss be enough to trigger another stroke?

As I steered the Caddy up the driveway and around to the house, I noticed her eyes were tracking, if erratically. She seemed to be aware of her surroundings.

"We're home," I said with forced cheer as I pulled the Caddy to a stop near the steps to the front porch. The back door was still blocked with boxes and bins, so I'd have to take her in the front door. As I helped her from the car, I pushed down resentment toward Tyler for not being there to help me. What if I dropped her?

It was touch and go, but she was stronger and lighter than I anticipated. Still, by the time we reached the front door, we were both breathing hard. I assumed her weight while I unlocked the front door and swung it open, then steered her over the threshold... and waited.

Her gaze darted around the room, to the clean wood floor and the uncovered windows letting in light, to the sparse but cozy furniture arrangement.

"Doesn't everything look nice?" I remarked.

She shuddered, then began to cry, a pitiful, wailing noise that tore at my heart. Tears streamed down her cheeks and she continued to whimper as I led her through the house to her bedroom. She moved stiffly, resisting me.

"Mom, don't cry," I soothed, but she wouldn't accept comfort... not from me. Her cries only escalated, and continued after I settled her into bed. I sorted through her medications and found the one to help her sleep, then practically forced her to take it. Her eyes continued to be unfocused, but it wasn't hard to read the expression on her face, even with the paralysis.

I recognized hate when I saw it.

October 3, Wednesday

I STARTED AWAKE. Was that a knock on the front door?

I rolled over, met air, then landed on the floor with an *oomph*.

As I lay there staring up at the ceiling, I realized this was what reality felt like—a punch to the lungs.

I wasn't in Mom's bed anymore. I'd moved to a lumpy—and narrow—loveseat in her room in case she needed me during the night, although the seventeen times I'd gotten up to check on her, she'd been sound asleep and resting more easily than I was.

It occurred to me she had probably done the same for me when I was a baby.

Payback was hell.

I was sure my fall had woken her, but when I gingerly pulled myself up to a standing position, she was still sleeping. Despite my mother's initial resistance to her clean surroundings, her subconscious must have recognized the bed she'd slept in most of her adult life, and acquiesced. She looked thin and drawn against the pale linens, but her breathing was deep and even. I hoped that was a good sign.

I massaged my hip—it was definitely going to bruise—then heard the knock again. I squinted at the clock, then squashed a groan at the late hour. That would be the home healthcare worker. I trotted toward the door, head swinging to take in the passably neat bedroom, bathroom, living room, and kitchen.

I couldn't say the same for myself, but I hoped the worker had seen worse. I glanced out the window to see the home service logo on the car sitting in the driveway and swung open the door.

The stocky, bald man on the other side of the door gave me a once-over, then smiled. "The first night a patient comes home is usually the worst."

I gave a grateful laugh, then ran a hand over my wild hair. "That's good to know."

He stuck out his hand. "I'm Owen McCoy."

"I'm—"

"Jane Hunnicut," he said, pumping my hand. "I know."

I squinted. "Have we met? I'm sorry—I've lived away for so long."

"I was a year behind you in high school." He cocked his head. "Picture me with a Justin Beiber bowl cut."

I grinned, then shook my head. "Sorry."

He gave a wave. "No worries. We ran in different crowds. You were the smart, quiet type and I was the smart, closeted type. You were friends with Emma Gaines, weren't you?"

I nodded. "We're still friends."

"I helped Emma when her mother was ill. She's so nice."

"Yes." I invited him inside, then closed the door.

Owen squinted. "And didn't you and Emma hang around with another girl?"

"Deidre Valentine," I murmured, wishing I had a dollar for every time I'd heard or said her name since I'd come back to Accident.

"Oh, right... that was a bit of a sensation when she ran away. I remember the police coming to school."

"Did you know Deidre?" I asked lightly.

He shook his head. "Just who she was. She stood out."

"That was Deidre," I agreed.

"I read both your books—you're very talented."

I pulled on the hem of my sleep shirt, feeling even more self-conscious over my state of disarray. "Thank you."

His eyes went soft. "I'm sorry about your mother."

I gestured toward her bedroom. "She's still asleep."

"Rough night?"

"For me," I said. "She seemed to rest."

"That's good. And this will give us time to talk about her care."

He glanced around, and I was glad the doors to my and Tyler's bedrooms were closed. They contained the worst of the hoard that remained, but the path to the washer and dryer and other areas were still jammed with stuff.

"Will it be just you taking care of your mom?"

I inhaled and nodded. "Looks that way."

"I remember you had an older brother... Tyler, I believe?"

"Yes. But it's my, um, turn."

He nodded knowingly. "So you have your hands full."

That was such an understatement, I laughed hysterically.

I expected him to recoil, but instead he reached out and squeezed my arm. "I know this is hard. But you get me for ninety minutes every day for six weeks. I'll do what I can to make this easier for you and your mom."

I exhaled and blinked back grateful tears.

October 4, Thursday

WITH OWEN'S HELP, I established a shaky schedule for bathing, feeding, and otherwise taking care of Mom. It was exhausting and humbling, made worse by my mother's resistance. She seemed to flinch every time I touched her. And because she didn't respond even to yes and no questions, I had to guess at what she needed and when.

Feeding her was the worst because I had to look at her face and her eyes, and endure her avoidance. I suspected she tolerated me only because I was the person with the food. Owen had encouraged me to talk to her and the care sheet I'd been given at the hospital suggested recovering stroke patients needed lots of stimuli. But I exhausted one-sided small talk quickly and more important subjects felt off-limits. By the second day, we settled into a strained silence as I tended to her needs and moved her unresponsive limbs.

When she fell asleep mid-morning, I took a deep breath and opened the door of my small bedroom. The soaring stacks of boxes and bags sent a stone to my stomach. I hadn't expected Mom to keep everything the same after I left, but neither did I expect this. It was as if she was trying to obliterate and negate everything I'd experienced growing up in the room.

I heard the rumble of an approaching vehicle—Will Story's giant truck. Unbidden, my pulse clicked higher, but by the time I'd walked to the front porch, I had it under control.

Mostly.

He waved and climbed out. "Hi."

I crossed my arms. "Hi, yourself."

"I came by to see if you need anything."

I hesitated, then blurted. "How about an explanation?"

He blinked. "Come again?"

"At your house, I saw a picture of you and your sister with Deidre Valentine."

He nodded slowly. "Yeah. And?"

"You acted as if you didn't know her."

"I never said that, although I didn't know her well."

I pressed my lips together. "The two of you dated?"

He shook his head. "It wasn't like that—she and my sister hung out some when Tiff was going to school in Birmingham." A wry smile touched his lips. "I think it was when Tiff was going through a bit of a wild period."

"Was that around the time Deidre... ran away?"

He shrugged. "Maybe. I remember asking Tiff why Deidre had stopped coming around and she said she'd left town."

He squinted. "Is that why you've been avoiding me, you think I had a thing for your friend?"

I squirmed. "No. I told you—I'm busy."

"How are things with your mother?"

"I'm muddling through."

"Anything I can do to help?"

I started to say no, then thought about the heavy boxes blocking my access to the washer and dryer. "There is something, if you don't mind a little heavy lifting."

He grinned. "Put me to work."

I led him inside and pointed to the wall of cardboard boxes marked "The Accidental Post."

"The town newspaper?" he asked.

"Right. I understand it closed down a few years back."

"I remember. So is this the archives?"

"Presumably, although I have no idea how or where she got them."

He pulled on his chin. "What are you going to do with them?"

"For now, I'll keep them in the garage—if you don't mind moving them."

"Not at all," he said, and reached for the first box. I held the doors open between the house and garage as he transported each one. He moved with athletic ease, in total command of his body— as I remembered from our romp. I tried to think of other things, but by the time he finished, I'd worked up a sweat that rivaled his. I offered him a glass of tea, and he accepted. We carried them to the front porch and sat on the steps. The temperature was still warm, but the cooler breeze held the promise of Fall.

"I noticed the pigpen is still empty," he remarked.

"I haven't had a chance to corral them back in."

"I could do that for you."

"Thanks, but Tyler said he'd do it."

"I don't mind."

"I said no thanks." I hadn't meant to speak so sharply. I wet my lips, then gave him a little smile. "You've done enough, and I really appreciate it."

He inclined his head, then handed me his empty glass and pushed to his feet. "Call me if you change your mind."

I nodded and watched him drive away, chewing on my lower lip.

What did it say that I wasn't ready to move the pigs back?

I sighed. Time to call the interfering detective.

October 5, Friday

"I WISH YOU HAD called me when you found it," Detective Jack Terry said over the phone.

"I called you when I found the quilt and you ratted me out to the Sheriff anyway," I retorted. "Besides, you said this was Sheriff Tomlin's jurisdiction."

"I didn't say you shouldn't have called the sheriff, I just wish you'd looped me in."

"I'm looping you in now."

He made a rueful noise of concession. "Now that the weather has cleared, I was planning to come back to Accident to fish this weekend anyway. I'll follow up with the Sheriff on the piece of bone. And is the veterinarian the same guy I talked to in the diner?"

"Yes, Will Story."

"*Dr.* Will Story, right?"

I rolled my eyes. "I suppose. Meanwhile, should I put the pigs back in the pen?"

"Do you have another option?"

"Yes, for a while."

"Then hold off for now," he said. "By the way, how is your mother?"

"She's home," I said. "But not much has changed."

"Hang in there, Ms. Hunnicut."

I gave a little laugh. "Do I have another option?"

I disconnected the call, then wondered, once again, if I'd done the right thing by confiding in Jack Terry. I couldn't decide if he was on my side, or if he was enabling my fixation on Deidre's case.

October 6, Saturday

"THOUGHT I'D COME and see for myself," Jack Terry said as he closed the door to his SUV.

He gestured toward the pigpen. "Can you show me where you found the bone?"

I nodded and led him over to the pen. "The stick is still there where the sheriff pulled it out of the mud." Much of the rain water had evaporated, leaving the mud the consistency of thick brown bread dough.

He unlocked the gate and walked into the mud, heedless of his black cowboy boots, then walked all around the stick, scanning the ground. Apparently he didn't see anything of interest because after a few minutes, he backtracked to the gate.

"Did you talk to the sheriff?" I asked.

He grunted. "Yeah. Told him I'd called you and pried the information out of you."

"Thanks," I said dryly. "What did he say?"

"He was short, told me he'd sent the bone off to be properly examined."

"You believe him?"

"I do. Like any local law officer, he might let some things slide, but I think he knows this could be serious."

I hoped so.

Detective Terry put his hands on his hips. "Have you tried talking to your mother about any of this?"

I shook my head. "She doesn't respond to even basic questions. And I think she's still getting over the trauma of me clearing out the house."

He perked up. "So she's aware of her surroundings."

"I believe so." Then I sighed. "But I don't know for sure."

"I'm trusting you'll let me know when I can talk to her?"

I nodded. I felt guilty about the information I hadn't shared about Tyler—the fact that his previous girlfriend insinuated his "type" was exotic, like Deidre, and that he'd folded a feed bag in the same diagonal way the buried quilt had been folded. Despite previous incidents of bad behavior, I couldn't bring myself to think the worst of Tyler. He was a better man than my father had been.

Wasn't he?

In the distance, the pigs were grazing in the abandoned garden. Even from here, the ground looked brutalized.

"Did the pigs do all that damage?" the detective asked.

"Not entirely," I admitted. "Before the rain, I decided to do some more digging in the area where I found the quilt." Actually, Will had helped me.

"Were you looking for anything in particular?"

I shrugged. "My friend Emma reminded me Deidre kept a journal… I thought maybe if she'd buried the quilt to come back for it, she might've buried her journal, too. But I didn't find anything."

"How about you, Ms. Hunnicut? Did you keep a journal around that time?"

I'd kept journals most of my teenage years, and hid them away in my room. In those pages I'd vented about my home life, my parents' arguing, how oppressed I felt. Early in my senior year, though, my mother had found them and burned them. It was the final straw in my mind, and why I'd decided to run away with Deidre.

I shook my head. "I don't have journals."

"Really? That seems strange for a writer."

I smiled. "Maybe. But you should know I've decided to write about Deidre's disappearance—a fictional account, of course."

He pursed his mouth. "Of course. Then again, truth can be stranger than fiction." He waved and walked back to his vehicle.

Touché, Detective. Touché.

October 7, Sunday

"HOW IS YOUR MUM?" Hugh asked over Skype.

His sweet face looked so comforting—and so far away, which was where I wanted to be—I choked on my reply.

"There, love," he murmured. "I didn't mean to make you down. Is it really so unbearable?"

I sniffed and shook my head, then nodded and burst into tears.

He made anguished noises. "Tell me what's going on."

"It's… just… so…"

"Painful? Heartbreaking? Tragic?"

"Quiet."

His eyes rounded. "Quiet, you say?"

I nodded. "And so… silent."

"But you love the quiet, Jane. You have a T-shirt that reads 'Silence is golden.'"

"This is different," I said. "We just stare at each other, and she looks at me like I've done everything wrong my entire life."

"If it's any consolation, that's every dinner at my parents' house."

I gave a little laugh.

"Is your brother helping?"

"No. Tyler's out of town."

Hugh frowned. "Rotten time for a holiday."

"It's probably not a coincidence. But I'm trying not to be angry—he has his own problems at the moment." Still, I was exhausted... and yes, a little angry because I was covering for him on more than one front.

"You said the home nurse has been helpful?"

I nodded. "A godsend. But he won't be coming round forever."

"But your mum is getting better, right?"

"Some," I agreed. "She seems stronger, is holding herself up longer."

"Is she trying to communicate at all?"

"No." My tears welled again. "It's awful."

He sighed again. "You must rally, Jane, for your mother."

I nodded. "I should go check on her. Any news about Trudy?"

He looked mournful. "Sorry, Love. I'm still looking."

I nodded, then ended the video call. When Hugh's face disappeared, I felt so lonely. And I felt so guilty for sleeping with Will Story... and even more guilty for enjoying it.

I wiped my eyes and stood, feeling a wall of dread when I turned toward my mother's room, a feeling made worse by not knowing how long things would be like this. I was taking care of Mom's basic needs, but I couldn't offer the comfort I suspected she longed for.

A scratching noise sounded at the door. I smiled—the cat had brought me another dead-animal offering, no doubt.

But when I opened the door, he walked by me and into the house, trotting toward my mother's bedroom door. It was ajar, and he squeezed inside. I followed, marveling, and when I opened the door, he was sitting on her lap in bed, rubbing his head on her drawn arm.

I wouldn't say my mother smiled—it was more of a twitch. But it was the closest she'd come to responding positively to anything since the stroke.

October 8, Monday

WHEN I SAW Tyler's delivery truck lurching up the driveway, I was shot through with anger—and relief. But mostly anger.

Which dissolved as soon as he opened the door and grinned, the handsome devil. "Hi, Sis."

I accepted his quick hug. "When did you get back in town?"

"Last night," he said, still smiling.

"I assume Stacey and the boys came back with you?"

He nodded, and looked so happy, it was impossible to be cross with him.

"I've turned over a new leaf," he said.

I assumed he meant he'd decided to honor his wedding vows and not have sex with other women. "Good," I said brightly. "I'm glad things are back to normal. I've missed you around here."

"How's Mom?" he asked, then before I could answer, he frowned. "Where are the pigs?"

"Um… grazing. I found a bone in the pigpen and the sheriff thought it was best to keep the pen clear in case… it's… you know…" I swallowed hard. "Not animal."

Tyler frowned. "Of course it's an animal bone—countless hogs have been slaughtered here over the years. I find bones in there all the time."

"You do?"

"Yeah. Why on earth would you call the sheriff over something like that?"

Coming from his mouth, it did sound foolish. "Well, there was the quilt," I stammered. "And I was afraid… that is…"

He made a sound of disgust. "What, that your ditzy friend Deidre is buried in the pigpen? Have you lost your mind?"

I pressed my lips shut. That was entirely possible.

"Jane," he said, fairly shouting, "I know you have a wild imagination, but are you listening to yourself?"

I was, and I sounded crazy. And bored. But mostly crazy. "You're right... I'm sorry."

"I'll round up the pigs," he said, sounding tired.

"I think we should consider selling them."

He turned back. "Why?"

"For the money," I said bluntly. "Besides, then you wouldn't have to take care of them."

"I don't mind," he said, then glanced toward the house with a wince. "It gives me a reason to stop by, and it makes me feel like I'm doing... something."

"Mom seems to be doing some better," I offered.

"Good," he bit off. "I'll stop in to say hello before I leave. Oh, and you have a package from England."

I took the box, not particularly looking forward to sorting through the past due bills Hugh had sent to me. Still, it made me the teeniest bit happy to see something to remind me of my old life... the life I was still hoping to get back to.

Inside was a bundle of mail, mostly bills, but some thoughtful cards, too, from friends who'd heard my mother was ill. And the addendum to my book contract to adjust my delivery date. That dropped another stone of worry into my stomach—December thirty-first was not looking so far away.

The last item made me cry out—a chew toy that had belonged to my beloved cockapoo Trudy, who had vanished just before I came back to the States. Hugh had attached a note.

Thought this might cheer you up.

It did... for a few seconds. But then I missed her even more, if that was possible. The cat that had taken up residence in Mom's room reminded me of the companionship and unconditional love I was missing.

I closed my eyes and inhaled the doggy scent of her to drive out the perpetual odor of the pigs.

October 9, Tuesday

I'D MADE IT a few feet inside the door of my old bedroom. Thus far, the boxes and bags had yielded the same types of items as the bins in previous rooms: clothes, magazines, and useless brick-abrack. Except I'd noticed a theme emerging: childhood. Specifically, the clothes were for a young girl, with an emphasis on sparkly dresses with stiff taffeta skirts and crushed crinolines, dresses I would've loved to wear when I was growing up. The drab brown dress my mother had bought me—and burned—came to mind. I wondered if she remembered it, too.

Other boxes were full of dolls and girlish toys like play dishes and plastic mermaid figures. One bin overflowed with broken Barbie dolls and assorted knock-offs, in different stages of dress and with knotted hair. I sighed, doubting Junk Man Jim could sell much of the stuff in this room. Board games, jigsaw puzzles, and stuffed animals seemed to multiply when I tried to sort through them.

There were untold boxes of children's books, and that made me smile. Books had been expensive when I was growing up, and with no library in town, they were hard to come by. But Mom would occasionally surprise me with hardcover books she'd scavenged somewhere. I would devour them, reading them over and over...

Until they would be confiscated and burned over some infraction. A ping of remembered hurt shot through my chest. My mother had been so conflicting... and conflicted.

The next box I cleared gave me access to the small night stand that sat next to my piled-up bed. I opened the drawer, hoping to find a treasured memento.

Instead I found my high school senior yearbook. Left behind purposefully because I didn't have particularly fond memories of high school.

But now I opened it eagerly.

October 10, Wednesday

I FINISHED TYPING the sentence on my laptop screen, then backspaced and reworded it, improving it not one whit.

I groaned and scooted the chair away from the table where I worked. The silence in the house was maddening, but I was afraid to turn on the radio or TV for fear I'd miss a noise from my mother's room, like her falling out of bed.

On impulse, I carried my laptop to her room and peeked inside. She was awake, staring toward the window. The cat lay curled asleep on her stomach. When Mom heard me, her eyes moved, but not toward me. Since her gaze didn't track, I still wasn't sure how much she was registering, or even understanding. But Owen seemed to think she was walking and eating better, and moving her drawn fingers on her own volition.

"You're awake," I said.

She didn't acknowledge my voice.

"I was thinking I might come in here to work, if that's okay with you."

Nothing.

I moved the tray table from the side of her bed to sit in front of the loveseat where I'd been sleeping, then situated my laptop and sat down to check the ergonomics. "Not bad," I said. I was directly in my mother's line of sight, but she didn't look at me.

Picking up where I left off, I retyped the sentence, finally satisfied, then typed another one.

But my mother's listlessness felt palpable. I stopped and glanced at the lump of her in the bed. Owen said she needed visual stimulation, but the only working television was in the living room. The couch wasn't comfortable enough for her to rest, and I didn't want to set her in a chair she might fall out of.

But her laptop was portable.

I retrieved the machine I'd bought for her and connected it to one of my streaming services—neatly ignoring the prompt that told me my account payment was slightly late—and found a movie I'd heard her talk about. I positioned the screen on the bed next to her.

She didn't acknowledge me or the screen, but it made *me* feel better to hear another human voice in the house.

I put my hands on my keyboard and typed a decent sentence… then another one…

October 11, Thursday

SINCE OWEN WAS converting me to the advantages of having a routine, I had settled on a personal routine of clearing my old bedroom in the morning hours, breaking to feed Mom and myself

192

lunch, then working on my manuscript in the afternoon on the tray table in her bedroom.

On her laptop I set up the entire twenty seasons of *Law & Order* to play without interruption so I didn't have to think about it again for a long while. While the "chung chung" of the scene breaks sounded in the background, I made headway on my pagecount, sometimes to the point of losing track of time.

I was ecstatic to be writing again, and although my turn of phrase felt a little rusty, I was experiencing something akin to the rush I used to feel when I sat down to my laptop.

I marveled that in the midst of the worst crisis of my life, I was able to write again.

And the story was moving along well, no doubt because the situation hit so close to home. When I wrote about the friendship of the three girls, I remembered the fun Emma, Deidre, and I had shared. It made me miss them. I picked up my phone to text Emma.

How are you?

A few minutes later she responded *Slammed with contractors and kids, can we connect soon?*

Emma and her husband Eddie were well off, and in the middle of redecorating their already gorgeous home where they'd raised three delectable children. I was happy for Emma, but I nursed a little pang of envy. Apparently on the day of the lesson on How to Be Happy, Emma had been paying attention, whereas I'd been daydreaming.

Yes, soon I texted back.

When I hit a snag in the story, I decided to skim the articles I'd found under Mom's mattress about Deidre's disappearance for a detail that might inspire me. When I opened the manila folder and began to scan the clippings, my mother made a noise. Not a noise of pain or constriction, but a noise that sounded as if she were trying to vocalize.

I looked up to see her staring in my direction. "Do you need something, Mom?"

But instead of responding, she simply closed her eyes. I couldn't tell if she was sleeping, or if she was cutting me off.

"Mom?"

No response.

"Mom, are you sleeping?"

No response.

I glanced down at the folder I held and pressed my lips together. Had she recognized it, and was she upset I was reading its contents?

I reread the articles, but none of them contained anything different than the basic details of Deidre being reported missing from school, was a presumed runaway, and if anyone had further information, to contact Sheriff Tomlin.

Mom's former married lover.

October 12, Friday

I'D BEEN WRITING at a good pace all afternoon, so I was ready for a break when I heard Will's truck make its way up the driveway.

"I'll be back in a minute," I said to Mom, who didn't acknowledge my voice. But when I stood, the orange and white cat leapt to the ground and followed me to the door. It wasn't housebroken and seemed to prefer to do its business outside.

I could respect that.

I resisted the urge to check my clothes and smooth my hair before walking outside to greet Will. No need to throw gasoline on the fire.

"Hi," Will called when he dropped down from his truck.

"Hi yourself."

One corner of his mouth lifted. "I see your pussy... cat... has improved."

"Yes," I agreed. "It's back to normal and doesn't need your attention anymore."

"Don't say that." He leaned over to rub the pet behind the ears. "Every cat likes a good scratch once in a while."

I smirked, but... *meow*.

"How's your Mom?"

I shrugged. "Maybe a bit better."

"Good. I came to check on your pig. I see you got them back in the pen."

"Tyler corralled them when he came home."

"I saw him driving through town. We're going fishing this weekend if the weather allows."

I had no comment—the sport was lost on me.

"Speaking of fishing," Will said, "that detective guy who rents a fishing cabin at Bayview was asking me questions about the bone you found."

I nodded. "He's the cop who originally investigated Deidre's truancy report. He's just poking around while he's in town fishing."

"That's pretty much what he said, verbatim."

He sounded suspicious. I decided not to respond.

Will looked down, then picked up my red, rough hand. "You're not using the salve I brought you?"

His fingers were warm and tanned against mine. "I ran out."

"Good thing I have more," he murmured.

In an instant, the moment turned sexy, and I didn't mind terribly. He intertwined our hands, then pulled me close for a long, languid kiss. When he pulled back, he smiled. "When can we have another sleepover?"

I made a rueful noise, then shook my head. "Not soon, I'm afraid. I can't leave mother overnight."

"I could stay here," he offered.

"There's barely room for me on the loveseat I sleep on—and it's in Mom's room. But I'll let you know when I get my girlhood bedroom cleared."

He grinned. "Deal."

I gestured to the house. "I should go... I don't want to leave her for too long."

"Okay." He kissed me again, then released me. I went back to the house feeling loose-limbed and wanted. When I walked back in her bedroom, I noticed my mother's cheeks were wet.

"Mom? Are you in pain?"

She didn't respond, of course, and I didn't see anything obviously wrong. I used a tissue to wipe her cheeks and chalked it up to something she'd seen or heard on the episode of *Law & Order* she was watching.

Until I realized where she was lying gave her a direct view out the window where Will and I had been standing. Had she seen us kiss? Was that what had upset her?

I frowned. But why?

October 13, Saturday

"HELLO? Is anyone home?"

I stopped typing and cocked my head. I hadn't heard a car pull up, but the female voice coming from the front porch seemed familiar. I pushed to my feet and walked to the door. When I opened it, Kelly Valentine, Deidre's younger sister, stood there in cut-off jeans and a Foster The People T-shirt. She was tall and leggy like her sister, doe-eyed and exotic.

"Hi, Kelly."

"Hi," she said, looking anxious. "I came to see if you've found out anything about Deidre."

I shook my head. "Not yet. But I'm glad you stopped by. When you were describing your mock story in Ms. Jeffson's class, you said the female student dated teachers, ministers, and married men."

"Yeah, so?"

"So, was that off the cuff, or were you talking about Deidre?"

"I was talking about Deidre."

"How do you know she was dating men like that?"

She shrugged. "I heard her fighting with my mom all the time. And any time Deidre's name has come up over the years, Mom accused her of being a homewrecker and messing around with men who were off limits."

Although I wasn't aware of Deidre doing that, I wouldn't put it past her. And Kelly's story jibed with Emma's story of Deidre's claim if everyone knew about the person she was seeing, it would be a huge scandal. Emma believed Deidre had written about it in her journal.

"Did Deidre or your mother ever mention these men by name?"

Kelly was thoughtful, then shook her head. "No. But I remember one of them using a nickname—Preacher Man."

I frowned. Deidre used to joke if she ever walked into a church, she'd be struck by lightning.

But maybe a local minister thought he could save her soul... and had lost his in the process?

October 14, Sunday

"HOW'S YOUR MUM?" Hugh asked.

I sighed. "About the same. Still not responding, still not communicating."

"Do you think she knows who you are?"

I lifted my shoulders in a shrug. "Sometimes. Sometimes, I wonder if she just knows I'm the person who feeds her, like a cat would know." I blinked back tired tears. "I'm sorry—that was a mean thing to say."

"It's okay," he soothed. "You must be exhausted."

I sniffed, then said, "Thank you for the package, and for sending one of Trudy's toys."

He nodded and looked forlorn. "About that..."

My heart caught. "What?"

"No bad news," he assured me. "But no good news either. So I was thinking I might... try to find a good home for all her stuff."

I frowned. "Give Trudy's stuff away? Her bed, her toys? Is that what you're doing with my stuff, Hugh? Giving it to a 'good home'? "

"Of course not." His face gentled. "I'm thinking of you, Jane. I thought it might be easier if I did it instead of you having to when you come back."

I registered a little spike of pleasure that Hugh was still expecting me to come back to London, but it didn't override my irritation. "Don't you dare get rid of her things. We'd be giving up on finding her."

He sighed. "Jane... it's been over three months. Don't you think if she was coming back, she would've done so by now?"

Like Deidre.

"No," I said stubbornly. "We're. Going. To. Find. Her."

Or at least find out what happened to her.

Trudy *and* Deidre.

"Don't give up," I pleaded. "Please don't give up."

October 15, Monday

I HADN'T SLEPT WELL. My dreams were of Deidre and Trudy being lost and the dreams kept crisscrossing. I was chasing both of them, then they had run in opposite directions. I had to choose which direction to go, knowing I would lose sight of both of them if I didn't choose, yet unwilling to pick one over the other. I turned back and forth until I was spinning in place while they slipped farther and farther away.

When I awoke pre-dawn, the covers on the loveseat were tangled, and I was in a sour mood.

Worse, Owen had to cancel his morning visit because of an emergency with another home patient. I understood, of course, but it left me bereft. I'd begun to count on his good-natured cheerfulness to lubricate the stiffness that existed between me and my mother. On the other hand, as Owen had wisely suggested, it gave me a chance to practice her physical therapy.

But my mother must have gotten used to Owen's morning presence, too, because from the get-go, she was resistant to my touch, and refused to make eye contact, or she would go completely listless.

"Close your fingers around mine," I encouraged.

No response.

"You did this for Owen yesterday," I said, irritated.

I tried to tamp down my frustration, but if she wasn't even going to try, she was never going to get better.

"Try to push against my hand," I said.

She wouldn't.

I tried another tack. "Okay, let's walk to the bathroom and back."

But she stiffened when I tried to help her out of bed.

"Are you in pain?" I asked.

She didn't respond, didn't look at me.

"Mom, I don't know how to help you if you won't communicate with me."

No response.

"Can you at least let me know if you understand what I'm saying? Blink or nod or make a noise?"

No response.

I retrieved a pen from my makeshift writing desk and put it in her good hand over a pad of paper. "Can you make a mark on the paper? Any kind of mark, just hold the pencil and try."

But when I released her fingers, the pen fell to the floor.

"Dammit!" I blurted. "Mom, I think you're being difficult on purpose because I'm here instead of Tyler or instead of a complete stranger! Is that it? Would you rather have a complete stranger take care of you than me? Because so would I!"

She blinked, but it could've been an involuntary response. I pulled my hand over my mouth. I'd spoken the truth, but I shouldn't have said it. "I'm sorry," I murmured.

I needed to cool off.

I set up the laptop for her to watch, then let the cat in to assume its place on her stomach. I decided to work off some frustration by clearing another couple of boxes in my old bedroom. With luck, by the end of the month, I'd be able to sleep in my bed.

When I lifted the lid from the next box that weighed a freaking ton, I was still pulsing with frustration over my mother's condition. We were in a conundrum. She didn't want me here, and I didn't want to be here, but we were out of options.

Unless I put her in a nursing home... and went back to England... and forgot about the can of worms she'd opened with her phone call to Detective Terry.

Fighting off a tension headache, I reached into the heavy box to find dozens of plastic and paper bags that appeared to contain books.

I opened the first bag and blinked.

My first book. Three copies, purchased at a bookstore in Birmingham.

That was strange. I'd sent Mom a signed copy—if she'd needed copies for friends, all she'd had to do was tell me.

I peeked into the next bag. Six more copies of my book.

I moved through the box, stunned to realize every book inside was mine.

Purchased from every bookstore and big-box store in the tri-state area.

I eyed three more boxes sitting nearby of similar size and weight.

Surely not...

But yes, more and more copies of my book, all of them crisp and new and unread. Jocelyn's words came back to me.

Sales for both of your books were really strong in the area around your hometown.

Because my mother had driven around buying them!

All told, there were nearly five hundred pristine copies of my hardcover book.... and the sales receipts in the bags showed they were all purchased the first week of publication. Realization dawned on me.

My mother had single-handedly put my book on the bestseller list.

I sucked back a wall of tears, then walked back to my mother's bedroom to find her unchanged, still lying, still staring.

From her nightstand I picked up her hairbrush and began to brush her gray-streaked hair in long, soothing strokes.

October 16, Tuesday

MY PHONE RANG and I was pleased to see my former teacher Ms. Jeffson's name come up on the screen. I connected the call with a smile.

"Hi, Ms. Jeffson."

"Hello, Jane. I was wondering if you're available to pick me up from the clinic?"

"I'm so sorry, but I can't. My mother is home now and I can't leave her."

"Of course, dear... I wouldn't ask you to do that. How is your mother?"

"Better," I said as cheerfully as I could manage.

"That's good news. Will you give her my best?"

"I will. Ms. Jeffson, somehow my mother came into possession of the archives of *The Accidental Post*, and I wondered if you'd be interested in having them. I'd give them to you, of course."

She made a thoughtful noise. "I wondered what had happened to the archives after the editor passed away and the office closed. But I can't think of a better holder of the archives than our resident best-selling novelist."

I winced, thinking of how dubiously I'd gotten the label of "best-selling" novelist. "If you're sure."

"By the way, Jane... did you ever hear from that high school friend of yours who ran away?"

"Deidre? No."

"The student of mine who asked you the question in class, she's Deidre's younger sister."

"Yes, I know. She and I have talked. Kelly's upset because her sister hasn't contacted her over all these years."

"Poor girl. Do you know if your friend has contacted anyone in town at all?"

"No... and I'm not sure how I'd find out." I gave a little laugh. "If the newspaper was still operating, I'd take out an ad asking for information."

"I suspect there are other ways to get the word out."

"You mean like on social media?"

"Yes... although, Accident isn't the most technologically advanced town."

"No," I murmured agreement, then pushed my tongue into my cheek. Old-fashioned towns called for old-fashioned tactics.

October 17, Wednesday

"I'LL BE BACK before it's time for you to leave," I promised Owen.

"No worries," he sang, then waved me off toward the Caddy. "I'll call the pharmacy and tell them to put your order at the front of the line."

Driving away from the house for the first time in days gave me an enormous sense of relief and freedom. I was going stir crazy in the house.

Which gave me a sense of how my mother must feel.

Among the prescriptions I was planning to pick up for Mom was a mild anti-depressant Dr. Kessler had prescribed. I hoped it would improve her energy level to speed her recovery.

When I parked and walked into the pharmacy, despite Owen's phone call, I was told it would be a few minutes' wait, so I shopped for toiletries Mom and I needed.

In the lotion aisle, I noticed a pretty blonde reading a bottle's label and realized with a start it was Will's sister, Tiffany. She'd answered the door of his house once and, mistaking her for his girlfriend, I hadn't introduced myself.

"Hello," I ventured.

She looked up and gave me a tentative smile. "Hello.... I know you from somewhere."

"I'm Jane Hunnicut. We talked briefly when I dropped off a box of produce for Will."

She set the bottle back on the shelf. "Oh, right. Will talks about you."

I nodded, hoping he'd left out the crazy parts. "When I was at Will's house, uh, another time... I noticed a picture of the two of you with someone I used to be friends with—Deidre Valentine."

Was it my imagination, or did her demeanor change—and not for the better?

But she offered me a little smile, nodding. "Deidre... right. She used to come to Birmingham and hang out with me on campus."

"I remember she had a crush on Will," I offered.

Tiffany laughed. "Will was too serious for her."

"Did she ever mention anyone else she was seeing?"

She squinted. "Why do you ask?"

I tried to be nonchalant. "I just wondered if she ever reached out to anyone after she left town. I was going to contact some of her old friends, and maybe there was a guy she didn't mention to me."

Tiffany pursed her mouth. "There was someone..." She looked as if she were trying to remember. "Deidre called him her secret fling, but she never mentioned his name." Tiffany shrugged. "But for all I know, she could've made it up—Deidre was like that."

I nodded. "So true. Well, thanks anyway. It was good to see you."

"You too. I'll tell Will I ran into you."

I returned to the pharmacy counter to get my order, then asked the clerk, "Do you know if there's someplace in town I can have copies made?"

She lifted her hand and pointed to the left. I looked over to see a copy machine in the corner with a "5 Cents" sign above it.

You gotta love small towns sometimes.

I thanked her and walked over to the copier, then fed in five dollars to get one hundred copies of the flyer I'd printed up:

If you have heard from my friend Deidre Valentine, who lived in Accident until 2007, please contact me. I have something of hers.

I'd listed my name and phone number at the bottom of flyer. The picture of Deidre had copied well in black and white.

I walked through the store and spotted a teenage boy carrying a skateboard. I held up the flyers and a box of thumb tacks. "I'll pay you ten dollars to put up these flyers all over town."

He considered it. "Make it twenty."

I frowned, but handed over the twenty.

October 18, Thursday

"THIS IS A NICE SURPRISE," I said, then gave Emma a hug.

She held up a casserole dish. "Taco pie, I thought you could use a break from cooking."

"Yum. That was sweet of you. Let me put this in the fridge."

"How is your mother?" she whispered as I closed the front door.

I looked around, realizing just how much of the hoard was gone since the first time Emma had stopped by and I wouldn't let her in. "Come say hello."

She waited until I put away the casserole, then followed me to my mother's room.

"I haven't been in this house in so long," Emma said, glancing around. "Nothing has changed."

"Uh-huh," I said absently. She'd think differently if she saw the floor-to-ceiling, wall-to-wall hoard mountain waiting for me in Tyler's old bedroom. "Mom, look who's here. It's Emma."

Mom stared toward her computer screen that played *Law & Order*, but her gaze was unfixed.

"Hi, Mrs. Hunnicut," Emma ventured.

"She brought us taco pie," I added.

No response.

Emma shot me a mournful glance.

"Mom, Emma and I are going to sit out on the porch for a few minutes. I'll be back in to check on you shortly."

"I didn't mean to intrude," Emma murmured.

"No, this is a nice break," I insisted, then snagged a book as we walked outside. "Look what I found in my room."

Emma grinned. "Our senior yearbook. Lordy, I haven't looked at it in years."

"Me neither," I said. "This should be fun."

I grabbed a soda for each of us, then we pored over the yearbook, laughing and remembering the good and the bad. For Emma, it had been mostly good. For me, the latter.

"Oh, look at us," Emma said, pointing to a picture of me, her, and Deidre in front of our lockers.

Emma looked gorgeously made up, and Deidre looked gorgeous without trying. I was the ugly duckling between the two swans.

Emma glanced up. "I saw one of the flyers you posted about Deidre. What's that about?"

I shrugged. "Just wondering if anyone else has talked to her since she left, and I realize I don't know everyone she might've been close to. You were the one who said she had a secret boyfriend."

"Alleged," Emma said. "You know how dramatic Deidre could be."

"Still," I said, turning to the teachers' section of the yearbook. "Do you think she was having an affair with any of them?"

She nodded, then pointed. "Yeah, maybe with Mr. Jackman... and Mr. Stewart always had a thing for her, used to walk her to the bus, remember?"

"Yeah, now that you mention it."

"But you don't think she'd reach out to either of them, do you?"

I shrugged. "Who knows? The flyer might not lead to anything, but if it does, I'd love to know she's well."

"Me, too," Emma said, her voice a bit wistful. She glanced all around. "It's so pretty up here." Then she stopped and grinned. "Oh, my goodness—the treehouse is still there?"

"Yeah."

"Can I check it out?"

"Sure. I'll go with you, but I can't be gone long."

We waded through the tall grass to reach the treehouse. Emma scrambled up the tree ladder with no hesitation, then hoisted herself through the opening in the deck. I followed her, pleased to see genuine joy on her face as she explored the inside of the structure. "This was always the most wonderful place to be."

I nodded. "Lots of adventures planned, if not completely carried out."

I saw Emma's glance snag on the wood table with our initials and the gouges, and waited for her to ask what had happened... but she didn't.

"Thanks for letting me take a look," she said breathlessly. "But I need to go, and you need to get back to your mom."

I followed her out onto the deck and while I waited for her to descend, I glanced toward Will's house... and smiled.

Tied to his doorknob was a red and blue Wonder Woman cape.

October 19, Friday

I WAS MAKING progress in clearing my old bedroom. When I reached my closet, I felt downright victorious.

I opened the closet door gingerly, worried varmints could be lurking inside—or worse, more hoard.

Instead, I was pleasantly surprised to see it was much as I'd left it when I'd gone to college, with left-behind shirts and jeans and sweaters from high school still hanging the way I still liked to organize things, by color. I pulled out a few of the items, smiling as memories flooded back. I withdrew a mustard yellow sweatshirt with the name of a local band, ACCIDENTAL BEAT printed on it. One of the band members had been a friend of my father's, so he had taken me and Tyler to one of their concerts, and we'd had a great time. I recalled he'd even allowed us to sip from his beer, and we'd felt so grown up. Outings with our father were rare and special.

I withdrew the sweatshirt and pulled it over my head, surprised to see it still fit.

And I was surprised to see there were some good memories lingering in this place that I'd forgotten in my determination to hate it.

October 20, Saturday

"Ms. HUNNICUT, how are you?" Jack Terry sounded as if he might've pulled a few beers from his fish cooler.

"I'm good, Detective. How are the fish biting?"

"Not at all," he said, "but I'm optimistic. Listen, I've seen your flyers up all over town—not a bad idea."

"Thank you."

"Has anyone contacted you?"

"Not a soul. You and I are both coming up empty."

"Oh. Well, it might take a while for word to get around."

"But I do have a couple of names for you to look into regarding that secret boyfriend Deidre might've had."

"I'm listening."

"There were two teachers at school who had the hots for Deidre—Mick Jackman was a history teacher, and Paul Stewart was the track coach and he taught Phys Ed."

"Okay, I'll make some discreet inquiries," he said. "Anything else?"

I hesitated. "It might not be anything, but I talked to Deidre's younger sister and she remembers Deidre and their mother arguing over someone Deidre was involved with that they called Preacher Man. Does that mean anything to you?"

"Nope," the detective said. "But I'll scour the file again. You never know what might be important. You keep fishing, Ms. Hunnicut, and I'll do the same."

October 21, Sunday

I WAS SITTING in the treehouse, waiting to Skype with Hugh. After a frustrating day with my mother, I needed a break.

When I heard the sound of Will's truck coming up the driveway, I was torn. I shouldn't be so glad to see him when I was waiting for Hugh's call.

On the other hand, Hugh had "suspended" our engagement.

On the other hand, Will had nothing to offer me but a life in Accident—he was committed to servicing the surrounding counties because of a scholarship he'd accepted.

On the other hand, Hugh was thousands of miles away.

I stood on the deck of the treehouse and waved to get Will's attention from the driveway. He saw me and grinned, then jogged across the field toward me. "Hi there."

I smiled down at him. "Hi yourself."

"Want some company?"

"I'm waiting for a long distance call."

His eyebrows flew up. "From your fiancé?"

I squirmed and knew this was my chance to tell Will I wasn't engaged.

Before I could answer, he said, "Then I'm definitely coming up," and climbed to the deck in record time.

I laughed. "You're going to get me in trouble."

"That's the plan," he said. "Hey, the guy in England gets lipstick?"

I pressed my lips together self-consciously. "It's for the screen," I said lamely.

He pulled me in for a slanting kiss.

I counted to ten, then pulled back. "Will, seriously, you can't be here. I need to talk to Hugh."

"Has he found your cockapoo?"

"No," I murmured. "She's still lost."

He gave an exaggerated shrug. "How can you like this guy if he can't even find your dog?"

I gave a little laugh. "That's not fair."

"All's fair in love and war."

I soaked that in for a few seconds—*hm*. Then my phone lit up with the call from Hugh and I shooed Will away. "You have to leave. Bye."

He pouted, then waved. "Okay, but I'm not giving up."

I waited until he descended the ladder before I connected the call with Hugh. His happy face filled the screen. "Hi, Jane."

"Hi," I said, trying to look equally happy. "What's new?"

He launched into a story about a work colleague, and I glanced over to watch Will walk to his truck and climb in.

"Jane?"

I looked back to the screen. "Huh?"

He gave a little laugh. "There must be something going on there more interesting than talking to me."

"No, not at all," I said in a high voice.

He leaned in and squinted. "Your lipstick is all smeared."

I mentally cursed, then used the back of my hand to wipe it off. "I've been drinking a soda, that's all."

Hugh frowned. "Soda's bad for you."

"Don't I know it," I replied.

October 22, Monday

My OLD BEDROOM was revealing itself to me in more ways than just being nearly clear of the hoard Mom had put there. Underneath all the junk, she had indeed, as Tyler had first said, left everything just the way I'd left it. I ran my fingers over the spines of the young adult novels I'd read and reread, pretending I was the heroine with paranormal powers, and the angst-ridden handsome loner guy in school was secretly in love with me.

I smiled, thinking back to the nights I'd lain awake worried about something that now I couldn't even remember. Time had a way of diminishing problems I'd once thought so dire.

I dearly hoped I would someday look back on this chapter in my life and marvel that I'd worried over the outcome.

I pulled one of the books from a shelf and thumbed absently through the pages, then frowned when a slip of paper fell to the floor. When I picked it up, I recognized my teenaged handwriting.

Joe P blew me a kiss today in Microbiology.

I smiled, having no recollection whatsoever of Joe P.

But I suddenly did remember the notes.

After my mother had found and burned my journals, I'd started writing little notes to myself and sticking them in my books. It seemed less likely to be found, and to get me into trouble.

On a whim, I pulled out all the books on my shelf and turned them upside down while flipping through the pages. By the time I reached the end, a small pile of notes were stacked on the floor. I flipped through them, amused by the nonsensical nature of the messages—boys I liked and thought liked me, someone calling me a name, or something funny a friend had said.

I loved that not even my mother had been able to keep me from writing.

I turned over another note to read *I think Tyler has a crush on Deidre—ew.*

I bit into my lip. Yes, *ew.* And dammit.

October 23, Tuesday

I LIFTED MY HEAD from my computer screen and peeked over at my mother. Her eyes were open and staring in the general direction of the laptop screen where episodes of *Law & Order* marched on.

It occurred to me the story I was working on was infinitely more interesting than the one on her screen, and this story actually concerned my mother. And in wake of the troubling things I'd learned about Tyler, it was past time to ask her some questions.

I walked over to pause the episode playing on the screen. "Mom, would you like to hear about the story I'm working on?"

No response, no flicker. The cat, on the other hand, appeared interested since his tail started to curl and uncurl.

I walked back to my laptop, chose a particular scene and began to read about my character digging up a quilt in a vegetable garden, a quilt that had belonged to a missing friend. A few sentences in, my mother made a noise.

I stopped and looked up. "Did you say something, Mom?"

She made another noise, but her eyes were averted.

I wet my lips. I didn't want to upset her, but I did want her to know what was happening, and largely because of her.

"Mom, does this sound familiar to you? You should know I'm writing a story based on Deidre Valentine's disappearance. I dug up a quilt in the garden a few weeks ago that belonged to her. I'm working with the detective you called in Atlanta to figure out who put it there."

She made another noise, and her eyes flitted in my direction.

Maybe I was getting through to her.

"Mom, I need for you to try to talk to me. Try to communicate."

No response.

I walked over and put the pen in her hand again, over a pad of paper. "Make a mark on the paper. Can you write what you want to say?"

I felt her fingers spasm around the pen. Encouraged, I pulled my fingers away.

But the pen clattered to the floor. And when I straightened, my mother's eyes were closed.

"Mom?"

No response.

I gently shook her shoulder. "Mom, please don't shut me out. I have to know what you know."

But she continued to feign sleep. Whatever she was thinking, whatever she knew, she was keeping to herself.

October 24, Wednesday

WHEN MY PHONE RANG, I was on my hands and knees scrubbing the wood floor of my old bedroom. When I saw Anne Warford was calling, I considered not answering.

But purposely not answering when an OCD specialist called seemed a little... compulsive.

Although, so did answering on the first ring.

So I waited for it to ring a couple of times, then I connected the call.

"This is Jane."

"Hi, Jane. This is Anne Warford. I was just calling to check in, I haven't seen you in a while."

"Yes. My mother was released from the hospital earlier this month. I've been caring for her at home."

"Ah. And how did she respond when she saw you had cleared out most of her collection of things?"

"It's hard to say because she's so uncommunicative, but she cried, and they weren't tears of joy."

"But they could've been tears of relief," she said.

I paused. "I... didn't think of that. She just seemed upset."

"And she probably was," Anne agreed. "Her emotions could've run the gamut from fear to anxiety to appreciation, but she couldn't express them."

"Okay," I said, wanting to believe her. "Regardless, Mom seems happy to be sleeping in her bed, and she probably hadn't been able to do that for years."

"That's positive," the therapist agreed. "But I really called to find out how you're doing."

"Oh, I'm... fine."

"Are you? Sometimes caretakers don't take care of themselves. And if they have their own compulsive behaviors, the behaviors can worsen."

I held up my raw, angry hands and squinted. And suddenly I realized I was cleaning a floor that didn't need to be cleaned.

Just like the bathroom floor in the London flat.

Poor Hugh. He was a saint.

"Jane, are you there?"

"Yes," I murmured. "I have to go. But thank you so much for calling."

I disconnected the call, then texted Hugh. *Thank you*

He responded *For what?*

For caring

He sent back a smiley face.

I frowned—the emoji men texted when they didn't know how else to respond.

October 25, Thursday

I HAD MEMORIZED the sound of nearly every car that had visited lately, so when a new vehicle noise reached my ears, I turned to look out the window.

To my surprise, it was a church van. While I watched, a tall man alighted, fiftyish, dressed in slacks and a short-sleeve button up shirt. He was carrying a Bible, which set off alarms in my head.

"Probably looking for a donation," I muttered to myself. But I made my way to the front door. I opened it before he could knock—better to meet him outside.

"Hello," I offered first. "Can I help you?"

He smiled wide. "Hello. I'm Phillip Lewis. I'm the minister of the church your mother attends."

My eyebrows climbed. "You must have the wrong house. My mother is Sharon Hunnicut."

"Yes, that's right. Sharon attended my church for the past few months before she fell ill."

I couldn't hide my shock. "I... didn't know."

"You must be Jane, the writer."

"Yes."

"I was pleased to hear Sharon had been released from the hospital. I just wanted to come by to visit with her for a few minutes and pray."

"I'm sorry, but she's asleep."

"Oh, don't wake her then." He smiled. "Perhaps I could pray with you."

I blinked. "I... er... okay."

He bowed his head, and I did the same, feeling totally out of my depth. I hadn't been raised in the church. In fact, the only time we'd heard the Lord's name in our house was when Mom and Dad were taking it in vain.

He murmured what sounded like a heartfelt prayer for my mother's recovery, and threw in a good word for my soul while he was at it. "Amen," he said.

I nodded. "Er... thank you. I'll tell my mother you stopped by."

"Good." He started to turn away, then he opened his Bible.

I braced for a sermon.

"Also... about this." He withdrew one of my flyers and held it up.

I couldn't hide my surprise. "You knew Deidre?"

"Not well. She visited my church a few times to get... necessities. Meals sometimes, or toiletries."

Deidre was always on the move, so it sounded believable, but I'd never heard her mention going to a church, even if it was for a free meal.

"Have you heard from her since she left in 2007?" I asked.

"Once, I believe."

My heartbeat picked up. "When?"

"It was a couple of years later, I want to say 2009. A phone call came into the church office and I answered. And I can't be sure, but I think the person on the other end of the line was Deidre."

"What did she say?"

"She said she was well, but she needed help."

"And?"

"And the call ended." He shrugged. "I'm sorry, that's all I have."

"Did you go to the sheriff?"

"No. Because the person who called didn't sound as if she was in danger, and I couldn't be sure who it was, frankly. It might've been a prank." He gave a little shrug. "Anyway, I thought I should mention it. God bless you."

I inclined my head. "Er... thanks."

He turned and walked back toward the van. I stepped back inside, trying to process the bizarre encounter.

My mother attended church?

Deidre might have reached out to Phillip Lewis to say she needed help?

Then I remembered something Kelly Valentine had said—that her mother and Deidre had argued about someone called Preacher Man.

October 26, Friday

OF ALL THE SOUNDS coming up the driveway, one of the sounds I enjoyed most was when Junk Man Jim's jalopy came bouncing along.

I ran out to meet him, hopeful he would take the things I'd cleaned and sorted in the garage, like before. He met me on the porch and handed me an envelope.

"What's this?" I asked.

"The cash you got coming to you," he said with a grin.

I wanted to kiss the toothless old guy.

Well, not really.

"Can you take some more things?" I asked.

"Let me take a lookey-loo," he said, whistling.

After he took a little tour of the jumble of spiffed-up junk, he nodded. "I'll take it all off your hands." Then he nodded to the boxes stacked up in the far corner. "Including the newspapers."

I glanced to the archives of *The Accidental Post*, then hesitated. "Those... aren't for sale. But I'll help you load the rest of these things."

He nodded and picked up a box to carry outside. I did the same, eager to see it all go, then trotted behind him toward the truck.

"Hey, you're the one who put up the flyer about that Valentine girl, ain't you?"

My head swung around. "Yes. Did you know Deidre?"

"I know her family," he said, then made a rueful noise. "Girl was raised like a wild dog."

I couldn't argue that point.

"And I only saw her enough to know who she was when she came to see me before she took off."

Now he had my attention. "Deidre came to see you?"

He set the box on the back of his truck, then scratched his balding head. "Sure did. Wanted to sell a few things for cash, said she was taking a trip."

October 27, Saturday

WHEN I WALKED INTO the diner, Detective Terry lifted a finger to get my attention, as if he wasn't the largest object in the room. I walked to the counter and sat down on the stool next to him. "I have to make this quick, I need to get back to my mother."

"Okay. I talked to both of the teachers you mentioned, but I don't think there's anything there."

"You don't think either one of them were messing around with Deidre?"

"In my opinion, it was wishful thinking on their part. Both of the guys are squeaky clean, and they didn't raise any red flags when I questioned them."

I nodded. "Okay, I have another name for you."

"You've been busy," he remarked, pulling out a pocket notebook. "Shoot."

"Phillip Lewis... *Minister* Phillip Lewis."

That got an eyebrow lift. "Preacher Man?"

"Maybe." I told him about the man's visit and what he'd said about the call he'd received.

"Sounds iffy," Detective Terry said. "But I'll check it out."

"And one more thing—apparently Deidre sold some things to Jim Powers who runs the flea market just before she disappeared, said she needed cash for a trip." I wet my lips. "So maybe she really did run away."

The detective scribbled another note. "Good work, Ms. Hunnicut."

"Thanks... I should go." I pushed to my feet, and waved as the waitress Tamara walked up.

"Hi, Jane. What can I get for you?"

"Nothing, thanks. I was just leaving."

"Oh." She looked disappointed, then she glanced all around. "I need to tell you something... in private."

Intrigued, I nodded.

"Outside," she said, tugging me toward a side door. "I need a smoke anyway."

I followed, curious as to what she had to tell me, and hoped it wasn't that she was still in love with my brother.

"I hear Tyler's back in town," she started.

"He's back with his wife," I cut in, hoping to pre-empt a confession.

"This isn't about Tyler," she said between puffs. "Not really."

"Okay, what?"

"It's about why I broke up with Tyler."

"I assume because he almost hit you?"

"No, believe it or not." She took another puff. "I feel real funny saying this to you."

"What?"

"The reason I broke up with Tyler is because your dad was hitting on me."

October 28, Sunday

I WAS SITTING IN the treehouse, waiting to Skype with Hugh.

But I was thinking about Will.

On cue, his truck come rolling up the driveway.

When he climbed out, I stood on the deck of the treehouse and waved. Will waved and grinned, then jogged across the field toward me. "Hi there."

I smiled down at him. "Hi yourself."

"Want some company?"

"I'm waiting for a long distance call."

He put his hands on his hips. "From your fiancé?"

I squirmed and knew this was yet another chance to tell Will I wasn't engaged. Instead, I nodded.

"Then I'm definitely coming up," he said, and climbed to the deck, hoisting himself through the opening. He walked up to me and smiled sexily. "You're wearing lipstick again."

"I am."

He pulled me in for a long, slanting kiss.

I pulled back. "You're smearing my lipstick."

"Guess that means you can't Skype with your boyfriend."

I studied his heated gaze and caved. "I guess so."

My phone lit up with the call from Hugh.

But I let it ring.

"You arrived just in time," I said, eliminating the space between us.

"I saw your flag," Will said, pointing to the yellow scarf I'd tied on a post.

"Oh, right," I murmured, then looped my arms around his neck.

October 29, Monday

I WAS GOING THROUGH the boxes of *The Accidental Post* newspapers, looking for my father's obituary. It took me a while to locate since it was a weekly paper and sometimes things didn't get posted on the exact date. When I found it, my eyes watered at the bareness of it—his name, age, the name of his wife and children, and that he'd briefly served in the United States Navy. I was glad it didn't give the name of the young woman he'd been sleeping with when he'd suffered a heart attack (Jewel something, I believe), but I'd hoped for more details about his life.

But then what was there to say? That Dermot Hunnicut couldn't seem to hold down a job? That he was steeped in melancholy and unfulfilled dreams?

I closed my eyes and the day of the funeral floated back to me. It had been an unusually cold day, generally reflecting the frigid state of our family.

The service had been sparsely attended, and considering the way my father had died, my mother was fine with that. I'd never seen my mother cry so violently, so her sobbing had taken me by surprise. And as I sat there, another memory floated into my head.

My mother saying the wrong person had died.

At the time I thought she'd meant it in the global sense, that it was wrong for my father to be taken at a relatively young age.

But in retrospect, I wondered if when she'd said the wrong person had died, she'd meant the girl he'd been screwing should've died instead.

And I wondered if there'd been another young woman my father had fooled around with.

Who *had* subsequently died.

October 30, Tuesday

I KNEW I possessed an active imagination, but while I was sitting there writing the story about the young woman who'd disappeared, I couldn't take my eyes off my mother. I was going to lose my mind if I didn't try again to ask her some direct questions.

I stood and went to sit on her bed, trying to get in her line of sight. "Mom, do you know what happened to Deidre?"

No response.

"Mom, I know you called Detective Terry and told him you had information about Deidre's disappearance. It's time you tell me what you know."

Her eyes moved to meet mine. She understood me.

She made a noise and her eyes strayed to the pen on the side table. I put it in her fingers and positioned her hand over a pad of paper. When I let go, she still held it... and moved it across the paper. With agonizing slowness, she created a garbled letter.

I squinted. "C? Or maybe G?"

She made a noise.

"Okay. G what?"

Slowly, she made another letter on the pad.

"O?" I asked.

She grunted, then dropped the pen.

"G... O?" I asked.

Another grunt.

"Go?"

A triumphant grunt sounded.

Go. Meaning me.

"You want me to go?" I asked, incredulous. "Really? Because if I go, that means you go into a nursing home, Mom. Is that what you want? To spend the rest of your days in a nursing home?"

She closed her eyes, shutting me out.

And it occurred to me that maybe she'd rather spend the rest of her life in a nursing home than reveal what she knew.

October 31, Wednesday

WE RARELY RECEIVED Trick or Treaters at the house because it was so isolated, but it was a nice evening and Mom was asleep, so I was sitting on the porch at dusk with a bowl of candy bars just in case Tyler brought his boys by. I was still smarting over my mother's invitation for me to *go*, and churning over my next move.

And since it seemed doubtful I would be besieged with costumed kidlets, I was helping myself to the candy bars.

When I heard a car coming, I leaned forward and turned on the light for the flashing pumpkin.

When I realized it was Will, I smiled and waved, happy to see him. When he climbed down from his truck, I felt a little tug in my stomach.

Ugh, this *thing* with Will Story was going nowhere good.

"Hi there," he called.

"Hi." I arched an eyebrow at his silly hat. "I see you're dressed as a cowboy."

He laughed. "Trick or Treat." He held up a new jar of hand salve, then he came in for a kiss.

But our really good kiss was interrupted by the approach of another car.

"Oh, good," I said. "Some Trick or Treaters, at last."

Will straightened, then squinted. "Looks like a man."

I didn't recognize the car, so I watched closely to see who would emerge.

When Hugh stepped out and waved, I gasped. "Hugh!"

"Hugh?" Will muttered.

I stood and leaped off the porch to run to him. He looked happy to see me, but was eyeing Will. I suddenly realized how sticky this was going to be.

"What are you doing here?" I asked, then hugged him tight.

"I wanted to see you," he said earnestly, then gave me a kiss to rival the one I'd just received from Will. "And I wanted to bring you something."

"What?"

He opened the back door of the car, and out bounded a brown shaggy mess of fur.

My heart vaulted. "Trudy!"

November 1, Thursday

I WAS FLOATING in the mallowy goodness of a happy dream, lying in a green field of Queen Anne's lace and clover. Dr. Will Story was there, too, wearing his dumb cowboy hat, grinning like a fool, and making my mouth smile, too. He leaned over me, then licked my face.

It wasn't wholly unpleasant, so I let him keep doing it, but when my nose began to itch, I started awake.

Trudy, my beloved brown cockapoo, stood on my chest. A flood of affection swamped me as the memory of my former boyfriend Hugh arriving from England with her washed over me. After she'd disappeared on my watch, I'd thought I'd never see her again. And I'd blamed myself for being so careless. My entire body lit up with relief and gratitude to see her shaggy teddy-bear face. "Hi, sweet girl."

She yapped happily to see me awake, then whimpered to go outside. Mom's bedroom was dark and the digital clock on her nightstand read 4:02 AM. But Trudy's little bladder was still on London time, so she was probably ready to burst.

"Okay," I murmured, swinging my legs over the edge of the loveseat where I'd slept since bringing Mom home from the hospital following the stroke that had summoned me to Accident, Alabama.

I'd stowed Hugh in my old bedroom, sidestepping the awkward question of sharing a bed with the excuse that I needed to stay close to Mom, but in truth I was less worried about my mother suffering a sudden relapse than I was about her long-term recovery. She seemed stubbornly resistant to communicating, and I didn't know if it was a cognitive problem or the fact that she didn't like what was happening to her and around her... possibly a little of both.

Regardless, it didn't seem right to fall into bed with Hugh since I'd been tongue-kissing Will when Hugh had driven up.

I pushed my feet into a pair of Mom's slippers and stood with a groan. I had been looking forward to moving to the bed in my old bedroom, newly cleared of the floor-to-ceiling hoard of stuff that had packed each room of my childhood home when I'd first arrived. I'd managed to clear most of the rooms, but it had been a back-breaking, heart-wrenching exercise that, four months in, remained incomplete. Still, I was thankful the house was presentable to Hugh. I hadn't told him about my former neatnik mother's acquired proclivity for useless crap. I was still struggling with the implications of it myself. Like Hugh, my knowledge of hoarders came from the horror stories I'd seen on television of people burying themselves alive inside their own homes. There was some general consensus that hoarding was triggered by emotional trauma. But I had not yet figured out what had caused my mother to begin "collecting." From what I could tell, it had begun a couple of years after my abusive father had died suddenly. My brother Tyler had insinuated it was because I'd moved to England. I'd since learned she had been rejected by a lover, the town's sheriff, around the same time. Perhaps it was a combination of those things.

Or something else.

I walked through the darkened living room, then unlocked the front door. As soon as I opened it, Trudy scrambled outside into the cool, dark air before I could attach her leash. "Trudy!" I whispered loudly as I stumbled onto the porch after her. "Come back!"

My heart beat wildly, panicked at the thought of losing her again. I half-fell down the steps, cursing myself for not bringing a flashlight. I told myself this wasn't London where Trudy could be snatched by the driver of a passing car who'd simply liked the look of the little dog. But rural areas harbored their own dangers... as my high school friend Deidre Valentine had learned.

When I heard a rustle of bushes and the telltale sound of a full bladder being relieved on the ground, I relaxed a bit. Trudy was safe.

I just wished I could say the same about Deidre.

Weeks of worrisome incidents were catching up with me. When I'd come home, I hadn't expected to be thrust in the middle of an old mystery. But it was getting harder to ignore the niggling thought that my mother's voice message to Detective Jack Terry that she had information about my friend's disappearance might have precipitated her near-fatal medical event.

And that her hoarding had been a manifestation of her desire to cover up what she knew. Did she suspect, as I was beginning to, that my older brother Tyler had something to do with it? Or even my father, who'd shown a predilection for younger women?

Or had my mother herself had a hand in Deidre's disappearance? If my dad had been messing around with Deidre, my mother wouldn't be the first woman to blame the other party for her husband's transgressions.

Not that I had any proof my father was the source of the scandalous affair Deidre had hinted at, an affair our friend Emma said Deidre had allegedly written about in her diary.

There were other contenders, after all. More than one male teacher had flirted with Deidre, although Detective Terry had made some inquiries and seemed to believe they had no knowledge of Deidre's whereabouts. And Deidre's younger sister had overheard arguments between Deidre and their mother about someone they called Preacher Man. Detective Terry was following up on that angle, too.

Meanwhile, I was keeping my qualms about my family's involvement to myself... although with the discovery of Deidre's flying geese quilt buried in our vegetable garden, and Tyler's past arrest for assaulting a girlfriend, the Atlanta detective probably had his own suspicions.

I was beginning to realize my folly in attempting to write a novel based on my friendship with Emma and Deidre and Deidre's subsequent disappearance. After months of writer's block, the pages were finally coming between bouts of hoard-clearing and nursing my mother... but in the process I'd lit a fuse to my imagination and it was running amuck.

My eyes had adjusted to the dim light of the low-hanging autumnal moon, but being able to make out the distant shapes of the things that had enclosed much of my life—the deceptively pretty white picket fence around the front yard, the smelly pig pen and the barn beyond, the expansive garden, the menacing burn pit, and the bittersweet treehouse—did not comfort me. Gooseflesh raised on my arms.

I hugged myself and called to Trudy. "Come, Trudy. Now!"

She bounded back to me and I scooped her up, then hurried up the steps, eager to get back inside. But even Trudy's warm wriggling body couldn't dispel the chill that had settled into my chest.

November 2, Friday

"THANK YOU for coming," I said as Will jumped down from his gigantic pickup truck.

"No problem," Will said, retrieving his black medical bag. "I was between afternoon appointments." He gave me a cautious smile. "Where is she?"

"Inside," I said, leading the way into the house.

Will wiped his boots on the mat in front of the door, ever the gentleman, then removed his hat and stepped inside. His gaze bounced around the neat, sparse living room, and I knew he was comparing it to when it had been packed to the ceiling with boxes and bins and furniture and accessories and a thousand other mismatched, hodgepodge pieces of junk. In one of the two chairs, Trudy lay on a blanket like a limp hairy brown rag. Her eyes were half open, and she attempted to raise her head as we approached, settling instead for a lackluster thump of her tail.

"How long has she been like this?" Will asked.

"Since yesterday," I said, lifting a finger to my mouth to nibble at a fingernail. After being reunited with my sweet Trudy, I couldn't lose her now.

From the bag he withdrew a stethoscope and put in the earpieces, then pressed the listening end to her chest.

"Is she okay?" I asked.

He gave me a wink, but didn't answer, just kept listening. Then he cupped his hand over her nose, checked her mouth, eyes and ears.

I made an anguished noise. "Will, is she okay?"

He smiled and nodded. "A little dehydrated, but overall she's fine."

I sighed in relief. "Then why is she like that?"

"Sleeping? Lethargic?" He removed the stethoscope and

returned it to the bag. "My guess is she has a bad case of jetlag."

I frowned. "Dogs get jetlag?"

He stood. "Sure. Animals have a bodily rhythm just like humans." He glanced toward the hallway. "Where's your boyfriend?"

I squirmed. "Hugh is… asleep."

"He's jetlagged, too?"

"I suppose so."

"Just keep bowls of water around." He grinned. "For Trudy, I mean."

I smirked. "Got it. And thanks. What do I owe you?"

He glanced at my mouth and I wondered if he might extract another kiss for payment. "I'll add it to your tab," he said easily, then headed toward the door. "We didn't exactly get to talk when Hugh and Trudy arrived. How did he find her?"

"I didn't," Hugh said from the doorway.

We both turned toward him. Hugh looked pale and tired and rumpled, but managed a smile.

"Hello," Will said with a nod.

"Hello," Hugh said, stepping forward for an awkward shake. He was barefoot and wearing cotton pajamas.

I had it on good authority (mine) that Will didn't sleep in pajamas.

"You said you didn't find Trudy?" Will prompted.

"No," Hugh said, positioning himself next to me. "A woman showed up at the flat and admitted she'd seen Trudy on the sidewalk and snatched her."

Will pursed his mouth. "Really?"

"Really," Hugh confirmed, in a slightly mocking tone.

I coughed. "Apparently she saw the flyers Hugh put up, but she didn't want to give her back."

"It was clear she had emotional issues," Hugh supplied. "But your theory that Trudy was dog-napped turned out to be correct."

"Jane told you about that?" Will asked.

"Yes," Hugh said, putting his arm around my shoulder. "Jane tells me everything."

My neck felt warm.

One of Will's eyebrows climbed a fraction of an inch.

"Really?"

"Really," Hugh said flatly.

My face was on fire.

"Mr. Story, I missed why you dropped by," Hugh said, his tone more of a question than a statement.

"*Dr.* Story," Will corrected amiably, "but you can call me Will, like Jane does." Will gave me a smile of familiarity.

"I phoned Will," I cut in quickly, "because Trudy is acting so lethargic."

"And what's the diagnosis?" Hugh asked, smothering a yawn.

"She's jetlagged," Will said. "She should get as much sleep as she can the next couple of days. You too," he added lightly, giving the pajamas a dead-pan look.

Hugh nodded to Will's outfit. "The other night I thought the cowboy clothes were a Halloween costume, but I see not."

I pressed my lips together.

"When are you leaving?" Will asked Hugh mildly.

"Sunday." Hugh's arm tightened around my shoulder. "I don't have the loose schedule of a country animal doctor. I can't be away from my work for long."

"Ah," Will said. "And what do you do?"

"Cyber security mostly." Hugh gave a little laugh. "Guess you don't have much need for that here in Accident."

"You're right," Will said with a slow smile. "We don't have any use for you here at all."

I pushed my tongue into my cheek. "Thank you, Will, for coming by."

"Anytime," he said, touching the brim of his hat as he walked toward the door. "My truck knows the way."

I wanted to kick him... and kick Hugh for breaking up with me and leaving me vulnerable to Will's charm... and kick myself for getting into this pickle.

When the door closed behind him, Hugh made a rueful noise. "I'd forgotten how arrogant good old Southern boys can be." Then he yawned widely. "I'm going back to bed."

Hugh turned and padded toward my old bedroom. Outside the roar of Will's truck seemed louder than necessary.

My head pivoted, looking back and forth.

November 3, Saturday

HUGH HANDED TRUDY up to me, then hoisted himself through the opening in the treehouse deck.

"So this is the infamous treehouse," he said with a wide grin. After another night's hard sleep, he seemed much improved, sporting color in his apple cheeks. It was a brisk, breezy day, with roly poly clouds and a beleaguered sun.

I nodded, flush with happiness Hugh had come and he'd brought Trudy to me. She, too, had revived. I rubbed her cold nose against mine, then set her down to explore. "This is where I spent most of my time between the age of ten and eighteen."

"I can see why," he said. "Your family must have had good times up here."

I shook my head. "Not so much. Tyler was too old and grown up for it when my dad built it."

"But your mother must have fond memories of it."

I squinted. "What makes you say that?"

"Her laptop password—Treehouse, zero five zero seven."

I'd asked Hugh to hack her password, and had forgotten what it was. But I gave a little laugh. "Mom was never up here that I knew of."

"Maybe when she was thinking of a password, it was the first thing she saw when she looked out the window."

I bit my tongue to keep from saying she'd been so surrounded by piles of hoarded stuff, she couldn't have seen out the window. "Maybe."

He circled in place to take in the panoramic view. "It's beautiful here, Jane. Why haven't you invited me before?"

I squirmed. "Looks can be deceiving. It wasn't the happiest of places to grow up."

"I know. And I'm sorry you had to come back like this. But your mum is improving?"

I nodded. "She's getting stronger, and I feel okay about leaving her alone for short periods of time."

"But she still isn't talking, or is she just shy around me?"

"Don't take it personally—she still isn't speaking." I didn't want to tell him she'd communicated cryptically last week by scratching out the word "GO" on a piece of paper to tell me to leave.

"I confess I'd wondered if she were better, but you were putting off coming back to England because of how I behaved."

I blinked up at his anguished expression. "No. I truly can't leave yet."

He nodded. "I see that now, although I was desperately hoping you and Trudy could leave with me tomorrow."

I sighed. "I'd like that too. There are so many memories here."

"You haven't unearthed any answers about your missing friend?"

"Not yet," I murmured. "Maybe she did run away. I would have if I'd had the guts."

He smiled, then pulled me to him for a really good kiss. Then he held me and I pressed my face into his chest, breathing in the familiar scent of him and his sweater. My eyes brimmed with tears—I missed him and wanted to go home... to my England home.

"Is that the animal doctor's house?"

I froze, then lifted my head and looked in the direction Hugh was pointing. In a clearing on the next ridge over, Will Story's unmistakable behemoth truck sat in the driveway next to his modern log home.

"So it is," I squeaked.

Hugh frowned. "Should I be worried about him?"

"What do you mean?"

Hugh's expression was half anger, half concern. "You know what I mean. Is something going on between the two of you? I assume the man wasn't here Trick or Treating the night I arrived."

I frowned. "You did leave me, Hugh."

"No," he said, lifting his finger. "I only moved out to give you time to work on some things."

"You said I had issues," I reminded him. "And I do, I know that now."

"I handled it badly," he said, clasping my hands. "I should've stayed to support you and help you deal with your problems. I love you, Jane. I want you to be well and happy... with me."

My heart swelled at his earnest words. "You do?"

He lowered his mouth to mine and kissed me like he did when we'd first met. My body flickered to life. Where had *this* man been?

When he pulled back, his eyes were shining. "Trudy isn't the only thing I brought you, Jane."

He stuck his hand in his pocket, and I braced myself for a bawdy joke about the "gift" he had for me. But when he pulled out a ring box, opened it, and lowered himself to one knee, I was struck speechless.

"Jane Hunnicut, will you marry me?"

I gasped at the diamond, my heart thudding in my astonished ears. The stone was dazzling in the rays of the slanting sun, yet Hugh's hopeful smile eclipsed them both.

"Yes," I said on a happy exhale.

November 4, Sunday

HUGH LOOKED AT his watch for the umpteenth time. "I'm going to miss my flight if we don't leave in the next ten minutes."

I gave the Caddy another crank. The engine whined, but refused to turn over. I pounded on the steering wheel. "Start, dammit!"

From the backseat, Trudy barked her support.

"I shouldn't have let the rental company pick up the car," Hugh fretted, sounding shrill. "What was I thinking?" He pulled out his phone. "I'm calling for an Uber."

"Uber?" I gestured to emphasize the fact that we were surrounded by farmland and livestock. "Do you see where we are? The nearest Uber driver will be in Birmingham, and it'll take them forty minutes to get here—at best."

He pulled his hand over his mouth. "What then?"

"I'll call Tyler. Maybe he's in the area." I pulled up my brother's number and connected the call. To my great relief, he answered on the second ring.

"What's up, Sis?"

"Hugh needs a ride to the airport, like, now. The Caddy won't start."

He groaned. "I'm delivering around Five Mile Creek today. Earliest I could be there is an hour."

I winced. "Any other ideas? Uber will take too long."

"Have you called Will?"

I winced again, harder. "I don't think that's a good idea."

Tyler laughed. "Maybe not, but sounds like you're outta options if Hugh wants to make his flight."

"Thanks," I mumbled. I ended the call, then reluctantly pulled up Will's number and connected the call. If he had his arm stuck up a donkey's rear end, there was no reason to even mention the option to Hugh.

Will answered on the first ring. "Hi, Jane. What's up?"

"At the moment, my blood pressure," I said. "The Caddy won't start and Hugh needs to get to the airport to make his flight."

"Say no more," Will said happily. "What time should I swing by?"

"We need to leave within ten minutes."

"I'll be there in five."

I ended the call, then turned a magnanimous smile toward Hugh. "Good news. A neighbor friend will be here in five minutes."

Hugh heaved a sigh of relief, then opened the door. "I'll get my bags."

I climbed out, too, then fetched Trudy and met him at the rear of the Caddy where he set his two sizeable bags on the ground.

Then Hugh frowned. "Wait—what neighbor friend?"

"Um..."

The rumble of Will's truck sounded in the distance.

Hugh scoffed. "Bloody hell, not the animal doctor."

I lifted my hands. "You could skip the flight and stay a few more days."

"Unfortunately, that's out of the question."

"Then be nice," I chided.

Hugh pouted, then picked up my left hand, admiring my engagement ring. "You're right. I can afford to be nice. I won."

I frowned at his comment, but my reaction was lost in a cloud of gravel dust as Will roared up the driveway.

He pulled the pickup to a jarring stop, then slammed into park and jumped down. "Your taxi has arrived."

I was dismayed at how pleased, yet irritated, I was to see him.

Hugh gave Will a strained smile. "Thanks, old chap."

"Happy to help you get back across the pond," Will said amiably, picking up Hugh's bags and chucking them in the pickup bed none too gently. "Let's go. There's room for Trudy, too." Then his gaze snagged on my ring. "Whoa, Jane... I haven't seen your big rock."

I squirmed—Will believed I was engaged all along, and I didn't see the need to clear up the confusion now.

"Nice, isn't it?" Hugh crowed.

"Very," Will said, but he was looking at me, not Hugh.

It occurred to me the ride home alone with Will would be excruciating. I turned to Hugh. "If it's okay with you, I'll say goodbye now, and stay with Mom."

Hugh's mouth twitched downward, but he nodded. "Whatever you think is best." He pulled me into his arms, then kissed me until Will cleared his throat.

"Sorry to interrupt, *old chap*, but we should be leaving."

Hugh pulled back. "Right." Then he cupped my face. "You and Trudy come home soon."

I smiled and nodded. While he bent to pet Trudy and give her a goodbye rub, I walked over to Will. "Thanks for this."

"Don't mention it."

I looked back to Hugh, who was still occupied with Trudy. "And Will..."

Will winked. "Don't worry—I'll behave."

I stepped back and picked up Trudy as both men climbed inside the cab. When the truck pulled away, they both waved goodbye.

Trudy broke into rapid-fire barking, ending in a mournful whine.

"I know," I crooned, cuddling her close. "I know."

November 5, Monday

"BE HONEST, how do you think my mom is doing?"

Owen McCoy, the home healthcare aide assigned to Mom's case, sipped from the mug of coffee I'd handed to him. We were in the kitchen, out of earshot.

"She's definitely stronger," he said cautiously. "And sometimes I think she understands what I'm saying... but other times, she seems almost catatonic."

I'd had the same frustrating experiences. Since writing the ambiguous "GO" message on a piece of paper, she'd refused to hold a pencil, even with her good hand. "What's the next milestone, and what can I do?"

"Honestly, Jane, if you can just get her to respond to you— even a grunt is progress."

"I'll keep trying," I promised. Although secretly, I wondered how much my mother was impaired, and how much she was pretending to be impaired.

When I died and went to hell, I'd be relegated to the fiery corner saved for evil daughters.

He took another drink and swallowed. "And I'd like to see her eyes track more when people and things are moving around her. Or even the action on one of the episodes of *Law & Order* on her laptop screen. Jesus, how many of those are there?"

"Thousands."

"Well, if she can't focus on Benjamin Bratt, we know there's still a problem."

I laughed, grateful for his good-natured humor.

The rolling growl that reached my ears was either an approaching thunderstorm, or Will Story's big-ass truck. And since it was a cloudless November sky...

Owen and I both glanced out the window as Will rolled up.

"Speaking of beautiful men," Owen murmured.

I scoffed.

"What, did that engagement ring of yours render you blind?"

"No," I said, drinking to sidestep responding, then frowned. "I wonder why he's here?"

"It's mystifying," Owen said dryly.

"He probably came to see the pigs," I offered.

"Uh huh," Owen said, then picked up the coffeepot and filled another mug. "Why don't you take the good doctor a cup of coffee?"

"He's not a real doctor," I groused, but I took the cup and headed toward the front door. By the time I walked out on the porch and down the steps, Will had lifted the hood of the Caddy and was leaned over the engine, wielding a wrench.

"Good morning," I called.

He lifted his head, then smiled. "Morning."

"Tyler is supposed to come and see if he can figure out why it won't start."

"I talked to him," Will said. "I think it might be the fuel filter, offered to check it out. Hope you don't mind."

"Not at all."

He leaned back in, banged around on something, then came out holding a small black drum. "I think this is your culprit."

"How can you tell?"

"It's supposed to be white."

"Ah. Where do I get a new one?"

"You probably don't need one. I'll hose it off and put it back in."

I extended the cup of coffee. "Thank you." I winced. "I seem to always be thanking you."

He took the cup with a grateful smile. "Don't mention it. How are you?"

"Fine."

"How's the book coming along?"

"Actually, that's fine, too," I admitted. "I set up a place to write in my mother's room, and it's been... productive."

"How is she?"

"Improving," I said carefully.

"She must be since you're planning to go back to England soon," he said, nodding to my engagement ring.

I took a drink of coffee. "Will, you should know... I wasn't engaged before."

He squinted. "You weren't?"

"No. Hugh and I had talked about getting married, but it was never official."

"Ah."

I wet my lips. "In fact, we broke up just before I came back to Accident."

"And you're telling me this now because?"

"Because I want to be clear that I wouldn't—won't—um, fool around if I were—am—really engaged."

He scratched his temple. "So no more fooling around?"

I swallowed hard. "Right."

"No more flags flying from the treehouse?"

"Right."

"No more Wonder Woman underwear?"

"Right. By the way, I can't seem to, um, locate them. Did I leave them at your house?"

"Nope."

I took another drink from my cup, and so did Will.

"I like him," he offered.

"Hm?"

"Hugh. He seems like a nice guy."

"He is."

"Then it's all good."

"Yes, it is. All good." I gestured toward the house. "I should get back inside."

He held up the filter. "I'll take care of this, then I'll be on my way."

"Okay."

"Okay."

I headed back to the house, conscious of Will's gaze on me. When I walked back into the kitchen, Owen was rinsing his cup in the sink. He arched an eyebrow in question. "Well?"

"He's cleaning my fuel filter."

"Uh huh."

November 6, Tuesday

I STOOD IN THE hallway outside the door of Tyler's old bedroom, debating whether to go inside.

Since my return in July, I had methodically made my way through the main rooms of the small house I'd grown up in—the kitchen, then the living room, then my mother's bedroom, then my own bedroom. Thankfully my mother's higher value of hygiene had compelled her to leave paths to the commodes and the showers of the two small bathrooms, although the paths had been bordered with enough toiletries, towels, and toilet paper to stock a convenience store. Junk man Jim Powers had relieved me of most of the hoard to resell at his flea market, probably to another hoarder.

Each room had held its own assorted memories, some good, but mostly bad. I was still reeling from the bittersweet discoveries in my old room, and I suspected deep in Tyler's room were the remnants of his teenage dysfunction. I had urged him to go through the items himself, but he had waved me off, saying he wanted no part of it, and reminded me again that if it were left up to him, he would take care of everything with a match and a can of accelerant.

I was tempted to just leave it—the room was isolated to a corner of the house, and no one was using it. I had writing to do and I could always spend the time doing physical therapy with Mom and pressing her to blink, grunt, nod, or please dear God in heaven give me some kind of clue she could understand me.

But the fact that it was the last piled-up room needled at me. I reasoned there were practical reasons to clear it out—a bug infestation or mold could spread to the rest of the house. And once I returned to England, one room of hoard might trigger my mom to start it all over again. But truth be told, my own compulsions were starting to kick in. Leaving the room as-is would render the rest of my clearing victory a failure.

I considered calling the therapist Anne Warford to talk it through, but I knew what she would tell me—that if I couldn't stop my unnecessary compulsive cleaning, I was the same as my mother. And unless there was a clear imperative to clean the room, I should leave it alone.

I put my hand on the doorknob. Perhaps there was another reason to clean the room... maybe I would find something that would support my growing unease that Tyler had something to do with Deidre's disappearance.

I dropped my hand. But did I really want to know?

I put my hand back on the doorknob. There was a chance I'd find something to support Tyler's claim that he knew nothing about Deidre's disappearance or her quilt being buried in the garden. He'd scoffed over my discovery of a leg bone in the pig pen and chalked it up to my overactive imagination, just like Sheriff Tomlin.

And the only thing that might prove Tyler had nothing to do with it would be finding proof someone else did.

My father?

I swallowed hard. My mother?

I dropped my hand, then turned and walked away.

November 7, Wednesday

MY HANDS WERE motionless on the keyboard. The words wouldn't come today. My mind was still running on a loop from the previous day's musings, and the specter of truth was blocking me from putting the fictional version of it on the page.

The ring of my phone startled me and Trudy. When I saw Detective Jack Terry's name on the screen, my pulse blipped higher. Maybe he had good news, although honestly, I wasn't sure what good news regarding Deidre's case would look like at this point.

Mom lay stiffly in her bed, seeming not to notice the shrill sound, and the cat that continued to lie on her stomach seemed equally disinterested. Still, I decided to take the call in the living room.

"Hello?"

"Hello, Ms. Hunnicut. It's Jack Terry. How's the fishing?"

I smiled. It was our private joke—after receiving my mom's voice mail that she had information on Deidre's disappearance, he had made a habit of coming to Accident to fish at Bayview Lake. And I had made a habit of fishing for information from the locals.

"Nothing on the stringer at the moment, Detective. Are you getting any bites?"

He grunted. "I talked to Jim Powers about his story that Deidre Valentine came to see him before she ran away to sell some items for cash."

"And?"

"And he seemed to have a clear memory of the incident, said he knew her and her family, and said it was definitely Deidre, and he'd tried to talk her out of running away."

"Did he remember what items she sold to him?"

"He said it was a few pieces of inexpensive jewelry, except for one item—a man's gold watch."

My stomach did a flip. "Wow. Did he ask her about it?"

"Yeah, but he said she was cagey, just said someone gave it her."

"Did he take a picture of the watch?"

He made a rueful noise. "No such luck. And he said he sold it the next day at his flea market."

"He remembered selling it?"

"Only because when the Valentine girl ran away, he went to the Sheriff to repeat what she told him about taking a trip and remembers he no longer had the watch."

I frowned. "Do you remember this from the initial investigation?"

"No, and it's not in my notes. But maybe Sheriff Tomlin thought it was a moot point, or maybe by that time the case has already been marked as a runaway and since it supported the theory, he didn't bother."

"Or maybe he was covering up for the owner of the watch?"

"Covering, maybe, but not necessarily for a crime."

I made a noise of concession.

"But Powers did remember another detail—that Deidre said she was heading to Dallas."

My heart lifted a bit. "Dallas, Texas?"

"Presumably. Did the two of you talk about that?"

I squinted, trying to bring my fuzzy memory into focus. "I don't think so. When we talked about running away together, we always said we'd go where the wind took us."

He groaned.

"I know. It was probably in the lyric of some song we were listening to."

"So maybe she was headed for Dallas, or maybe she just told Powers that in case someone tried to find her."

My shoulders fell, dejected not to be able to visualize a place where Deidre might have landed. "That's true."

"Anyway, I also talked to the minister about the phone call he received a couple of years after Deidre disappeared that he thought was her."

"And?"

"And the guy seems genuine enough, and he repeated the same story he told you about supplying Deidre with meals and toiletries from the church's supplies. He still says he doesn't know if the caller was Deidre, and he admitted feeling guilty for not going to the Sheriff or her family with the information."

"But you don't think he's covering anything?"

"My gut says no, especially since if he was guilty of something, why would he come forward and shine a spotlight on himself. Unless—"

"Unless what?"

"Unless he knows someone in his congregation was involved, and he can't say anything because of spiritual confidentiality. Maybe this is his way of pointing us in the right direction."

I was struck silent. My mother was a member of his congregation.

"Ms. Hunnicut, are you there?"

"Um, yes, Detective. Just processing."

"How's your mother?"

"Um... improving in some ways, not so much in others."

"Is she communicating?"

"Not yet."

"You'll let me know when I can ask her a few questions?"

I swallowed hard. "Absolutely."

"Okay, well, I need to take another call. I'm not sure when I'll get back to Accident, but you know where to find me."

"Yes. Thanks."

He ended the call, and I slowly made my way back to my mother's room. She hadn't moved, but the fingers of her good hand—her left hand—were stroking the cat's fur.

"That was the detective in Atlanta you called about Deidre," I said.

She didn't respond in any way, was still staring vacantly toward the laptop screen where Detective Lenny was making a darkly humorous wisecrack about their suspect.

"He wants to talk to you as soon as you feel better."

Her eyes closed, and stayed closed.

November 8, Thursday

EMMA GAVE ME a brief hug, then pulled back and reached for my left hand. "Let me see this ring!"

I let her gush over the diamond ring that promised me to Hugh Green. I basked in her pleasure—and in mine. I have to admit, just looking at it made my heart swell. He did want me, compulsions and all.

"Congratulations!" she cried, then gave me another hug.

"Thanks... it was a nice surprise."

"But you were already engaged, right?"

"Um... in theory," I hedged. "Europeans aren't as hung up on the whole engagement ring thing."

Emma beamed. "Well, I'm glad the man came around to good old American values."

"Right," I said, nodding. Because nothing said I love you like a cold hard rock.

"Come in, come in." She waved me past the front door of her huge home. "Eddie is getting ready to leave, and I have two whole hours until the kids get home from school."

"Unfortunately, I don't want to leave Mom alone for too long."

She hummed in understanding. "Do you have time for a cup of coffee?"

"Sure."

I followed her through the palatial entryway into the more palatial kitchen, where every finishing detail was top of the line. Her husband Eddie—Dr. Eddie Hopper, a real people doctor—was sitting at the breakfast bar watching business news on a small TV and eating the last few bites of a sandwich. He looked up and smiled. "Hi, Jane."

"Hi, Eddie. Sorry to intrude on your lunch."

He gave a dismissive wave. "You're always welcome here. Besides, I'm getting ready to take off."

I noticed he was dressed in outdoor clothing. "Going fishing?"

"Kayaking, actually." Then he grinned. "With your buddy Will, in fact."

I managed a flat smile. "He's not… my buddy."

"The man talks about you nonstop."

"Jane just got engaged," Emma broke in, giving Eddie a meaningful look.

I held up my left hand, helpfully. "To my boyfriend in England."

His expression morphed to surprise, then forced cheer. "Well… that's… terrific!"

"Thanks."

Then he squinted. "Does Will know?"

"Yes. In fact, he gave my boyfriend a ride to the airport."

He nodded. "That's Will." Then he wiped his mouth, stood and leaned forward to kiss Emma. "Bye, sweetie."

"Please don't drown," she said.

"I won't, dear."

He winked at me. "Guess I know what Will will be talking about today. I'll try to cheer him up." He strode out of the kitchen, and Emma laughed.

"Will does have a thing for you, you know."

"I'm not sure that's true, but it'll pass."

"For you, too?" Emma asked lightly.

"Already has," I assured her.

Emma sighed. "Too bad… Will's a nice guy."

"Yeah, he is."

"He's good to his sister—do you know Tiffany?"

"I've met her a couple of times."

"She and her husband are having problems, so she and her daughter have been staying with Will."

"I believe he mentioned that. Did you know she knew Deidre?"

Emma nodded. "They were close at one time, I believe. Deidre used to hang out with Tiff when she went to college in Birmingham."

"Seems like an odd mix."

"I agree. Did you know Tiff was Miss Alabama?"

"No. But she's pretty enough."

"Yeah. Speaking of Deidre, Jim Powers told me she'd sold some things to him before she ran away, and mentioned she was heading to Dallas... did you know that?"

Emma shook her head. "I don't recall." Then she grinned. "But then Deidre always had a thing for cowboys, remember?"

A memory chord vibrated in my brain. "Maybe."

Emma angled her head. "Too bad she's not here... she'd be cheering up Will Story."

I gave a little laugh, then sobered. Hm.

November 9, Friday

I WAS WAITING for Tyler when he came to feed the pigs. Lately, he'd been in and out before dawn, and I wondered if he was avoiding me... and Mom.

But mostly me.

"Good morning," I said when he stepped out of his delivery truck. Tyler delivered packages all over the area, and seemed to like his job.

He appeared surprised to see me, but grinned. "Hi, Sis."

That was Tyler—so charming. But it made me rethink that he was avoiding me—was I projecting? "How are Stacey and the boys?"

His smile widened. "Really, really good."

I smiled back, happy to hear that he and his wife seemed on the road to reconciliation. "I'm glad."

He headed toward the barn to get feed for the pigs. "How's Mom?"

"About the same," I said, then pressed my lips together as I followed him into the barn. "But actually, I wanted to talk about Dad."

Tyler turned. "What about Dad?"

"I've been thinking about the, um, woman he was with when he died."

Tyler made a face. "Don't go there."

"Do you know anything about her?"

He sighed, then picked up a bag of feed. "Her name was Jules, or Julie or something like that. She moved away after it happened. She was a tramp."

I winced. "So what does that make Dad?"

Tyler made an irritated noise as he walked past me to carry the feed bag outside. "Stop it, Jane."

I trotted to follow him. "Tamara White told me the reason she broke up with you is because Dad was hitting on her—is that true?"

He dropped the bag of feed on the ground with a thud, and yelled, "I said *stop it*, Jane!" His face was contorted with anger.

I blinked.

He withdrew a pocket knife and stabbed the feed bag, then sliced it open and dumped it into the troughs. The pigs were already gathered, grunting and waiting. Tyler wadded up the bag and walked back to his truck to toss it inside. "Stop rehashing the past," he said, jabbing the air to make his point. "You moved away and everyone else moved on. You should too."

"Let sleeping dogs lie?" I asked, mocking him.

His shoulders fell, and he suddenly looked sad. "Yeah. Dad wasn't perfect—he made mistakes. But Jesus, he's dead. I've made mistakes, too, but I'm happy now." He looked mournful. "Jane... can't you just let people be happy? And then maybe you'd be happy, too."

Tyler climbed back into his truck and closed the door with a bang.

I stood frozen, marinating in his words of disdain and judgment long after his truck had disappeared.

November 10, Saturday

I WAS DRIVING through the town of Accident, on the way to the pharmacy to get a prescription for Mom, when I saw Will's gigantic truck coming the other way. He slowed, then stopped.

I smiled to myself, wryly. Stopping traffic to talk to someone was commonplace in Accident. Sometimes it took a half hour just to drive a few blocks, and no one seemed to mind.

I stopped obligingly, then rolled down my window, craning to look up at him from the much lower Caddy.

"Hi," he said, pushing back his hat.

The movement made me think of my conversation with Emma about Deidre liking cowboys. "Hi, yourself. Cleaning the fuel filter must have done the trick—the Caddy's never driven better."

He grinned. "Good." Then he glanced at my hand. "I see you're still engaged."

"Yep."

"Just checking," he said, then gave a little wave and drove away.

I gave an exasperated sigh, then drove toward the pharmacy. Will was only teasing anyway—men like him talked a flirtatious game, but if I told him I was staying in Accident and wanted to make a life with him, he'd probably disappear like a smoke ring.

As I drove by the diner, I noticed Tamara White was standing by the dumpster, smoking a cigarette and talking animatedly to a big guy in a uniform—Tyler.

I frowned and slowed. Even though his back was to me, I could see that he, too, was animated—and angry. And it didn't take a lipreader to guess what they were talking about.

Tamara cocked her hip and said something to Tyler that must've pissed him off even more because in an instant, he was in front of her, twisting his hand in her apron bib to force her closer to him.

Panicked, I didn't know what to do, but my hand automatically went to the car horn. I blasted the air, startling myself and apparently them, since Tyler released her. They both turned to look in my direction, and I waved. Tyler straightened, then stalked toward his truck that was parked nearby. I waited for him to start his vehicle, and even allowed him to pull out in front of me. He gave a little wave as he went by, then drove away.

I looked back to Tamara. She gave me an "I told you so" look, then turned back to her cigarette.

November 11, Sunday

I STOOD IN the hallway outside the door of Tyler's old bedroom, debating whether to go inside. The scene I'd witnessed yesterday had stuck with me... I had plenty of proof that Tyler's mood could turn on a dime—one minute he was handsome and charming, and the next he was ugly and full of rage.

I put my hand on the doorknob, and turned it.

The door opened, then stopped on the edge of one of the dozens of boxes stacked to the ceiling. But I felt compelled to squeeze inside.

The smell of old things assailed me—dust, moisture, and moth balls. The entire house had smelled this way when I arrived.

Tyler's room was still blue, as I remembered it, but the color had faded in places. He had one of the nicest windows in the house, and a pretty view toward the back property line, but the window was obscured by hoard. Everywhere I looked was so much junk, spilling out of bulging boxes it had been stuffed into.

When the feeling of overwhelm began to descend, I opened the first container I could reach—a battered black boot box. I opened it, expecting trash, but realized quickly it was Tyler's personal stash of photos.

They were mostly yearbook photos—the stock kind that the standard school photographer would take of everyone in school. The kids with means, though, would seek out their own photographer for custom yearbook photos, and some of them were quite glamorous—or gawdy, depending on a person's taste.

I rummaged through the photos, seeing a few faces I recognized, but most of the names escaped me. Within a few moments, though, I realized there was something strange about all the photos.

They were all of girls. Tyler had been a popular athlete in high school, with many male friends. But there were no pictures of any guys.

I bit into my lip, wondering if he'd segregated the photos, if I might find another box containing photos of his male friends.

But I suspected not.

I kept rummaging, and stopped when I came across a picture of a girl who was familiar to me—Emma. I kept rummaging and found another of her, then one of Deidre, then another of Deidre, then two more of Emma, one with a red heart drawn around her face.

I took out my phone and texted Emma.

Going through some mementos of Tyler's and found a photo of you... did my brother have a crush on you?

A few seconds later, she replied *LOL! Tyler was always a flirt, but he knew Eddie would kill him if he ever made a pass! How big was my hair in the photo?*

I smiled. *Enormous*

Good!

I laughed, then stowed the phone, and turned back to rummage through the pictures again. I found another photo of Deidre, and pulled it out. Then frowned.

Devil's horns had been drawn on her head.

It was the kind of thing any boy would do, especially if he'd been spurned.

But what if it meant something?

I glanced around the room and zeroed in on the other thing that niggled at me.

In my room, the outer layers of hoard was junk Mom had accumulated at various yard sales and flea markets, and the personal items I'd left were deep inside.

But here was a box of Tyler's photos, easily within reach.

As if Mom had gone through them recently... or often?

November 12, Monday

WHEN THE PHONE rang and my editor Jocelyn's name came up on the screen, I was happy to answer it.

And I couldn't remember the last time that had happened.

"Hi, Jocelyn."

"Hi, Jane," she said, her voice light. "Are you still in Alabama?"

"Yes."

"And how is your mother?"

"Improving," I said cheerfully. "But I expect to be here for a while longer."

"I'm sorry," she said, then after a beat added, "But the atmosphere must be working for you because I have to say, the first two hundred pages you sent me are some of the best you've written."

I smiled, shot through with pleasure. "Thank you. I'm glad you're pleased."

"So am I," Jocelyn said with a laugh. "I must confess when you first pitched the idea of writing about your childhood friendship and the mystery of your missing friend, I wasn't sure you could pull it off. But so far, I think this story has the makings of a bestseller."

Especially, I mused wryly, if my mother was well enough to buy hundreds of copies by the time the book was released.

"This could be your comeback book, Jane."

"That's very good news," I said, beyond relieved.

"And you're still on track to deliver the rest of the manuscript by the end of December?"

"Lord willing and the creek don't rise."

"Pardon?"

I winced, realizing I'd blurted a common rural saying. "Um, I mean yes." Barring some unforeseen tragedy, like my brother being arrested for murdering my friend.

"Good," Jocelyn said. "I'm enjoying reading the story with no idea of where it's going, although right now, I think the brother murdered her friend."

"R-Really," I said noncommittally. Hearing it aloud sounded positively brutal.

"You do have an ending in mind, don't you?"

"Absolutely," I lied. Have I mentioned that novelist are good liars?

"And there's not enough likeness to reality that we'll be sued?"

"Right," I said. "Most of this stuff is pure conjecture."

"Phew. Okay… keep going—I can't wait to see what happens next."

I ended the call and glanced over at my mother's rigid, unresponsive form, then murmured, "Me, too."

November 13, Tuesday

I WAS MAKING some headway in Tyler's room, emptying bins and boxes of stuff Mom had obviously bought because it reminded her of his childhood—untold numbers of baseballs, basketballs, footballs, plus various racquets, bats, and helmets. There were at least three boxes of worn smelly athletic shoes, none of them Tyler's size. And there were bins of hunting and fishing magazines, as well as rusty tackle boxes full of tangled fish lures and rubber worms. Some of it went to the garage for Junk Man Jim to peruse on his next visit, but most of it went into trash bags for the dump.

So far I hadn't found anything else that might have belonged to Tyler personally. But I had yet to make enough ground even to reveal his bed or boyhood furniture.

When the phone rang, I bit back a curse, loath to stop and lose momentum. I wanted to get this job done so I could get back to writing, and back to my mom's physical therapy.

I glanced at the phone and smirked. The therapist Anne Warford.

A thump on the head from the universe?

I sighed and connected the call. "This is Jane."

"Jane, hello, this is Anne Warford calling to check in."

"Hello, Ms. Warford. My mother is improving some."

"Glad to hear it," she said politely. "And what about you?"

I surveyed my red hands, so chapped and raw, it was painful for me to type on my laptop. "I'm good."

"So you've been able to control the compulsion to clean?"

"Absolutely."

"That's good. The next time you bring in your mother for a checkup, stop by—I'd like to see for myself."

I frowned. "You don't believe me?"

She gave a little laugh. "You misunderstood. Of course I believe you—I just meant I'd like to see you and catch up."

I relaxed. "Oh."

"And when your mother has recovered enough to consider therapy, maybe the two of you could come in together."

I frowned. "I don't think that will be necessary."

"Okay. It's just a suggestion."

"Thanks just the same," I said tightly.

"Sure. Take care, Jane."

I disconnected the call with the stab of my red, raw finger. The nerve! My mother had the problem, not me. I was only trying to clean up her mess—literally.

November 14, Wednesday

I WAS TAKING a break from cleaning Tyler's room, walking Trudy. Every time I looked at her, I was filled with happiness. I was so grateful to Hugh for bringing her to me—it made being here more tolerable.

I glanced at my engagement ring, dull from residue from all my grubbing around. I shouldn't be wearing it, but it helped me to remember Hugh, and how much I loved him. I had so many things sprinting through my mind lately, I needed reminders of what was important. And the ring was a big step up from a sticky note.

A distant rumble sounded, and my pulse quickened as I glanced toward the driveway, expecting Will's truck to roll into view. Instead I realized the rumble was a plane flying overhead. I bent my head back and watched it move across the sky, leaving a plume of white smoke in its wake. I looked forward to the day I was on a plane heading back to England.

And away from this burdensome place.

Trudy barked and I realized she'd found something. She was pawing at a shiny object in the gravel, near the garage. I walked over and bent down for a closer look.

Eyeglasses. Silver wireframes, now bent beyond use and ground into the rocks. Scattered around them were small pieces of broken lenses. I frowned. Mom didn't wear glasses... did she?

I remembered something Owen McCoy had said. *I'd like to see her eyes track... if she can't focus on Benjamin Bratt, we know there's still a problem.*

I pulled out my phone and dialed Tyler. Considering how we'd left things, I didn't expect him to answer, but he surprised me.

"Hi, Sis. What's up?"

"Hi, Tyler. I found a pair of eyeglasses in the driveway, broken. Are they Mom's?"

"Hm… now that you mention it, I think she was wearing glasses the last couple of times I saw her."

"I don't remember her wearing them when we Skyped."

"She was kind of vain about them, she probably didn't want you to know."

I sighed. "Why didn't you tell me? All this time she's been going without glasses—she probably can't see well."

"Sorry," he said. "Guess I forgot."

I pinched the bridge of my nose. "Okay, I'll try to find her doctor, and order a new pair."

"Let me know if I can help."

I wanted to say "too late." Instead I swallowed my anger, knowing he'd only come back with a remark that I should've known, too.

I ended the call and surveyed the mangled frames, wracked with guilt. I scanned the area where Trudy had found them and recalled Mom had been near her car when she'd suffered the stroke. Someone she was supposed to pick up had sounded the alarm and she'd been found lying in the driveway. I visualized her falling hard and her glasses flying off. And in the melee of people and the ambulance arriving, the frames probably had been driven over multiple times… and how many times had I driven over them myself?

I choked back a sob, wondering how vulnerable Mom must have felt… must still be feeling.

November 15, Thursday

WHEN JACK TERRY'S name came up on my phone screen, once again I was hoping for good news.

"Hello, Detective."

"Hello, Ms. Hunnicut. How are things on your end?"

I glanced over at my mother lying in her bed. "About the same. Do you have news?"

"Some. I was able to track down the bus passenger logs around the time Deidre Valentine ran away. And I found her name on a log for a trip from Birmingham to Dallas, Texas."

I exhaled. "So she did run away?"

"Someone purchased a ticket in her name. There's no way to prove she was actually on that bus, but all the evidence supports that scenario."

"Are you going to follow up in Dallas to see if you can locate her?"

"No," he said gently. "Like you said, it looks as if she did run away, just as she told many people she was going to do."

"What about the blood stain on the quilt?" My voice sounded high and manic even to my ears.

"We don't know it's blood," he chided. "I have to agree with the Sheriff at this point. Unless I learn something that compels me to believe a crime was committed, it ends here."

My mouth watered to tell him about the random pieces of incriminating information I'd learned about Tyler, but I knew how it would sound spilling out of my mouth—like a fiction writer spinning tales.

"So I guess that's it," he said. "At least until your mother is able to answer some questions."

"Right," I managed to get out. "I'll let you know."

"Okay, Ms. Hunnicut. I'll wait to hear from you. For now, I'm closing the file on Deidre Valentine."

November 16, Friday

I FELT LIKE A perv hanging around the school parking lot, waiting for the doors to open and the kids to pour out. But I needed to talk to Kelly Valentine, and she'd said this was the safest place to meet—she didn't want her mother to know we had talked and I wasn't too keen on venturing back into the hollow where Deidre had grown up.

When the dismissal bell sounded, the doors burst open and a stream of noisy, colorful bodies exploded from the building. I kept an eye out for Kelly's tall, lanky figure and long, dark hair. She was easy to spot. I shouted her name and when her head turned toward me, I experienced déjà vu—she looked so much like Deidre, it was eerie.

She waved and jogged toward me, giving me a wary look.

"We need to talk," I said.

She juggled an armload of books. "I don't have much time," she said, nodding to the buses lined up.

"I'll make this quick. A police detective found Deidre's name on a bus passenger log the day she went missing for a trip from Birmingham to Dallas."

"Dallas, Texas?"

I nodded. "So it looks as if Deidre did run away after all."

Kelly's face crumpled, then she shook her head. "No. She would've called me, she would've written... she would've come back to get me and take me with her."

I could feel her anguish, the sense of hurt and betrayal. I ached for her because she was counting on Deidre to rescue her from a desperately unhappy home life.

"I'm sorry," I murmured.

"Don't be sorry," Kelly said, her grief morphing to anger. "Because you're wrong."

She turned and ran away from me, wiping her eyes.

November 17, Saturday

"HOW IS YOUR MUM?" Hugh asked.

I was sitting in the treehouse, Skyping with Hugh. "She's the same."

He sighed. "I miss you. I want you and Trudy to come home."

I held Trudy up so she could see Hugh and he could see her, too. "We both want to be there. Hopefully soon."

"Hey, your hands look terrible—you aren't cleaning again, are you?"

251

I instantly curled my fingers into my palms. Without the salve Will had supplied, my hands were more raw and itchy than ever. "Just normal household stuff."

"Are you sure?" he asked suspiciously.

"Yes," I lied.

"How's the book coming along?"

"Great," I lied again. My hands were too painful to type. But thankfully, I was almost finished cleaning Tyler's room, and once it was done, there would be nothing else to clean, and my, um, *issue*, would be gone.

"Hey," Hugh said, leaning into the camera and wagging his eyebrows. "Can we... you know?"

But I wasn't feeling it—the treehouse was cold and creaky, and I wanted to get back to the house... to clean.

"I can't. Maybe next time?"

He nodded amiably. "Bye, Love. Bye, Trudy!"

I ended the connection, then closed my laptop. I was sitting at the little wood table inside. I ran my fingers over the place where three sets of initials had been carved—JH, EG, and DV—for me, Emma, and Deidre. But at some point, someone had chiseled out Deidre's initials, as if they were obliterating the memory of her. It was a petty act of vandalism.

I sighed, reminding myself the evidence pointed to the fact that Deidre had run away, so I needed to start believing it, too, no matter how anticlimactic it seemed. Deep down, I guess I was feeling rebuffed like her sister Kelly—unwilling to believe that Deidre could've reached out all this time, but had chosen not to.

I stood and walked out onto the treehouse deck, calling for Trudy to follow. My head turned on its own accord to glance at Will's house, now more visible since flame-colored leaves had begun to fall. I realized people were standing in front of his house. I used my phone to bring the people into focus.

Tiff and a big man I didn't recognize—her husband? Considering the familiarity in their body language, it would seem so. A child hovered next to Tiffany—her daughter, I presumed, and she appeared to be afraid.

The man was shouting, and making threatening gestures toward Tiffany. She leaned forward and said something back that he must not have liked because he raised his hand as if he was threatening to hit her. She retreated and gathered her daughter next to her, then turned and attempted to go in the house, but the man grabbed her by the arm.

I saw Will's truck zoom into the picture. He was out of the vehicle practically before it stopped, charging the man and pulling his hands off Tiffany. Will punched the man in the jaw and he dropped to the ground. Then Will straddled him and wrapped his hands around his throat. The man flailed, but Will didn't relent. In the background, the shrill screams of Tiffany and her daughter reached me. Tiffany touched Will's back and he finally relented. He pushed to his feet and slowly, the other man began to move. Will dragged him up, then gave him a push toward a vehicle, and the man left.

My heart was pounding. The man certainly deserved Will's anger—but from my vantage point, Will had almost killed the guy.

Just how much violence was the animal doctor capable of?

November 18, Sunday

I WAS ELBOW-DEEP into a box of ratty old sweatshirts when I heard a car pull into the driveway. I'd cleared a corner of the window in Tyler's room, so I peeked out, surprised to see the Sheriff's vehicle rolling to a stop.

My pulse blipped higher. I harbored mixed feelings for Sheriff Tomlin. Early on I'd suspected him of covering up Deidre's disappearance—or at best, not caring. Then I'd learned he and my mother had had an affair when he was separated from his wife, but that had ended when he and his wife had reconciled. He'd admitted to me he'd wondered if the rejection had triggered my mom's hoarding. To make up for ending the affair, he had smoothed over Tyler's arrest for assaulting a former girlfriend.

Detective Terry seemed to think Sheriff Tomlin was no more corrupt than any other small town law man, but overall wanted to do the right thing. I still didn't know what to make of him.

As I made my way to the front of the house, I wiped my hands on the tail of my shirt, wincing at their raw sensitivity. He knocked and I swung open the door.

"Hello, Jane."

He looked friendly enough today. "Hello, Sheriff, what brings you by?"

He held up a plastic bag holding the bone fragment I'd found. "This."

My heart began to pound. "Why don't you come in?"

I didn't want to have the conversation on the porch, and besides, I wanted him to see the house was still absent of the hoard that had prompted an anonymous report to his office and a message from him to my mother threatening to have her cited.

He moved his portly body through the doorway, and glanced around in apparent approval. "I see you've got the place looking nice."

"Thanks. About the bone?"

"Oh, right." He extended the bag to me. "It's animal bone—specifically, swine, no surprise there. Happy now?"

I nodded, but honestly, I felt a little deflated. Which was crazy because it was good news. How morose had I become? I remembered Tyler's accusations that I didn't want to be happy. Maybe he was right. "Thank you, Sheriff, for humoring me."

"You're welcome," he said, then gave me a little smile. "How's your mother?"

I looked in the direction of the bedroom, wondering if she could hear his voice. "She's improving, I think."

He wet his lips. "Would you mind if I said hello?"

I blinked. "Not at all. She's sitting up in bed, just down the hall to the right."

"I, uh, remember," he said sheepishly.

My face warmed. "Right."

Call me a nosy daughter, but after a few minutes, I was curious about what he might be saying to Mom, and it occurred to me I probably shouldn't have let him go by himself. What if she didn't want him there?

I crept down the hall, then stopped when I heard his voice.

"... she's a fine girl, Sharon. I can see why you're so proud of her. Maybe a little too curious for her own good, but she kind of reminds me of you." He laughed.

I frowned. Was he talking about me?

"Anyway, I just wanted to say hello, and... well, woman, I still love you." He sniffed mightily, then I heard footsteps. I turned and trotted back to the living room to cover my eavesdropping. But my mind was reeling.

He loved my mother, the way a man loves a woman. It was a shock to my sensibilities to think of her in those terms.

And it made me even more sad for the way her life had turned out.

November 19, Monday

"BUT I MISS YOU so much," Hugh said, pouting. "Jane, when are you going to make some decisions concerning your mother? You can't stay in Accident indefinitely."

I was in my old bedroom, Skyping with Hugh. "I know," I said, nodding. "It's on my mind every day, too."

"I want to set a wedding date soon."

I blinked. "You do?"

He laughed. "Yes, Jane, I do. Call me crazy, but I want to start our life together."

I smiled. "I want that too." Then I angled my head and unbuttoned the top of my blouse. "Do you wanna... you know?"

Hugh grinned. "I thought you'd never ask."

I unbuttoned the second button, then stopped when a rumbling noise reached my ears. My nipples instantly hardened, and my pulse ramped up.

"Are you okay?" Hugh asked.

I realized it was only the sound of the clothes dryer kicking off, and smiled to cover the little jolt of disappointment. "Where were we?"

November 20, Tuesday

"IT'S SO KIND of you, Jane, to come and pick me up from the clinic," Ms. Jeffson said from the backseat of the Caddy. "I know you must have your hands full taking care of your mother."

"The home healthcare aide is with her this morning," I said. It was Owen's last week—he would be missed. "And I needed a little outing. It's good to see you."

"It's good to see you, too. How is the book progressing?"

"It's going well most days, thank you. I've finally gotten into a good routine, and it feels good. And my editor seems really pleased with the first half of the manuscript."

Ms. Jeffson smiled. "That's wonderful. So you've found your muse."

I lifted an eyebrow. "Hm?"

"Your muse," she said in a tinkling tone. "Accident is your muse, how about that?"

I frowned and was processing her pronouncement when I caught her reflection in the rear view mirror and noticed a grimace of pain.

"Are you feeling okay?" I asked gently.

She nodded, still grimacing. "It's getting worse now, but I'm okay."

"Getting worse?"

"I have cancer," she said as pleasantly as if she'd said, "I have curly hair."

Sadness stabbed my heart and I inadvertently hit the brake. "I didn't know... I'm so sorry." I had taxied the woman from the clinic a dozen times, yet it hadn't occurred to me she might be seriously ill.

She gave a dismissive little wave. "It's okay, Jane. Don't feel sorry for me. I've lived a wonderful life, and if I'm lucky, I'll be around a little while longer to enjoy even more of it." She smiled wide. "I'm so happy I'll be seeing all my family in two days."

I smiled back. "That's nice. Is it a special occasion?"

She squinted. "It's Thanksgiving, dear."

My eyes widened. "Thanksgiving is in two days?"

Ms. Jeffson tittered. "My, you have been away for a while."

November 21, Wednesday

"I HAVE ONE turkey left," the man behind the meat counter said. "And it's twenty-two pounds."

I winced. "Twenty-two pounds. I don't need one that big."

He shrugged. "Sorry."

"How about a turkey breast?"

"Out."

"Turkey roll?"

"Out."

"Sliced turkey deli meat?"

He gave me a flat smile. "Miss, it's the day before Thanksgiving and we close in fifteen minutes. How about a nice pork tenderloin?"

I frowned and he turned his attention to the person who'd walked up behind me.

"Any more turkeys?" she asked hopefully.

I knew that voice. I turned to see Will's sister Tiffany standing there looking all Miss Alabama. No wonder the guy had dismissed me.

"One," the guy said, beaming as if he'd shot it himself.

"But I was just about to buy it," I cut in.

He frowned. "You said it was too big."

From out of nowhere, Will appeared with a cart and an adorable little girl walking next to him. "Hi, Jane. This is my niece DeeDee."

"Hello," I said, and she gave me a shy smile.

"Is there a problem?" Will asked.

"One turkey, two women," the guy behind the counter supplied.

"We could split it," Will suggested.

"And each have half a bird?" Tiffany asked. "No. Why don't we invite Jane to our house?"

I balked. "Oh, I couldn't... my mother is bedridden."

"Oh, I'm sorry," Tiffany murmured.

"But why don't you and Will and DeeDee come to eat with us?"

"I don't know," Tiffany said, looking at Will.

"Tyler and his wife are coming," I said to Will. "DeeDee will have someone to play with."

Will glanced at Tiffany, then she shrugged. "Okay, sure.

Will's smile sent warmth to unwholesome places. "Thank you, Jane. We'll see you tomorrow."

When they walked away, I turned back to the man behind the counter and announced triumphantly, "I'll take the turkey."

He nodded.

"Now... can you tell me what to do with it, exactly?"

He sighed and shook his head.

November 22, Thursday

THANKS TO THE internet, I was able to get the turkey in the oven and a few passable side dishes going, but even so, I was a nervous wreck to host the big meal. Thankfully Stacey and Tyler arrived early with the boys, and I was surprised to find Stacey helpful and easy-going. I felt bad for not extending myself to her sooner. But I didn't blame her for being standoffish considering how my mother—and my brother—had treated her.

"Look what I have," Tyler said, holding up a shiny pair of wire frame glasses.

"Mom's prescription," I said with a smile. "She'll be happy to have these." I put them in my pocket to give to her when she woke up and things settled down. We were going to sit her at the table, and hope for the best.

When Will and Tiffany and DeeDee arrived, the house felt more full and happy than it had in... never, I realized suddenly. The house had *never* been full and happy. Our holidays had been just as contentious as other days of the year. This, I realized, looking around at the smiling faces, was a treat.

Will sidled up to me, looking handsome in a blue shirt and an easy smile. My heart lifted at the sight of him. He dropped a quick kiss on my cheek, then held up a jar of salve.

I winced, and folded my hands into my apron. "Thank you... I've been cleaning."

"It looks nice in here," he said, glancing around the big room that was our living room and today, our dining room. I had set the table where Mom had Skyped from, relegating the kitchen table for preparation.

"Thanks, but I've actually been clearing out the last room of Mom's, um, collection—Tyler's room."

Tyler stuck his head between us. "Did someone say my name?"

"Jane said she was cleaning out your old bedroom," Will offered

Tyler made a face. "Really?"

Will laughed. "I'll bet there are all kinds of treasures in there. Have you found anything good?" he asked me.

"Not yet," I said, studying Tyler's face. He looked sour, but he held his tongue.

"Hey," Will said to Tyler. "Do you want to go hunting with me and the guys the next couple of weekends? We got a cabin at Bayview, and it's nice."

Tyler looked at Stacey. "Would you mind?"

She smiled up at him. "Not at all."

He gave her a kiss. I was happy to see they were healing the hurt between them. And I vowed to stay in touch with Stacey.

Will and Tiffany had brought a few dishes, too, and when the table was set, I felt a pang of pride. My first Thanksgiving dinner. I hoped Mom would be proud, too, even if she couldn't partake of all the food.

I slipped away from the party to her bedroom. "Our company is here, and Thanksgiving dinner is on the table. Doesn't it smell good?"

She was lying in the bed, listless. But I'd dressed her in a nice gown and warm housecoat, and combed her graying hair into a becoming bob. I moved the wheelchair to the side of the bed and helped her into it.

She was, I realized, definitely getting stronger—she hardly needed my help. "Tyler and his family have come, and we have some other guests."

I wheeled her up to the dining room table and everyone quieted, then chorused welcomes. Once everyone had found a place at the table—Will had managed to snag the chair next to mine—I remembered Mom's glasses.

"Mom," I murmured in her ear. "I found your broken glasses in the driveway and Tyler picked up a new pair for you."

I pulled them from my pocket and set them on her face. She blinked and I could see her eyes darting, the pupils dilating. Her head bobbed and she gripped the arms of the wheelchair as if to regain equilibrium. Then she began to flail and grunt.

"Is she okay?" Will asked.

Tyler got up to stand near the chair, looking helpless.

I clasped Mom's hands, but she was strong and resisted. Her mouth moved and she grunted, then said, "Go... go... go..."

I uttered soothing words, then stood and wheeled her back toward the bedroom as she sputtered, "Go... go... go..."

November 23, Friday

"I'M AT THE hospital," I said to Hugh, trying to keep my voice level.

"What happened?"

"It's mom... she had a setback yesterday and she cried all night, was inconsolable. She won't eat or drink, so I know she's dehydrated. I had no choice but to call an ambulance. They're keeping her overnight for observation."

"I'm so sorry, Jane. Can I do anything?"

"No, but thank you." I choked back a sob. "She might have to go to a nursing home after all."

He made a mournful noise. "Maybe the doctors will be able to help her."

My phone beeped and I glanced at the screen. "That's Tyler beeping in. I'll call you soon."

"Okay," he said. "I love you."

I smiled, grateful for his support. "I love you, too." Then I hit the button to connect Tyler's call. "Hi."

"What's happening there?"

"I haven't seen the doctor yet. I'll let you know."

He sighed. "I'm sorry about Thanksgiving, sis. It was a terrific idea."

I gave a little laugh. "I guess I was aiming too high for a happy holiday at the Hunnicut house."

He laughed too. "It wasn't a total loss, we still had a nice meal. What do you think got Mom so upset?"

"I don't know," I answered honestly. "Maybe since she could see, it was the first time she realized her hoard was gone."

"And that's why she kept saying, 'go, go, go'?"

"Maybe. She could've meant 'gone.' "

"That makes sense, I guess. Should I come to the hospital? I could cancel the hunting trip."

"No use in both of us being here. But do you mind stopping by the house to feed and walk Trudy?"

"I'll do that."

"Thanks."

I ended the call, feeling utterly defeated. Maybe Mom's brain simply wasn't working well. And maybe she wasn't going to get better. And maybe by coming back and trying to fix things, I'd done more harm than good.

November 24, Saturday

I WAS DRIVING through town, on my way back home from spending the night at the hospital. The doctors had no answers yet, were still testing Mom and giving her fluids. They had sent me home, probably because the nurses remembered how much my mother had objected to having me around.

My emotions had been all over the place in the last few days, and now I was numb. All I wanted to do was get to the house and fall into my bed and sleep for days.

As I passed the laundromat, I saw Joann, the older woman who worked there, sweeping the sidewalk and waved. She recognized me, and waved her arms to get me to stop. I pulled over, assuming she'd heard about Mom and wanted to know what was going on so she could feed the gossip mill.

"Hi, Jane," she said with a big smile. "I have something of yours, wait right here."

I was too tired to be intrigued, so I just sat there until she came running back out… waving my Wonder Woman panties.

"You left these here the last time you did your laundry," she said helpfully.

"Yes. Thanks," I said, then stuffed them into my purse.

"You haven't been in the laundromat for a while."

"Oh, I was finally able to get to Mom's washer and dryer," I said.

She frowned. "Hm?"

"Repaired," I amended. "I was finally able to get Mom's washer and dryer repaired."

"Oh, good," she said, seemingly unfazed that it meant less business for her. "But I wanted to talk to you about this." She held up one of the flyers I'd posted asking anyone with information about Deidre to contact me.

My pulse blipped higher. "What about it?"

"I knew that Valentine girl. She used to come in the laundromat all the time to wash her clothes. Poor thing, didn't have much of a home life."

"Uh hm."

"Anyway, I remember when she came in, she sometimes had a man with her."

Now I was wide awake. "Who was he?"

She shook her head. "I don't think I ever heard his name, and frankly my memory isn't what it used to be. But I recall seeing his picture since then."

"Where?"

"He was in a photograph with a blond beauty queen, Miss Alabama… isn't that strange?"

November 25, Sunday

I WAS SITTING in the treehouse, waiting to Skype with Hugh when I heard a rumbling noise. I checked the sky for planes, then gave in to the lift in my pulse to see Will's big truck roll into view.

He climbed out and headed for the pig pen, gave Petty a cursory going-over, then walked toward the house. But I could tell from the set of his head (in that ridiculous hat) that the man had something on his mind.

Didn't we all?

I shouted from the treehouse to get his attention, and he waved, then headed across the grassy field, now knocked back to ankle-height by fall temperatures and a fading sun.

"Hi, there," he called, looking up.

"Hi, yourself," I said from the railing. "I thought you were hunting this weekend."

"Had to come back for a breech foal at the Macintire farm."

"I hate when that happens. Everything okay?"

He nodded. "Mother and daughter are fine. Want some company?"

"Sure."

He climbed up and hoisted himself through the deck, then offered me a sad smile. "Tyler said your mom is back in the hospital."

"Yes. The doctors aren't quite sure what's wrong, but they're keeping her for a few more days." I didn't add that among the tests was a psychiatric evaluation. "Have you shot anything yet?"

He smiled. "Oh, you mean the hunting trip? Not yet." Then he sobered. "But Tyler's been... drinking some and... talking."

I was instantly worried. "About?"

"About Deidre Valentine."

I was instantly *more* worried. "What's he been saying?"

"That you've been poking around a lot, and basically looking for trouble."

Will had helped me dig up the garden where I'd found Deidre's quilt, so it wasn't a surprise to him. "Deidre was my friend," I said. "And I promised her little sister I'd try to find out what happened to her." Then I sighed. "But Tyler's right—all my prying and prodding only made things worse for her family, especially since it looks as if Deidre really did run away."

Will wet his lips. "The thing is... I always wondered if Tyler had something to do with it."

I blinked. "Seriously? Why?"

He shrugged. "Things he said about women in general, and about Deidre in particular."

I squinted. "If you thought Tyler was capable of something like that, then why would you be friends with him?"

Will averted his gaze and the answer hit me.

"You befriended my brother hoping he'd confide in you?"

He winced. "It wasn't like that... exactly. I actually like your brother, but he does have a dark side."

"So does your brother-in-law."

He arched an eyebrow.

I gestured to the clearing on the next ridge where his house sat like a picture in a magazine. "I saw the fight... you could've killed him."

"In the moment, I wanted to," he admitted, then pulled his hand down his face. "Thank goodness Tiff stopped me."

"Did Tiffany's husband know Deidre?"

He pursed his mouth. "Yeah, I guess Carl knew Deidre. But Deidre disappeared in May of 2007?"

"Right."

He shook his head. "Carl was working for a private military company then—he wasn't even in the country."

Another dead end.

"Did you finish cleaning Tyler's room?" Will asked mildly.

"Almost."

"Did you find anything... incriminating?"

"No," I said, then added. "Not yet."

He leveled his gaze on me. "So you're looking for something?"

"Maybe," I admitted.

He shifted his stance. "And it's crossed my mind your mother knows something, too... that it might've caused her to start hoarding a few years back. That maybe she was hiding something."

I narrowed my eyes. "How do you know when my mother started hoarding?"

His face blanched. "You showed it to me, I assume it would've taken her a while to accumulate that much stuff."

I pulled back. "You knew, didn't you?"

264

He averted his gaze, then nodded. "Tyler asked me to come up and look at the pigs a couple of times, and I noticed the windows were covered with... stuff."

I gasped. "You were the one who reported it to the Sheriff's office?"

"No, I didn't. But your mom obviously needed help."

I set my jaw as Will's motivations became clearer. "You cozied up to Tyler because you thought he would spill his guts about Deidre... and you cozied up to me for the same reason. Were you in love with Deidre?"

"What? No, of course not."

"Leave," I said, pointing. "Now."

"Jane—"

My phone started pinging with the Skype call from Hugh. I connected it. "Hugh, give me a minute. Will Story stopped by and he was just leaving."

Hugh frowned. "I'll wait."

Will held up his hands and retreated. "Bye, Jane."

I watched him leave, my heart racing like mad. I was breathing hard, my head reeling from his revelations. I felt like a complete fool.

"Jane?" Hugh asked, sounding concerned.

"I'm here," I said, conjuring up a reassuring smile. "I'm here."

November 26, Monday

I WAS IN THE bathroom, scrubbing the commode bowl with a steel wool pad, removing the shadow of rust that seemed permanent... but I was determined to get rid of the stain. I was starting to feel as if I would always be trying to remove the stain of my family's dysfunction.

Lying under the sink, her paws over her nose, Trudy whined, as if she sensed my mood and realized something was wrong. I remembered another time she'd lain on the floor, watching me clean maniacally—when I'd scrubbed every inch of the tiny tiles of our bathroom floor of the London flat.

When a drop of blood pinged into the toilet water, I stopped and watched it curl downward in a little crimson cloud that turned into a pink swirl. When another drop plopped in, I lifted my hand and surveyed the damage the steel wool had done, tearing into my raw skin like little razor blades. Rubber gloves would've spared me, but the pain felt like a release. Tiny shards of the silver metal were imbedded in the open wounds that were now bleeding. I grunted in concession to the pain, then stood and flushed the commode.

I heard the clink of metal against porcelain and didn't realize what had happened until I saw my engagement ring being sucked to the bottom of the bowl and whoosh out with the bloody water.

My panicked gaze went to my empty finger to confirm what I already knew.

November 27, Tuesday

I WAS RACING to the finish, down to only a few drawers and shelves in Tyler's old room. But I was feeling euphoric because I'd worked my way through all the hoard in the room, and all of Tyler's boyhood things without finding anything incriminating. I was giddy with relief, knowing I could at least feel good about searching every nook and cranny of the house, and coming up empty. The marked up photo of Deidre didn't mean anything, not really. I could remember doing similar things to pictures of classmates for no reason other than to feel better about myself.

The sooner I finished cleaning, the sooner I could move Mom into a nursing home, the sooner I could sell this house full of bad memories, the sooner I could escape the pull of Will Story, the sooner I could leave Accident, Alabama, and the sooner I could return to my life in England. I would finish my novel, marry Hugh Green, and live happily ever after.

When I wiped the last drawer of Tyler's bureau, I sat back on my heels in triumph.

Done.

I smiled and pushed the drawer to close it, then frowned at the resistance. I realized I'd knocked it off the runner, so I pulled out the drawer to realign it. In the dark recess, I saw something had fallen on the wooden track rail. I reached inside and pulled out a brown leather cord. Dangling from the end was a small gold key.

Recognition slammed into me. I'd seen the key a thousand times as Deidre had fingered it, moving it back and forth on the brown leather cord around her neck.

The key to her diary.

November 28, Wednesday

"THANKS FOR THE address, Stacey," I said into the phone.

"No problem," she said. "I told Tyler they need to find a better hunting cabin next time. The cell service there is terrible."

"I'd rather talk to him about this in person anyway."

"If it's about your mother, I'll load up the boys and track him down."

"I'm already heading toward the lake," I said. "But thank you."

I ended the phone call with a shaky finger. I'd lain awake all night ruminating about what to do. Should I take the diary key to the Sheriff... so he could tell me once again it was no proof of a crime... or call Detective Terry who would tell me the same thing, only in a nicer way?

Instead I'd decided to confront Tyler in a place away from his family, and if any of his hunting buddies were around—Will included—they could hear it, too. Maybe there would be a *Murder, She Wrote* moment where Tyler admitted everything and fell to his knees begging for forgiveness.

I knew I was being manic—I was light-headed from lack of sleep and I hadn't eaten. I was feeling as if I was reaching some sort of breaking point and wondered if this was how Mom felt just before her stroke.

I drove into the Bayview Lake property and followed a circuitous route. The cabin Will and his friends had rented was in a more remote area than the one Detective Terry had rented. Here it was heavily wooded, and the cabins were more spread out. Along the way I drove past a couple of roads that had been gated off from traffic with "Danger Flood Zone No Trespassing" signs, and numerous Deer Crossing signs. When I reached the address, I saw Will's truck among the vehicles parked there, along with Tyler's delivery truck that he was allowed to use off-hours. The cabin was perched on a rocky ledge of the lake shore. Through the bare trees I could see the sparkle of green water below.

I parked the Caddy and hesitated. Storming a cabin full of men with guns suddenly didn't seem like the brightest idea. I climbed out and by the time I reached the door, I'd decided to talk to Tyler privately.

I knocked on the door and waited, second- and third-guessing myself. When Will opened the door, we both blinked.

"Hi," he said.

"Hi." I brought up my chin. "I need to talk to Tyler."

"Come in," Will said.

"I'd rather he come out."

Will looked concerned. "Is your mother okay?"

"Will you get Tyler, please?"

Will nodded, then disappeared. Booming voices and laughter sounded from inside. Just as I suspected, the hunting and fishing parties so many men had at these cabins were really just parties for wearing camouflage gear and drinking.

When Tyler appeared at the door, he was holding a beer and I could tell it wasn't his first. "Jane, is everything okay?"

"There's no change with Mom," I said quickly.

"What then?"

"I found this in your old room." I held up the brown leather cord, with the key dangling.

"Okay," he said, reaching forward to take it. "What is it?"

"It's the key to Deidre's diary," I said through gritted teeth. "How did you get it?"

His expression changed. "Deidre's diary? That's what this is about?"

"Yes, and I want an explanation."

He gave an angry scoff. "There's no explanation, Jane. I don't know why it was in my room—maybe I found it."

"Found it?"

"Maybe," he said hotly. "I don't know. What are you getting at?"

My heart was pounding and I drew myself up. "Tyler... did you hurt Deidre?"

His face flushed, then mottled. "Are you shitting me? You think I did something to your friend?"

I could feel my nostrils flare. "I'm asking."

"Well, here's my answer," Tyler said.

He pulled his arm back and flung the key toward the water. I watched in horror as it spun round and round, flying long, then landed with a splash.

He turned and jabbed his finger in the air. "Your friend ran away, Jane—end of story. I wasn't even around when she disappeared—I was in a fishing tournament here at the lake with Dad."

My stomach crimped. Now that he said it, I remembered he and Dad had gone fishing because I'd reasoned that with fewer people at our house, it would be easier for me and Deidre to slip away to our grand adventure.

"I'm... sorry," I murmured.

You're as crazy as Mom," he shouted. "I wish you'd never come back." He retreated into the cabin and slammed the door.

That made two of us.

Three, counting Mom.

November 29, Thursday

I WAS SITTING in Mom's room at my makeshift desk, trying to write, but I kept glancing up to her empty bed. The doctors thought she'd suffered a mini-stroke, but they weren't sure. Mom was still refusing to eat, so they were feeding her with an IV.

I set my fingers on the keyboard and began to type gibberish, hoping something would come to me. I acknowledged wryly that the nonsense on the page was a good metaphor for my life at the moment.

Maybe Tyler was right—maybe I was losing it. And maybe that's what the therapist Anne Warford was getting at—maybe I was more like my mother than I cared to admit.

A knock on the door startled me. I was spooking more easily these days, taking care to lock doors and windows. Trudy jumped up, barking.

"You're supposed to let me know before someone gets to the door," I scolded. But when I got to the window, I saw a familiar bicycle lying on its side in the driveway.

When I opened the door, Kelly Valentine gave me a big beaming smile.

I smiled. "Hi, Kelly. You must have good news."

"I do." She held up her phone. "Deidre called!"

I blinked. "She did? When? Where is she?"

"I didn't talk to her," the girl said. "She left me a voice message a few hours ago. Do you want to hear it?"

I nodded eagerly. She punched a few buttons on her phone, then played it over the speaker.

A female voice sounded. "Hi, Sis... it's me, Deidre."

My pulse rocketed—the velvety voice was unmistakably Deidre's.

"I know it's been a while," the message continued, "but I wanted to let you know that I'm okay, and I'm coming to see you... soon. I love you."

The message ended, and Kelly looked at me expectantly. "It's her, right?"

I nodded, smiling. "It's Deidre."

Kelly squealed. "She's coming to see me. I knew she would."

I nodded, thrilled that Deidre was alive, and happy she was finally honoring her promise to her sister. My chest pinged with excitement. "Did you call her back?"

Her smile dimmed a bit. "Lots of times... but it keeps going to automated voicemail."

"Can I copy the number?"

She nodded. "I looked it up—it's a Texas area code."

I typed the number into my contacts list and added Deidre's name. It felt a little surreal.

"I have to go," Kelly said happily, backing away. "Should I tell Deidre anything for you when she comes to see me?"

"Just that Emma and I would love to see her if she has time."

"Okay! Bye!"

I waved, feeling light headed from the revelation, stinging with shame and remorse. I was hellbent that something horrible had happened to Deidre, and that various family and friends had been involved—my brother, my father, Will... even my mother. How many bridges had I burned?

The first person I called was Emma.

"Good news," I said when she answered. "Deidre left a voice message for her sister—she's coming to see her."

"Really?" Emma asked, her voice high with surprise. "Oh, my goodness, that's terrific! Did she say where she's been all this time?"

"No, but the number she called from was a Texas area code, so she must've gone to Dallas after all."

"And found a cowboy," Emma added with a laugh. "Did she say when she's coming?"

"She didn't, but I told Kelly to tell Deidre that you and I would like to see her."

"Definitely. Won't that be fun? I wonder if she's changed."

"Probably some, like us."

"True... I wonder if she has children."

"Wow, it's hard to think of her as a mother, but maybe," I conceded. "I just hope she reaches out when she comes to town."

"So do I. Will you let me know if you hear from her?"

"Sure."

I ended the call on a smile. Then I took a deep breath, pulled up Detective Terry's number, and connected the call to tell him how utterly, completely, wildly wrong I'd been about absolutely everything.

November 30, Friday

I WAS SITTING with my hands on the keyboard, trying to force the words to come. It had been a long, unproductive day, and I was beyond irritated with myself. I had my ending to the story—Deidre had simply run away, after all—so why couldn't I write it?

Because I couldn't be happy about a happy ending?

To be fair, I was still churning over my lost engagement ring, too, trying to figure out how I was going to break the news to Hugh.

And my mother's unexplained setback had me in knots.

Trudy yapped, signaling she needed to go outside. Relieved at the reprieve, I walked through the quiet, empty house and out onto the porch. Dusk was disappearing quickly and the air held a distinct chill, a reminder of the advancing season. I followed Trudy into the yard, encouraging her to hurry while I rubbed my hands over the goosebumps on my arms.

My phone buzzed with a text message and I glanced at the screen.

Deidre Valentine.

My pulse jumped in surprise and pleasure. I'd called the number Kelly had given me and left a voice message after the automated tone, saying hello to Deidre and if she came back to Accident, I'd love to talk to her and catch up. But honestly, I hadn't expected a response. After all, if Deidre had wanted to reach out, she could've done so years ago.

Hi, Jane. It's Deidre. Got your vm. I'm in Accident, saw your flyer, would like to see you.

I smiled. *I'm at the house—come on up.*

On my way out of town... can we meet somewhere?

Sure... I could call Emma. She'd like to see you too.

Maybe next time. Would like to talk in private.

I hesitated. The voice I'd heard on Kelly's phone was definitely Deidre... so why was I suddenly leery? *Meet me in the place where you and Emma and I hung out after junior prom.*

The cemetery... 30 minutes?

I relaxed. It was Deidre... only the three of us knew that bit of trivia. *Ok... can't wait to see you.*

Same here.

"Want to go for a ride, Trudy?"

She barked adorably and followed me to the Caddy. On the drive to the cemetery, I chalked up my jumping nerves to the uncertainty of reunions—they rarely turned out to be as satisfying as one hoped.

And it occurred to me since Deidre had read the flyer saying I had something that belonged to her, she might expect me to bring it. I would have to explain the Sheriff had her flying geese quilt... and we'd have a big laugh over the suspicions surrounding her disappearance.

I parked at the mouth of the cemetery, in the most public area. My heart was pounding with anticipation. I'd waited only a few minutes when a gray car pulled in and drove toward me. I noticed the car rental plate on the front and wondered if Deidre had driven all the way from Texas.

The car stopped next to mine, driver side to driver side. I zoomed down the window, and the other window zoomed down... but all I saw was the barrel of a gun.

"Get in," a voice said. *"Now."*

I recognized the voice and in the span of a few seconds, the pieces of the puzzle fell into place.

"Oh, God," I murmured. "Not you."

December 1, Saturday

"WAKE UP... come on, Jane... wake up!"

I resisted waking because a heavy sense of dread held me down. Something was terribly wrong.

"Wake up, dammit!"

A firm hand shaking my shoulder brought me to the surface. I slowly blinked my eyes open, knowing I wouldn't like what I saw.

Eddie Hopper, Emma's beloved husband, glared down at me in the dim light of a lantern. "I thought you were dead."

And I thought you were a good man.

I couldn't speak because of the tape covering my mouth, so I had to be satisfied with sending daggers at him with my sleep-crusted eyes. I couldn't tell if he was relieved or irritated I was still alive, but fear hummed in my blood like menthol. My mind was still foggy from whatever was on the rag he'd held over my face when he'd abducted me. I vaguely remembered getting off one good long scream at the cemetery before things had gone black. In hindsight, I shouldn't have agreed to meet at the graveyard because if things went sideways, there was no one to help.

But then I'd been expecting to meet Deidre, my long-lost friend, not the person who had been her apparent assailant. My stomach roiled at the implication... Deidre was dead and Emma was living with a monster.

Eddie scowled deeper. "Don't look at me like that, Jane. I didn't want to do this. But you wouldn't leave well enough alone. You had to come back and start asking questions and poking around." He pulled his hand down his face, then walked away, his shoes scuffing against a rough surface.

My mind was chugging like a wheel through molasses, trying to comprehend what he was saying and how everything fit together. Deidre's secret lover she'd hinted would be scandalous if anyone found out—it was Eddie. And it was—in his warped opinion—my own fault I was in this predicament.

I forced myself to calm enough to gradually become aware of my surroundings. I was lying on my side on a scratchy blanket over a lumpy mattress so thin I could feel the springs beneath it. My wrists were bound behind me and my ankles were also tied. My fingers and toes were numb, so I'd been trussed up for a while. Overnight? My bladder said probably. We were indoors, but the air was cold and deathly still, absent the white noise of electricity. An out building of some kind? And either it was dark outside or any windows were covered.

Eddie was agitated, pacing with the lantern. The glow of it allowed me to ascertain we were in a small wood structure with a fireplace and sparse, rustic furnishings. A rifle leaned against a wall, and I remembered the barrel of a gun pointed at me through the car window. My heart seized when I realized my cockapoo Trudy wasn't with us... and what he might've done to silence her. I pushed away the thought, hoping she'd run from him at the cemetery. But being lost and loose in a rural area held other dangers—she would be terrified.

As was I.

The scent of fish permeated the cool air. We were near the lake, I realized... probably in one of the countless hunting cabins that were rented and privately owned. Which meant someone could be nearby... near enough to hear me scream?

I lifted my head, groaning at the pain in the back of my neck from sleeping in an unnatural position. Eddie came back to me, frowning. I grunted against the tape, hoping he would remove it, and tried to pull myself up to a seated position.

"Be still or I'll put you back to sleep."

I stilled. And I wondered why I'd ever thought Eddie was handsome—in the yellow light of the lantern his features were harsh—and cruel.

He gave me a sad smile. "No one's looking for you, by the way... they'll find a typed note in your car that you decided to disappear because you couldn't live with yourself any longer after what you did to Deidre."

My eyes widened.

He looked pleased with himself. "Kind of ingenious, don't you think? And it makes sense. She spent the night at your house the day before she disappeared... and you were the last known person to see her... and you dug up her quilt in your garden—the quilt everyone will think you buried."

Scarily, he was right. My mind tumbled ahead of him, visualizing how the other pieces of evidence could be similarly positioned. I could've been the one who gouged Deidre's initials out of the wooden table in the treehouse, then tossed the chisel in the firepit... I could've drawn the devil's horns on her picture... I could've kept the key to her diary.

But why would I hurt my friend? I shook my head against the blanket, grunting.

"Oh, yes," he corrected me cheerfully. "Because you suspected Deidre was having an affair with your father, who was known to, shall we say, have a weakness for young women."

In my mind the incriminations kept unfolding... Detective Terry would think my mother had called him to point the finger at me, so to distract him, I'd sent him on a wild goose chase.

Eddie made a thoughtful noise. "I'll keep you here until everything dies down, then I'll have to do to you what I did to Deidre." He reached forward and caressed my cheek. "Don't worry—it won't be so bad."

My blood ran cold. He was completely mad, a man with a split personality. What had he done to Deidre? And what would he do to me before he offed me and tossed my body somewhere it might be found months from now—or never?

Hot tears welled in my eyes, blurring my vision. More than one writer had committed suicide under the pressure of delivering a manuscript—would everyone think my deadline had helped to push me over the edge? Hysterically I wondered if I'd be a bestseller posthumously due to macabre interest versus my mother buying every copy she could hoard.

What would Hugh think? And my mother and brother?

And Will?

My heart squeezed over all the life I wouldn't get to live. Like Deidre.

A faint sound reached me. Eddie heard it, too, because he made a startled movement. The noise sounded again, this time more loudly... but still indecipherable. I blinked furiously to clear my vision. The room went dark—Eddie had extinguished the lantern. And he'd moved away from me. As my eyes adjusted to the dark I saw him near the wall—near a window?

Again the noise sounded, and this time I could make it out—the bass howl of a dog... no, more than one dog.

"Hunting dogs," Eddie murmured.

My pulse hammered higher. Hunting dogs were notorious for running on their own for hours on end, rounding up prey and herding it back to their master. So the presence of dogs didn't necessarily mean a human was nearby... but it was possible.

I screamed into the tape over my mouth, which produced almost no sound but nearly punctured my eardrum. I worked my jaw furiously and managed to rip the tape painfully from my upper lip. I stabbed at the loose end with my tongue, but quickly realized I wouldn't be able to push the tape off.

But I might be able to pull it in.

I gnashed my teeth against it, snagging an end, then worked to chew it into my mouth. It was slow going—and painful. I choked on my own saliva and the bitter taste of the adhesive. It crossed my mind I might asphyxiate myself to death on the wad of tape... but since that seemed preferable to whatever Eddie Hopper had in store for me, I kept going.

"Be quiet," he hissed. "Or I'll have to shoot you."

And the sound of a shot in these woods wouldn't necessarily raise an alarm. Still, the crescendo of the approaching hunting dogs emboldened me—especially when I heard a voice shouting, "Jane... Jane!"

Will?

With a rush of adrenaline, I ripped the rest of the tape into my mouth, gagged, then spit it out. I gulped air and my lungs quivered as I dragged in oxygen. "Help!" I shouted. But it came out as a hoarse whisper.

Suddenly Eddie was standing over me with the rifle pointed at my chest. "Shut up!" he hissed. Even in the dark, I could see the lethal glint in his eye.

A crashing noise sounded and the gun went off with a loud crack. I flinched. But when Eddie fell to the floor, I realized he'd been shot, not me.

The room was suddenly filled with the echo of barking dogs, human voices, and bouncing beams of light. Everything sounded gluey and I felt light-headed, but I focused in on the faces of the people who had come to my rescue: Detective Jack Terry, Sheriff Tomlin, and Will.

I gave him a lopsided smile and he stroked my hair while the other men loosened my bindings.

Then I focused on the faces of the animals that had come to my rescue: a tall baying red bloodhound with floppy jowls and ears... and—

I blinked to be sure I saw what I thought I saw.

It was Trudy!

December 2, Sunday

"YOU ARE ONE lucky lady."

Detective Terry stood next to the hospital bed where I sat, dressed and waiting for my ride home. His face was grim. "If Dr. Story hadn't noticed your dog running along the side of the road, we might not have found your car when we did."

I winced. "So you didn't believe the note Eddie planted that I'd disappeared?"

He grunted. "Even if I'd wanted to, Will wouldn't let me. He insisted you'd never leave your pet like that."

I smiled. So true.

"Then the man produced a hunting dog that can track a human scent like a law enforcement canine."

I was still soaking it all in. "How's that possible, when Eddie had me in his vehicle?"

"Apparently people riding in cars shed skin cells through the exhaust." He shook his head in wonder. "Damnedest thing I've ever seen, that hound running along the road following your scent over all that terrain, over all those miles, from a single glove we found in your car. Led us right to the cabin."

"I owe that dog my life," I murmured.

"And his handler," Jack said. "Will never missed a beat—he knew just how to help his dog find you."

I swallowed hard. "Yes, I owe Will, too."

He frowned. "You shouldn't have gone to the cemetery alone."

"I thought I was meeting Deidre... I was sure it was her voice on her sister's phone. And when I got the text, I told the person to meet me in a place only she and Emma and I knew about."

"And Emma's husband," he added.

I nodded in concession. "Did Eddie live long enough to say anything about Deidre?"

The detective shook his head. "He was dead by the time we got to him. Sheriff Tomlin is a good shot—thank goodness."

Remembering how close the barrel of Eddie's rifle had been to my chest, I had to agree. "Who gave the news to Emma?"

His mouth twitched downward. "The sheriff. He said she took it pretty hard. She had no idea her husband was... what he was."

A lump rose in my throat. Emma must be devastated.

"You'll have to give a formal statement when you're out of the hospital," Jack said. "But in the meantime, did Hopper tell you anything pertinent about the Valentine girl?"

I bit into my lip. "Only that he was setting me up to take the fall for her disappearance. And... he said he was going to do to me what he'd done to her."

Jack grimaced, then he shifted. "So when do you get out of here?"

"As soon as my brother gets here." I gave him a smile. "Other than being dehydrated and a few bruises, I'm no worse for the wear."

He frowned, then pointed to my red, scaly hands. "Is that because your wrists were tied?"

I folded my fingers into my palms. "No. I've been, um... cleaning... a lot." So much so, I'd accidentally flushed my engagement ring down the commode. I had the same compulsive tendencies as my mother, except hers was to hoard, and mine was to unhoard. If it wasn't so dysfunctionally complementary, it would be sad.

He gave me a knowing smile. "How is your mother?"

"Still recovering from her setback. She's going to be in the rehab unit for a few more days, then hopefully she can come home."

"Do you think she left me that voice message because she had suspicions about Hopper?"

"I don't know. I confess I thought she was going to point the finger at someone else."

"Your brother?"

I winced and nodded. "I'm not proud of my suspicions."

"I had my suspicions about Tyler, too," Jack said. "But I'm glad I was wrong."

A rap at the door sounded, then opened a few inches to reveal Will Story's cowboy hat... as well as the man himself underneath it. "Can I come in?"

I couldn't contain my happiness... or my smile. "Sure."

Jack Terry pivoted to shake Will's hand when he walked in. "I was just leaving," the detective said. "Take care, Ms. Hunnicut. By the way, do you still plan to return to London?"

I wet my lips, then nodded. "Of course."

His gaze went from me to Will, then back. "Okay. I trust we'll talk again before then."

Will waited until the door closed before offering me a smile. "How are you?"

"Alive, thanks to you."

He grinned. "And Virgil."

"That's your dog's name?"

"Yeah. I have four hunting dogs, but Virgil is special. I raised him from a pup."

"You trained him to track?"

"It's born in him. I just learned how to bring it out. A couple of years ago, he tracked a little girl who'd wandered away from her family campsite, but I honestly didn't know he had it in him to do what he did to find you." His jaw hardened. "Jane... I don't think I've ever been so scared as when I found your car at the cemetery."

"Trudy led you there?"

"Yeah. I saw her on the side of the road and stopped to pick her up, but she ran back to the graveyard."

"That's why she was with you when you found me."

He crossed him arms. "Actually, cockapoos have hunting and herding in their genes."

"Really?"

"Yeah. Having Trudy along kept Virgil going." He winked. "Behind every successful man is a woman barking at his heels."

I laughed, then sobered. "Speaking of successful men, did you ever suspect Eddie Hopper had secrets?"

Will's eyes clouded. "No. And I've been beating myself up over thinking Tyler was involved in Deidre's disappearance."

I sighed. "Tyler hasn't exactly hidden his worst character traits, something Eddie had obviously mastered."

"Have you talked to Emma?"

I shook my head. "Not yet."

"I hear the funeral is Tuesday… a private ceremony."

I nodded. "That's understandable." We'd had a private burial for my father to avoid the tongue-wagging about the lascivious way he'd died, and Emma's situation was far worse.

"Ready to go?" he asked.

"Tyler's picking me up."

He smiled. "I offered to… if that's okay."

I'd been hoping to have a heart-to-heart talk with Tyler, but I supposed since we'd gone more than twenty-five years without one, it could wait. I smiled back at Will. "I'd like that."

Our gazes locked and my vital signs stuttered. But I chalked it up to the life-threatening situation we'd shared. When I stood, I swayed unexpectedly, and he reached for my arm to steady me. "Easy. I've got you. There's a wheelchair in the hall."

"I don't need one," I protested.

"Humor me," he said, leading me out into the corridor.

I relented, allowing him to ease me into the wheelchair and push me toward the elevator.

I dug my nails into my thigh. This knee-weakening feeling around Will was because I was grateful to him for saving my life.

Not because of any other reason.

December 3, Monday

"I DON'T BELIEVE what I'm hearing," Hugh said.

On my laptop screen, his eyes were as round as saucers and under his freckles, his complexion was green.

"Jane, tell me you're making this up, that this is a chapter in your novel!"

"I wish I could," I said ruefully. "But it happened. I'm okay, though, partly because of my sweet Trudy." I nuzzled her close for a kiss and a cuddle. "And partly because of you," I pointed out brightly, "for bringing her to me."

He looked dubious. "It sounds to me like Dr. Cowboy is the one who saved your life."

"It took a village," I insisted.

"I think I should come back there," he said, half rising from his chair as if he might dash off to the airport on the spot.

My heart overflowed with appreciation. "That's so sweet, Hugh... but really, you can see I'm fine." I hoped he didn't look too closely, though, and notice I wasn't wearing my engagement ring. I still hadn't decided how I was going to break the news to him. Ridiculously, I was holding out hope I wouldn't have to.

He looked pained. "Jane, when are you coming back?"

"As soon as I get things settled with Mom," I assured him. "She's coming home in a week, and then I'll see where things stand with her recovery. I have feelers out to two nursing homes that might have availability at the end of the month." I didn't add the morbid detail of why: the placement coordinator explained that deaths in nursing homes spiked over the Christmas holiday.

"Good," Hugh said. Then he backpedaled. "I mean, I'm sorry about your mum, of course, but I miss you, love."

"I miss you, too... and our flat... and London. But hopefully I'll be there to ring in the new year." I was eager to get away from Accident, Alabama, a place that had held few good memories before, and held even fewer now.

Hugh still looked dazed and confused. "So... this Dr. Hopper fellow killed your friend Deidre?"

I pressed my lips together. "That's the general theory. DNA on the quilt is being compared to Deidre's DNA, and to Eddie's."

"You mean her blood and his... bodily fluid?"

"His semen, yes." It still icked me out to think about Deidre messing around with Eddie behind Emma's back.

He winced. "Are the police looking for your friend's body?"

I sighed, then nodded. "Our garden is being excavated." I didn't mention the pig pen and the burn pit were part of the dig because the thought of Deidre dying in either of those places was too awful to comprehend. On cue, outside the backup beep of the backhoe sounded shrilly, over and over. Through the window I observed Sheriff Tomlin supervising with a dour expression. He'd also been instrumental in keeping reporters and news vans off the Hunnicut property.

"They believe this man killed her and buried her on your property?"

"They need to rule it out," I said quickly. "They're also searching around the home where he lived during that time."

"But she could be buried anywhere."

I nodded.

He pushed his hand into his hair and sighed. "I can't imagine you're getting any work done on your novel."

"Not in the last few days," I admitted.

"But your editor is probably excited about this latest development," he said drily.

"Actually, Jocelyn is on vacation, so she doesn't know I was... um..."

"Kidnapped? Abducted?"

"I was going to say snatched," I said, which proved I was still having a hard time accepting the fact that Eddie Hopper was a cold-blooded killer. "Meanwhile, I'm making progress on the manuscript." Except I still hadn't figured out how to end the story.

That wasn't true, exactly. I knew how the story ended... I just didn't want to write it.

December 4, Tuesday

SINCE EARLY MORNING I had been working on my manuscript, but between the noise of the continued excavation outside and my constant checking of the clock, I wasn't getting much accomplished.

I typed a sentence and left the participle dangling while I idly glanced back to the time. I sighed. Sometime today Emma was burying her husband and the father of her children. I felt torn, wanting to reach out to her, yet not wanting to intrude. I suspected she wasn't answering her phone, and I didn't want to leave a voice message. Texting seemed much too casual. On the other hand, I didn't want to crash the private ceremony… or go to her house where she was probably sequestered with her grieving kids.

While I churned, I heard the sound of a car coming up the driveway. I tensed, sure it was another reporter. Since I'd seen Sheriff Tomlin's car leave a few minutes ago, I was on my own to turn them away or ignore them altogether.

I pushed to my feet to get a better look at the car and its occupant from a side window, then gasped to see Emma alighting from the vehicle. I deduced she'd come from the funeral because she was dressed in black head to toe, including large sunglasses. Her lush red hair was pulled into a severe bun. She surveyed the large machines that were systematically scooping out chunks of earth and depositing them in a large wooden box. Another machine shook the box until the soil fell through the screen at the bottom. Throughout, the box was monitored in case something was sifted out of the dirt.

I saw the moment Emma realized what they were looking for. Her hand went to her mouth and she leaned forward, as if she might be sick. I rushed to the door and hurried outside to meet her. By the time I walked to the edge of the porch, she had recovered somewhat and was moving toward the house. When she saw me, she stopped.

I stopped, too, not sure what to do. My heart was breaking for her, but I also wondered if she felt I was to blame for Eddie's death. He'd said I'd forced his hand by coming back to Accident and asking questions about Deidre's disappearance. Did Emma feel the same?

Slowly she walked toward me and climbed the steps to stop within arms' reach of me. She stood still, but her mouth was trembling and her body was shaking… with anger? I couldn't tell because of the sunglasses. She lifted her hand and I braced myself for a face slap.

Instead she threw her arm around my neck and pulled me into a fierce hug. She was crying, and so was I.

"I'm so sorry for what he did to you," Emma said.

"I'm so sorry for what he did to *you*," I murmured.

"I'm so sorry for what he did to Deidre."

"I'm so sorry for what Deidre did to you."

"I'm so sorry for not staying in touch."

"Me too... so sorry."

We stood there for a long while, rocking back and forth, trading sorrys.

December 5, Wednesday

WITH THE ASSISTANCE of the school guidance counselor, I was able to arrange to meet Deidre's sister Kelly during her study hall.

But I was dreading the encounter. The last time I'd seen the young woman, she'd been bubbling over with the news Deidre had left her a voice message that she was coming to visit soon. She'd played the message for me and I'd agreed it was Deidre... I'd been so sure.

Yet considering what had transpired since, it was clear the person calling couldn't have been Deidre. Kelly and I both had been fooled, and it had nearly cost me my life.

But somehow I suspected Kelly wouldn't be so easily persuaded there were worse things than finding out her sister wasn't coming home.

Sure enough, when Kelly walked into the guidance counselor's office, she was wearing a defiant expression. Tall and willowy with long dark hair and chocolate eyes, she was the spitting image of her sister at that age. It made me breathless to remember Deidre just like this, fiery and ready to take on the world... only to be extinguished by Eddie Hopper.

When the guidance counselor excused herself, Kelly nailed me with a sullen gaze. "I know why you're here."

"The sheriff said he'd spoken to your family."

"Yeah. He told me Dr. Hopper kidnapped you and was going to kill you for asking questions about Deidre."

I pressed my lips together, then nodded. "That's right."

"And that he... killed Deidre."

I chose my words carefully. "Dr. Hopper didn't tell me he killed Deidre, but he implied he'd done something to her, yes."

Her eyes welled with unshed tears. "The sheriff said they're digging all over looking for her body."

I nodded. "Including around my house."

"But that's bullshit. Deidre's alive! She left me that voice message."

I felt guilty for having beat the drum of Kelly's hopefulness. "Did you play the message for the sheriff?"

Two tears escaped and ran down her cheeks. "No... my mother was listening to it, and accidentally erased it." Her voice broke off on a sob.

My heart contracted for her. She'd lost her last imagined connection to her sister.

"But you heard the message," she cried. "You said it was Deidre!"

"I... thought it was her," I admitted gently. "But now I realize it was because I wanted so much for it to be her."

She shook her head so adamantly, her hair swung into the air. "No... Deidre can't be dead. She just can't be." The girl began to cry in earnest. "She has to come back to get me... she has to take me away from here. She promised."

I reached out my hand to her, but Kelly turned and ran out of the room, wiping at her tears.

December 6, Thursday

"HI, JANE." Nurse Diane Shipple Yancy's eyes and mouth were rounded like a cartoon character's. "I'm surprised to see you out and about."

I conjured up a smile for my former classmate and Tyler's former fling. She'd no doubt heard the rumors about my ordeal. "I came to visit my mother."

She put her hand on my arm. "How are you doing?"

"Fine."

She leaned in. "I'm so sorry to hear what Eddie Hopper did to you."

"Er... thanks."

"I mean, can you believe it? Walking around and acting like an upstanding doctor and husband and father, and all that time, he was a murderer."

I agreed, but I didn't want to fan the flame. "Uh huh."

She squeezed my arm. "How is Emma taking it?"

I frowned. "Hard."

Diane made a mournful sound. "How will she be able to hold her head up in town?"

I frowned harder. "Emma has nothing to be ashamed of... this is all on Eddie."

The blonde looked unconvinced. "You don't think she suspected anything?"

I set my jaw. "No, I don't."

"Not even when we were in high school? She and Deidre were so close."

I nodded, then pivoted to move past her. "I need to see my mother before visiting hours end."

She made another sorrowful noise. "I guess the upside of your mom being sick is she doesn't know the police are digging up your yard looking for Deidre's body."

I gave her a tight smile. "Yes, silver linings. Excuse me." I maneuvered around Diane and found my mother's room.

She was alone. The other bed in the room was empty, and the television screen was dark. Tyler and I agreed it was better if she wasn't exposed to the local news, so we'd asked for it to be removed from her bill.

But the silence felt melancholy.

She was lying stone still, her hands on her stomach. My heart squeezed. I suspected she was missing her own bed and her cat. I rapped on the doorframe, then stepped into her line of sight. "Hi, Mom. It's me... Jane."

Other than blinking, she gave no indication she knew I was in the room.

"Where are your glasses?" I asked cheerfully, then rummaged around in the drawer at her bedside until I found them. I placed them on her face, happy to see the right side drooped less than the last time I'd seen her. "There."

Her eyes tracked across the room, stopping just short of me, as if she couldn't look me in the eye... or didn't want to.

"You look much improved," I said. "Your color is better."

She made a little sound. My mother had always been proud of her looks. Her response made me think she could understand me, a suspicion backed up by her test results. Dr. Kessler said since my mother's last setback on Thanksgiving Day, her brain activity had improved significantly and her motor skills had progressed, but her cognitive response didn't correspond.

Meaning, either the doctor was wrong, or Mom was being stubborn.

I held up a plastic bag. "I brought dry shampoo and your favorite hairbrush."

Her mouth twitched.

I took that as a green light, then positioned her pillow so she sat higher. She pushed herself up with her good hand. I lifted the strands of her lank graying hair and sprayed the roots with the powdery substance, then massaged it into her scalp with my fingers. She moved her head slightly to accommodate my ministrations, and made a few noises.

"Does that feel good?" I asked.

She didn't respond.

I picked up the brush and began to draw it through her hair, distributing the shampoo. "Mom," I said carefully, "some things have happened I think you should be aware of."

She didn't respond.

"Eddie Hopper is dead," I said gently.

She made a small noise, but it could've been pain since I'd encountered a tangle. "In fact," I continued in a calm voice, "the sheriff shot Eddie after he abducted me and took me to an empty cabin at the lake. Eddie thought I was asking too many questions about Deidre Valentine. He said he was going to do to me what he'd done to her."

My mother's hand stopped mine. She squeezed my wrist and made a mewling noise.

I set down the brush, and swung around to sit on the edge of the bed. My mother was looking at me, her eyes full of tears. I was encouraged, but eager to relieve her suffering.

"I'm okay," I assured her. "I'm telling you this because if you've been keeping something bottled up inside about Deidre's disappearance, you can let it go. We don't know what happened to her exactly, but it's clear that Eddie Hopper is to blame, not... anyone else."

She made a strangled noise in her throat, then her tears began to flow freely.

A chime sounded, and an announcement came over the public address system that visiting hours had ended.

"I have to go," I murmured, then added, "I love you."

But she had gone stiff again. I removed her glasses and dabbed at her tears. Her expression was glazed—she'd retreated inward.

When I left her room, I was questioning my decision to tell her about Eddie and Deidre. If Dr. Kessler was wrong and my mother's brain was still scrambled, the bits and pieces about a man dying and a woman disappearing and another woman being abducted might simply have frightened her.

It was only after I was in the Caddy heading home that a realization hit me: The hand my mother had lifted to stop mine was her paralyzed hand. The stroke that had afflicted Sharon Hunnicut had been real... but how much of her stalled recovery had she been faking?

December 7, Friday

I WAS WORKING on my manuscript—editing and reworking the beginning and the middle in my self-sabotaging attempt to avoid the end—when I heard a rumbling noise separate from the machinery still operating outside my window. My pulse tripped higher and Trudy perked up, too, leaving her spot near my feet to lift her head and give a happy yap.

"Calm down," I murmured as I watched Will's big truck roll into the driveway.

Trudy looked up at me quizzically.

"I was talking to myself," I conceded, then moved toward the front door.

She walked with me onto the front porch, but cowered back at the loud noise of the backhoe and other activity. We watched Will walk over to a deputy and extend his hand in a firm shake. They exchanged a few words, and the deputy shook his head to, presumably, let Will know they hadn't found anything during the excavation except an old tractor tire and a few bricks.

Thank goodness. Aside from the fact that I didn't want to think about Deidre's body being here the entire time, I knew we'd never sell the house and the land if someone thought it had been the graveyard for an almost serial killer.

But the digging wasn't over yet. And admittedly, I was surprised they hadn't at least found Deidre's diary... although it might have simply decomposed in the soil.

Decomposed—ugh.

Will lifted his hand to the deputy, then moved toward the house. I leaned against the railing and offered him a smile and a wave.

He grinned and touched the brim of his hat. "Hi, Jane."

Jesus God, he looked good. "Hi, yourself." I nodded to his mud-spattered jeans and boots. "Been wrestling gators?"

He laughed. "Ha... no. Helping Boyd Halihan pull a cow and her new calf out of the mud. It's a good thing cattle are domesticated because they wouldn't make it in the wild."

Inside I was shaking my head over our small-town small talk, so different than when I mixed with my London friends. My life there seemed more than a world away.

"Where are the pigs?" he asked, gesturing to the plowed up pen.

"In the shed for now. I told Tyler this would be a good time to sell them."

"Yeah, he mentioned it."

"You talk to my brother more than I do."

Will removed his hat and ran a hand through his flattened hair. "I admitted to Tyler I suspected he'd had something to do with Deidre's disappearance, and I apologized."

Something I still needed to do. "What did he say?"

"He accepted my apology, said he'd done things he wasn't proud of, and he could understand why I might think that."

I nodded, glad my brother and Will were still friends. "So did you come just to inquire about the pigs?"

"No," he said, climbing the steps and cooing to Trudy, who came running, her tail wagging. "I came to see about my girl."

I smirked at her blatant enthusiasm as Will petted her head and ruffled her fur. She rubbed herself up against him like a little hussy. "She's fine," I said.

He looked up. "I meant you."

I froze, then swallowed hard. "I... I'm fine, too."

He gave me a once over. "You look fine."

I gave a little laugh. "I recovered these jeans and this sweater from Mom's hoard."

His eyes went all sexy. "You forget I know what's underneath. Did you ever find your Wonder Woman underwear, by the way?"

Despite the chill, I was suddenly feeling overheated. "Yes." And dammit, how did he know I was wearing them?

"Hey," he said, reaching out to lift my left hand. "Where's your engagement ring?"

My face flamed, and I pulled back my red, rough hand. "I, um... lost it."

His eyebrows climbed. "When Hopper kidnapped you?"

"No." Although that would be an excellent lie for when I had to fess up to Hugh. "I, um... accidentally flushed it down the toilet."

He smothered a grin. "Accidentally, huh?"

Irritated, I scoffed. "Yes."

"Maybe you did it subconsciously," he offered. Then he splayed his hands. "Or maybe it's a sign from the universe."

"It's neither," I assured him.

He winced. "What was Hugh's reaction?"

I fidgeted with the cuff of my sleeve. "I haven't told him yet."

"Yikes... that's gonna be awkward."

Unbidden, my eyes filled with tears.

His expression softened. "Hey, hey... I was only teasing. He'll understand it was an accident."

I sniffed, feeling miserable. "I hope so. I'm going to tell him when we Skype Sunday."

Will nodded, then set his hat back on his head, his signal he was leaving. "How's the book coming along?"

I was happy for the change of subject. "Good. I'm almost finished."

"You're going to make your deadline then?"

"If I can come up with an ending."

He gave me a wink. "Can't go wrong with happily ever after."

While I pondered his too-simple advice, he leaned over to give Trudy's head a goodbye pat. "Take care, girl."

He strode back to his truck, whistling.

"I will," I murmured.

December 8, Saturday

I WAS STARING at my manuscript, but the words were beginning to blur. Every time I tried to tackle the ending chapters, Will's corny advice ran through my head.

Can't go wrong with happily ever after.

My phone rang and I glanced at the screen. UNKNOWN. I cursed under my breath and hit decline. What had I been thinking to put my cell number on the flyers I'd put up about Deidre? Every reporter in the tristate had my number now and were relentless in trying to get an exclusive on the story.

I wasn't opposed to telling it, but I wanted things to die down a little... the excavating was still underway, although the sheriff's deputy had informed me the search around Eddie Hopper's childhood home had ended, with nothing to show for it.

Besides, I was trying to finish writing my own story.

Can't go wrong with happily ever after.

I squeezed my eyes shut and groaned. I was letting Will mess with my mind... and my career.

Then as if I'd conjured him up, I heard the thumping bass of his goliath truck rolling up the driveway. Trudy heard it, too, and jumped to attention.

"Hm, two days in a row," I said to her. "The man must really like... you."

She yapped her agreement and followed me out to the front porch. Will was swinging down from his truck, then turned and waved to the driver of another truck pulling up behind him. In the back of the second truck was a metal tank of some kind. A man wearing hip-waders got out and greeted Will, who was also wearing the hip-high-rubber-boots-and-overalls onesie. Then Will waved and jogged over to me.

"Hi, Jane."

"Hi yourself. What's going on?"

He smiled. "I hope you don't mind, but I called a buddy who maintains septic tanks and told him about your little, um, accident." He gestured to the backhoe. "I figured since the machinery was already here, why not dig up the cover for your tank and look for your ring."

I was equally elated and nauseated. "You'd do that?"

"Sure."

Humiliation and wonder warred in my chest. Then I lifted my hands. "That would be... great."

Still, I was skeptical... and I didn't want to watch. So Trudy and I retreated to the house and I stared at my computer screen, trying not to think about the details of the search and rescue mission taking place outside.

My phone rang three more times, and three more reporters left voice messages about interviewing me. I declined them all, but it reminded me to phone the DA's office and schedule a time to make a formal statement about my encounter with Eddie Hopper. I wasn't looking forward to reliving it, but it needed to be done.

When I heard a whooping sound outside, I looked out the window to see Will, waist deep in the uncovered septic tank, holding his hand in the air in triumph. It was totally gross, but I gave a little squeal of relief. Will and the other guy high-fived, then Will dragged himself out of the muck holding the found item—my ring, presumably—in his gloved hand.

I met him at the front porch steps.

Will's grin was white in his mud-splattered face. "I found it!" He presented me with the black goo-covered ring. I gave him the best smile I could manage in the wake of the unspeakable stink wafting from it—and him.

"Thanks," I choked out.

"You're welcome. I want you to be happy, Jane."

His unspoken words hung in the air, like the stench around us: *Even if it means digging through crap to retrieve a ring another man gave you.*

December 9, Sunday

"I SEE YOU'RE wearing your ring," Hugh said with a wide smile.

I glanced down at the sparkling diamond I'd soaked and scrubbed and disinfected at least a hundred times since Will had handed it over.

"Of course," I said nonchalantly, then held it up so Hugh could see.

"We should start thinking about a date for the wedding."

I blinked. "Really?"

"Jane, we've dated for a long time, and lived together. We don't need a long engagement."

"Right," I agreed, nodding.

"How are things otherwise?" he asked.

"Otherwise?"

"You were kidnapped, love… by someone you knew… and the man was shot dead in front of you—that has to affect you."

I nodded. He was right—it should have affected me. "Well, I've been having nightmares," I offered. True, but they were more about Deidre than about Eddie Hopper. I squinted—why was that? Because we hadn't yet found her body?

"Jane?"

I blinked. "What?"

"I said you should probably talk to someone, a professional."

I nodded. "Good idea."

"How's your mum doing?"

"Better," I said, hoping it was true. "She's coming home Tuesday, and she'll have a health care aide for a few days, maybe through Christmas. By then I hope to find a place for her to live if need be."

"So you're still planning to come back to London by the end of the year?"

I nodded. "I'm coming back... absolutely... I'm coming back."

December 10, Monday

I DECIDED TO take advantage of what could be my last free day for a while to have breakfast at the Accidental Diner.

My appearance caused a bit of a stir. To be more precise, everyone stopped and gawked until I took a seat at the counter. The waitress Tamara sidled up with a coffeepot and a wink. "Don't mind them. This town loves good gossip."

"Don't I know it."

She turned over the upside-down mug in front of me, then filled it. "How're you doing, Jane?"

"Not bad... considering."

"Eddie Hopper was a surprise," she said. "I think I'd prefer a man who doesn't hide his bad side, thankyouverymuch."

I arched an eyebrow. "How about a man who doesn't have a bad side?"

Tamara laughed. "Not many of them walking upright."

I blew on the top of the steaming coffee, then took a sip. "Has my brother been around lately?"

She offered a flat smile. "Not since the day he came to rip me a new one for telling you about your dad hitting on me."

"You don't have anything to feel bad about."

"That's what I told Tyler." She frowned. "And I thought he was going to smack me."

"So did I. I saw you out by the dumpster. He left when I honked."

She nodded. "Yeah... but something happened to him before that."

I squinted. "What do you mean?"

She cocked her head. "I don't know. Tyler was angry and yelling and I thought he was going to hit me, and then he just... stopped. Before you honked."

"Before I honked?"

"Yeah, it was weird. It was like watching someone change… he just melted. Then we saw you, and he got into his truck and left."

"I'm just glad you're okay."

"Me too. I can't stop thinking about Deidre Valentine… how awful her death must have been."

I nodded. It was on a constant loop in my head, too. Maybe Hugh was right—maybe I needed to talk to someone.

"Ooh, don't look now," Tamara said, "but here comes one of those upright men."

I turned to see Will walking in the door with his sister Tiffany and his niece DeeDee. He smiled and waved, but Tiffany seemed distracted as she led her daughter to a booth. I surmised she was still having marital problems.

"Hi, Jane," Will said.

"Hi yourself."

"Have you finished your book yet?"

I wet my lips. "Not yet. But I'm getting there."

Can't go wrong with happily ever after.

He reached over and picked up my left hand. My engagement ring sparkled back.

"Just checking to make sure you hadn't flushed it again." He grinned, then walked away to join his sister.

Tamara's eyes followed him and she grunted. "Girl, I'd give anything to have a man look at me the way that man looks at you."

I swallowed a mouthful of bitter coffee. The man was bound to this place and these people. "Can I get a menu, please?"

December 11, Tuesday

I GRIPPED the steering wheel of the Caddy, fighting to stay awake as I drove toward the house. I'd had another sleepless night of Deidre tormenting me in my dreams. And checking Mom out of the hospital had further zapped my energy.

"Mom," I said carefully, "you should know that because of what happened with Eddie Hopper, the Sheriff has renewed the search for Deidre." I swallowed hard. "The search for her body, I mean."

From the passenger seat, Mom's head turned toward me slightly.

"And because I found Deidre's quilt in the garden, he decided to excavate the rest of the garden... and some other areas on the property. I don't want you to be surprised by all the activity when we get to the house."

"O... kay."

I almost swerved off the road. My head pivoted to look at her. "Did you just talk?"

She nodded. It was a tiny nod—more of a chin dip—but a definite response.

"Mom," I said excitedly, "this is great!" I was half laughing, half crying. "How do you feel? Are you in any pain? Are you eager to get home? Do you remember what happened to you?"

She didn't respond. In fact, she lay her head back and closed her eyes.

"Okay," I yammered on. "Get some rest. We'll talk later."

I was wide awake now, full of optimism at the prospect of communicating with my mother again—which was kind of strange considering how long we'd gone without truly communicating before her stroke.

December 12, Wednesday

I WAS WORKING at my makeshift desk in Mom's room when I heard vehicles come up the driveway. I looked out the window to see Sheriff Tomlin's car and Jack Terry's SUV. Dread settled in my stomach. This could either be good... or bad.

Although, since Deidre was gone forever, wasn't it all bad?

I glanced toward Mom to find her fast asleep, the cat curled next to her, then I pushed to my feet and headed toward the front door with Trudy pattering behind me. I opened the door before they knocked, then said hello and waved them inside. Winter was finally getting around to Alabama, and the wind had turned whip-cold.

The men offered their greetings and I ushered them into the kitchen where we could talk over coffee.

"Do you have news, gentlemen?"

"The excavation is done," the sheriff said.

My pulse ramped higher. "You found something?'

He shook his head. "No. But I'm satisfied her—" He stopped himself, then corrected. "I'm satisfied there's nothing here."

I was giddy with relief, yet I sensed there was more. "But?" I asked as I set down mugs of hot java.

They each nodded their thanks and took a drink.

"But," Jack Terry said, "the lab results are back from the quilt you unearthed."

"And was the stain blood?"

"Yep," the sheriff said. "Deidre Valentine's blood. We matched it to a baby tooth her mother kept."

I closed my eyes briefly. Deidre's mother had a hard edge, but it spoke volumes that she'd kept her daughter's baby teeth. And what a horrible reason to have to hand one over to the police.

"Was there anything else on the quilt?"

"Semen," the sheriff bit out. "Belonged to Eddie Hopper."

God forgive me, but I was a little surprised the only semen on it was Eddie's. Maybe Deidre hadn't been as wild and worldly as she'd claimed.

"We've also traced the gold watch Deidre sold to Jim Powers back to Hopper."

"So what happens now?" I asked.

"Hopper could still be charged with Deidre's murder posthumously, the DA hasn't decided."

"Some of that might depend on the statement you give," the sheriff said.

"But what good will it do even if he's charged and convicted?" I asked.

Detective Terry made a rueful noise. "Justice for the family... closure."

I drank from my cup. We could all use a little closure. Maybe it would stop Deidre from haunting me at night.

"How's your mother?" Sheriff Tomlin asked.

I looked at him over my cup, the man who'd had an affair with her, and had left her broken-hearted. "She's getting better. She's talking some."

The man's expression lifted. "She is?"

"I'd still like to ask her some questions," Jack said. "Maybe she knows something about the case, something that would be helpful to the DA."

But not before she and I had a pow-wow about it and some other things. "I don't think she's ready for that yet, Detective. But I'll let you know."

December 13, Thursday

"YOUR MOTHER is much improved," Owen McCoy said, putting on his coat.

"I'm glad you think so," I said, walking with him to the door. I was so pleased he was her home health care aide again. "Did she talk to you?"

"Only a word or two, but I can tell she understands, and she's much stronger. The paralysis in her face is better, and she's squeezing a ball with her hand. If she continues at this rate, she'll be up and around in no time."

"Hopefully," I said.

At the door, he turned back. "By the way, Jane... I heard about what Eddie Hopper did to you... and to Deidre Valentine. I'm so sorry."

I nodded. "So am I. We all misjudged Eddie."

"Poor Emma, she doesn't deserve this."

"I know. I wish something good could come of it, but I just don't know what."

He squeezed my shoulder. "You're okay, and that's a good thing."

I smiled. "Thanks."

I said goodbye, then walked back to my mother's room. She was sitting up in bed, watching *Law & Order* on her laptop. If I didn't know better, I might not be able to tell she'd had a stroke. Her eyes were tracking and focused. In her right hand, she squeezed a soft ball over and over.

"Hi, Mom... do you feel like talking today?"

She glanced up at me, then opened her mouth. "W... want... K... can't."

"You want to, but can't?"

She gave a tiny nod, relieved I'd understood her. She had to be frustrated at not being able to express herself. Inspired, I picked up a pen and pad of paper. "How about writing me a note? Can you do that?"

Her eyes lit up, so I positioned the pen in her right hand over the paper. She held on for dear life, and managed to make a haphazard mark. "Is that an 'H'?"

She shook her head.

"An 'R'?"

After two more wrong guesses, she dropped the pen, frustration written on her face. I moved the pen and paper to her left hand, but because it wasn't her writing hand, the mark she made wasn't much better.

"A 'Y'? A 'T'?"

She dropped the pen again, her eyebrows knit.

"You'll get there," I said.

"Tie," she said.

"Tie? Do you mean Tyler? He promised he'll come visit soon. Christmas is always his busiest time, he's working so many hours."

She shook her head. "Tie... puh."

I frowned. "Tie... puh... tiepuh? Type?"

She grunted and moved her head in a minuscule nod.

I glanced at the laptop. "You want to type on the keyboard?"

Another nod, this one triumphant.

I smiled in wonder. Why hadn't I thought of that?

I fashioned a lap desk for her out of a pillow, then placed her hands on the keyboard. "Is that okay?"

Instead of answering, she started tapping keys, first erratically, then more slowly. A lopsided smile bloomed on her face, and I realized how much I'd missed it.

"Good," I said. "We'll both type."

I sat down at my own keyboard and stared at the blinking cursor, urging me on to The End. I listened to the clicking coming from Mom's laptop and sighed. Maybe she could finish my book for me.

December 14, Friday

"THIS IS A nice change," I said to my mother. "Me reading your words."

She managed a little smile, but I could see the fear around her eyes. I realized how nerve-wracking it would be to let her novelist daughter read something she'd written.

"Don't worry," I said. "I don't expect it to be perfect... you're practically typing with one hand behind your back."

I skimmed the text jammed together on the pages I'd printed, trying to pick out words between the typos and the repeated letter strikes and the lack of spaces. "Jane... need to tell you things."

I glanced up for her confirmation and she gave a tiny nod, then visibly relaxed.

I looked back to the paper. "Miss you much... sorry... miss you... love you." I broke off, suddenly too choked up to continue. When I glanced back to Mom, she was asleep. The writing had exhausted her... and she seemed content I would understand what she'd written. I continued reading to myself.

She looked forward to our Sunday video calls... she was lonely... Tyler was distant and had his own family... she suspected he was cheating, like Dad, and it made her say cross things when she visited. They had stopped inviting her... she was lonely... planted a bigger and bigger garden... found the quilt, remembered it was Deidre's... started to worry and spin stories... I'd gotten my imagination from her.

That made me smile.

She was cleaning Tyler's old room and found the picture of Deidre... then the diary key... and had started to suspect the worst... that Tyler had hurt Deidre, or that Dad had... or maybe the two of them together... Tyler tried to be good, but Dad was a bad example.

I stopped—ugh. What a terrible thing for a woman to wrestle with.

And she was so, so, so sorry because she hadn't been the kindest mother.

I'd come to that conclusion myself, but seeing her admission softened my heart.

She'd decided to put everything back where she'd found it... buried the quilt... buried the other things by hiding them under stuff she'd bought... and that felt better. So she'd bought more stuff and buried them deeper... then bought more stuff. She was ashamed for anyone to know about the hoarding so she kept it a secret. Then she'd started attending church and her conscience began to bother her.

Another revelation.

She'd thought of Deidre's mother often and knew how tormented she'd be if I'd disappeared, so she'd called Detective Terry... but then she got sick. When she woke up, I was here and she knew her secret was out. When I told her I was clearing out the house, she wasn't afraid I'd find something incriminating... she was afraid I'd throw something out—the quilt, the pictures, the key—without realizing how important it might be.

My mother sighed in her sleep.

I smiled. The knowledge that Eddie Hopper had been responsible for Deidre's disappearance—not Tyler and not Dad—must have lifted a boulder of guilt and worry from her chest.

She was at peace.

December 15, Saturday

I WAS STANDING at the kitchen window when Tyler came up the driveway in his delivery truck. I grabbed two cups of coffee and met him by the pigpen.

He opened the door and swung down, his expression tight. "Hi, Sis."

"Hi, Tyler. Thanks for coming."

"Happy to put the pigs back in the pen," he said, already moving toward the shed. He glanced around at all the displaced dirt, now tamped back down and covered with grass seed and straw. "Wow, they really dug up the place, didn't they?"

"Yeah," I said, handing him a mug. He set it on a fence post. "I'll have to take it with me, I'm already late."

I jogged to keep up with him. "Tyler, can I talk to you?"

He stopped at the shed door and lifted the plank that served as a makeshift lock. "I thought that's what we were doing."

I exhaled for patience. "Tyler can you stop for just a minute and let me apologize?"

He stopped and turned back with a sigh. "For what?"

"For... thinking the worst of you." Tears pressed at the back of my eyes. "I accused you of doing something bad to Deidre, and I was wrong. And I'm so sorry."

He pressed his lips together. "It's okay, Sis. Apparently, you aren't the only person who thought so." Then he winced. "And I did kind of have a thing for Deidre."

"You did?"

"Yeah, but she always shot me down. And I was pretty immature about it."

I squinted. "Did you gouge out her initials in the treehouse table?"

"Yeah, a long time ago. Sorry—it was dumb." He sighed. "I've done some shitty things, worse than defacing a table. I can't change the past, but I'm trying to do better." He averted his gaze, then looked back. "I'm getting help."

"What kind of help?"

"Counseling," he said. "Anger management, for starters, and Stacey and I are seeing a marriage counselor."

I blinked. "That's... great."

"It's why I've been so scarce around here—it's been hard to squeeze it all in. But I'm hoping Stacey and I'll be in a good place soon so we can step in to help Mom. Then you can go back home to England."

My mouth opened and closed. "That's... great."

Then he looked pained. "Are you really doing okay? I swear, if Eddie Hopper wasn't already dead, I'd kill him with my bare hands." Then he looked sheepish. "Just don't tell my anger management therapist I said that."

I smiled. "I'm really okay. But the therapy is helping?"

"Yeah. I've been working though some things, like how I feel about Dad. He wasn't all bad, you know."

I nodded, then reached for my pocket. "That reminds me. I found some pictures of you and Dad I thought you might like." I handed him the handful of photos and he smiled.

"Yeah, I remember this one… and this one." He stopped and held up a photo of him and my father holding a fish. Tyler looked to be in his late teens. "And this is the tournament I told you about."

"What tournament?"

"The fishing tournament Dad and I were at the week Deidre disappeared."

"Oh, right."

"There's Hank and John and George behind us." Then he frowned. "And there's Eddie, the sonofabitch."

I craned for a look. "Eddie Hopper?"

"Yeah."

"Eddie was at the tournament the whole week?"

"No. He got there as we were leaving, I think. It was his dad's cabin we were using, so he came and went."

I frowned. "The cabin Eddie took me to—the Sheriff said it belonged to someone out of state. Was it the one Eddie's dad used to own?"

"Nah. His dad's cabin was on the part of the lake that flooded and was cut off. It's probably not there anymore. And if it was, you could only get there by canoe." He held up the photos and grinned. "Thanks, Sis."

Tyler opened his arms and I stepped inside for a rare hug. I expected him to pull away after a few seconds, but he kept hanging on. And so did I.

December 16, Sunday

I TOSSED AND turned all night. I would've thought that after hearing Mom's story and after clearing the air with Tyler, my own conscience would be at peace. Instead Deidre pursued me. It was as if she was willing me to find her body. I felt helpless. Eddie could've taken her anywhere… the county was full of valleys and caves and mines and quarries. Not to mention the lake, which was huge and had hundreds of fingers reaching back into the land. If he'd dumped her body there, she would likely never be found.

Toward dawn I dozed fitfully, then startled awake, my heart racing. Something—a detail, a cast-off thought—was hovering in the corner of my mind, waiting to be remembered.

Then the fragment stealthily slid into my memory—something Tyler had said about the cabin Eddie's father had owned.

That cabin was on the part of the lake that flooded and was cut off... you could only get there by canoe.

Or kayak?

The day I had gone to Emma's house for lunch, Eddie had been there, oozing charm... and he'd been getting ready to go kayaking.

I rolled over and picked up my phone from my nightstand, then pulled up a number and connected the call.

Will's sleepy voice came on the line. "Jane? Are you okay?"

"I'm fine. Do you by chance have a canoe?"

"A canoe?"

"Or a kayak?"

"Yeah, both."

"Good. Can you bring the canoe and pick me up in say, twenty minutes?"

He sighed. "You do know it's the middle of December? And it's freezing outside?"

"Thanks—I'll wear a coat."

"What's this about?"

"I'll explain when you get here."

I disconnected the call and jumped into clothes, then wrote a note for Mom while I brushed my teeth. I took Trudy for a quick walk in the frigid morning temperatures, then filled a thermos with coffee and was ready when Will drove up, a green canoe tilted sideways in the bed of his truck, with paddles and life jackets tossed in haphazardly.

"This had better be good," he said.

It the light of day, I was having second and third thoughts, but I calmly explained what I was thinking—that Eddie might've taken Deidre to his father's cabin and committed his evil act there. "Do you remember where it was?"

"Yeah, I was there a time or two." But he looked dubious. "You think Deidre's body is somewhere in or around the cabin?"

"Doesn't it seem possible?"

"I suppose… but why don't we call the sheriff?"

I winced. "Because I want to see for myself if it's still there."

He gave a little laugh even as he turned the truck toward the lake. "Fess up—you needed an excuse to call me."

I smiled into my coffee. That too.

With little traffic on the road, we reached the lake in short time. Will drove a winding path around the lake with the ease of a local. When he slowed at a side road that was blocked, a memory chord vibrated. "I remember seeing this road, with the sign that it was impassable."

"It's been closed for close to ten years," Will said. "I can't imagine there's anything left of the cabins that were once there."

I turned pleading eyes his way.

"But let's find out," he added.

He parked the truck and I helped him unload and carry the canoe to the water. If the air was cold, the water was glacial. My wellies kept my feet dry, but not warm. I was shivering in my life jacket by the time we shoved off.

By mutual consent, we dug our paddles into the water, eager to get our blood moving. The sun was coming up, sending pink light over the water. Will pivoted his head to get his bearings, then steered the canoe in the right direction. Within ten minutes, a handful of white dilapidated cabins came into view. Most of them squatted in water up to the windows, but two sat back in a copse of trees on a rise just high enough to keep them out of reach. They were on their own little deserted island.

"It's one of those two," Will said, pointing with his paddle.

My heart was thudding in my chest. "So Deidre could be here somewhere."

"Do you want me to call the sheriff?"

"Not yet," I said. "Can we look around?"

"I'm not sure that's a good idea."

I nodded. "But can we look anyway?"

His expression was grim, but he guided the canoe over to the grassy island. I stepped out before the canoe stopped, and got a bootful of icy water. I gritted my teeth, telling myself if I'd come this far, I needed to keep going. If Deidre came to me in my nightmares tonight, at least I could tell her I'd looked for her.

Will jumped out and beached the canoe. We tossed down our paddles, then picked our way through rotted brambles, rocks, and washed-up trash to the two cabins.

"Do you remember which one was his?"

"No." Will stepped up to the first one and tried the doorknob. It turned, then the door fell inward. He pulled a flashlight from his belt and shined it inside. A bird flew out and I screamed like a little girl. Will paused to laugh, then we stepped inside. The floor was rotted and the walls were giving way. Animals had built nests among the ropey cobwebs. A few remnants of furniture were strewn about. Will walked the two rooms, then shook his head. "Empty."

But my eyes were riveted to the floor—I was looking for a grave, after all.

"This isn't the Hopper cabin," Will said, picking up a wood sign that read, "THE CALLEY FAMILY CABIN." "It must be the other one."

We hurried to the other cabin. I was already chilled to the bone. Will tried the rusty doorknob, expecting the door to give way, but it held.

"It's locked," he said, then stepped back and used his booted foot to kick it open.

I was impressed.

The interior was black. Will shined his flashlight inside to scare away any birds or other varmints, then he stepped inside. I hung back, partly because my limbs were frozen.

"*Jane.*"

From the sound of his voice, my heart sank to my feet. He'd found her. I choked back tears, unable to move.

Will appeared at the door, and wordlessly, he extended his hand to me.

I shook my head. "No, I don't want to see her, no... I can't."

"You have to," he said, reaching for me.

I moved toward him, crying. I owed it to Deidre to see this through. I braced myself to view her bones, then stepped inside and followed the beam of his flashlight.

Then I gasped. It was Deidre, in a barred room. Thin, bedraggled... but very much alive.

December 17, Monday

"BRAVO, MS. HUNNICUT," Jack Terry said. "This is the case of the century, and you solved it."

I preened. Maybe it wasn't the case of the century, but of the decade, for sure.

Will and I had met the detective at the sheriff's office to give our statements. I was operating on next to no sleep, and was feeling slightly dazed from the events of the past twenty-four hours. I couldn't remember when I'd eaten last, and my reserves were depleted. Thank goodness Will was able to function.

"How is Deidre?" he asked.

"Considering all she's been through, Jack said, "she's in surprisingly good health. Hopper fed her well and kept her in supplies." He looked to me. "The reason we didn't find the diary you mentioned is because Ms. Valentine had it... and apparently she's kept one all these years. I guess Hopper wanted her to have some sort of past-time." His expression turned grim. "But after he was killed, she ran out of food and water. She was days away from perishing. I'd hate to think what would've happened if the two of you hadn't followed up on your hunch."

"It was all Jane," Will said, and turned his gaze on me.

I hugged myself. How cruel would it have been for Deidre to die now after suffering years of captivity? I was still trying to wrap my mind around what Eddie had done to her... and how he'd managed to live a double life. And his words still chilled me:

I'll keep you here until everything dies down, then I'll have to do to you what I did to Deidre.

I'd narrowly missed the same fate she'd suffered.

"When can I see her?" I asked.

"Give her a couple of days," Jack said. "She's still recovering in a private ward of the hospital. Her family has been allowed to visit, but there's a lot to sort out here. The press has descended on the town, so the two of you should be prepared to be bombarded."

"I'll stay close," Will murmured to me.

I didn't have the energy—or the desire—to protest.

December 18, Tuesday

HUGH'S EYES bugged out of his head. "This is like something out of the Twilight Zone!"

I nodded, still numb.

"So this sicko guy held her captive all these years?"

"Uh-huh. For over ten years."

He grimaced. "He wanted a sex slave?"

I'd thought as much too. "No, thank goodness. As strange as it seems, he didn't abuse her sexually, not after he kidnapped her." That was some consolation, at least. There were no pregnancies, no children.

"He just wanted to *keep* her?"

"I suppose so." Not unlike the woman who'd kidnapped Trudy, I realized. In Eddie's twisted mind, Deidre was well-cared-for... except for the whole freedom thing. He'd wanted her, so he'd taken her, and he hadn't wanted to give her back. I shuddered.

Hugh was still shaking his head. "I just can't believe it."

"I'm still trying to process it all myself," I admitted.

"Jane, I'm coming back to Accident right now."

I shook my head. "Don't. It's a circus here. I'm holed up at Mom's and getting lots of rest."

"And you're taking care of her, too?"

"We're taking care of each other. And Will—" I broke off.

"What about Will?"

"He's been... helpful."

Hugh frowned. "I still don't understand why you called him instead of the police."

"He had a canoe," I said, as if that explained everything.

Hugh squinted.

"I should go," I said. "I'll keep you updated."

"Wait—are you still coming home at the end of the year, Jane?"

I gave a little laugh. "Are you kidding? I can't wait to leave this place."

December 19, Wednesday

"YOU HAVE TEN minutes," Nurse Diane Shipple Yancey said. "And no more."

I nodded solemnly as I reached for the handle of the door to Deidre's room.

Diane leaned closer to me. "This," she gushed, "is the most exciting thing that's ever happened to me in my life!"

I squinted. "Except it's not happening to you, is it?"

She straightened with a frown, then huffed away.

I chastised myself—just because I was on edge didn't mean I had to be snippy. And Diane was only expressing what everyone in Accident felt—this was a big, honking story, and it belonged to our little town.

I inhaled, then pushed open the door.

Deidre was sitting up in bed, laughing with her younger sister Kelly. They both turned when I walked in. I waited, trembling.

Deidre stood, arms open.

I went to her and we hugged. I felt as if I were clinging to a mirage.

When she pulled back, she was crying, and I was crying, and Kelly was crying.

"The doctors say I'll be doing this for a while," Deidre said, wiping her eyes.

I couldn't stop looking at her. She looked the same, except gaunt and pale. Her hair was overlong and shaggy, but she was so beautiful, she could pull off just about anything. I had been worried sick about the state of her mind before I walked in, but her eyes gave me hope. Her eyes sparkled with the same fire I remembered. In fact, she was even more animated.

"See, toldja she was alive," Kelly said happily. "The voice message really was from her!"

"Sweetie," Deidre said, "why don't you go get a soda and give me and Jane a few minutes to catch up?"

"Sure. Bye." Kelly left with a wave.

I looked at Deidre. "She never stopped believing you were alive. She's so much like you."

Deidre's eyes went dark. "He threatened to take her, too."

I gasped. "No."

She nodded. "Unless I made the phone call to Kelly from a phone he brought me… and not say anything to tip anyone off."

Eddie had been trying to create the impression she was alive and well somewhere else, so people would stop looking for her.

"It's how he controlled me," she said, her voice vibrating with anger. "Early on, I managed to get a phone and call a church before he caught me."

I nodded. "The minister told me… he thought it was you, but couldn't be sure."

"After that, Eddie kept a closer watch on me… and threatened me with Kelly when he had to."

I swallowed hard. "I'm so sorry."

"It's not your fault. I have you to thank for my freedom… and my life." She entwined our fingers. "Jane… how can I ever thank you?"

"By living your life to the fullest."

"Don't worry," she said earnestly. "I intend to."

The door opened and I thought Kelly had returned. But when we looked up, Emma stood at the doorway, her face unreadable.

None of us said anything for the longest time. I considered leaving, but I was in the middle of this, too. The tension in the room was palpable.

Then Deidre stepped forward and, as she'd done with me, opened her arms toward Emma.

Emma went into her embrace sobbing. They hugged and rocked back and forth, exchanging sorrys and I love yous. After a few minutes, Deidre lifted her head. "Oh, good God, Jane, get over here."

I went, laughing. The threesome was restored.

December 20, Thursday

"HELLO?" a female voice trilled into the phone.

"Ms. Jeffson," I said, "this is Jane Hunnicut. I hope I'm not intruding."

"Jane, hello. Not at all. How are you? I understand you've been through quite an ordeal lately."

"I have," I admitted. "And I'm fine. Actually, that's what I wanted to talk to you about."

"I'm intrigued," she said. "And I'm listening."

"I've been overwhelmed with reporters wanting to interview me, Deidre too. And Emma, God help her."

"I can only imagine," the woman said.

"So I was wondering… how would you feel about putting out a special edition of the *Accidental Post* to cover the story? Definitive interviews of the hometown people whose lives were affected, conducted by the hometown newspaper."

"What a wonderful idea!"

I smiled into the phone. "Of course, I couldn't pull it off without your help, and maybe some of your students. Would you mind giving me a hand?"

She gasped in delight. "I'd be honored, Jane."

December 21, Friday

"JANE, JANE, JANE!" Jocelyn sang into the phone. "The publicity department is going bananas over the news that you're in the middle of the real life mystery that you're writing about… and you *solved*." She laughed merrily. "England might have to pass the torch of Agatha Christie to our newest mystery writing sensation, Jane Hunnicut!"

I was pleased at her enthusiasm, but decided to play coy. "So you think this exposure will be good for book sales?"

My editor screamed. "Are you kidding? Sales will be over the moon! I see translations, I see audio, I see TV and movie adaptations! Jane, this book will definitely be your big comeback."

December 22, Saturday

I WAS SITTING at my laptop, my hands flying over the keys. After all, I had my ending now… and in a nod to Will, the real story was about as happily ever after as it could get.

Across the room, my mother was tapping on her own keyboard. Then she stopped and I heard the sound of the printer kicking on.

"Is it something you want me to read?" I asked.

She nodded.

It had become our routine. Her speech was improving daily, but talking was still too laborious for her to have a long conversation. So if she had something on her mind, she typed it up and printed it for me to read.

Dutifully, I went to the printer and held up the sheet of paper. "Should I read it aloud?"

She nodded.

"Okay..." I skimmed the type, noting how much her accuracy had improved. "Let's see... how are things with Hugh?"

She nodded.

I shrugged. "They're good. He's eager to set a date for the wedding when I get back. But don't worry, I want to make sure you'll be able to attend."

She nodded, and gave me a little smile, then moved her hand in a 'go on' motion.

I smirked, then looked back to the paper. "Let's see... wouldn't you rather be with—" I looked over the top of the paper. "Will?"

She nodded.

I scoffed. "Mother, I'm engaged to Hugh. He's the man I'm going to marry. Will is... local. We had a moment, but that's over now."

"If... you... say... so," she said.

I frowned. "I say so."

She made the "go on" motion again.

I looked back to the paper. "I have a confession to make." I looked up, eyebrows arched. My pulse clicked higher—what could this be? I looked back to the paper and skimmed. "I reported myself to the sheriff's office for all my stuff." I glanced up to her. "You wrote an anonymous letter reporting yourself for being a hoarder?"

She nodded.

"Why would you do that?"

She wet her lips. "Wanted... to... get... well."

My chest expanded with pain and pride. "Oh, Mom."

"And…"

I waited.

Her mouth twitched downward. "Wanted… to… see… Tommy."

I frowned. "Tommy?" Then it hit me. "The sheriff?"

She hesitated, then nodded. Her flush of embarrassment tugged on my heart.

"Mom, you're not the first woman who's been foolish in love." I moved to the side of the bed and leaned down to give her a hug. When I realized she was crying softly, I hugged her tighter.

I don't think I'd ever loved my mother more.

December 23, Sunday

"IT'S GOING TO BE just wonderful!" Ms. Jeffson said, scanning the page proofs of the special edition of the *Accidental Post*. "When it comes out, let's all go stand and give them out on the corner, the way we used to in the old days."

I gave her a sad smile. "I won't be here… I'll be in London by then."

She looked crestfallen. "Oh, Jane. When you go back to England and when I'm gone, no one will be left to resurrect the newspaper."

"You're not going anywhere anytime soon," I said, willing it to be so in light of her terminal diagnosis.

The bouncy woman who had shaped my literary mind returned my sad smile. "I'm not so sure about that."

My heart crimped, but before I could say anything too melancholy, she winked.

"But this special edition of the newspaper is the best going away present you could've given me."

December 24, Monday

IT WAS CHRISTMAS EVE and we were decorating the small fir tree Tyler had brought by.

To be clear, I was decorating the tree while Mom watched from her wheelchair. We were both enjoying a cup of eggnog when I heard the familiar rumble that caused my body to purr.

My mother smiled, and I noticed how much better her paralysis had gotten.

"I'll be right back," I said, then I carried my eggnog to the porch and waited for Will to bring the truck to a crunching halt. When he sprang down, he was wearing a Santa hat on top of his cowboy hat and carrying a big red bag.

"Hi, Will."

He frowned. "I'm not Will—I'm Santa Claus! Ho, ho, ho!"

I laughed at his fake voice. "Okay, Santa, what's in the bag?"

"All kinds of goodies," he said, still in character. He stopped at the bottom of the steps, and pulled out a small gift box. "For you, little girl... for being so good... at everything."

I giggled at his silliness. "What is it?"

"A souvenir, so you don't forget Accident."

"Sounds intriguing, Santa. Can I open it?"

"Not now, little girl. You have to wait until Christmas!"

"Okay," I said, tucking the gift under my arm. "But I don't have anything for you."

"There's only one thing I want," Will said, reverting back to his own voice. "Stay, Jane. Stay in Accident, with me."

I blinked, stunned. "I... I... wow."

He looked at me, his eyes serious, expectant.

The man was tempting, no doubt... but the woman who settled down with him would be settling for Accident... and that wasn't me. "Will, I can't."

His eyes clouded, then he nodded and broke into Santa again. "Well, ho, ho, ho! You have yourself a merry Christmas, little girl!"

Guilt suffused my chest. "Would you like to come in for some eggnog?"

"I have to get these presents delivered," he sang. "I'd better get back to my sleigh!" He picked up the bag and jogged back to his truck, then drove off with a wave.

I walked back inside, still reeling over his request. Then I scoffed. The man hadn't said he loved me, he'd simply asked me to stay in Accident.... with him. What did that even mean?

I closed the door behind me and noticed Mom had nodded off. After tucking a blanket around her, I opened the giftbox...

And pulled out a cowboy hat Christmas tree ornament. I smirked and carried it over to hang on a branch.

This much of the man I could handle.

December 25, Tuesday

ON CHRISTMAS DAY, my mother and I were enjoying a late breakfast when Sherriff Tomlin's car rolled into the driveway. My mother instantly tensed and touched her hair. My heart ached for her—the man obviously still affected her.

When I opened the door, he was holding his hat in his hands. "Hi, Jane. Merry Christmas."

"Merry Christmas, Sheriff. What brings you out on a holiday?"

"I just wanted to check on you and make sure everything is okay."

"Thanks, Sheriff. Everything's fine. Even the pesky reporters are taking the day off."

He nodded. "Good. And Jane, I wanted to say..." He fidgeted with his hat. "Well, I'm sorry I doubted you over the Valentine girl. I hate to think about what might've happened if you hadn't come back to Accident and started asking questions. You do us all proud around here."

I was stunned by his admission... and his heartfelt praise. "That's real nice of you to say, Sheriff. Thanks for stopping by."

He nodded, then he flushed all the way up to his bushy eyebrows. "Actually, before I go, I was hoping I could talk to Sharon."

"Of course."

"In private."

I looked at him and he looked back.

"I asked my wife for a divorce, and she said yes."

I narrowed my eyes. "Don't break my mother's heart again."

His smile rearranged every feature on his face. "I won't."

I stepped aside and allowed him to walk past me, smothering a grin of pure joy.

December 26, Wednesday

I WAS STANDING on a stepladder taking down the Christmas decorations when the sound of a rattletrap vehicle reached us. I looked out the window to see Junkman Jim's jalopy rolling up.

"It's Jim Powers," I said. "I wonder what he's doing here." I hadn't called him about the smattering of things left in the garage. But maybe he had some cash for Mom from things he'd sold.

"I... called... him," my mother announced.

"You did?" I was surprised—and pleased—she was using the phone.

She was getting her confidence back, and some of that probably had to do with Sheriff Tomlin. The man had stayed most of the afternoon yesterday. I'd been riveted to watch her interact with a love interest. Even confined to a wheelchair, she had become bubbly and vivacious. I honestly couldn't remember ever seeing her like that with my father.

Happy.

"Get rid... more stuff... in garage," she said.

I smiled. "That's a real change."

"Think... stroke... made... me... smarter."

I laughed, then helped her wheel out onto the porch to talk to the man. I let her handle the exchange, watched her starting to get back to the woman she'd been before the stroke.

She was getting well. I'd noticed she'd been researching obsessive-compulsive disorders online. Anne Warford the therapist had been spot-on about the hoarding triggers. Now that Mom's mind was clear of suspicions and guilt, she was in a better frame of mind to deal with her emotions in a more positive way.

I was starting to feel as if she would be okay after I left.

Which was good, because it was almost time for me to leave.

December 27, Thursday

I WAS OUTSIDE walking Trudy when Will roared up the driveway. She was happy to see him. So was I, but without the tail wag.

"Hi, Jane," he said, swinging to the ground.

"Hi yourself. Thanks for the tree ornament. It was very… specific."

He smiled. "You're mighty welcome. Did you have a nice Christmas?"

"The best," I said, and meant it. "You?"

"Almost the best," he said with a wink that made me feel all warm inside, like a cup of hot cocoa. I would miss him some, I conceded.

"I came to say goodbye," he said. "Tyler says you're leaving on New Year's Eve?"

I squirmed. "That's right."

"Sure hate to see you go."

"Thanks," I murmured. "But things are under control here."

Trudy yapped at Will, then rolled over for him to rub her belly.

"You're shameless," I chided.

Will laughed and bent down to rub her stomach, then made a thoughtful sound.

"What?" I said.

He palpated the pale skin of her belly. "She's pregnant."

"What?" I frowned, incredulous. "That can't be!"

"Has she been spayed?"

"No… I haven't done… that… yet," I sputtered. "She's never around other dogs…. and Hugh had her checked out after she was returned."

Will winced. "Then I think Virgil might be the culprit. Looks like she's about four weeks along."

"Your hound dog?"

He grinned. "He is that, alright."

Hugh would lose his mind when I told him Trudy was knocked up by a country hound. I shook my finger at Trudy. "Bad girl!"

Will laughed again. "She didn't do anything you didn't do."

Of course a veterinarian would compare our romp to our dogs' romp. "I didn't get pregnant."

"We could try again."

I frowned. "I thought you came to say goodbye."

"You distracted me." He removed his hat and put it over his heart dramatically. "Goodbye, Jane. Parting is such sweet sorrow." Then he put his hat back on his handsome head. "But I have to say, it makes it easier knowing you're taking a little part of me and Virgil back with you."

I was so exasperated, I couldn't speak, could only watch him turn his humongous truck around and drive off.

December 28, Friday

WHEN I PULLED into the cemetery, I got the heebie jeebies thinking about the last time I'd come here. Eddie couldn't hurt anyone anymore, but his charming evil had run so deep, it would likely haunt us all for a while. I couldn't help but look over my shoulder while I fast-walked to my father's grave. The low-hanging gray clouds and blistering wind didn't help.

When I reached the small plot, I knelt to clear a few sticks and leaves from around the bottom of his headstone.

"I can't stay long," I said. "I'm packing and getting ready to leave Accident. I just wanted to let you know we're all good, I think. You'd be proud of the man Tyler is becoming. And Mom is getting well, and she's more happy than I've ever seen her. And I…"

I trailed off, not sure what to say about myself. "I… learned a lot about life when I came back. I learned no one is all good or all bad. You did the best you could, and I love you for trying."

I pushed to my feet and blew him a kiss, just like when I was a little girl. "Bye, Daddy."

December 29, Saturday

I WAS TYPING on my laptop, and Mom was typing on hers when suddenly she stopped.

I looked up to find her staring at me. "Everything okay?"

She nodded. "Proud… of… you."

I smiled. "That makes me feel good, Mom."

"Good… writer."

That made me laugh. "I'm glad you think so. You know I found all the copies of my books you bought."

Both corners of her mouth lifted—a small miracle—then she put her finger to her lips.

"Yes, it'll be our secret."

"The... good... kind."

"Yes, the good kind of secret."

Her eyes watered. "Thank... you... for... coming back."

I abandoned my laptop and went to sit next to her in the bed. "I was happy to."

She shook her head.

I sighed. "Okay, at first I wasn't happy about it, because I was in a bad place in my own life."

She lifted an eyebrow.

"My writing career wasn't going well, and I wasn't writing. And... I had some compulsive behaviors of my own."

She lifted both eyebrows—another small miracle.

"I was cleaning," I admitted. "Way too much."

When she laughed, it startled me. It had always been a rare sound, and I hadn't heard it since I'd been home. "I know, right? You were hoarding, and I was cleaning like a madwoman. In fact, I was driving Hugh crazy. He moved out."

Her brows knitted.

"And then Trudy was dognapped."

"Dog... napped?"

"It's a thing, trust me. Anyway, all that happened just before I got the call that you were sick."

She looked pained.

"It was a rough patch," I admitted. "But Hugh and I are back together, and Trudy came home, and I'm very close to typing The End to my novel."

She reached for my hand and folded it into hers. "No... more... bad... secrets."

"Deal."

I lay my head back against the pillow and we just listened to the house be happy.

I'd finally made peace with this place, with my mother, with my brother, with my father. I'd been looking forward to leaving ever since I'd come back to Accident, Alabama.

So why was it feeling like it was going to be hard to leave?

December 30, Sunday

IT WAS MY last evening at home. The cold, windy day had given way to a frosty dusk, but still, I felt compelled to climb up to the treehouse. It needed its own goodbye.

So I bundled up and for the last time, I climbed up the ladder and hoisted myself through the deck. Then I walked into the little house where Deidre and Emma and I had spent so many hours planning and plotting our lives. In hindsight, it had been an exercise in futility since we'd all wound up in vastly different places than we thought we would be.

Especially Deidre. All three of us thought she would travel the farthest, climb the highest, and grab every brass ring she passed. I believed it was why Eddie had taken her—because he wanted to extinguish her light, to have it all for himself.

But from what I'd seen of her, he hadn't succeeded. I think Deidre was still going to live enough life for ten people. And Emma would bounce back—the woman was as strong as a flowering tree. And I...

Why did that part always stop me? My future was laid out in front of me... London, Hugh, marriage. A beautiful city, a good man, nuptial security.

I shivered.

The sun was setting and the temperature had dived. I walked back out onto the deck, then chanced a last glance toward Will's house.

From his doorknob flew a long yellow ribbon.

For me?

I sighed. For me.

December 31, Monday

I LOOKED AT my watch. "Where is Tyler?"

"You're so... eager to leave," my mother said.

Feeling contrite, I turned back to her. "That's not true. I'll be back soon. But I don't want to miss my plane."

At the sound of a familiar rumbling engine, my mother's head turned toward the window. "Here comes... taxi."

I muffled a groan. Will and I had said our goodbyes. I didn't need another tension-filled ride to the airport to make things more... murky.

"Be nice," Mom chided.

I smiled. "Just for you." Then I dropped a kiss on her cheek and gave her a hug. "I love you. I'll let you know when I land."

Mom's eyes watered, but she nodded. We were good.

I picked up my big pink suitcase in one hand and Trudy's carrier in the other, and walked out of my childhood home feeling like an adult for the first time in my life.

Will brought the truck to a halt in the gravel, then jumped to the ground and lifted his arms. "Tyler and I thought why not bring this thing full circle."

I smirked. "Tyler just didn't want to drive me to Birmingham."

"True," Will said. "But I want to visit my sister and niece, so I don't mind."

Still, I wavered.

"I promise not to be a sore loser," he added.

I smiled, shaking my head at his absurdity. "Okay... and thank you."

"Hey, did you finish your book?"

Happiness ballooned in my chest. "Yes! I'll email it to my editor when I land."

"Congratulations! And did it end happily ever after?"

I hummed. "Not exactly. I decided to go with a more literary ending."

He pursed his mouth. "Too bad."

I frowned at his broad back as he stowed my suitcase in the truck bed. I wasn't about to tell him I'd written two endings—one with a more literary open-ended conclusion, and one with happily ever after. I'd decided to pick which ending to send to Jocelyn once I got back to London.

Will set Trudy's carrier in the middle of the cab, then helped me up into the passenger seat. His hands were warm and familiar now, unlike the first time I'd been catapulted inside the monster truck. That seemed like a lifetime ago.

He banged the door closed, then ran around and jumped into the driver's seat. "Buckle up."

I did, and I braced myself for a long, tense ride. But I needn't have worried. Here I was, churning with all kinds of heavy, unnamed emotions, while he was carefree and happy, singing along with songs on the radio and talking to Trudy through the opening in her carrier.

In fact, by the time we arrived at the airport drop-off, I was a little irritated he hadn't spent the time more… productively.

Will ran around and helped me down, touching only my hand, which had, thanks to his salve, finally healed. Then he bounced away and retrieved my suitcase while I fetched Trudy.

When he set the piece of pink luggage on the curb, he grinned. "I guess this is it, then."

"I'll see you again sometime," I said. "I'll be back to visit."

"But you'll be married to a limey," he joked. "It won't be the same."

I gave a little laugh. "Goodbye, Dr. Will Story."

He sighed, then his expression turned serious. "I sure wish you'd change your mind about… well, pretty much everything."

A lump of emotion rose in my throat. Right here, right now, I wanted this man. But it would pass. Meanwhile, I had a future waiting for me in England.

"I can't… I have to get back to my life."

His eyes clouded, then he nodded. "I told you I wouldn't be a sore loser, so on that note, I'll say goodbye, Jane. It's been fun." He touched the brim of his ridiculous hat, then turned and climbed into his truck. He waved as he drove off, tapping his obnoxious horn for good measure.

Trudy craned her neck to watch him go… whining.

"Don't," I scolded her. "Remember, that man got you pregnant."

I picked up her carrier and my suitcase, then walked to curbside international bag check.

"How many bags?" the man asked.

"Just one," I mumbled, handing over my ticket.

"Okay, one bag to London, England," he said. He wrapped a temporary luggage tag around the handle. "Is that all?"

I stared at the luggage tag. Why did London suddenly seem so foreign to me?

"Ma'am?"

I looked up. "Hm?"

"I said, is that all?"

"No," I said. "I've... reconsidered."

The man frowned. "You've reconsidered your destination?"

"No. I've reconsidered leaving." I gestured to the luggage tag. "Could you take that off, please?" I pulled out my phone and brought up Will's number, then connected the call.

He answered on the first ring. "Jane, is everything okay?"

My heart was beating in my ears. "No. I've changed my mind about... pretty much everything. I need for you to come back."

Silence.

Too late, I realized I should've waited for Will's reaction before telling the luggage handler I'd changed my mind. The man was in the process of removing the tag and un-checking my big pink suitcase. I got his attention and held up my finger in a "wait" signal.

"Will?" I asked, wincing, hoping, loving. The end of my story depended on what he would say next.

"Don't move," he said. "I'm coming back!"

- The End -

A NOTE FROM THE AUTHOR

Thank you so very much for taking the time to read my story COMEBACK GIRL! What do you think is in store for Jane and her man... and for Trudy?! I'll miss writing about Jane and her twisty-turny life—it's sometimes hard to leave characters after I've lived with them for so long. I hope you enjoyed this serial, and I hope you'll join me for future serials I have planned.

Reviews are so important to authors and our books—especially series. Online bookstores give prominent placement to books that receive lots of positive reviews because they value what their customers say, and so do other customers. Reviews help me to attract new readers so I can keep producing more stories for you. Plus I really want to know if I'm keeping you entertained! If you enjoyed COMEBACK GIRL and feel inclined to leave a review at your favorite online bookstore, I would appreciate it very much.

And are you signed up to receive notices of my future book releases? If not, please visit www.stephaniebond.com and enter your email address. I won't flood you with emails and I'll never share or sell your address, and you can unsubscribe at any time.

Thanks again for your time and interest, and for telling your friends about my books. As long as you keep reading, I'll keep writing!

Happy reading!
Stephanie Bond

OTHER WORKS BY STEPHANIE BOND

Humorous romantic mysteries:
COMEBACK GIRL—*Home is where the hurt is.*
TEMP GIRL—*Change is good… but not great.*
COMA GIRL—*You can learn a lot when people think you aren't listening.*
TWO GUYS DETECTIVE AGENCY—*Even Victoria can't keep a secret from us...*
OUR HUSBAND—*Hell hath no fury like three women scorned!*
KILL THE COMPETITION—*There's only one sure way to the top...*
I THINK I LOVE YOU—*Sisters share everything in their closets...including the skeletons.*
GOT YOUR NUMBER—*You can run, but your past will eventually catch up with you.*
WHOLE LOTTA TROUBLE—*They didn't plan on getting caught...*
IN DEEP VOODOO—*A woman stabs a voodoo doll of her ex, and then he's found murdered!*
VOODOO OR DIE—*Another voodoo doll, another untimely demise...*
BUMP IN THE NIGHT—*a short mystery*

Body Movers **series:**
PARTY CRASHERS (full-length prequel)
BODY MOVERS
2 BODIES FOR THE PRICE OF 1
3 MEN AND A BODY
4 BODIES AND A FUNERAL
5 BODIES TO DIE FOR
6 KILLER BODIES
6 ½ BODY PARTS (novella)
7 BRIDES FOR SEVEN BODIES
8 BODIES IS ENOUGH
9 BODIES ROLLING
10 BODIES LYING

Romances:
FACTORY GIRL—*Long hours, low pay, and big dreams.*
DIAMOND MINE—*A woman helps her beloved choose a ring—for another woman!*
SEEKING SINGLE MALE (for the holidays)—*A singles ad mixup leads to mistletoe mayhem!*
ALMOST A FAMILY—*Fate gave them a second chance at love...*
LICENSE TO THRILL—*She's between a rock and a hard body...*
STOP THE WEDDING!—*If anyone objects to this wedding, speak now...*
THREE WISHES—*Be careful what you wish for!*

The Southern Roads series:
BABY, I'M YOURS (novella)
BABY, DRIVE SOUTH
BABY, COME HOME
BABY, DON'T GO
BABY, I'M BACK (novella)
BABY, HOLD ON (novella)
BABY, IT'S YOU (novella)

Nonfiction:
GET A LIFE! 8 STEPS TO CREATE YOUR OWN LIFE LIST—*a short how-to for mapping out your personal life list!*
YOUR PERSONAL FICTION-WRITING COACH: *365 Days of Motivation & Tips to Write a Great Book!*

ABOUT THE AUTHOR

Stephanie Bond was seven years deep into a corporate career in computer programming and pursuing an MBA at night when an instructor remarked she had a flair for writing and suggested she submit material to academic journals. But Stephanie was more interested in writing fiction—more specifically, romance and mystery novels. After writing in her spare time for two years, she sold her first manuscript; after selling ten additional projects to two publishers, she left her corporate job to write fiction full-time. To-date, Stephanie has more than eighty published novels to her name, including the popular BODY MOVERS humorous mystery series, and STOP THE WEDDING!, a romantic comedy adapted into a movie for the Hallmark Channel. Stephanie lives in Atlanta, where she is probably working on a story at this very moment. For more information on Stephanie's books, visit www.stephaniebond.com.